Elizabeth Hoyt is a *New York Times* bestselling author of historical romance. She lives in central Illinois with her husband, two children and three dogs.

For more information visit Elizabeth's website at www.elizabethhoyt.com

ELIZABETH HOYT

Scandalous Desires

piatkus

PIATKUS

First published in the US in 2011 by Grand Central Publishing,
A division of Hachette Book Group, Inc.
First published in Great Britain as a paperback original in 2011 by Piatkus
Reprinted 2011

ISBN 978-0-7499-5450-5

Printed and bound in Great Britain by
Clays Ltd, St Ives plc

Papers used by Piatkus are from well-managed forests
and other responsible sources.

MIX
Paper from
responsible sources
FSC
www.fsc.org FSC® C104740

Piatkus
An imprint of
Little, Brown Book Group
100 Victoria Embankment
London EC4Y 0DY

An Hachette UK Company
www.hachette.co.uk

www.piatkus.co.uk

*For my daughter, Honor, who wanted me to
write a book about either a cross-dressing hero or
a psycho-killer heroine. Yeah. That's not happening,
but this book is for you anyway. I love you! ;-)*

$\mathcal{A}$cknowledgments

One of the best things about being an author is getting a behind-the-scenes look at how books are put together. I had the exciting opportunity to attend the cover shoot for *Scandalous Desires* and I'd like to thank all the professionals involved: my super editor, Amy Pierpont; her excellent editorial assistant, Lauren Plude; Grand Central Publishing's art director, Diane Luger; the photographer, Shirley Green; the cover shoot stylist, Sharon; the cover illustrator, Alan Ayers; the models, Ewa daCruz and Emmanuel Fremin; and, finally, my fabulous agent, Susannah Taylor.

I had a wonderful time and you all did a magnificent job. Thank you!

Acknowledgments

One of the best things about being an author is getting a behind-the-scenes look at how books are put together. I had the exciting opportunity to attend the cover shoot for *Seduction's Demand*, and I'd like to thank all the professionals involved, my super editor, Amy Pierpont, her excellent editorial assistant, Lauren Plude, Grand Central Publishing's art director, Diane Luger, the photographer, Shirley Green, the cover shoot stylist, Sharon, the cover illustrator, Alan Ayers, the models, Ewa and Cruz and Emmanuel Froman, and, finally, my fabulous agent, Susannah Taylor.

I had a wonderful time and you all did a magnificent job. Thank you!

Scandalous Desires

Chapter One

Now once there was a king who ruled a tiny kingdom by the sea. He had no sons, but he did have three nephews, and the youngest one was called Clever John....
—from *Clever John*

LONDON, ENGLAND
APRIL 1738

Wolves, as Silence Hollingbrook well knew, are savage beasts, little given to pity or honor. If one must face a wolf cleverly disguised in human form, it did no good to show fear. Rather, one must throw one's shoulders back, lift one's chin, and stare the damned beast down.

At least that was what Silence told herself as she eyed "Charming" Mickey O'Connor, the most notorious river pirate in London. As she watched, Mr. O'Connor did something far more alarming than any real wolf.

He smiled at her.

Silence swallowed.

Mickey O'Connor lounged like the pirate king he was on a gilded throne of red velvet at one end of a lavishly corrupt room. The walls were lined with sheets of gold, the floor was a fabulous mosaic of different colored marbles, and around her, piled high, were the spoils of thieving: trunks overflowing with furs and silks, crates of tea and spices, and treasures from every corner of the globe, all of it stolen from the merchant ships that came into London's docks. Silence stood in the midst of this illicit opulence like a petitioner.

Once again.

Mr. O'Connor plucked a sweetmeat from a tray offered by a small boy, holding it between long, beringed fingers as he examined her. One corner of his wide, sensuous mouth curled in amusement. "'Tis always a pleasure to gaze upon yer sparklin' hazel eyes, Mrs. Hollingbrook, but I do wonder why ye've come to see me this lovely afternoon."

His mocking words strengthened Silence's spine. "You know very well why I'm here, Mr. O'Connor."

The pirate lifted elegantly winged black eyebrows. "Do I, now?"

Beside her, Harry, one of Mickey O'Connor's guards and her escort into the throne room, shifted his weight nervously. Harry was a big man with a battered face—a man who'd obviously lived a rather rough life—yet he was just as obviously wary of Mickey O'Connor.

"Easy now," he muttered to her beneath his breath. "Don't want to get 'is temper up."

Mr. O'Connor popped the sweetmeat into his mouth and chewed, his black eyes closing for a moment in pleasure. He was a beautiful man. Silence could see that even if she found him quite repugnant herself. His eyelashes were thick and black, surrounding dark, liquid eyes, his complexion a smooth olive, and when he smiled...well!

The dimples that were revealed on his cheeks made him look both as wicked as the devil and as innocent as a small boy. Had a Renaissance master wanted to paint all the seductive allure of Satan, he would've painted Charming Mickey O'Connor.

Silence inhaled. Mr. O'Connor might well be as evil as Satan himself, but she'd braved him once before and survived—even if she hadn't walked away entirely unscathed. "I've come for Mary Darling."

The pirate's eyes opened lazily as he swallowed his sweetmeat. "Who?"

Oh, this was too much! Silence felt her face heat as she shook off Harry's restraining arm and marched right up to the foot of the small dais on which the ridiculous throne stood. "You know very well *who*! Mary Darling, that sweet little baby girl I've taken care of for over a year. Mary Darling, who knows only me as her mother. Mary Darling, who you took from the foundling home where we both live. Give her back to me *at once*!"

So great was her ire that Silence found herself out of breath at the end of her little tirade and pointing her finger nearly in Mr. O'Connor's face. For a moment she froze, her finger only inches from his nose. Everyone in the room seemed to hold their breath. Mickey O'Connor had lost his smile, and without that expression to lighten his face, he looked quite, quite frightening.

Silence let her hand fall.

Slowly, the pirate straightened from his chair, his long limbs uncurling gracefully like a predator. He stood, his polished black jackboots *thunking* to the floor, and stepped down from the dais.

Silence could've backed up, but that would've shown

fear. And besides, she thought she might've become rooted to the spot. The scent of lemons and frankincense drifted in the air. She lifted her chin in defiance as Mickey O'Connor's smooth, tanned, *bare* chest nearly touched her nose—the man was so vain he left his extravagantly ruffled shirt unlaced—and looked him in the eye.

Mr. O'Connor bent, his mouth lightly touching her ear, and murmured, "Well, and why didn't ye say so in the first place, darlin'?"

And while Silence gaped up at him, he straightened, his gaze still locked with hers, and snapped his fingers.

A door opened and Silence finally found the willpower to tear her gaze from those black, impenetrable eyes. And then she forgot all about Mickey O'Connor. A servant girl had entered, and in her arms was the sweetest, most wonderful being in the whole world.

"Mamoo!" Mary Darling shrieked. She began a frantic bouncing in the servant girl's arms. "Mamoo! Mamoo! Mamoo! *Up!*"

Silence rushed to catch the toddler before she could completely squirm from the girl's arms. "I have you. I have you, my love," she murmured as Mary Darling wrapped soft, pudgy arms about her neck and squeezed.

Silence breathed in the scent of milk and baby, tears pricking her eyes. When she'd found the toddler gone—when she'd feared that she'd never see Mary Darling again—her heart had seemed to shrivel into a tiny, frozen thing.

"Mamoo," Mary Darling sighed, and unwrapped her arms to pat Silence's cheeks.

Silence ran her hands over Mary Darling's black curls, touching and squeezing and rubbing, making sure the little girl was as well as when she'd last seen her, half a day before. The previous six hours had been the most frightening of her life and she never wanted to repeat—

"Ahem," a masculine voice murmured nearby, and Silence suddenly remembered where she was.

She clutched Mary Darling to her breast and whirled to face the river pirate. "Thank you. It's most . . . most kind of you to have given her back to me. I really can't thank you enough." Silence took a step backward, afraid to take her eyes from Charming Mickey's face. "I . . . I'll just be leaving—"

Mr. O'Connor smiled. "Oh, certainly, sweetheart, do as ye wish, but the little one will be a-stayin' with me, I think."

Silence froze. "You have no right!"

The pirate lifted one inky eyebrow and reached out to finger Mary Darling's black curls. His tanned hand was large against her little head. "Oh, don't I? She is me daughter."

"Bad!" Mary Darling glared at Mickey O'Connor, dark eyes meeting dark eyes, black curls framing a face that might've been a feminine miniature of Mr. O'Connor's own.

The resemblance was quite devastating.

Silence swallowed. Mary Darling had been abandoned on her doorstep almost a year ago to the day. At the time she'd thought that the baby had been left with her because Silence's brother, Winter, ran the Home for Unfortunate Infants and Foundling Children. Now she wondered if there had been a much more diabolical reason. Fear that she was about to lose Mary Darling forever made her clutch the baby closer.

"You abandoned her upon my doorstep," she tried.

He cocked his head, eyeing her with ironic amusement. "I left her with ye for her safekeepin'."

"Why?" she whispered. "Why me?"

"Because." He let his hand drop. "Ye were—*are*—the purest thing I've ever seen, me sweet."

Her eyebrows drew together, confused. He didn't make any sense, and besides, they'd wandered from the main point. "You don't love her."

"No. But I'm a-thinkin' that don't matter when *ye* do, Mrs. Hollingbrook."

Silence felt the breath catch in her throat. "Let me leave with her."

"No."

Mary Darling squirmed again with one of those mercurial shifts of moods that toddlers are prone to. "Down!"

Silence let her slip from her arms, watching as the little girl carefully stood against one of the huge trunks of booty. She looked so small. So precious. "Why are you doing this? Haven't you done enough to me in this lifetime?"

"Oh, not nearly enough, m'darlin'," Mickey O'Connor murmured. Silence felt more than saw him reach out his hand toward her. Maybe he meant to fondle her hair as he had Mary Darling's.

She jerked her head out of his way.

His hand dropped.

"What are you about?" She folded her arms and faced him, though she kept Mary Darling within sight.

He shrugged, the movement making his shirt slip further off one muscled shoulder. "A man in me position has many an enemy, I fear. Nasty, mean creatures who don't let the thought of innocence or youth stop them from doin' terrible, murderous things."

"Why take her from me now?" Silence asked. "Are these enemies new?"

His mouth curved into another smile, this one entirely without humor. "Not at all. But me enemies have become more…er…*persistent* in the last month, ye understand. 'Tis merely a matter o' business—one that I hope to soon tidy up. But in the meantime, should me enemies find the wee child…"

Silence shivered, watching as Mary Darling grabbed for a dark fur and pulled it half out of the trunk. "Damn you. How could you have put her in this danger?"

"I didn't," he said without any signs of conscience. "I gave her to ye, remember."

"And she was safe with me," she said desperately. "What has changed?"

"They've discovered where she and ye live."

She shifted her gaze to him and was disconcerted to find him only a foot away. The room was big, and besides Harry and the sweetmeats boy, a gang of pirates sat around Mr. O'Connor's throne. Was he worried they'd be overheard?

"Let me keep her," Silence whispered. "She doesn't know you, doesn't love you. If there's truly a danger, then send men to guard her where we live, but let her stay at the home. If you have any decency in you at all, you'll let her go with me."

"Ah, love." Mickey O'Connor tilted his head, long coal-black locks of hair slithering over his broad shoulders. "Don't ye know by now that *decent* is the last thing anyone would be a-callin' me? No, the lass stays with me and me men, here where I can keep me eye on her night and day until I can put an end to this bit o' bother."

"But she thinks me her mother," Silence hissed. "How can you separate us when—"

"And who said anythin' about separatin'?" Mr. O'Connor asked with feigned surprise. "Why, darlin' I said the babe had to stay with me, I never said ye couldn't as well."

Silence inhaled and then found she had trouble letting the breath out again. "You want me to come *live with you*?"

Mr. O'Connor grinned as if she were a pet dog that had finally learned a trick. "Aye, that's the way o' it, sweetin'."

"I can't live with you," Silence hissed furiously. "Everyone would think…"

"What, now?" Mickey O'Connor arched an eyebrow, his black eyes glittering.

She swallowed. "That I was your whore."

He tutted softly. "Oh, and we can't be havin' that, now can we, what with yer reputation bein' all snowy white and all?"

Her hand was half-raised, the fingers balled into a fist before she even realized it. She wanted to hit him so badly, wanted to wipe that smirk from his face with all her soul.

Except he was no longer smiling. He watched her, his face expressionless, his eyes intent, like a wolf waiting for the hare to break from cover.

Trembling, she let her hand fall.

He shrugged, looking mildly disappointed. "Ah, well, it'd be a great inconvenience to have ye livin' under me roof anyway. I 'spect ye've made the right decision."

He turned away from her, sauntering smoothly toward his throne. She'd been dismissed, it seemed. He no longer found her interesting enough to play with.

In that moment, with rage and grief, and yes, love, swirling all inside, Silence made her decision.

"Mr. O'Connor!"

He stopped, still turned rudely away from her, his voice a rumbling purr. "Aye?"

"I'll stay."

Ah, but victory felt so fuckin' lovely. Mick smiled, his back still toward the little widow. She was so outraged, her dusty black feathers all ruffled, she probably didn't even feel the net tangled about her prim little feet. And yet, how easy it'd been to make her walk into his palace of her own volition, simply by kidnapping the babe.

He turned, eyebrows arched as if surprised. "Ye'll be stayin' with me, is that what yer sayin', Mrs. Hollingbrook?"

Her pointed chin was raised as if to challenge him in his own palace, poor foolish wench. She was an odd creature, Silence Hollingbrook, pretty, of course—or he'd not have looked twice at her in the first place—but not his usual type, oh no. She didn't flaunt her charms, didn't try to lure a man with titties overflowing from a low bodice or a wicked wink. She didn't try to lure at all, come to think of it. She held her womanliness locked up tight like a miser, which, on the whole, was a bit irritating.

Irritating and alluring at the same time—made a man want to find the key to her locks, truth be told.

Mud was splashed on the hem of her plain black frock; her shawl and cap were tattered, and yet her eyes stared at him all defiant like. Ah, but what eyes they were—large and wide, and a glorious hazel—made of golden brown and grass green and even a bit of gray blue. Hers was a face that might haunt a man's dreams, make him wake in the night sweating and lonely, the flesh between his legs heavy with longing. Why, it made him think of those ghost tales his mam used to tell him when he was but a wee lad, crying for lack of a dinner and the burning from the welts upon his back. Wailing women, dripping water in the night, searching for their lost loves.

Mind, the tales might've been lovely, but his belly had still ached with hunger, his back had still stung with pain when he'd woken in the morning.

"Yes," Mrs. Hollingbrook said, her nose tilted proudly in the air, "I'll come and live in this...this *place*. Just to take care of Mary Darling, nothing else."

Oh, it was hard not to grin at those words, but he was strong, keeping his expression as solemn as a judge's. "And what 'else' might ye be thinkin' about?"

The color flew high into her pale cheeks, making her eyes sparkle. Making his cock twitch. "Nothing!"

"Yer sure now, Mrs. Hollingbrook?" He took a step closer, testing, watching for her to flee, for despite his enjoyment of this sparring, 'twas a serious matter that she stay beneath his roof. Her very life might depend upon it.

But she stood her ground, his little widow. "I'm quite certain, Mr. O'Connor—"

"Oh, do call me Mickey, please," he murmured.

"*Mister* O'Connor." Her eyes narrowed on him. "Despite what the rest of St. Giles thinks, you and I both know that my honor is quite intact, and I'll thank you to remember that fact."

She was a brave one, was Silence Hollingbrook. Her small chin outthrust, her hazel eyes steady, her pale lips trembling. Any other man might've felt a twinge of guilt, a trickle of remorse for the sweet innocence he'd taken and smashed to the ground like a fine china dish.

Any other man but he.

For Mick O'Connor had lost any vestige of guilt, remorse, or soul on a winter's night sixteen years before.

So now he smiled, without any conscience at all, as he lied to the woman he'd hurt so cruelly. "Oh, I'll be sure and remember, Mrs. Hollingbrook."

She heard the mockery in his voice—her lips thinned—but she soldiered on. "You said that you'll soon have your business tidied up."

He tilted his head in interest, wondering what loophole she thought she'd found. "Aye?"

"And when you're done with your . . . your enemies, then Mary Darling will no longer be in danger."

He merely watched her now, waiting patiently.

She inhaled as if to fortify herself. "When that happens—when your enemies are defeated and Mary isn't threatened anymore—I want to leave here."

"O' course," he said at once.

"With Mary."

Oh, now, but the lass wasn't daft, was she? "She's me own flesh and blood," he said softly. "The only soul in London related to me—or at least the only one I'll acknowledge. Will ye be partin' a fond papa from his wee little one?"

"You've said you don't love her." Mrs. Hollingbrook ignored his pretty words. "I can provide a loving home for her, a wholesome, *decent* life."

Well, and he'd already admitted to a lack of decency, now hadn't he? The corner of his mouth curved, a bit too sharply. He glanced at the babe, playing with the furs from a chest. Her down-bent head was topped with hair the exact shade as his own—and his mam's, come to think of it—and yet the sight didn't cause anything to stir within his chest.

He looked back at Mrs. Hollingbrook. "When I say the danger's past, when *I* say ye can go, then aye, ye may take the babe with ye."

She sighed a bit. He had the feeling she didn't like it, not at all—he'd not put a date on the day she could go—but she'd already made the bargain, hadn't she?

"Very well. I shall have to return to the home to retrieve my things and Mary's. We'll come back here as soon as—"

"Ah, ah." He shook his head with amusement. Did she think he'd toddled into St. Giles yesterday? "The lass stays here with me. Ye can take two o' me men with ye to bring back whatever ye'd like."

She must've known she was pushing the matter. She merely pursed her pretty lips, nodded, and bent to kiss the oblivious baby on the top of the head. "I'll be right back, sweetheart."

Then she turned to stalk to the door.

Mick admired the outraged sway of her hips for a second before jerking his head at Harry to follow the little widow. Harry touched his forehead and hurried after her. He'd get his cohort, Bert, and between the two of them guard Mrs. Hollingbrook to and from the home.

There was a squeak somewhere around the level of his knees. Mick glanced down and saw the babe's face turn a bright shade of beet red as she watched Mrs. Hollingbrook leave the throne room. It was his only warning.

And then all hell broke loose.

* * *

"You don't have to escort me all the way back to the home," Silence muttered irritably some moments later.

"'Imself says we do, and so we do," Harry said somewhat obscurely.

He took one step for every two of hers and might've been out for a late afternoon stroll. The buttons of his frayed brown coat strained over his barrel chest and he wore a bright red scarf wound around his neck, the ends flung debonairly over his shoulders. The scarf was at odds with his battered face and massive broken nose—Harry looked like a pugilist who had lost one too many rounds. The early spring wind was chill with a nasty edge of damp, but Harry didn't seem to notice as he stumped along, his old cocked hat at a jaunty angle.

The same couldn't be said for his companion.

"And 'oos mindin' the palace, is what I'd like to know," grumped Bert. He was half a head shorter than Harry and was hunched inside the collar of his bottle-green coat like a turtle. A huge gray scarf wrapped around and over both his face and the seedy wig he wore, making his head look disproportionately swollen. "Sendin' us off in the middle o' the day with a wench!"

"There's a dozen o' the crew at the palace," Harry pointed out. "And Bob."

"Bob! Jaysus, Bob," Bert said in disgust. "Couldn't guard a kitten, could Bob."

"When 'e's not three sheets to the wind 'e can," Harry said judiciously.

"'E's always fuckin' drunk!"

"Watch yer tongue," Harry said, and then as an aside to Silence, "'E's missin' 'is afternoon tea is Bert, and it makes 'im tetchy like. Normally the most placid o' men is our Bert."

Silence, watched as "our Bert" spat through his missing two front teeth, almost hitting a passing mongrel. She was rather doubtful that the man was ever in a good mood, tea or no tea, but she wisely decided not to share this thought. For whatever reason Harry seemed to have taken a liking to her, and she was loath to spoil their accord.

If she was to live with Charming Mickey O'Connor she would need a friendly face.

Dear God. Only now as she walked the grimy streets of St. Giles, did the full impact of her decision hit her. She'd pledged to live in the same house as the most notorious man in St. Giles—a man she'd spent over a year hating and fearing. Whatever shreds of respectability she'd been able to pull together over her battered reputation in the last year would be truly torn asunder now. But what choice did she have? One look at Mary Darling's face and she would've walked through fire.

Silence shivered and pulled her cloak more firmly about her person. Mickey O'Connor had never actually hurt her—not physically anyway—and she had Harry as an ally. She would draw on her own strength, keep to herself, and avoid the company of Charming Mickey and his men as much as possible until his enemies were defeated and she could go home.

Pray that was soon.

She turned into a small lane and the modest door to the Home for Unfortunate Infants and Foundling Children came into sight. It was the *temporary* Home for Unfortunate Infants and Foundling Children, sadly, ever since a fire had burned down the original home a year ago. A new building was being built for the home, but a series of setbacks had delayed their move to the new place.

The door was flung open before Silence could touch it.

"Have you found her?" Nell Jones, the home's trusted maidservant, looked eager, but her bright blue eyes dimmed when she saw Silence's empty arms. Nell's pretty face was flushed, one blond lock fluttering around her ear—her disorder a measure of how worried she was about Mary Darling.

"I did find Mary Darling," Silence said hastily. "But... well, it's a long story."

"And who are these two?" Nell asked suspiciously, eyeing Harry and Bert.

"Gentlemen what 'as seen yer mistress safely 'ome," Harry said. He removed the battered tricorne from his head, revealing a thinning patch of straggly brown hair, and bowed rather elegantly, considering his size.

"Huh," Nell sniffed, though her tone was less strident. "Best come inside, then."

The entryway to the home was narrow and cramped and the two men seemed to take up not only what little room there was, but the air as well.

Nell stared at them disapprovingly for a moment and then turned to a small boy loitering curiously behind her. "Joseph Tinbox, take these, er, *gentlemen* back to the kitchen and ask Mary Whitsun to make them a pot of tea."

"Why, that's quite kind o' ye, ma'am." Harry beamed.

Silence was surprised to see Nell fight to keep her face stern.

"Mind nothing goes missing in there," the maid said gruffly. "I know everything in that kitchen down to the vinegar shakers."

Harry placed his hand over his heart. "I'll keep me eye on Bert, 'ere. See that 'e don't pocket a spoon or nothin'."

With an indignant snort from Bert, Joseph Tinbox led them off.

"Hurry," Silence said as she made for the stairs. "I had to leave Mary Darling behind and I want to get back quickly."

"Back where?" Nell cried as she followed Silence up the stairs, panting.

"To Mickey O'Connor's house."

"Dear Lord in Heaven," Nell muttered. "Is that where you rushed off to after reading the note? To see that devil?"

Silence had returned from the shopping that morning to find that Mary had somehow disappeared from the home. Everyone in the house—all eight and twenty children, three maids, and the lone manservant—had immediately begun searching for her. But it wasn't until a mysterious note had been delivered hours later that Silence had even thought of Mickey O'Connor.

"The note was from Mr. O'Connor saying he might have something I'd want," Silence said breathlessly as they made the top floor of the house. The room she shared with Mary Darling was up here under the eaves. "He's Mary's father."

"What?" Nell had finally caught up with her and she laid a hand on Silence's arm. "How long have you known this?"

Silence bit her lip. "I've suspected it for some time. You remember Mary's mysterious admirer? The one who used to leave presents for her on the step?"

"Yes." Nell sank onto the narrow bed in Silence's room, her pretty face creased with worry.

"A couple of months ago, just before Christmas, he left me a lock of black hair." Silence pulled a small trunk from under the bed. She straightened and looked at Nell. "The lock matched Mary Darling's hair."

"And you think Mickey O'Connor left it for you?"

"I don't know." Silence shrugged. "But I think it must've been him. I thought I saw him watching me and Mary Darling once or twice last fall."

"If he's her father, why did Mickey O'Connor leave her with you?"

"He says he was trying to protect her from his enemies." Silence began to throw clothes into the chest. "Perhaps he thought her safely hidden with me. Perhaps he was merely playing a game to amuse himself."

Nell shook her head as if dazed. "But what of the baby's mother? Surely she had some say in the matter?"

Silence froze, her hand outstretched for one of Mary's frocks hanging on a hook. She turned her head and stared at Nell. "Her mother—my goodness, he never even mentioned the woman."

"Perhaps she's dead." Nell frowned. "Do you think Mickey O'Connor was married? I never heard of such, but he's a secretive scoundrel."

"I don't know." Silence took the frock with shaking fingers and placed it carefully in the trunk before closing the lid. "I only know that I must go live with him now."

"What?" Nell jumped to her feet in alarm.

Silence locked the trunk. "He says that Mary is in danger from his enemies and he won't let her leave his house. If I'm to be with her, I must live with him."

Nell lifted one end of the trunk even as she moaned. "But after what he did to you—"

"I haven't any choice, don't you see?" Silence walked to the door, the heavy little trunk between them.

"But the home—"

"Oh, goodness!" Silence stopped and stared at Nell.

She'd been so busy worrying over Mary Darling, she'd not thought of what her actions would do to the home. In the last year the Home for Unfortunate Infants and Foundling Children had gained the patronage of several aristocratic ladies—ladies who cared terribly about appearances and reputations. The home depended on their donations. If they found out that Silence was staying with a man—a *pirate*—without benefit of marriage...

Silence's eyes widened. "You mustn't let anyone know where I am. We can say that I've gone to attend an ill aunt in the country."

"And Mr. Makepeace?" Nell muttered as they began to descend the staircase. "What shall I say to him?"

Silence stumbled, nearly dropping her end of the trunk. She'd forgotten she'd have to deal with Winter's disapproval as well. Her brother had made a journey to Oxford on business and thus had been away from the home when Mary Darling's absence had been discovered. This morning Silence had wished desperately for her brother's support in searching for the little girl. Now she was thankful he was away. Winter was a mild man, a schoolmaster by trade, as well as manager of the home, but she had no doubt at all that he would've locked her in her room before letting her go to Mickey O'Connor.

Just the thought made her hurry her step. "I'm truly sorry, Nell, to leave you with the chore of telling Winter but I can't stay. I need to go to Mary Darling."

"Of course you do," Nell said stoutly.

Silence shot her a quick smile. "None of this is your fault and Mr. Makepeace will understand that."

"I surely hope so, ma'am."

By the time they'd descended the rest of the stairs Silence was perspiring from exertion and anxiety. Winter wasn't expected back for days, yet she couldn't help jumping when the door to the kitchen opened.

"Take that, shall I?" Harry asked as he strolled out, a bun in one hand. He grasped one of the trunk's handles and easily swung it to his broad back.

Nell straightened, hands on hips and glared. "Watch you don't drop the mistress's things."

"O' course not," Harry said easily, earning himself a disgusted grunt from Bert.

Nell looked at Silence and her face seemed to crumple. "Oh, ma'am!" She threw her apron over her face and let out a loud, hiccupping sob.

"It's all right, Nell, really 'tis," Silence said helplessly.

She didn't know whether or not she believed the words herself, but what else was she to say? Tears were pricking her eyes now as well. She'd lived at the home for just over a year, learned of her husband William's death last fall here, discovered she was more than a wife here—that she could stand on her own two feet and be of use to others. Now she was leaving suddenly and without warning. She felt as if the very ground beneath her feet was unstable. She had no home now—hadn't since William's death, really—all she had was Mary Darling.

"I'll be back," she whispered, not even sure she spoke the truth.

Nell pulled down her apron, her face reddened and damp, her blond hair trailing from its pins. She marched up to Harry and stuck a finger in his chest. "Just you watch out for her, you hear me, you great lout? A hair on her head gets harmed and it's *you* I'll be coming after."

The threat was ludicrous, Harry towered over Nell. Silence blinked, Bert scowled, but Harry himself was quite solemn. He took Nell's hand gently in his big paw and spread her fingers until he could rest them on his great chest, just over where his heart might be.

"Never you fear, ma'am," was all he said. "Never you fear."

And then Silence was out the door, the wind whipping her skirts flat against her legs as she headed into a new life.

CHARLIE GRADY, BETTER known as the Vicar of Whitechapel, poured himself a tankard of beer. Some might find it strange—his taste for beer—seeing as how he controlled the distilling of damn near every drop of gin in Whitechapel and indeed the whole East End of London, but there it was. Charlie liked beer, so beer he drank.

And if anyone *did* find his taste in drink strange, well … no one was foolish enough to tell him so to his face.

"What have you found?" he asked, watching as the foam in the pewter tankard slowly subsided. He didn't need to look up to know that Freddy, standing before Charlie's table, was studying his own big feet.

"'E moved the babe into 'is palace today." Freddy was a big bruiser, smarter than he looked, but not much for expansive talk.

Charlie grinned, only half of his face moving. "Always a smart one was Charming Mickey. He must have a real fear for what I'd do to the babe to take her out of his hiding place and move her to the palace."

Freddy shuffled uneasily. "There's more."

"Aye?"

"A wench came to see 'im."

Charlie laughed, the sound a strange sputter. "That there isn't news."

His gaze flicked up in time to see Freddy look hastily away.

Freddy flushed, the red mottling his pitted face. "This one is different."

"How do you figure?"

"She's the one 'oo lived in the orphan's 'ome—the respectable one. The one takin' care o' the babe."

Charlie cocked his head, feeling the pull of old scars on the left side of his face and neck. "Ah, but that is news. Charming Mickey don't like the respectable ones much, now does he?"

Freddy knew better than to answer, so Charlie took a sip of his beer, the tart taste of hops washing down his throat.

He set his tankard back on the table and picked up the dice with his left hand—the one with the thumb and fore-finger turned to claws. He'd had the dice for long years now and they were worn smooth, the paint gone from the carved pips, the edges rounded. They were old friends in his palm and when he threw them gently, they rolled with barely a sound on the bare plank table.

Deuce and trey. A five. Ah, now, five could be good or very good, depending. Depending.

Last fall he'd had plans to move into St. Giles. Take over the gin distilling there and become king of gin in all of London. Those plans had stumbled because of an aris-tocrat not afraid of blowing up his own still—and taking half of Charlie's men with it. But Charlie'd had time to regroup since then.

And besides, he had another focus now.

"My Gracie's dead and buried. What she wanted, what she kept me from doin'...now that's dead, as well." Charlie stared with fascination at the greasy bits of bone. They seemed to wink up at him slyly. "All bets are off and Charming Mickey O'Connor would do well to look after his females."

He looked up in time to catch Freddy's horrified gaze directly.

"Best have our spy find out how much the lady means to Mickey, hadn't ye?"

Chapter Two

*The king had a palace, naturally, and beside the palace
was a large and lovely garden. Every morning it was the
king's habit to stroll about his garden and inspect
the fruit trees, which were his pride and joy. Imagine
then, the king's shock when one morning he came upon
his favorite cherry tree and found the ground
underneath littered with cherry pits....*
—from *Clever John*

It was dusk by the time Silence, Harry, and Bert made it
back to Mickey O'Connor's gaudily opulent "palace." The
moment they stepped inside Silence heard the screams.

She knew that angry shriek.

Silence took the stairs two at a time, not even slowing
at Harry's worried, "Oi!" from behind her. The screams
were growing louder the nearer she got to Mr. O'Connor's
throne room. She pushed open the great double doors and
swept right past Bob, the skinny guard, and marched to
where Mickey O'Connor stood in the middle of the room
with a bawling Mary Darling in his hands.

No wonder the little girl was crying! The pirate held
his screaming daughter out at arm's length as if she were
a stinking chamber pot.

"What have you done?" Silence demanded and snatched the baby from his hands.

Mary Darling had stopped shrieking at the sight of Silence, but she still cried, her little face red and swollen, her shoulders shuddering with uncontrollable sobs. Silence recognized this state of affairs: Mary had been wailing for quite some time.

She kissed the baby's damp cheek, murmuring soothing nonsense and then turned an accusing eye on Mickey O'Connor.

He threw up his hands. "Don't be lookin' at me like that. I didn't touch the brat and no one could get her to stop wailin'!"

Silence covered Mary's ears. "How dare you?"

Mickey O'Connor scowled, for once looking less than charming. "She started bawlin' the moment ye left. Like a great, barmy banshee, she was. Near to deafened me, I tell ye."

"Well, perhaps she doesn't like it here." Silence tucked Mary's still shaking head under her chin and cuddled the baby. "Perhaps she doesn't like *you*."

Mr. O'Connor snorted. "*I* don't like her, and that's a fact, no *perhaps* about it."

Silence gasped. "But she's your daughter!"

"And what does that have to do with the matter?" Mickey asked with a sardonic twist to his lips. "Her dam was a whore I kept for less than a sennight. The first I was hearin' o' the babe was when the wench died and left a note that I was the father. An old bawd came and dumped the babe on me, but not afore demandin' a guinea for the pleasure. For ought I know her mam lied and the babe is none o' me flesh at all."

Silence stroked a hand over Mary's soft curls, truly shocked. Had he no feelings at all? "Is that what you truly think?"

"Matters not at all, does it?" He turned away, one wide shoulder shrugging elegantly. "Daughter or not, flesh or not, *like* her or not, she's me own now, so don't be a-gettin' any ideas to the contrary. Now follow me like a good lass and I'll be showin' ye to yer room."

He strode away as if he did indeed expect her to follow like "a good lass." Had Silence any choice she would've remained where she was. But since Mary was already half-asleep on her shoulder, she tramped after the awful man with Harry and Bert bringing up the rear.

He led her out through the double doors—Bob ran to open them as Mickey O'Connor approached so he didn't have to stop. Mr. O'Connor didn't acknowledge the courtesy, merely striding past like a king, but Silence nodded her thanks to the skinny guard as she hurried after.

Mickey O'Connor stalked down a short hallway and then through another door that led to the back of the house. A big man stood guard here as well. The gold walls and marble floor stopped at the door, but that didn't mean this area of the house was any less richly appointed. The carved wood panels of the walls shone richly with beeswax and the floor beneath their feet was thickly carpeted. Mr. O'Connor mounted a set of stairs, Silence panting behind, trying to tamp down the frisson of dread remembrance. Mickey O'Connor had taken her this way once before, and she hadn't emerged again entirely whole.

The sound of the pirate's heels as he led her and the smell of fresh beeswax on the panels suddenly made the memory of that night rise up, overwhelming her like water closing over her head.

William, her dear husband, had been accused of stealing the cargo from his ship—the cargo that Mickey O'Connor had taken.

So Silence had come to St. Giles, wrapping herself in foolish bravery, love for William, and a fatal naïveté. She'd pleaded with Mickey O'Connor for William. She'd thrown herself on the mercy of a wolf, forgetting that wolves didn't understand even the idea of mercy.

Mr. O'Connor had told her that he would replace the cargo—but that in return she'd have to spend the night with him. He'd stood up from his throne and led her from the throne room and through these very hallways.

By that time she'd been very nearly in a panic. She was a good woman—a virtuous woman—and she had no choice but to think that he would debauch her. Instead, he'd brought her to his magnificent bedroom, seated her by the fire, and called for supper. Servants had brought the most beautiful meal she had ever seen. Sweets and rich meats and hothouse fruits. He'd insisted she eat and she'd obeyed him, though the food had tasted like ashes in her mouth.

Afterward, he'd bid her lay in his big bed, stripped the shirt from his body...and then he'd ignored her, reading papers by the fire, half unclothed. When she couldn't stand it any longer she'd sat up. "What do you mean to do with me?"

He'd glanced up in feigned surprise, the shadows the firelight had cast across his face making him look nearly demonic. "Why, nothin', Mrs. Hollingbrook. What did ye think I'd do with ye?"

"Then why did you bring me here?"

He'd smiled—not a nice smile. No, this was a smile such as a wolf would give just before he tore into the doe's throat. "What will ye tell yer husband when ye return to his arms tomorrow?"

"Tell him? I'll tell him the truth: that we dined together, but that nothing else happened."

"And he'll believe ye?"

"Of course!" She'd been outraged. "William loves me."

He'd nodded. "If he loves ye, he'll believe ye."

His words had been like a curse. Even then—sitting on that ridiculously lush bed, just beginning to feel the relief that she wouldn't have to sacrifice her pride to this man— even then, she'd shivered with foreboding.

The next morning Mickey O'Connor had made her undo the front of her dress until her breasts were nearly revealed. He'd had her take down her hair and tousle it about her face. And then he'd made her promise to walk up the street like that.

As if she were a common whore leaving his bed.

It had been hard—until then the hardest thing she'd ever done in her life—but she'd walked up that street, past the catcalls of the whores returning home for the night. She'd found her sister, Temperance, waiting for her at the end of the street, worried sick about what had happened to Silence over the night. Silence had collapsed in her sister's arms, hoping that the terrible spell was over.

But that walk up the street in disarray had not been the worst—not by a long shot. For after that night she'd found that no one believed her. Not Winter, not Temperance, not the butcher on the corner, not her neighbors in Wapping.

No one.

Not even her darling husband, William. They all had thought Charming Mickey O'Connor had raped her. William had hardly been able to look at her before he left on that last voyage. He'd turned his head aside as if the sight of her shamed him—or as if she repelled him. And as she had watched her love leave, that last time on a ship that in six months' time would be lost at sea, Mickey O'Connor's words had echoed in her mind:

If he loves ye, he'll believe ye.

Silence blinked and saw that they were climbing past a wide landing. She caught sight of familiar gilded double doors and glanced hastily away. Mickey O'Connor led her to the next floor up and then to the first door in the hallway there. He opened it with a flourish to reveal a neat bedroom with pink walls and white trim. Silence stopped short in astonishment. A bed with embroidered flowered hangings stood in one corner. Beside it was a cot with spindled rails all around the outside—obviously a child's bed. There was even a small sitting area with a settee before the fireplace. Harry was already placing her trunk at the foot of the bed while Bert took a chair outside the door.

All in all the room was very nice—and terribly out of place in this den of iniquity.

Silence turned to Mr. O'Connor with a frown. "Who usually resides in this room?"

He'd leaned a broad shoulder against the fireplace mantel as he watched her examine the room. "Why, no one, darlin'. Did ye think I kept a passel o' virgins here to sacrifice to me wicked lust?"

She could feel herself color at his mocking words. "I merely wondered."

"Ah, well, wonder no longer. This room is for ye and ye alone." He arched one satanic eyebrow. "Have ye any other questions?"

"Um . . . no."

"Then I'll leave ye to make yerself at home. Supper's at eight o'clock. Sharp, mind. Harry'll show ye the way." He'd straightened from the mantel as he spoke, and now he strode out the door without so much as a backward glance.

Silence stared, rather stunned, as the door closed softly behind the river pirate. "Wretched man!"

There was a soft gasp from near the bed and Silence noticed for the first time that a girl sat by the cot. It was the same maidservant who had brought Mary Darling into the throne room.

Behind Silence, Harry cleared his throat with a sound like boulders rubbing together. "This 'ere's Fionnula, 'oo's been set to carin' for the babe."

"Ma'am." Fionnula dipped in an awkward curtsy, abandoned halfway down. She was a pretty girl, perhaps no more than eighteen, her fair skin freckled, her hair a lovely reddish blond, springing out from its pins in a cloud of curls about her face.

"Mrs. 'Ollingbrook is goin' to stay 'ere with the little lassie, Fionnula," Harry said. "Orders o' 'Imself, so mind what she says, 'ear?"

Fionnula nodded, apparently struck mute by Harry's instructions.

"Well, then," Harry said after an awkward pause. "Ah . . . I'll jus' push along. 'Imself 'as given orders that me and Bert'll be watchin' after ye while yer 'ere, Mrs. 'Ollingbrook, so if'n ye need anythin', jus' give us a 'oller. We'll be outside the door."

And Harry left, as well.

Silence scowled at the door through which the men had disappeared. "Sometimes I suspect that men are great idiots."

Fionnula gave a surprised giggle, hurriedly muffled.

Silence smiled sheepishly at the girl. It was hardly Fionnula's fault that Mr. O'Connor was such an autocratic pirate.

"The babe's fair worn out," Fionnula said, nodding at Mary still in Silence's arms. Her Irish burr was pronounced.

"She is, isn't she?" Silence whispered. She carried Mary to the cot and gently laid her down, hovering a moment to see if the toddler would wake.

But Mary was exhausted from her crying bout and slept deeply.

Silence straightened and moved to the fireplace, motioning Fionnula to follow. "So you were looking after Mary today?"

"Aye," the maid said shyly. "She was fair mad to've been taken from her home. She's a handsome lass, though. The spittin' image of Himself."

"That she is," Silence murmured as she sank into the settee. She hadn't had a moment to rest since she'd discovered Mary missing and weariness was making her limbs liquid. "Is this your room now, too?"

Fionnula's eyes widened. "Oh, no, ma'am. 'Tisn't anyone's as far as I know, savin' yerself. I have a cot in the attic, same as the other maids, but Himself has said I'm to sleep through there now." She gestured to a small door on the wall.

"Oh, yes?" Silence got up to peek into Fionnula's room. It was barely big enough to hold a cot and a row of pegs on the wall. Certainly it was far more Spartan than Silence's and Mary's room. She came back and flung herself down on the settee again and looked at the maid curiously. "When did you come to work for Mr. O'Connor?"

"A bit more'n a month ago." Fionnula's fair face suddenly flamed. "I...I have a friend who lives here."

By the blush on the maid's face, Silence thought the "friend" must be a man. "Surely not Harry?"

Fionnula giggled. "Oh, no, ma'am!"

"Or Mr. O'Connor?" Silence asked with a strangely heavy heart. Had he sent his kept woman to watch over her?

"Goodness, no," Fionnula said. "The ladies that Himself entertains are fancy pieces, quite lovely like. I'm not nearly as beautiful or as high in the instep as they."

"Oh. Of course." Silence got up to unpack her meager trunk.

The reality of her situation swept over her. She'd placed herself entirely in the power of an evil man—a man whose only use for women was to have them "entertain" him. This wasn't what she wanted for Mary Darling—or herself. Once again she'd let Mickey O'Connor get the upper hand. For a moment panic rose in her chest, nearly suffocating her.

"Are ye all right, ma'am?" Fionnula asked hesitantly.

Silence glanced up and saw the little maid watching her worriedly. "Oh, yes. Just a little tired."

She rose to put away a pile of stockings, but as she did she came to a decision: she might be in Mickey O'Connor's palace again, but that didn't mean this time had to end like the last. This time the pirate would find that Silence Hollingbrook had a mind and a spirit of her own.

And she would never blindly obey him again.

* * *

THE LITTLE WIDOW's presence in his palace gave him an odd itch 'tween the shoulder blades, Mick mused later that evening as he spread out a great map upon a table. 'Twas a crawling feeling, two parts curiosity, one of lust, with a dram of uneasy wariness stirred in.

Strange, that, since he'd spent the last year slyly planning to get Silence Hollingbrook exactly where she was—under his power and under his roof. It'd been a whim in the beginning. He'd eyed the squalling babe held in the greedy old bawd's arms, and known at once that the babe would have to be hidden from the Vicar. *And why not her?* he'd thought. *Why not the righteous Mrs. Hollingbrook?* Perhaps it was a way to claim some of that pure virtue she'd blazed at him in his own throne room. To steal by proxy what he could never earn. It had given him a bittersweet satisfaction: to hide the flesh of his flesh with the woman he'd harmed most in the world. To tie Silence to him with bonds of her own maternal love.

Aye, and now at last he'd brought her back to his palace and by rights he ought to be feeling a triumphant bit of glee, hadn't he?

Not an odd, crawling sensation instead.

"She seems content enough." Harry's broad, ugly face wrinkled as if he were thinking on whether "content" was really the word he wanted. "I left 'er with Fionnula."

Mick shot him a sardonic glance before returning his gaze to the map spread upon a great gilded table before him. Rumor had it that the table had been meant for a royal palace. But that was before Mick had demanded it in tithe from a captain who'd tried to wriggle out from his just obligations to Mick and his crew. Made it all the sweeter to have it in his own planning room, then.

"Left her alone?" Mick asked with an edge to his voice. Silence was in his palace now—a treasure he'd protect like any other.

"Naw," Harry said hastily. "Bert's guardin' 'er."

"Good," Mick grunted. "I'd be best pleased if'n she and the babe were within eyesight o' one o' ye at all times. She's to be guarded well, mind." He spread the map, leaning on it with both arms outstretched and studied it. "Where's this dock yer contemplatin'?" he asked the third man in the room.

"Down here," Bran Kavanagh said, waving his hand over the lower Thames. "It's rumored that the owners are in debt. They'll sell cheap."

The lad leaned forward eagerly, forgetting that he liked to pretend an air of sophistication. Bran had been with Mick for the last six years or more. He was a pretty lad of twenty or so, all light blue eyes and red-brown hair pulled back into a queue. Made the girls quite swoon over him—much to Bran's discomfort, for the lad was a solemn one.

Except as now when he had a scheme brewing in his brain.

Mick examined the area Bran had indicated. "What're ye thinkin' we can do with it?"

"We can buy the docks and charge for the use of them," Bran said at once. He'd been contemplating his plan for a while, it seemed. "Or sell them again at a higher price in the future. It's a bit of insurance against lean times."

"Mmm," Mick murmured. He hadn't told Bran, but he already had "insurance." "I do like the idea o' insurance."

Bran grinned, quick and hopeful. "Then you'll buy the docks?"

Mick sighed, hating to disappoint the lad, but business was business. "If I go a-buyin' docks and such, then I'll be havin' to hire secretaries and managers and the like to run the damn things. Might be more expense than profit."

The corners of Bran's mouth turned down—the boy hadn't yet learned to hide his emotions properly. "If you wait, they'll sell to someone else. We'll have lost the docks and another mayn't come up for sale for years."

"And if I jump too soon, I'll lose me money," Mick said. "It's an interestin' idea, Bran, me lad, but I'll have to think on it a bit."

"But—"

Mick shook his head once, staring at the boy sternly. "And besides, I've other matters to settle first—ones involvin' the Vicar."

Bran looked away. "As you like."

"I do like," Mick said mildly as he rolled up the map. "What have ye found out for me?"

Bran sighed. "I saw his men lurking around the orphans' home this afternoon after Mrs. Hollingbrook left. You got the babe out just in time, I'm thinking."

"Lurkin' in plain sight?"

"Aye," Bran replied. "The Vicar's men have become quite bold. They tramp about St. Giles in packs of four or five without a care in the world."

"Fuck 'em," Mick growled. "St. Giles is mine and I'll see those bloody whoresons run out." He stretched his neck. "And how did the Vicar find out about the babe in the first place is what I'm wonderin'."

"You did have men watching her," Bran pointed out.

Mick looked up, eyes narrowed, only to find Harry nodding thoughtfully.

"Might've led the Vicar straight to the babe," Harry said.

Mick grunted. He didn't like the thought that 'twas his own error that had led the Vicar's men to the orphanage and the babe. There was another possibility, too: Had one of his men betrayed his secret to the Vicar?

"Then he knows that I have the babe within me palace," Mick said slowly.

Bran nodded grimly.

Mick sighed. "Well, 'twas never me plan to hide the fact that I had her safe. He knows he must attack me palace to get to her—and that, I'm thinkin', he'll be loath to do." He looked at Bran. "What have ye found out about the Vicar himself?"

"The Vicar's got dozens of men around him at all times," Bran replied. "He guards himself better than you, come to that. It'll be a right job to get to him."

"Ah, but get to him we must," Mick said. "'Tis near the end o' winter and he'll be runnin' low on grain for his damned gin stills. Have some o' me men find out who's supplyin' him. I'll offer the suppliers an incentive to quit doin' business with the Vicar."

"Very well." Bran hesitated, then blurted out, "But I don't see why you two are at war. He has his gin distilling and you have the river. How do your interests cross?"

Sad brown eyes rose up in his inner mind, the lilt of an Irish voice, *Me darlin' Mickey.*

Mick grimaced, pushing the memories aside. "It's a personal matter. One ye needn't worry about."

Bran frowned as Mick put away the map. "That's your

own affair, but we're spending time on the Vicar and getting no money in return."

"Aye, and I'm aware o' it," Mick said. "If I could end this, I would. But I'm afraid the Vicar isn't such a reasonable gent as m'self."

"Then you'll have to kill him." Bran's light blue eyes were young—and utterly ruthless.

"I would, but as ye've pointed out, the man guards himself well." Mick tapped the table for a moment in thought, then came to a decision. "We're better off takin' the roundabout way. Cut off his grain, starve him, and run him out o' St. Giles for good. In the meantime, send some o' me men about to roust any o' his crew they find in St. Giles."

Bran nodded. "As you wish."

Mick arched an eyebrow. The boy was still lingering though he'd been given his orders. "Somethin' else on yer mind?"

"What about this Mrs. Hollingbrook?" Bran's upper lip curled. "I can see keeping the child—*if* you think she's truly yours—but why insist the wench stay, as well? She's a distraction."

Mick's jaw tightened. "Pardon me, but I wasn't aware I need explain m'self to ye, lad."

Bran's face went a fiery scarlet. A muscle beneath his right eye jumped and then he turned and left the room abruptly.

Harry had been leaning on the wall in the corner, but he stirred now. "The boy's impatient."

"That he is," Mick muttered.

"'E's clever, is our Bran," Harry said with an air of consideration. "But a bit rash."

Mick cocked a sardonic eyebrow at Harry, waiting.

Harry straightened. "'E may not like Mrs. 'Ollingbrook,

but Bran does 'ave a bit o' a point. Are ye sure 'tis best to keep 'er 'ere?"

Mick's reaction was immediate and gut-deep. Silence was his and he would hold her. No one was going to change that.

"Second-guessin' me, Harry?" Mick asked with silky menace.

The big man flinched, but didn't back down. "Now, ye know I'd never do such, Mick. But, see, she's a soft thing, is Mrs. 'Ollingbrook, though she 'ides it be'ind a sharp tongue. She's a lady, through and through, and easily 'urt. Ye 'ad yer way with 'er once afore. Is it necessary like to play with 'er again?"

Mick glanced down at the papers he'd picked up. They'd crumpled beneath the force of his grip. *Hazel eyes weeping in the night.* "I find m'self in a strangely good mood this evenin', Harry, otherwise ye know I'd not be allowin' such questionin'."

"I know that, I do," Harry said earnestly.

"Then ye know also that I'll be answerin' yer damned questions jus' this once," Mick said, his eyes pinning Harry. "I trust ye remember the girl found upon me doorstep jus' last week?"

"I do."

"She'd been in me palace only nights afore, though I didn't take her to me bed," Mick rasped, remembering the body of the girl. Her face had looked like it had melted off her head. *Jaysus.* That wouldn't happen to Silence Hollingbrook, not while he still lived. "Can ye imagine what the Vicar would do to someone I might…care about?"

Harry looked away uneasily. He'd been the one to find the body. "Aye, but Mick, the Vicar don't know ye fancy 'er, does 'e?"

"I don't know." Mick felt his jaw clench at the admission. "I thought the babe secret and safe as well—and she wasn't, was she?"

Harry shook his head soberly.

"Either he knows already or he soon will—he's not stupid is the Vicar. It's very necessary that I keep Mrs. Hollingbrook here with me," Mick said softly. "Do we have a problem?"

Harry swallowed. "No."

"Good." Mick nodded. "And Harry?"

Harry, who had turned to the door, froze. "Aye, Mick?"

Mick smiled thinly. "Whatever else I might be doin' with Mrs. Hollingbrook, I'm not playin'."

The information didn't lighten Harry's expression. He was wearing a frown on his ugly face when he left the planning room.

Mick cursed and flung himself onto a velvet settee. Months of scheming had finally born sweet, juicy fruit and yet he still had a feeling of ... What? Some strange emotion, some odd sense that he hadn't truly won. Mick snorted. And what sort of pirate felt any emotion at all? He had the wench in his grasp, held fast in his own domain where he might examine her at his leisure. Find out why the little widow Hollingbrook brought such an uncommon itch to his skin, making him as restless as a caged wolf. He'd forgotten the face of the lass he'd bedded just the night afore, yet Silence Hollingbrook's wide hazel eyes had haunted his sleep for months.

Muttering to himself, Mick rang for his accountant, Pepper. The balding sparrow of a man came to him promptly enough and for the next hour or so Mick listened to the man drone on about ships and building materials until his head fairly ached. Yet at the end of that time, had anyone asked, Mick realized he wouldn't have been able to report what Pepper had said.

Sighing, Mick sent the accountant away again, then washed his face and hands and headed to supper.

The dining room was a cavernous hall—Mick liked to have all his people eat the evening meal together— and thus the room was usually quite loud. But as Mick entered tonight, what conversation there'd been quickly quieted.

He looked about. Bran was seated next to Fionnula. Pepper was across from him, a book open on his empty plate. A couple of Mick's current women tittered together in the corner, while Bert glared at them from across the way. And a dozen or so of Mick's night crew took up the far end of the long tables set end to end. To a man they were a dangerous, shifty lot—and yet not a one could meet his eye. Even the sweetmeats boy, Tris, was seated behind Mick's chair, ready to serve him.

Everyone was there in fact, except Mrs. Hollingbrook. Mick strode to Fionnula. "Where is she?"

The girl trembled. "She said that she couldn't come down to sup."

Mick bent and whispered softly, "Couldn't or *wouldn't*?"

The girl gulped and said bravely, "Wouldn't"

Mick inhaled, feeling rage boil within his breast. He turned heel and left the room without a word. *No one* ignored his summons to supper—a fact Mrs. Hollingbrook was about to learn the hard way.

Silence had just finished feeding Mary Darling her dinner when Mickey O'Connor burst into the bedroom without so much as a knock. She glanced up, startled, and then stiffened at the grim set of his mouth.

Mary Darling frowned sternly, looking quite a bit like her sire at the moment. "Bad!"

Mickey O'Connor narrowed his eyes at the baby and then turned to Silence. "'Tis supper time—or hadn't ye heard?"

She lifted her chin. "Yes, I'd heard. Fionnula informed me."

"Then why aren't ye downstairs with everyone else, darlin'?" he asked much too gently.

He stood preternaturally still, his head cocked as if listening to her breathing.

Silence found herself licking her lips nervously. She reminded herself of the promise she'd made just this afternoon: she would not blindly obey this man again. Refusing to dine with Mickey O'Connor might seem like a small defiance, but it was the only one she had. "I prefer to eat in my room with Mary."

"All those who live under me roof dine together downstairs."

She tilted her chin. "Do they?"

"Yes, they do," he said. "Get up."

His tone was so commanding that she almost did just that. Silence exhaled carefully and lifted Mary from her lap. She set the toddler on the floor and Mary immediately began exploring the room, holding on to the settee seat as she went.

She met his eyes. "No."

"What?"

He'd heard her well enough so Silence merely folded her arms in answer. The posture also served to hide the trembling of her hands.

He stared at her a moment and there was anger on his handsome face, but there was also a kind of animal curiosity as well. "Why not?"

She inhaled, trying to calm the rapid beat of her heart. "Maybe I don't want to break bread with pirates. Maybe I don't want to dine with *you*. Maybe I simply prefer my quiet room. Does it matter? Whatever my reasons I will not obey you."

He'd stilled and she found herself holding her breath, as if waiting for an attack. He stood in front of the fire, the light limning the tight fit of his breeches on muscled legs, his hands fisted by his sides, his big shoulders bunched and ready. His face was absolutely motionless, and she thought again how beautiful he was—beautiful and dangerously feral.

"Well, then, Mrs. Hollingbrook," he finally drawled, "that's yer choice sure enough, but ye'll not be eatin' at all until ye grace me supper table."

Her mouth dropped open in outrage. "You'll starve your own child?"

He sliced the air with the blade of his palm, his rings winking in the firelight. "I never said the babe won't be eatin'. I'll have enough victuals sent up for her, but not yerself, me darlin'. Feast on that fact, why don't ye?"

And with that he stalked from the room.

Of all the absurd, autocratic commands! For a moment Silence stared at the closed door, shocked. He couldn't just order her starved, could he? Except, of course, he *could*. Mickey O'Connor lived like some primitive king and like a king he was obeyed absolutely in his own home. Her gaze darted to the small tray that had been sent up earlier with Mary's supper. A few bits of cheese, and a bowl smeared with the remains of stewed apples still sat there. Silence could nibble on that, but Mary often decided to have a snack before bedtime. Silence would never deprive the baby of her food.

She blew out a frustrated breath. Why did Mr. O'Connor care anyway where she chose to dine? If he truly was surrounded by his gang and a bevy of beautiful females, he'd hardly notice if she were there or not. The whole thing came down to control: Mr. O'Connor wanted to have her at his supper table simply to show that he could make her do as he wished. Well, it would do such a dictatorial man good to find that he couldn't always have his way.

Besides, he wouldn't truly starve her, would he?

On that rather disquieting thought Silence finally roused herself to ready Mary for bed. Mary only fussed a little bit as her hands and face were washed and a clean chemise was pulled over her head. Halfway through their bedtime game of patty-cake Mary yawned and by the time she was settled in her little cot she was nearly asleep. Silence sat by the cot, quietly rubbing Mary's back until the little girl's knuckle crept to her mouth and her rosebud lips pursed in sleep.

Silence smiled ruefully. Mary was so angelic in sleep. One would never realize the tyrant the toddler could be when awake. And Silence had come so close to losing her today. Her breath caught on the thought and she leaned down to carefully brush a kiss against the tiny flushed cheek.

She rose then, and went to look at the tray before the fireplace. The last bits of cheese had been eaten before the game of patty-cake, but there was still a puddle of stewed apples in the bowl. Silence rubbed her stomach. She'd missed luncheon in the frantic search for Mary and now her stand against Mr. O'Connor's despotic ways seemed a bit...shortsighted.

She was reaching for the bowl when the door to the room opened. Silence snatched back her hand guiltily and whirled to find Fionnula creeping into the room.

"Oh!" the maid said, gasping softly at Silence's sudden movement. "I didn't mean to startle ye, ma'am."

"That's all right." Silence exhaled. "I was just preparing for bed."

"Of course, ma'am," the maid said shyly. "I'll just tidy up, shall I?"

Silence watched wistfully as Fionnula picked up the tray and brought it to the door, handing it to a servant outside.

"Thank you," Silence murmured.

"Not at all," Fionnula replied. "Will ye be needin' anythin' else tonight?"

"I don't think so," Silence began.

But Fionnula hastily answered. "Oh, but I fetched ye a fresh cloth with which to refresh yerself. I knew ye'd use the one here to wash the wee babe."

The maid had come closer as she said this and she now handed Silence a bundled cloth. Silence took it and immediately realized that something was hidden in the folds. Her gaze darted to Fionnula's face in question. The maid's eyes widened in warning as she glanced significantly toward the still-cracked door.

"If that's all, I'll just be biddin' ye good night."

"Yes." Silence hastily set the bundle on a table. "Thank you, Fionnula."

The maid went into her own bedroom and Silence crossed to the outer door. Bert was sitting in a chair against the wall on the opposite side of the hall.

Silence nodded to him. "Good night, Mr....er, Mr. Bert."

Bert scowled, but nodded grudgingly.

Silence closed her bedroom door very firmly. Goodness! She was beginning to wonder if the guards were there to ensure her and Mary's safety or to keep them from wandering. Shaking her head, she went to the bundle on the table and carefully unwrapped it. There lying on the pristine cloth was a slice of seedcake and a bit of roasted beef. Her stomach growled at the sight. What would Mr. O'Connor do if he learned of Fionnula's disobedience? Silence would have to talk to the maid tomorrow—tell Fionnula that she must not risk herself on Silence's behalf. But for now...

Well, right now she was very grateful for the supper.

She ate the cake and meat and washed it down with water from a pitcher on the table by the bed. Then she bathed as best she could. She doused the candles and removed her clothes in the dark. Clad only in her chemise, she climbed into the big canopied bed.

For long moments Silence lay, staring sightlessly in the dark. This morning she'd woken to a usual, chaotic day at the home. Tonight she lay cut off from all her family and friends. As she listened to the soft whisper of Mary Darling's breathing she made this vow: she would endure whatever she must for the baby's sake.

And whatever happened, she would not break under Mickey O'Connor's rule.

MICK WOKE IN the darkest part of night, the time when men forgot their bravery of the day and wonder if their souls still lived upon this lonely earth. He stared into the blackness, listening to the breathing of the wenches in his bed, thinking about the dream that had disturbed his sleep.

Her hazel eyes had been weeping, great teardrops of sorrow and accusation, which was a damned funny thing considering she'd never wept on that night over a year ago now. Why she should haunt his dreams so, he could not fathom. He'd killed men, some so young they still grew only down upon their cheeks. If he were to be haunted, surely it was those ghosts, long consigned to hell, that should be drifting through his sleep.

Not the color-shifting eyes of a woman who yet lived.

She was a part of him now somehow, whether he wanted it so or not. He'd not felt so close to a female since his mam—his mind skidded away from the thought. The heat and the stink of sex from the girls on either side of him suddenly made his stomach turn. Mick rose silently, padding on bare feet to pull on a pair of breeches. He left his room and stole through the darkened corridors of his palace until he reached Silence's door. Harry watched as Mick approached, though the guard didn't say a word. Carefully Mick turned the door handle. The door opened without squeaking for he'd ordered the hinges oiled well.

Her room was smaller than his, but somehow the air seemed fresher, less close. He could hear the sound of the child's heavy breathing in sleep and softer, slower, the woman's. He went to stand next to the bed and even though the room was unlit, he could make out, faintly, her slight form beneath the covers. The sight somehow calmed his soul. She lay in his bed, in his house, and no matter what bargain she thought she'd made with him, he knew the truth.

He had no plans to let her go—ever.

Chapter Three

The king roared with royal rage and called
his three nephews.
"Whomever of you can find this nighttime thief shall
be my heir!" cried the king.
Well the nephews all looked at each other and then they
each gathered weapons and settled themselves beneath
the cherry tree to wait for night and the thief....
—from *Clever John*

Silence's third meal of the day came just after two of the clock the next afternoon and from a quite unexpected source.

"Mum's the word, mind," Bert said gruffly, laying his finger aside of his nose.

Silence didn't even have time to thank the guard before he hurriedly stomped from the room.

She blinked, rather bemused at the bounty she'd received from Mickey O'Connor's servants. She'd never thought that the pirate's own people would defy him to bring her food. Uneasily she wondered what Mr. O'Connor would do if he found out about the underground rebellion against his orders not to feed her.

Shaking her head, she opened the rather grimy hand-kerchief Bert had thrust into her hands and contemplated the contents: three walnuts, a crumbled bit of pigeon pie, and a smashed cake with pink icing. Earlier she'd been given a slice of gammon and a muffin from Fionnula, and a scandalously out of season plum and a duck's wing from Harry.

The outer door to the room began to open and Silence hastily shoved the kerchief and its contents beneath a pillow on the bed. She turned, half-expecting to see the pirate himself, but it was a younger man who faced her. He was quite good-looking—nearly as handsome as Mickey O'Connor, but much more solemn, a bit shorter and only about twenty years old, if that.

The young man looked startled to see her as well. "Ah...er, I was looking for Fionnula."

"Oh," Silence said. "You must be her friend."

He blushed at her blurted words and looked suddenly even younger.

"I'm Mrs. Hollingbrook," she said to set him at ease. "Fionnula has gone down to fetch some hot water for Mary Darling's bath."

He nodded curtly. "I'll just be going."

"She'll be back soon," Silence said. He really did seem ill at ease. Perhaps he wasn't overly used to talking to outsiders? "Why don't you wait?"

"Ah..." He blinked, glancing past her. "Well, I—"

Suddenly he darted around Silence and scooped Mary Darling up. "Mind the hearth, lass. 'Tisn't safe for pretty little fingers."

"Goodness!" Silence hadn't noticed Mary near the fire, but the toddler had been quite inquisitive this afternoon. Mary had soon bored of remaining in one room and had been fretful and restless since noon.

Silence looked at the young man gratefully. "Thank you, er..."

"Bran," he said, smiling down at Mary Darling. "Bran Kavanagh." The little girl usually protested mightily at strangers, but she seemed charmed by Bran, looking curiously into his face.

Silence had to admit that when he smiled he was quite dashing. "She likes you."

"Aye." He fished a bit of string from his pocket and tied it in a loop before deftly threading it through his fingers and showing Mary the resulting cat's cradle. "The little ones often do. My mother had a dozen children and I looked after the ones younger than me."

"You're Irish?" His accent wasn't nearly as strong as Fionnula's or Mr. O'Connor's.

He glanced up warily, a lock of auburn hair falling over his forehead. "Bred and born right here in London, but, aye, both my mother and my father were from Ireland. Father was a weaver in Spitalfields."

"What happened—" Silence started, but Fionnula came in the room carrying a kettle of steaming water at that moment.

The maid stopped short on sight of Bran, her face lighting up. "Oh! I didn't know you were here."

"I just came to tell you I'd be gone tonight." Bran set Mary gently down by the settee and gave her the loop of string. "I thought you might want to know."

Fionnula knit her eyebrows, looking worried. "Is it the Vicar again?"

Bran frowned, darting a glance at Silence.

"What vicar?" Silence asked, looking between the two. "You have pirate business with a man of the cloth?"

"No, no," Bran said hastily. "The Vicar of Whitechapel isn't part of any church. He's a gin maker and he's..." Bran paused as if trying to find the word that wouldn't offend Silence's delicate ears.

"He's evil," Fionnula said. She crossed herself. "Pure evil."

Silence shivered at the solemn dread in Fionnula's voice and glanced at Mary, happily playing on the settee. "He's Mickey O'Connor's enemy, isn't he? One of the people Mr. O'Connor thinks might hurt Mary."

Bran didn't reply, but his grim glance at Mary was answer enough.

"Ye'd best be off, then," Fionnula said softly.

He nodded and left without further comment.

Silence blew out a breath and bent to pick up Mary. There had been a tiny, niggling suspicion at the back of her mind that Mr. O'Connor had made up all his talk of enemies who might hurt Mary. Perhaps he was playing some game of his own and simply wanted her and Mary in his palace for reasons she couldn't comprehend. That small suspicion was now laid to rest. The fear in Fionnula's face had been too genuine, Bran's voice too sure as he spoke of the Vicar. Whoever he was, the Vicar—and the danger he posed—would seem to be quite real.

Well, Mickey O'Connor might be an overbearing pirate, but they were safe enough in his palace. Silence sighed and began undressing Mary Darling for her bath, her thoughts turning to another matter. "Bran seemed quite nice."

"Yes." The maid was blushing still as she carefully poured the hot water into a basin and tested it with her elbow.

"And quite handsome," Silence said carelessly.

Fionnula jerked and some of the water splashed on the floor. She stared at the puddle and then raised worried eyes to Silence. "He's too pretty for me, 'tisn't he?"

Silence blinked. She'd meant to tease, not hurt. "Oh, no, I didn't mean that."

"But he is," Fionnula said dismally. "His eyes are so blue and he has such a handsome face. I see other girls lookin' at him and I just want to tear their hair out."

"Does he look back?" Silence asked as she placed Mary into the shallow bath.

"Nooo," Fionnula drew out the word as if unsure.

"Then I wouldn't worry," Silence said as she began to sponge Mary's little back. Mary was still busy with her string, dipping it into the water and draping it over her tummy. "I'm sure he finds you quite pretty."

Fionnula nibbled her lower lip as if unsure, then brightened. She took a bundle from her apron pocket.

"I got some more victuals for ye, ma'am," she whispered as she handed the bundle over.

"How kind of you," Silence said brightly as she unwrapped her fourth meal—either her third luncheon or perhaps an early supper? It was hard to tell. At this rate she might actually grow plump while on Mr. O'Connor's starvation diet.

She couldn't help but wonder if Mickey O'Connor was entirely oblivious to his people smuggling her food against his express command. She shivered at the thought.

What was the pirate's punishment for mutiny?

WINTER MAKEPEACE WOKE the next morning with a groan at his aching muscles. His room was still dark—the new day wouldn't dawn for another hour or more—yet he knew it was exactly half past five of the clock, for that was the time at which he'd trained his body to wake. He sat up in his narrow cot, feeling the twinge of thighs and buttocks, the result of spending all yesterday riding a horse.

Since he lived in the Home for Unfortunate Infants and Foundling Children and the day school where he taught small and not very disciplined boys was only a stone's throw away, he had no need to ride a horse usually. However, his trip to Oxford had necessitated the renting of a nag. He rubbed his legs for a half minute or so and then stood, pushing the aches from his mind. They were of no consequence and would fade soon enough.

He had to duck his head as he bent over the washbasin to sluice his face. His room was under the eaves and the roof sloped sharply. But months of living in the cramped space had accustomed him to the irregularities of the room, so now he could move about without knocking his head on a beam, even in the dark.

Winter dressed in white shirt, black waistcoat, black breeches, and black coat and threw open his attic window to toss the wastewater from his ablutions into the alley below. The sky was turning a pinkish gray, silhouetting the haphazard rooftops of St. Giles. He gazed at it only a moment before shutting the window firmly and lighting a candle. For the next hour he worked steadily at a narrow desk, writing and reading. Some of his work was in preparation for the day's lessons, but he also was in correspondence with scholars of philosophy and religion both in England and on the continent. In fact, his recent trip to Oxford had been to call upon an old acquaintance—an elderly philosopher who was on his deathbed.

When the sky had fully brightened, Winter stood and

stretched before pinching the candle out. Picking up the pitcher, he locked his bedroom carefully behind him and paused for a moment to glance at his sister, Silence's, bedroom door. No light shone beneath it. She was probably still abed. He contemplated waking her, then decided against it. Silence could use the extra minutes of rest.

He clattered down the stairs, nearly running into a small boy lurking rather suspiciously on one of the turns.

Winter grabbed him by the collar—he'd learned early in his career of teaching young hellions that it was best to catch and then ask. "Why are you not at breakfast with the other boys, Joseph Tinbox?"

Joseph, his freckled face cowled by the jacket Winter held, rolled his eyes up at him. "I was jus' now goin' down, Mr. Makepeace."

"Indeed?" Winter inquired skeptically. He set down the pitcher and made a lightning fast snatch at the object Joseph had been attempting to hide behind his back. "And what plans did you have for this sling?"

Joseph's eyes widened in what was a very good imitation of innocence at the leather strap dangling before his eyes. "I found it on the stairs, truly I did."

Winter cocked his eyebrow, staring at the boy.

Joseph's gaze slid away from his own.

"Joseph," Winter said quietly. "You know that I do not condone lying in this house. A man's word is a treasure he holds within himself no matter how poor his outer garments. To squander it recklessly is the mark of not only a fool, but a cheat as well. Now tell me. Is this sling yours?"

The boy swallowed, his small throat working. "Yes, sir."

"I am displeased to hear that you've been playing with a sling," Winter said calmly. "But pleased that you have spoken the truth to me. As punishment for the former, I would like you to sweep out the kitchen hearth and scrub clean the outer tiles around the fireplace."

"Aw!" Joseph began, but gulped back his groan at a look from Winter. "Yes, sir."

"Good." Winter let him go, pocketed the sling, picked up the pitcher, and gestured for the boy to precede him down the stairs.

They descended in silence, but as they made the bottom step, Joseph hesitated.

"Sir?"

"Yes?" Winter glanced at Joseph. He was shifting his weight from one foot to the other.

"I'm sorry, sir."

"We all make mistakes, Joseph," Winter said gently. "It is how one acts afterward that distinguishes the righteous man from the dishonest one."

Joseph's brow crinkled as he contemplated that statement. Then it cleared. "Yes, sir."

The boy walked into the kitchen, his habitual jaunty step nearly restored.

Winter felt his lips twitch in amusement as he followed. This was not the first such talk he'd had with Joseph, and he did not expect it would be the last, but at heart the boy was a good lad.

The home's kitchen was bright and loud with the chatter of children. Two long tables took up the center of the crowded room, one for the boys, one for the girls. Joseph Tinbox went to the boys' table and hopped onto one of the long benches.

"Good morning, Mr. Makepeace," Alice, one of the home's maids said, pausing as she hurried by.

"Good morning to you, Alice," Winter said, handing her the pitcher.

"Oh, thank you, sir, for saving me the trip upstairs." Alice flashed a smile that lit up her rather careworn face before rushing to catch a spilled cup of milk.

"Children," Nell Jones, the head maidservant at the home, raised her voice above the cacophony. "Please bid Mr. Makepeace good day."

"Good morning, Mr. Makepeace!" a ragged chorus immediately responded.

"Good morning, children," Winter said as he sat on a bench.

Nell hurried over with a bowl of porridge and a teapot.

"Thank you," Winter murmured as he sipped the scalding tea. He glanced across the table to a small dark-haired boy sleepily picking his nose. "Did you sleep well, Henry Putman?"

All the boys at the Home for Unfortunate Infants and Foundling Children were christened Joseph and all the girls Mary—except for Henry Putman. When Henry had come to the home—at the advanced age of four—he had urgently argued to keep his own name. And since unlike most of the orphans he'd been old enough to speak, his wish had been granted.

At Winter's greeting, Henry hastily dropped his hand. "Yes."

The older boy sitting next to Henry elbowed him.

Henry glanced at the older boy in outrage.

"Sir!" hissed the older boy.

"Oh!" Henry exclaimed. "Yes, sir. I slept good. 'Cept for a dream."

Winter, well aware that the subject of children's dreams

could take up most of breakfast, only murmured an, "Indeed?"

But Henry had found his voice. "'Bout frogs, it was. Big frogs. Big as *cows*."

Henry spread wide his arms to demonstrate the size of the mythical frogs, nearly upsetting his neighbor's bowl of porridge.

Winter caught the bowl with the ease of long practice.

The older boy had other concerns. "Frogs can't grow that big. Everyone knows that!"

Winter addressed the elder boy mildly. "Joseph Smith, perhaps you can inform Henry of your thoughts regarding the relative size of dream frogs in a more polite manner."

For a moment both boys were silent as they worked through his statement and Winter was able to take a bite of his porridge in near peace.

Then Joseph Smith said, "I don't believe frogs grow as big as cows."

To which Henry Putman replied, "They do in my dreams."

Which seemed to settle the matter.

A sudden squeal made Winter glance at the girls' table and he noticed that Silence still hadn't come down for breakfast. He caught Nell Jones's eye and motioned her over.

"I believe it may be time to wake my sister."

Nell's blue eyes shifted down and away and Winter felt a vague sense of unease. "Um, well, as to that sir..."

"Yes?" he prompted when the maidservant seemed to have trouble finding her words.

Nell screwed tight her eyes. "She's not here."

Winter blinked. "What?"

"Mrs. Hollingbrook left the home the day before

yesterday," Nell said rapidly as if to get a nasty task over as quickly as possible. "And Mary Darling is with her."

The children had begun to quiet, sensing with the animal instinct of the young when danger or excitement was around.

"Where," Winter asked very softly, "is my sister?"

Nell gulped. "She's gone to live at Charming Mickey O'Connor's palace."

SILENCE HAD JUST finished feeding Mary Darling a small bowl of porridge that morning when she heard the faint sounds of male shouting. Fionnula glanced up. Silence paused, a spoonful of the last scrapings from the bowl still held outstretched toward Mary. The toddler had lost interest in her breakfast and was busy fingering the sticky bowl, studiously ignoring the spoon.

Silence tapped her on the shoulder. "Mary, finish your porridge."

The shouts rose again, one of them sounding familiar.

A chill went through Silence. She dropped the spoon and ran to the door.

"Ma'am, ye can't—" Fionnula called behind her as Silence yanked open the door.

The scowling face of Bert met her gaze.

"Who is below?" she demanded.

He opened his mouth, but she was already shoving past him.

"Oi!" Bert yelled in indignation.

Silence ran down the stairs, fearful of the quiet below. What had they done with him?

She made the lower hall, skidded through the doors, and ran into a large male back, blocking her way.

"Oof!" she muttered, trying to dodge around Mickey O'Connor's form. She just caught sight of Winter—standing very still in the middle of a pack of pirates—then Mr. O'Connor hauled her back against his chest and set his hands on her waist to hold her.

Silence inhaled sharply at his touch. The exotic scent of frankincense surrounded her. She hadn't seen him since their argument the night before last over supper and already she seemed to have forgotten the intensity of his presence.

Winter's mouth flattened. "Unhand my sister."

"Eager as I am to bow to yer smallest command, Mr. Makepeace," Mickey O'Connor drawled above her, his chest rumbling against her back, "I can't in all good conscience do so when the lady herself hasn't asked me."

Winter looked at her. "Silence?"

She swallowed. Winter looked like thunder. He stood clad in his habitual somber clothes, his empty hands fisted by his side, a round, black hat on his head. Like all her brothers he preferred his dark brown hair undressed and tied back simply. The armed pirates circling him were almost comically more dangerous looking. Yet somehow he'd made it past the front door and this far into Mickey O'Connor's well-guarded palace.

Perhaps it was a measure of Winter's quiet authority that the pirates hadn't stopped him.

Silence turned within the circle of Mr. O'Connor's arms and looked up into his face. He was so close she could see each individual inky eyelash and notice the tiny wrinkles fanning from the corners of his deep brown eyes. "Let me talk to him."

Those perceptive eyes narrowed at her—the pirate didn't look at all happy.

"Please," she whispered.

"As ye wish." Mickey O'Connor spread wide his arms and looked over her head. "Five minutes, Mr. Makepeace. No longer. Ye can talk to yer lovely sister in me library."

Mickey O'Connor has a library? For a second, Silence was distracted by the thought of this outrageously virile man bent studiously over dusty books.

The image was dashed the moment they were shown into the library, however. Naturally Mr. O'Connor would have a library like no other she'd ever imagined. It was a middling-sized room, but from the carved rosewood ceiling overhead to the thick Persian carpet underfoot, the entire place was fantastic. Ancient statuary stood about the room, no doubt plundered from ships. Here there was a Diana in flight, her hunting hounds bounding beside her. There a bust of some ancient bearded dignitary. And the books! Every surface held open books, each one fabulously illustrated. From a folio of exotic animals to a tiny prayer book, delicately illuminated in gold.

"Goodness!" Silence breathed in awe, looking around the exquisite room. "Have you ever seen such a wonderful place, Winter?" She frowned. "Though it could do with some comfortable chairs."

"At the moment I'm a bit more interested in you than in the room, sister," Winter said drily.

Silence flushed and looked at her brother. His straight brown brows were drawn together in worry.

She inhaled and smoothed a hand down the apron she'd put on this morning out of habit—only now did she notice that it was a bit crooked. "I'm sorry to have left the home so abruptly. I know it must have distressed you—"

"Distressed." Winter said the word flatly.

Silence bit her lip.

"Are you being held here against your will?"

"Oh, no," she said.

He nodded. "I'm not a man given to hysteria. If I were, I'd be bald at this moment from having torn out my hair on the way over here. Mickey O'Connor, Silence?"

His last three words were soft, but there was a wealth of meaning behind them. Winter had seen her after she'd left Mr. O'Connor the last time. He knew what had been done to her.

And he suspected much worse.

"He's Mary Darling's father," she said.

His eyebrows lifted in inquiry.

"He says that Mary must stay here because she is in danger from his enemies. But he has let me stay as well, to take care of her."

Winter closed his eyes briefly and when he opened them again they were filled with sorrow. "If the child is truly his, then you have no hold on her. You must give her up."

"No!" She swallowed and lowered her voice. "You don't understand. Mr. O'Connor has promised to let me have Mary Darling—let me have her *forever*—once his enemies are no longer a threat. Don't you see? I can take her away from here."

"I think I'd rather trust the word of a snake than Mr. O'Connor."

"But—"

He stepped forward and gently touched her on the elbow. "He's using you, sister. Perhaps he only sees you as an amusement, perhaps his plan is far worse, but in either case you can be sure of one thing: Mickey O'Connor is interested only in pleasing himself. He cares for neither you nor Mary Darling."

"All the more reason for me to stay," she whispered. "I love Mary, Winter. She's as much a daughter to me as if I'd given birth to her. I wouldn't be able to leave her here by herself even if I had no hope of eventually bringing her home. But since I do ... Well, then, it's only a matter of hanging on."

"Your reputation will be in tatters if you stay here."

"My reputation already is in tatters."

"Because of *him*." Winter rarely raised his voice, rarely showed emotion of any kind, but he spat the word "him" with deep loathing.

Silence's eyes widened. She knew Winter disliked Mr. O'Connor, but she'd had no idea of the antipathy her brother held toward the pirate.

"Winter—"

"He'll destroy you and he'll destroy the home because of you." Winter's words were tight and controlled. "We cannot afford speculation about your virtue right now, sister. Think of the home if you will not think of yourself."

She closed her eyes, feeling sick. She was letting him down, betraying his trust, but... "I'm sorry. I'm truly sorry about the home, but it's *Mary Darling*, Winter. Please. She's all that I have left."

"*Christ.*" Her brother turned and walked to a bookshelf, staring blindly at the rows of expensive embossed leather spines.

For a moment there was quiet in the library.

Silence bit her lip, watching her brother. Waiting to see if she'd broken his trust irrevocably. Winter was the youngest of her brothers, the one closest to her in age—and closest to her heart.

If she hadn't been studying him she might not have seen his shoulders lower a fraction of an inch. "I know what Mary Darling means to you, sister. I've witnessed your grief and the renewal of your inner joy this last year. Much of it was due to the baby. If this is the only way to keep Mary Darling, then stay."

She sighed, opening her mouth to thank him.

Winter swung suddenly to look at her and she saw that his normally calm eyes blazed. "But I saw what Mickey O'Connor did to you. I saw the damage in your eyes. I cannot stop you from this mad plan, but do not expect me to dance with joy at the prospect of you in Mickey O'Connor's foul hands."

Behind them a single clap shattered the intimacy of the library.

Silence swung around.

Mickey O'Connor lounged in a narrow doorway cleverly hidden in the carved paneling. "I appreciate yer stamp o' approval, Makepeace. It warms the cockles o' me heart, it does."

Winter had gone very still next to Silence and for some reason she had the feeling he was holding himself in check, keeping himself from violence only by the thinnest of threads. Silly, really. Winter was the least violent man she knew.

But she placed a restraining hand on his arm anyway. "Please."

"I will do as you wish," Winter said to her, though his gaze never left Mr. O'Connor's face. "I'm leaving today, but next time I come I'll take you with me. Until then, if you feel yourself in peril at any time, send word to me and I will come for you—night or day."

"Yes, Winter," she said meekly, realizing that her brother needed to feel that he had some control over the matter.

Mickey O'Connor's black eyes slid to hers mockingly.

Fortunately, Winter didn't seem to see the look. He bent to kiss Silence on the cheek, murmuring as he straightened, "Remember: any time."

She nodded, unable to speak because of the lump that suddenly clogged her throat. She'd known that Winter was fond of her, but his actions today had spoken of real brotherly love: he'd stormed Mickey O'Connor's palace by himself for her. She'd never realized that he loved her so, and suddenly she felt the paradoxical loss of something she'd not known she'd had before now. He was leaving her here—only because she asked it of him. Only because he truly loved her.

"Me men will be showin' ye out, Makepeace," Mr. O'Connor said, "Jus' to make sure ye don't get lost 'tween here and me front door."

Winter glanced at the pirate and for a moment Silence held her breath as the men exchanged some kind of unspoken communication.

Then Winter turned and left the room.

Silence glared at Mickey O'Connor. "You didn't need to goad him."

"No?" The pirate straightened away from the doorway, ambling closer to her.

"No." Silence frowned at him. "We've already made our bargain and I have no intention of reneging on it. Winter has only my best interests at heart. By goading him, you could've started a rather nasty argument."

He shrugged. "But see, me darlin', that's where ye and I must disagree. Yer brother is a hard man. Had I not stood upon me principles, he'd've had ye out o' here before ye could blink."

Winter a hard man? What a very strange notion. Silence shook her head. Men could be very odd at times. She watched as Mr. O'Connor brushed his fingers idly over a huge volume of colored maps, his many rings flashing.

"I never would've guessed you had a room such as this," she said.

His black eyebrows winged up his forehead in cynical amusement. "Yer sayin' these things are too refined for a crude pirate?"

"No," she exclaimed, although of course that *had* been what she meant. "I . . . I just thought . . ."

Her voice faded as she watched him trail a long finger over the tip of Diana's nude breast.

He turned and caught her staring. "Aye, Mrs. Hollingbrook?"

Her face was aflame, but she met his gaze. Winter hadn't backed down from this man and neither would she. "There's no need for a room such as this."

"No need?"

She struggled to put her thoughts into words. "Your throne room is outrageously ostentatious, but you let others see it. It's almost a public place because you receive visitors there. The ostentation has a purpose. You intimidate with it. But this library . . ."

"Aye?"

"There's no need for it because you don't use it to impress others."

His head was cocked as he stared at her curiously. "What a very interestin' women ye are, Mrs. Hollingbrook. If I don't use me library to impress, then what do I use it for, if ye don't mind me askin'?"

"That's just what I wondered," she said. "Why have this library?"

The stark question seemed to catch him by surprise. He watched her a moment, hesitating, then seemed to come to a decision. He crossed to where another big book lay. Silence followed curiously, looking over his elbow as he opened the book.

An emerald beetle was revealed, perched on the stem of some exotic plant. The color was so startling, so vivid, the insect looked ready to crawl off the page.

Mickey O'Connor traced the edges of the page lightly. "One night maybe eight years or so ago, I found a book like this one in a chest taken off a ship comin' from the West Indies."

"You mean you stole it," Silence said severely.

Mickey grinned at her, flashing strong white teeth. "Belonged to one o' them plantation owners over there, I hear. Man who owned hundreds o' slaves laborin' to grow his sugar and make him his fortune. Aye, I stole from one such as he, and not a night's sleep have I ever lost over it."

Silence looked back down at the illustrated book. She certainly didn't approve of thieving, but then again she didn't approve of the trade of human beings, either. "You said you, uh, *found* a book like this one eight years ago."

"Aye," he said, returning his own gaze to the emerald beetle. "Found it, and opened it, and was amazed. I'd never seen such, ye understand. It was filled with pictures o' butterflies. Butterflies aren't exactly plentiful in the parts o' London I grew up in, and butterflies such as these"—his elegant fingers caressed the page as if remembering—"well, it almost makes a man believe in God, it does."

Silence swallowed. She'd been raised in London as well, but there had been trips to parks and outings to Greenwich and other towns. She'd seen butterflies and more—tame deer, wild birds, lovely gardens, and flowers. What kind of boyhood had he had never to have seen a butterfly?

"Where were you raised in London?" she asked softly.

"St. Giles," he said, still tracing the gilt pages. "Not more'n a stone's throw from here."

She tried to picture him as a boy. He'd have been beautiful, of course, lean and graceful. The thought made her uneasy. Beautiful youths didn't last long in St. Giles. "You lived with your family?"

"Me mam...and *him*."

She frowned at the emphasis on the last word. Was he talking about his father—or another man? She glanced at him, but ended up asking the easier question. "Do your parents still live in St. Giles?"

He gave her an ironic look and closed the big picture book. Obviously he had no intention of answering her.

Irritating man. She looked around the little library. "Which book is it?"

"What?"

She gestured to the overflowing bookshelves. "Where is your butterfly book?"

He shook his head. "I don't keep it here."

"But then—"

"What a curious thing ye are." He turned to place the book on a shelf.

She inhaled, feeling frustrated. "What is it you want from me?"

When he turned, his face had gone blank. "What makes ye think I want anythin' from ye, me darlin'?"

But she wasn't going to let him slide away from this question. She took a step closer and he made a movement almost as if he would retreat from her. "You didn't have to give Mary Darling to me. Didn't have to involve me in your life at all. What is it you're doing?"

He glanced away from her, a muscle clenching in his jaw. "I'm protectin' ye and the babe, nothin' more. All ye have to do is stay in yer rooms and be content."

Stay in her rooms? Be *content*? Silence's eyes widened incredulously. "Do I look like a doll to you?"

His eyelids lowered, his beautiful black lashes sweeping his cheeks before he glanced back up at her again. "Nay, yer a lovely woman, ye are. I'd not be mistakin' ye for any playthin'."

Her lips parted at his intimate tone.

His sensuous mouth curved at her confusion. "Supper's early tonight—seven o' the clock, mind. I trust we'll be graced with yer lovely presence."

Silence stiffened. He wouldn't catch her off guard so easily. "On the contrary, I have no intention of dining with you, Mr. O'Connor."

The smile was abruptly gone from his face, leaving it rather frighteningly grim. "Then ye'll fast in yer rooms, me darlin', until ye can see fit to change yer mind."

And with that he pivoted and strode from the room.

Chapter Four

*But a very strange thing happened. As dusk fell in
the king's garden, all three of the nephews began to
nod and soon they all slept. In the morning they woke
and none of the three could remember a thing. The
nephews had to confess rather sheepishly to the king
that they had not caught the thief. But when Clever
John ran his hand through his hair, a bright green
feather fell to the ground. . . .*
—from *Clever John*

"But ye can't!" Fionnula hissed early the next morning.

"Who says so?" Silence asked stubbornly as she took a
quick look up and down the hall outside her room. Harry
was eating breakfast and she'd just sent Bert to call a servant. She only had a minute at most while the guards were
occupied.

"Himself, that's who," Fionnula cried in a muted wail.
"He's given orders that yer not to leave the rooms until ye
consent to dine with him."

Silence snorted softly. "Mickey O'Connor is not my
master."

"He mayn't be," Fionnula said, "but he's used to bein'
obeyed."

"Then Mr. O'Connor is in for a surprise."

Silence slipped from the room with Mary Darling in her arms and ran lightly toward the back of the hallway—away from the stairs where Bert had gone. She stopped at the corner to catch her breath before continuing more sedately.

A touch at her shoulder nearly made her scream.

"Where are ye plannin' on goin'?" Fionnula whispered.

"I don't know," Silence admitted, "but Mary needs new surroundings to explore. Perhaps a sitting room?"

Fionnula looked doubtful. "I don't think Himself spends much time sittin'. He's not exactly gentry."

"The library, then. That's below us." Silence looked worriedly at Fionnula. "But I don't want to get you into trouble. Perhaps I ought to tie you up? We can say I've overpowered you."

Fionnula rolled her eyes. "As if anyone would believe that."

Behind them came a noise like an enraged bull. "Oi!" Bert had discovered her absence.

Silence couldn't restrain a start, but at least she didn't break stride.

Mary bounced in her arms, looking over Silence's shoulder. "'Ert!"

They reached the stairwell just as Bert caught up with them.

"Now see 'ere," the guard panted. "Where d'ye think yer goin'?"

"To the library," Silence said airily as she started down the stairs.

Bert scoffed. "Right next to 'Imself's plannin' room, that is. Ye'll not get two steps past the stairwell."

The news made Silence's pulse race. She was already at the landing, but she didn't stop, sailing through the doorway and into the lower corridor. Charming Mickey O'Connor might discover her disobedience—she was counting on it, in fact—but that wouldn't detain her. It was important that she assert her rights, her will to not be treated like some pawn at the beck and call to Mickey O'Connor's whims. In fact—

Hard hands caught her waist and Silence couldn't help a squeak of surprise and alarm. She was lifted quite off her feet with Mary Darling still clutched to her breast.

"What is Mrs. Hollingbrook doin' out o' her rooms?" Mickey O'Connor's voice rumbled behind her, far too calmly.

Silence craned her neck and saw that the pirate held her at arm's length, his face quite expressionless. She gulped and faced forward again, only to see Fionnula frozen while Bert opened and closed his mouth like a landed fish.

"Don't blame Bert or Fionnula," Silence blurted out. "This is my fault—"

"I never thought otherwise," Mr. O'Connor snapped. "Take the babe."

Fionnula darted forward, eyes wide and before Silence could protest Mary was in the maidservant's arms.

Silence frowned. "Now see here—"

"Not a word," the pirate whispered, and somehow his lowered voice was even more frightening than a shout.

He swung her and suddenly Silence found herself on her stomach over Mickey O'Connor's shoulder—a most ignominious position—one broad hand clamped firmly over her bottom to hold her in place.

"Put me down," she said with as much dignity as

possible, considering that all the blood was rushing to her head.

He didn't bother to reply. Instead, he simply turned and strode down the hall.

"Mr. O'Connor!" Silence found she had no choice but to brace her hands on his hips if she didn't want her nose to bounce off his extremely firm rear end.

He didn't reply as he mounted the stairs—seemingly without effort despite steadying her weight with only one arm—but Silence thought she might have heard him muttering to himself under his breath.

Or possibly cursing.

She gulped. She'd defied him outright this time—and humiliated him in front of his man and Fionnula to boot. There was a very real possibility that his ire might take a physical form. But she'd made up her mind not to bend to his will and she'd stick to her guns—no matter the cost.

So it was with a feeling of both defiance and trepidation that Silence found herself tossed on the bed minutes later. She bounced on the soft mattress, struggling to push her hair out of her hot face. She must present a firm but calm countenance to the pirate.

Still she couldn't help gulping when at last she looked up.

Mickey O'Connor loomed over her, arms crossed, feet braced wide apart. "What in the name o' all that's holy did ye think ye were doin'?"

She tilted her chin. "Going for a walk."

He bent, thrusting his handsome face into hers. "When I gave ye orders to stay in yer rooms?"

"Yes." She licked her bottom lip.

For a moment his gaze dropped to her mouth before snapping back up to meet her eyes. "*No* one disobeys me in me own home!"

For a moment she wasn't sure she could speak. He was crowded into her, his very breath hot upon her cheek. He was so much bigger than she. So much more physically powerful.

But she had determination. "Evidently someone does now."

His nostrils flared and for a moment all she could do was hold her breath.

Then he abruptly straightened and stomped to her door. He wrenched it open and glared at her. "Stay in this fuckin' room or I swear ye'll be regrettin' it."

The walls shook as he slammed the door.

Silence exhaled and flopped back on the bed. She felt as if she'd weathered a thunderstorm, but one thought rang gleefully in her mind:

She, Silence Hollingbrook, meek widow of no particular means, had just faced down Charming Mickey O'Connor, the most feared pirate in London.

SUCH A STUBBORN *little thing she was!* Mick stalked along the corridor to the stairs. When he came to a rag and bucket, carelessly left by a maid, he kicked it over. The clatter of the falling bucket was gratifying, but didn't tame his foul mood. Why wouldn't she sit meekly in her rooms? Why wouldn't she fucking *obey* him? He hadn't a bloody clue what he would do if she defied him again. The thought of giving her any sort of pain was simply out of the question and if he couldn't physically punish her...

Mick stopped at the bottom of the stairs and glared sightlessly at a tiny picture on the wall. It was an ancient Madonna and child, their halos layered in gold, Mary's face was pinched and disapproving and an odd shade of green. The widow had been in his home a mere two days and already she was overthrowing his orderly life.

There was the sound of a throat clearing behind him.

"What the bloody hell is it, Harry?" Mick growled without turning.

"Ah, beggin' yer pardon, sir, but Bert is upset that Mrs. 'Ollingbrook got past 'im and I was thinkin'—"

Mick shook his head once. "I'm not discussin' *her* right now."

"Ah . . ."

"Is there anythin' else?"

"Bran was wantin' to know when ye'll be talkin' to the owner of the *Alexander.*"

Mick turned at that. "After me supper, but afore midnight. Let the man get sleepy in his great house a-thinkin' Mick O'Connor has forgotten that he didn't pay tithe on his last bloody ship."

Harry pursed his lips. "Sleepy or not, 'e'd be a great fool not to be well guarded in 'is own 'ome."

"No doubt." Mick started down the corridor. "Which is why I'll be bringin' Pat and Sean as well as Bran."

"Think that'll be enough?" Harry hurried to keep up with him.

"Aye. We'll be a-waitin' in his room for him when he goes to bed." Mick reached his rooms and flung open the door. "The shock of seein' four armed men in his bedroom will, I think, be enough to soften him up right finely."

Mick stopped dead in the middle of his bedroom. His

bed was a huge piece of furniture with posts as big around as a man's thighs. He'd slept comfortably there with two other bedmates—and had he wished, could've fit another three. The bed was so massive it usually dwarfed whoever occupied it. But not the big dog draped over both his pillows. The animal lay with its pale belly exposed, forepaws up in the air, its great head turned to the side, jaws agape and tongue lolling.

"What," Mick said softly, "is Lad doin' in me bed?"

Hearing his name, Lad opened small, piggish, upsidedown eyes, gazing with idiotic adoration as his whip-thin tail thumped the covers.

"Ah." Harry scratched behind one ear. "Well, see, 'e was lookin' so forlorn, like, out in the courtyard by 'imself. Seemed an awful shame to leave 'im there all alone."

"Off!" Mick roared at the dog.

Lad's transformation was instantaneous. His tiny triangle ears folded back, his eyes narrowed worriedly, and he rolled so that he could crawl toward the edge of the bed on his belly.

"Is that mud on his paws?" Mick asked in outrage.

Harry glanced at the dog. "I do believe it is," he said as if making a discovery.

"Christ!" Mick watched disgustedly as Lad made the edge of the bed and slithered off, thumping to the floor. The dog seemed to think that his apology was done—or perhaps he'd already forgotten that Mick was mad at him—for he gamboled over as frisky as a lamb.

"He's not even me dog," Mick muttered.

Lad sat, one back leg sprawled out to the side, tongue hanging from his mouth, and grinned up at him. He completely ignored Harry, his supposed master.

"The dog 'as a wonderful affection for ye," Harry said brightly.

"Well, I haven't for him," Mick said. "Take the beast out to the courtyard and get the maids to clean me bed."

"O' course, o' course," Harry said, not moving. He cleared his throat delicately. "And Mrs. 'Ollingbrook?"

Mick swung on him. "What about her?"

Harry blinked. "Ah . . . I thought a nice walk about the place wi' the babe might make 'er feel less cooped up."

Mick snorted so loudly Lad cocked his head. "That woman isn't goin' anywhere until she bends to me will."

"Then she won't be joinin' us for supper this evenin'?" Harry asked, hope dying hard in his hangdog eyes.

"Not unless she has a sudden change o' heart," Mick said sourly. "In fact both she and that hellion babe will be stayin' in her rooms with only food for the babe until she makes up her stubborn mind to come sup at me table."

Harry tilted his head back to study the ceiling.

"What?" Mick demanded.

"Well, it's jus' that I've noticed in dealin' wi' the fair sex that it sometimes does a man well to show a little kindness."

"Have I not given her a bed and a room fit for a queen?" Mick asked softly, dangerously.

"Ye-es—"

"And have I not been most accomodatin' o' her?"

"Well—" Harry looked doubtful.

Mick sliced his hand through the air. "All I ask is that she sup wi' me. No other wench has disobeyed me thus to me own face."

"Aye, but most wenches ye be dealin' wi' are doxies or servant girls," Harry pointed out in a reasonable tone. He took a step backward nonetheless. "Mrs. 'Ollingbrook is neither."

For a moment Mick merely stared at his henchman. Jaysus, when had his life become so complicated that he took to pleading his case with Harry? He had Silence in his house. He had her where he wanted her. It wasn't supposed to be like this. She wasn't supposed to turn his life upside down.

"Why can't she live in me palace and be happy?" Mick muttered.

Harry shrugged massive shoulders. "Mayhap because she's a woman. They do 'ave minds o' their own, I find."

"Me orders stand," Mick declared. "She may not be a whore or a servant, but she'll bloody well learn to obey me."

Harry and Lad stared at him with strangely similar bloodshot brown eyes, sad reproach in both their gazes.

Mick flung out a hand irritably. "Get on with ye!"

Dog and man turned toward the bedroom door.

"And keep that dog out o' me house!" Mick roared after them.

BY THAT NIGHT Silence was going quietly mad in her bedroom.

"He can't keep me locked up here like some prisoner!" she muttered to Fionnula.

"Yes, ma'am," the girl said with admirable equanimity considering she'd been listening to Silence complain for most of the day.

Silence grimaced. "I'm sorry. It's just that this is so... so *medieval*. Who does Mickey O'Connor think he is? Some pagan god?"

"Oh no, ma'am," Fionnula replied earnestly. "I don't think he considers himself a god. Now a prince or even one of those sultans they have about in those heathen lands..."

"It's thinking like that that makes him as arrogant as he is." Silence paced to the windows. They were draped in lovely rose curtains, perhaps to hide the fact that they'd been boarded up. She could just make out a sliver of the street below if she applied her eye to a crack in the boards. "This is impossible! If he doesn't care if I go mad from confinement, he should at least think of his daughter."

Mary Darling whimpered as if in answer. Already this evening the little girl had thoroughly explored the room, been warned away from the fire a half a dozen times, and been rescued out from under the bed twice. Now she sat, fretfully playing with the spoon and dish leftover from her supper.

Silence's stomach rumbled at the sight of the empty porridge dish. She'd told Fionnula that she could no longer accept her smuggled food—not after defying Mickey O'Connor this morning. Fionnula, Bert, and Harry were already in enough trouble because of her.

"Ye could come down to sup with him," Fionnula pointed out cautiously.

Silence turned to glare at the girl. "Not as long as he orders me to do so."

Fionnula ducked her head.

"I'm sorry." Silence winced. It was hardly the girl's fault that Mr. O'Connor was such a despotic beast.

Silence wrapped her arms about her waist. She'd already acquiesced to living with him. She was a lone woman with very little power in Mickey O'Connor's palace. Refusing to dine with him really was the *only* way she could assert herself.

"It's too much," Silence muttered to herself and stomped out the door.

"What are ye about?" Fionnula cried as she scooped up Mary and hurried after.

"Ma'am?" Harry rose in alarm from the chair outside her room. Bert was apparently in disgrace—she hadn't seen him since she'd escaped this morning.

"I'm going to have a word with the sultan," Silence said with determination to them both. She turned and marched down the stairs before they could voice any more protests.

A moment later she opened Mickey O'Connor's bedroom door with a jerk, bracing herself. It was with something of a letdown that she realized the room was empty.

"He's off on his business," Fionnula panted from behind her, Mary still in her arms. "They were all talkin' about it at supper tonight. Come away now, ma'am. 'Twouldn't do to be found in here."

Silence ignored the warning, transfixed by the room. She'd been in here, of course, on that night nearly a year ago. He'd led her into this extravagantly decorated room, fed her, bid her enter his huge bed, and while she'd watched, had begun to unbutton his fine lace shirt. His long, elegant fingers had seemed to mesmerize her. She remembered staring, her mouth going dry with fear, as he'd bared his upper chest and then, his sardonic eyes locked with hers, he had lifted his arms, grabbing his shirt behind his back to draw it—

A sudden movement on the bed nearly made her scream. As it was Silence was unable to suppress a squeak of alarm. "What in God's name is that?"

Fionnula peered around her. "Lad! Do get off the bed."

An enormous dog raised its head, tiny eyes looking worried. The animal jumped clumsily to the floor and started for them.

Silence backed away quickly, ready to slam the door shut. "Is it dangerous?"

"Naw," Harry said, "I've never seen Lad 'urt anythin'—unless ye count an old soup bone."

"But he's so big." Silence eyed the animal worriedly. Lad was a none-too-clean fawn color, his little flop ears much too small for his massive head. She could see each rib on the dog's side—as well as the muscles that moved beneath his tawny coat. A sudden thought struck her. "Mr. O'Connor has a pet?"

Fionnula scrunched up her nose. "I don't know that I'd call Lad a pet. More like he just hangs around the place."

Harry cleared his throat. "Lad's me dog, actually."

"But he sleeps in Mr. O'Connor's bed?" Silence began skeptically, but at that moment the inevitable happened—Mary Darling caught sight of the dog.

"Gog!" she cried and bounced so hard that Fionnula set the baby at her feet.

Lad ducked around Silence and made straight for the baby.

"No!" Silence started forward to haul the animal back by the scruff of the neck—Lad wore no collar.

But before she could reach him, the animal stopped before Mary and wagged his tail tentatively as he looked down at her.

Mary chortled with glee and grabbed his muzzle with both her hands. "Gog!"

"Oh, my God," Silence breathed, her hand hovering

over the big dog's neck. She'd throw herself on him to tear him away from her baby if she had to. She wrinkled her nose. Even if the beast smelled like a stable.

Lad stood still, save for his tail wagging ever faster. Mary had his jowls in her tiny fists, but the big dog didn't seem to mind. As Silence watched he swiped the baby's chin with an enormous tongue.

"Told ye 'e's not dangerous," Harry said proudly.

"He might not be a danger," Silence conceded, "but he certainly needs a bath. He reeks."

"Well, he does usually spend most of his time in the courtyard," Fionnula admitted.

"Then what was he doing in Mr. O'Connor's bedroom?"

"Lad has taken a fair likin' to Himself," Fionnula said, shrugging. "Even though it was Harry who rescued him from the bull-baitin' pits."

Harry nodded in agreement.

"Lad was a bulldog?" Silence asked in horror. The sport was a popular one, particularly among the poorer denizens of London, but Silence had always thought it terribly cruel.

"'E was bred a bulldog," Harry rumbled, "but 'e were no good at it. Seems 'e were afraid o' the bulls. I took 'im off a man about to drown 'im."

"Oh," Silence said softly. Lad was large and ugly and very smelly, but it seemed a shame to drown any creature, even an especially unbeautiful one.

As if he knew her thoughts, Lad sat and wagged his tail.

Silence placed her hands on her hips. "Well, no matter how he came here, one thing is for certain. This dog needs a bath."

*   *   *

"D'YOU THINK HE'LL pay the tithe now?" Bran asked Mick that night.

They were tramping back to the palace in the company of Pat and Sean, four abreast down the middle of the street. Any they ran into in the dark made a wide berth around them.

"Aye," Mick replied with satisfaction.

The owner of the *Alexander*, a large, round man with sallow, hanging cheeks, had gone a rather sickly green when he'd walked into his bedroom to find it full of pirates. He'd nodded vigorously to everything Mick had said to him, while clutching his banyan about himself like a frightened virgin.

"Then that's done," Bran said.

"Not quite," Mick replied as they turned into an alley. They were nearly to the palace now, but he couldn't help but feel that they were being trailed. Well, this was as good a place as any—and he had his men at his back. Mick flexed his arm, feeling the sheathed knife bound to his forearm. "He's agreed to me tithe, but I don't think he understands the error o' his ways. We'll be raidin' the ship when it makes port."

"Aye," Bran began, nodding.

A shape suddenly dropped from above, landing just in front of the four men.

"Jaysus Christ!" Sean shouted, leaping back.

Mick had his knife already drawn and was looking around warily, watching to see where the other attackers might come from. Several yards back two shadows drifted into the entrance to an alley. Mick shifted, keeping both the attacker in front and the men behind in his sight.

The shape in front straightened and became a man.

Mick squinted. The figure wore a harlequin's motley and a wide-brimmed hat with a feather. Beneath the hat the upper part of his face was concealed by a black half-mask, the nose grotesquely long and curved.

In one hand he held a sword.

"The Ghost o' St. Giles," Pat whispered, crossing himself.

"We're right honored," Mick drawled. Pat might be superstitious, but the man before him looked real enough to him. "But yer barrin' our path."

The ghost cocked his head, eyes glittering behind the mask.

Mick's eyes narrowed. "What do ye want?"

At that the ghost smiled and pointed to his eyes. Slowly his forefinger swiveled until it was pointed at Mick. The message was quite clear.

"Fuck that." Mick lunged for him.

The ghost made an impossible leap, grabbing a balcony overhanging the alley. He swung himself up, nimble as an acrobat, and continued climbing up the side of the building.

"Jaysus," Sean breathed. "I'd 'eard 'e could climb where no mortal man can."

"Don't be a fool," Bran snapped. "Anyone with enough training and practice could do that."

Sean looked doubtful. "Don't think I could."

"Nor I." Pat backed a couple of steps, looking up the building's side. "Couldn't jump like that if me life depended on it. Were almost as if 'e 'ad wings, it were."

"Aye." Sean sounded admiring. "Right nimble 'e was, if 'e weren't a ghost or phantom or some such. Think 'e were givin' ye the evil eye, Mick?"

"No, I don't," Mick said shortly. He glanced behind him, but their followers seemed to have disappeared without making any move on them, perhaps made cautious by the Ghost. Uneasiness crawled up Mick's spine. He could handle an attack against himself, but that wasn't his weak point.

And the Vicar knew it.

Mick looked at Bran. "On the morrow we're movin' Mrs. Hollingbrook and the babe."

Bran nodded without comment.

"Best we were back," Mick said.

So saying he continued down the alley, though he didn't sheath his knife again. His thoughts turned to the unexpected confrontation. The ghost wanted him to know that he was keeping a watch on Mick.

The only question was: why?

"'IMSELF WON'T LIKE this," Bert growled. He'd returned from exile just in time to be caught up in Silence's plans for Lad the dog.

Silence hitched Mary farther up her hip and tramped determinedly down the overdecorated corridor. "I can't believe Mr. O'Connor enjoys having a filthy dog running about his house. Besides, you told me he wasn't home."

"Expected back any minute," Bert said with gloomy relish.

Silence suppressed a shiver of alarm at that information. She was sticking to her guns, but all the same she wasn't sure she wanted a repeat of this morning quite so soon.

She cast an apologetic glance at Bert. "We'll act swiftly, then."

She ignored Bert's continued grumbles as she followed Harry toward what he'd assured her were the kitchens. Lad trotted along beside her, happily oblivious to his impending soapy fate, while Fionnula brought up the rear.

Silence cleared her throat. "Fionnula said that Mr. O'Connor had gone off on some kind of business."

Harry glanced back at her. "'E's talkin' to a merchant ship owner."

"Talking?"

Bert grunted. "More like explainin' the facts o' life to 'im—*what*?"

Harry had stopped short and turned to glare at his compatriot.

Bert shrugged, both hands palms up by his side. "'E's a *pirate*. If she don't know that by now she's either a 'alf-wit or daft."

Silence cleared her throat to get the men's attention. "What do you mean by 'explaining the facts of life,' Bert?"

"'E gets a tithe, right?" Bert said patiently. "From every merchant ship that docks in London."

"*Every* ship?" Silence raised her eyebrows.

"Used to be 'e 'ad a bit more competition," Harry said judiciously. "But a couple o' years ago Black Jack Wilde took a swim in the Thames—"

Bert tched. "Middle o' winter it were, too. Didn't find 'im 'til spring."

"And Jimmy Barker went missin', which meant most o' 'is crew joined us." Harry pursed his lips as if thinking, then cocked an eyebrow at Bert.

Who nodded. "They was about it. After that 'Imself became the biggest pirate on the Thames. So, yeah, *every* ship."

She'd had no idea the extent of Mickey O'Connor's empire. Silence pressed her lips together as she turned to continue down the hall to the kitchens.

Bert hurried after. "So this owner o' the ship…er…er…"

"*Alexander*," Harry supplied.

"Right ye are," Bert said, "the owner o' the *Alexander* 'as been remiss, as it were, in 'is tithe, so 'Imself 'as gone to see 'im and explain 'is duties to 'im."

Silence snorted. "You mean he's gone to threaten the poor man."

"Bert's right," Harry said gently. "'E *is* a pirate."

And with that flat statement they entered the kitchen. It was a big room, lined in light gray stone, an enormous hearth at one end. Two maids, sitting at a table in the middle of the room looked up at their entrance. A huge, stout man at the hearth swung around. He was entirely bald and the color of a well-cooked lobster, his front and lower half swathed in a not very clean apron.

"'Ello, Archie," Harry said chattily. "This 'ere's Mrs. 'Ollingbrook what 'as come down to give Lad a bit o' a bath."

Archie's brow beetled ominously and the maids suddenly found the tabletop very interesting. "Ye know I don't allow that there beast in me kitchen."

Harry frowned, about to say something, but at that moment Mary Darling joined the conversation. "Down!"

"Shh, sweetheart." Silence bounced the baby on her hip, trying to comfort her, but Mary's face was growing as red as Archie's.

Archie stared at the baby for a split-second, his face entirely blank, before he turned and rummaged in a cupboard.

"Down! Down! *Down!*" Mary chanted as Silence hugged her.

Archie loomed in front of them. "Sugar biscuit?" he asked gruffly and held it toward the baby.

Mary's transformation was miraculous. She grinned,

showing her four perfect teeth, two on the top, two on the bottom, and grabbed for the sweet.

"Thank you," Silence said gratefully to the big man.

Archie shrugged. "'Spose ye can use the master's tub for the dog. But ye'll need to clean up afterward, mind."

"Oh, of course," Silence said hurriedly.

In a moment she'd settled Mary, her biscuit, and a tin cup of milk with Fionnula while Bert and Harry dragged out a big copper bathtub. Silence's eyes widened at the sight. The orphanage had a small tin tub that she could just fit into, but she'd never seen a bathtub as magnificent as Mickey O'Connor's.

Lad trotted around the room, sniffing at corners and being yelled at once or twice by Archie as the tub was filled. The maids—Moll and Tess—seemed to think bathing a dog to be a great lark. They giggled as they found soap and laid out cloths.

When everything was ready, Harry called Lad. The dog gamboled over, as happy as a lamb, and for a moment Silence had a twinge of guilt.

Then Harry tried to put the dog into the tub.

There was a curse, a bark, and a wild scrambling, and then Harry was down in a puddle on the floor and Lad was across the room, bone dry.

The maids dissolved into laughter.

Mary banged her tin cup on the table. "Gog!"

Fionnula had one hand over her mouth, attempting to control her laughter.

Even Archie's thick lips twitched.

"Oh, I am so sorry, Harry," Silence said breathlessly. She bent to help the guard up. "Are you hurt?"

Bert grunted. "What ye get for tryin' to pretty up a cur."

Harry glared at his compatriot. "I'm fine, ma'am."

Bert snorted.

Harry stood and yanked on his waistcoat to straighten it. "Now ye jus' come 'ere, Lad me boy."

Lad rolled his eyes from a corner of the kitchen. He appeared to be trying to squeeze his body into a crack in the wall, or perhaps simply become invisible, but since he was quite a large dog, the task was impossible.

Harry advanced on the dog.

Lad trotted out of his path, his tail tucked firmly between his legs.

Silence bent down. "Here, Lad," she called in a high, sweet voice.

Lad perked his ears and went to her, glancing anxiously over his shoulder at Harry.

"Now then, Harry," Silence murmured soothingly as she fondled Lad's misshapen ears, one of which appeared to be missing a piece, "if you take his back half very firmly and I lift his front…"

Harry grabbed, Silence lifted, and Lad was deposited into the bath before he quite knew what had happened. Immediately, he made an attempt to get out again, but Silence had had an idea that he'd try something of the sort and was ready.

"Oh, no, you don't," she said in the same soothing voice—the voice she'd perfected bathing small, reluctant boys at the home. "You're not coming out until every speck of dirt has been removed from your hide."

Lad seemed to recognize that tone. He sighed heavily, his ears drooping.

Half an hour later, Silence stood back and blew a lock of hair out of her eyes. Her entire front was damp, her hair was half undone and she felt a trickle of sweat down her spine. Harry had lost his scarf and coat and the front of his waistcoat was dripping, the result of a premature shake on Lad's part. Mary Darling had fallen asleep in Fionnula's arms sometime during the proceedings, her half-eaten biscuit still clutched in her hand, and the maids and Archie were enjoying a pot of tea between them at the kitchen table. Apparently a dog bath was the most entertainment they'd seen in ages.

Silence eyed her charge critically. "What do you think?"

"That," Archie said, "is one clean dog."

"Certainly cleaner than 'Arry," Bert muttered.

"Naw," Moll drawled, "ye forget the bath 'e's 'ad washin' that dog."

Both maids went off into peals of laughter.

Harry straightened his dripping waistcoat with dignity. "I do believe Lad is done," he said to Silence.

Silence nodded. "Well, then, out you come, Lad."

The dog didn't need more urging. Lad scrambled from the tub in a tidal wave of water and then immediately shook, spraying everyone in the room.

The maids shrieked, Bert cursed, and Archie just grimaced in disgust.

"Well, then," Harry said cheerfully, "now yer all as clean as me."

Silence started to giggle before Lad shook again. The dog was grinning, his tongue hanging out of his mouth, and trying to run around the kitchen—except he kept skidding on the puddles of water, his rear end sliding to the side.

"Oh, dear, the floor is rather a mess," Silence murmured. She crouched, trying to wipe up the lake with some of the cloths.

"What," came a deep male voice, "is this?"

Silence froze, her hand still outstretched, clutching a damp, dirty cloth. *Oh, dear Lord.* Slowly she raised her eyes and found herself face-to-thighs with Mickey O'Connor's extremely tight breeches.

"Ah...," she started, with absolutely no idea of what she was about to say.

At the same time, Harry cleared his throat. "See, I jus' thought the dog—"

"Enough," Mickey O'Connor interrupted Harry in that same much too calm voice. "Take the babe, Fionnula, and put her to bed. Everyone else, out o' me kitchen."

Silence started to stand.

"Ah, ah," Mr. O'Connor said. "Not ye, Mrs. Hollingbrook."

She swallowed, watching as the servants and Harry and Bert trooped out of the room. Lad, apparently not the brightest dog in the world, sat down next to Mickey O'Connor and leaned against his leg.

Mr. O'Connor looked at the dog, looked at the damp spot growing on his breeches where the dog was leaning, and sighed. "I find me life is not as quiet as it used to be afore ye came to me palace, Mrs. Hollingbrook."

Silence lifted her chin. "You're a pirate, Mr. O'Connor. I cannot believe your life was ever very quiet."

He gave her an ironic look. "Aye, amazin', isn't it? Yet since yer arrival me servants no longer obey me and I return home to find me kitchen flooded." He crossed to a cupboard and took down a china teapot, a tin of tea, and a teacup. "*And* me dog smells like a whorehouse."

Silence glanced guiltily at Lad. "The only soap we could find was rose scented."

"Aye?" Mr. O'Connor glanced at the dog. Lad looked back, obliviously adoring, his tongue hanging from his mouth. "Poor, sad beast. He's lost his bollocks and don't even know it."

Silence blinked. She'd braced herself for shouting and anger, but so far Mickey O'Connor hadn't shown either.

She watched as he spooned tea leaves into the teapot and crossed to the fireplace to fill the pot with hot water.

"D'ye take sugar?"

"Yes, please," she answered.

He nodded and placed the teapot and teacup on the table before fetching a little bowl of sugar.

Silence looked at the lone teacup. "Aren't you having any?"

Mickey O'Connor snorted. "I'd be drummed from the pirate's guild if'n I were seen takin' tea."

Her lips twitched at the thought. "Then why make it for me?"

He looked at her, his eyes black and a little tired. For the first time she wondered how his "business" had gone that night. "I thought ye'd like it, Mrs. Hollingbrook. After all, ye must be near starved after two days with only the food Fionnula and the others could smuggle ye."

Silence bit her lip. "I asked her to stop today."

He cocked his head curiously. "Did ye now?"

Silence sat and poured herself a cup, adding a spoonful of sugar. She *did* like tea. When she sipped, the tea was quite good. She glanced up to find him propped against the kitchen cabinets watching her with a brooding air.

"Thank you," she said. "How did you learn to make a good cup of tea when you don't drink it yourself?"

His mouth tightened and he looked down at his boots.

For a moment she thought he wouldn't reply. Then he sighed. "Me mam was fond o' tea when we could get it. I'd make it for her."

His words were terse, but the picture he drew was sentimental. What a lovely boy he must've been to be so thoughtful of his mother. Silence frowned. She didn't like thinking of him like this—as a vulnerable child, a loving son. It was much simpler to only think of him as a pirate.

"Yer tea is gettin' cold," he murmured.

She drank some more and his mouth softened.

"Tell me somethin'," he said, his voice a deep, quiet rumble. "I saw ye once with the Ghost o' St. Giles almost a year ago."

"So you *were* watching me." She set her teacup down.

Last fall she'd been caught in a riot in St. Giles and only escaped harm when the Ghost of St. Giles had saved her. She'd seen Mickey O'Connor across the street at the time and wondered why he was there.

He shrugged, unperturbed. "Aye, sometimes. Ye had me daughter after all."

"Oh." His explanation was rather deflating.

"D'ye know him?"

"Who?"

"The Ghost o' St. Giles," he said patiently. "Who is he?"

"I don't know. He wore a mask the night he saved me from the rioters."

"And that's the only time ye've seen him?" His question was intent.

"I've seen him from afar, but it was certainly the only time I talked to him, although he never spoke to me." Silence looked at him, confused. "Why do you ask?"

He shook his head, frowning absently. "No matter."

Lad sighed loudly and slid down to lie on the floor.

Mr. O'Connor looked at the dog. "I should put him out in the courtyard."

"But we just bathed him."

He shot a rather frightening look at her from under his brows. "Aye, so ye did. Be a shame, I guess, to let him roll in the mud so soon." He tilted his chin at her teacup. "Are ye finished?"

She took a last sip. "Yes."

"Good." He nodded and shoved away from the cupboard. "I'll escort ye to yer room, then."

They walked all the way back to her rooms in silence, Lad padding happily behind.

When they reached her door, Mickey exchanged nods with Harry, sitting outside, and turned to Silence. "Good night, then."

"Good night," Silence said, her hand on the doorknob. "And thank you for the tea. It was truly delicious."

One corner of his mouth curved. "Me pleasure."

She began to close the door, but he stayed it with one broad hand. "One more thing. Tomorrow ye and the babe are movin' rooms."

Silence blinked. "Why?"

"We were followed tonight," he said, his eyes angry. "I want ye closer to me so I can keep an eye on ye m'self."

She frowned over that alarming news as he turned and ambled gracefully away. It wasn't until he was nearly at the end of the hall that she remembered something.

"Where will our new rooms be?" she called after him.

He cast an inscrutable glance over his shoulder. "Next to mine."

Chapter Five

*The second night the nephews resumed their guard with
renewed determination. They placed thorns beneath their
clothes to keep themselves awake, refused to sit, and paced
about to stimulate their senses. But despite all
their efforts, once again they fell asleep. And in
the morning once again they had to confess their
failure to the king.
And this time when Clever John rose he found a yellow
feather behind his ear....*
—from *Clever John*

The moon was but a pale sliver in the sky when Mick
stepped into the wherry the next night. He wore two pistols stuck into a belt strapped across his middle, as well
as a half dozen knives hidden about his person. Tonight
they raided a ship whose captain had decided to keep half
of Mick's tithe for himself. Mick signaled the other boat
and the wherrymen silently pushed off from the dock.
Only the quiet sound of the oars dipping into the water
broke the night's hush.

Mick hunched down in the stern of the boat, watching
as the massive hulk of the *Fairweather* drew near. She
was a fully rigged ship, not more than five years old and

a beauty. He'd always had a certain fascination for the tall ships that docked in London harbor. They were like living giants, slumbering on the dirty waters of the Thames.

The wherry made the side of the ship and the rope ladder already waiting there. The water sloshed against the hull as Mick swarmed up, leading his men. He climbed over the rail and saw the two guards, huddled together.

"Good evenin,' gentlemen," Mick murmured as he straightened. "Only ye two aboard?"

"Aye," the elder of the two, a bantam fellow of thirty or so, nodded nervously. "Jus' like ye said."

"Good." Mick casually tossed a small bag to the men. It clinked as the elder man caught it. "Ye'll have the rest when me and me men depart."

Mick waved a hand to his crew.

Immediately, his men spread out over the ship, swiftly climbing below where the cargo lay.

Mick sauntered to the poop deck and ducked inside the door there. The captain's cabin usually lay at the stern of the ship and the *Fairweather* was no different. Mick grunted with satisfaction when he found a solid oak door that was finer than the rest in the corridor. Of course it was locked, but a few quick shoves with his dagger against the wood near the lock opened the door very nicely. He prowled inside.

The captain of the *Fairweather* obviously liked to take his luxuries with him when he sailed. An enameled snuffbox lay on a table next to a brass inkwell and stand. Mick glanced at them and turned to a small chest near the bed. This was locked, as well, but he opened it easily. Inside were a few gold coins, a fine brass sextant, and some maps. Mick rifled through the contents until his hand found a rectangular object wrapped in oilcloth at the bottom of the chest. He drew it out and sat back on his heels to unwrap it.

The oilcloth fell away in his hands to reveal a slim volume, the leather dark with age, gilt decorating the cover, but no title. Mick turned the book over in his hands before opening it. Within were finely written pages—in a language he could not decipher. He turned a couple of pages and came upon a tiny, exquisite illustration.

Mick's eyebrows arched and he smiled.

He rewrapped the little book carefully and stuck it into an inner pocket in his coat. Then he continued looking about the room.

Ten minutes later he'd found nothing more interesting than an amazing array of clay pipes. Mick left the captain's quarters and went up on deck. He'd taught his men to be swift when they went raiding and he wasn't disappointed now: Bran stood overseeing the removal of several barrels into the waiting boats.

"Almost done?" Mick asked as he came up to Bran.

"Aye." The boy turned to grin. "We got nearly all the tobacco."

"Good." The *Fairweather*'s captain would pay a steep price for his greed. Mick tossed another small bag to the waiting guards. They looked none too bright, but if they had any sense they'd be gone by the time the captain came on board tomorrow. "Then let's away."

Bran nodded and was over the side and down the ladder in two blinks. Mick followed, feeling the boat dip under his weight as he stepped in. He gestured and the wherrymen shoved away from the *Fairweather*.

The puny moon shed little light on the water and they

rowed in near darkness, the only sound the dip of the oars into the river. Still, as Mick neared the dock, something made him peer intently into the gloom. All looked the same as when they'd left it only a half hour before—a few barrels squatted together in the shadows, a tumbling-down warehouse looming behind. There was nothing to alarm him, yet he felt the hairs rise on the back of his neck.

Then something moved behind one of the barrels.

"Ambush!" Mick roared as he drew one of his pistols.

His shot coincided with one from the dock and the wherryman in front of him slumped over the oars, blood pouring from a hole in his head. Suddenly the night was lit with the sparks of gunfire. Mick fired his other pistol, then took the dead man by the arm and threw his body out of the boat.

He shoved one of his own men into position. "Row for shore, hard as ye can!"

A shout and a splash as one of his pirates went into the Thames. God willing, the man was already dead, for most of Mick's men couldn't swim—and drowning was a hard way to go. Mick growled and drew one of his daggers, sticking it between his teeth. Then he threw off his boots and coat and slipped over the side of the wherry like an eel.

The water was as icy as a dead woman's kiss and smelled of the sewers that emptied into the river. No matter—he'd swum the Thames before and tasted her foul brew. Mick glided through the water, only his eyes breaking the surface, his face going numb. He made the wharf before the boats and could see now clearly their attackers. One man crouched near the water's edge, firing from two long guns, another loading for him.

The gunman was the first to go into the river.

There was a splash and a gurgle and then the man was lost below the fetid surface. His mate stared as Mick swarmed the dock.

"Fuck," the gun loader cried. "It's Charmin' Mickey 'imself!"

"How de do?" Mick grinned and stuck his knife between the man's ribs.

The gun loader's eyes widened a moment, but Mick hadn't time to watch. He shoved the man—dead or alive—into the Thames's cold embrace. When he turned back, his boats were almost at the dock, some of his men still shooting. The attackers fled into the dark.

All but one.

He was only a silhouette, standing without fear even in the midst of gunfire, and Mick sensed more than saw who he was.

"Charlie Grady," he whispered.

"Charming Mickey." The shadow dipped his head as if in acknowledgment. "How long will you stay in business if you lose a man or two every time you go out on a raid?"

"Fuck ye," Mick breathed.

"The same to you," Charlie murmured. "Oh, the same to you, Mickey O'Connor. "

Then the pirates were on the docks and Charlie Grady was gone.

"Who was that?" Bran panted by Mick's side. "I couldn't see in the dark. Did you know him?"

"Aye," Mick said, his chest expanding and falling as he gulped air. "That was the Vicar o' Whitechapel."

BY THE TIME Mick and his men made it back to the palace, he was gritting his teeth to keep from chattering.

"Who was it?" he asked Bran as they came in the doors, trying to get a reckoning on the men he'd lost tonight. He'd sent the rest of his crew to store the barrels of tobacco and sugar. "I saw Pat Flynn, but didn't make out the other."

"Two others," Bran said grimly. "Sean Flannigan went over the side and didn't come back up again, and Mike O'Toole caught one in the face. Was dead at once."

"Damn me," Mick said, grimacing. Losing three of his best men in one night was enough to make him want to howl. "Pat had family, didn't he?"

Bran nodded as they tramped through the dark halls toward the kitchen at the back of the palace. "Pat had a woman and two little girls."

Mick shuddered, the cold shaking his bones. He'd taken off his wet shirt at the docks and put on his dry coat and boots, but the chill of the Thames seemed to have seeped to his very core. "Make sure Pat's woman has enough to live on until she can find another man."

Bran looked at him doubtfully. "That might take years."

Mick shot him an evil look. "And if it do?"

Bran shrugged uneasily. "Makes no matter to me, but you're throwing good money away—Pat's woman would be happy with ten pounds and a pint of gin."

Mick halted in the middle of the hall and swung on Bran. He thrust his face into the younger man's and growled, "Pat Flynn died obeyin' me orders. He was a good man. They *all* were. I'll see them buried proper with black gloves and mourners and all. And if I want to keep his woman and children in enough style that they dine upon beef and sugarplums every night for the next three years, I'll damn well do so."

Bran had flushed under Mick's diatribe. "Of course," he said without any inflection in his voice at all. "We'll do exactly as you wish."

Mick narrowed his eyes. If ever he'd have a rebellion on his hands it would come from Bran. The lad was the canniest of all his men, and a natural leader as well—a fact that had made Bran Mick's second-in-command at such a young age. Soon, Mick would have to give him more to do, guide Bran's restless, clever mind.

But not tonight. The Vicar had made his intentions plain and Mick couldn't afford any show of weakness—not even with Bran. The boy had to be reminded who was in charge.

"Good. See that it's done," Mick said, and turned to continue toward the back of the house.

Archie the cook was mopping the floor when they entered the kitchens.

"Start me some water boilin'." Mick strode to the fire and began stripping off his wet clothes. "I want a hot bath and a fire roarin' in me room."

He was down to his smallclothes now and Mick took a ladle of water and began sluicing his body and hair to get the worst of the river stink out. He felt tainted, as if he stank not only from the river, but from contact with the Vicar, as well. Mick shuddered, pouring water over his head. He couldn't let the Vicar destroy another woman. *Her brown eyes had been haunted as she'd turned her tear-stained face from his.* He shook away the phantom.

He wouldn't let that happen with Silence.

Mick threw aside the ladle, caught up his coat again, and turned to the hall. God, he was tired and cold.

Cold to his very soul.

*　　*　　*

SILENCE LISTENED TO the commotion in the next room as she lay in bed that night. She and Mary Darling had been moved early this morning into a room that had a prominent door connecting it to Mickey O'Connor's own room. She'd half-expected to see him all day—but apparently the pirate had been too busy with his own affairs. Only now, late at night, had Mickey O'Connor returned home.

Mary Darling was asleep in the corner, her railed cot having been brought with them. The new room was bigger and much finer than the rooms Mickey O'Connor had originally placed them in. The walls were a soft, feminine blue gray that suited her much better than the pink of the room upstairs, and an elegant arrangement of chairs stood before the fireplace.

Silence sighed and rolled over, fussing with the pillow under her head. Truth be told, she hadn't been able to sleep because her belly was aching. She'd again refused the food that Fionnula and the guards had tried giving her today. It simply wasn't right to put others at risk for her own needs.

Which might be true, but that lofty ideal didn't help her hunger tonight. Silence pressed her palms to her aching stomach. She was so hungry that she'd even contemplated sneaking down to the kitchen to steal food. Her eldest sister, Verity, who had raised Silence and Temperance after Mama died, would be appalled.

Actually, Silence was appalled. Here she sat in the near dark cowering from Mickey O'Connor.

Was she a coward?

On that thought she rose and was across the room toward the connecting door almost before she could think.

The sounds from the other room had stopped a while ago. Mr. O'Connor had either left or he was alone—perhaps enjoying an after-raid snack.

The thought made her stomach grumble.

Silence took a deep breath and opened the connecting door.

And then she had trouble exhaling.

Mickey O'Connor the pirate king was in the huge bath that they'd used the night before for washing Lad the dog. One arm dangled over the side of the tub, a goblet of amber liquid held carelessly in long elegant fingers. His ebony hair was wet and curling against his neck and shoulders. Those shoulders were broad, covered in smooth, olive skin, and spanned the width of the tub and more. And where before she'd thought that his chest was entirely devoid of hair, now she saw that small whirls circled his brown nipples and a thin line of hair trailed just below his naked navel, disappearing into the water where no doubt it led to other naked things.

Well, of course he was *naked*, Silence thought, trying to pull herself together. He was in his *bath*. Who took a bath fully clothed?

She had some vague idea of backing out of the room again, but he'd already seen her.

"Mrs. Hollingbrook," the pirate drawled, taking a sip from his goblet. "I was jus' sittin' here wonderin' if ye'd spent the day powderin' and curlin' Lad's fur and here ye are. To what do I owe the pleasure?" His voice had suddenly assumed an upper crust English accent on the last sentence, making the words even more mocking.

Silence lifted her chin. She wasn't going to turn tail and run from a pirate—even if he *was* naked. She darted a look at Lad—snoring in front of the fire—and decided it was best not to answer Mr. O'Connor's mocking inquiry. "I've come to demand you tell me what is going on."

He looked at her from under heavy eyelids. "Have ye, now?"

"I have." She set hands upon hips. "It's positively medieval, locking me up, refusing me food, never bothering to ask what I want or need."

"Need," he mused, his gaze slowly examining her form in a manner that caused her to go hot all over, "now that I'm thinkin' we might not agree upon—what ye *need*—but do tell me what ye might be wantin'."

She threw her hands up. "I want—and *need*—to eat!"

"Ah, but I've said more than once that yer welcome to sup with me."

She was shaking her head. "You know—"

"I know that Fionnula and Harry and half me staff o' bloody servants have seen fit to go against me by smugglin' food to ye." His voice suddenly held a nasty edge.

She froze, her eyes widening in fear for the others. "You can't—"

"I can't what?" he drawled. There was something dark in him tonight—something she'd not seen before. "I can't turn them off, can't toss them into the street, can't make them disappear? The Thames is an easy place to lose a body. A man can slip beneath those dark, cold waters and sink without a trace."

"Why are you doing this?" she whispered.

He shrugged one elegant shoulder, making the water ripple in the tub.

She took a step closer. "What happened on your raid tonight?"

He turned his face away, taking a sip from his goblet. "What a perceptive little thing ye are, Mrs. Hollingbrook. The raid went quite well, actually, thank ye for inquirin'. Got a load o' tobacco and sugar and the only cost was the lives o' three o' me men."

"My God," she breathed. "What happened?"

He waved a hand, rings flashing. "Nothin' to concern yerself with, I do assure ye."

Surely it wasn't usual for him to lose three of his men in one night? If it was, he'd be constantly recruiting more pirates. Something was wrong.

"Who were they?"

"What?"

"The pirates." She winced and gestured rather helplessly with one hand, her voice softer. "Your men. Who were they?"

For a moment she thought he wouldn't answer.

Then he took a long swallow from his goblet. "Pat and Mike and Sean. Not the brightest o' me men, sure, especially Pat, but he had a family and he was always quick with a joke, was Pat."

She waited, but he didn't say more.

"I'm sorry," she whispered.

He grimaced. "Sorry three pirates are dead? Why, Mrs. Hollingbrook, ye surprise me, ye do."

Her eyes narrowed. "I don't—"

He didn't stop to listen to her, talking over her instead. "Now then, tell me: shall I have the honor o' yer company tomorrow night at me supper table? Shall ye dine upon sweetmeats with me, Silence, mine?"

His words sounded obscene somehow. She frowned, frustration rising in her. He wasn't listening; it was as if she couldn't be heard. "I'm not yours and I never gave you leave to use my Christian name."

"Oh, but do I need leave, now?" Mickey O'Connor whispered. "Yer in me room—and not for the first time, love."

She inhaled sharply. How dare he remind her of that night? Suddenly it was too much: the hunger, the edge of darkness in his voice, and this room—this too familiar room. No one had believed she'd been untouched after that night.

No one had heard her.

She looked at the pirate luxuriating in his bath and a great rage swelled up in her, a mixture of hunger, frustration, lost love, and fear for Mary Darling.

And scorn. Oh, there was plenty of scorn, as well.

"Do you know what you cost me?" she demanded, her voice low and trembling. "When you played your cruel game with me?"

He looked at her, but didn't say a word. His black eyes reflected no light, fathomless and without expression. Was his heart made of stone that he could play with lives—*her* life—so carelessly and not feel a thing?

Silence balled her fists, trembling. "It was as if I became a cipher after that night. No one I loved believed me. You *silenced* me. What you did to me cost me everything I valued in life—my family's respect, my marriage, my love."

"And was yer marriage so perfect before ye came to me?"

She gasped, the breath catching in her breast in rage. Of course her marriage had been perfect, hadn't it?

Hadn't it?

"We had true love," she said, drowning out the tiny voice of doubt in her mind.

He turned his face from her, which only made her angrier. In four strides she was beside him, kneeling on the rug next to the tub of water. She reached out and took his face in her palms, turning it so he had to look at her, his lean cheeks cool and a little rough beneath her hands.

"Yes, *love*." She hissed the word like a curse. "I loved my husband, my William, and he loved me. That is until that night you kept me here. You destroyed what we had as thoughtlessly as a boy pulling the wings from a butterfly."

His wickedly sensuous upper lip pulled back in a sneer. "What is love?"

She leaned close to him. "Something you will never have. Something you're incapable of feeling. I pity you, Mickey O'Connor, for I may have lost my true love, but at least I had him for a time. You'll *never* feel love."

His sneer had grown and his voice was low and terrible. "I may not feel love, but I do feel *this*."

He grabbed her hand and thrust it beneath the bathwater.

She struggled so violently that the water splashed over her bodice and the rug, but he was stronger than she. He forced her palm down against his male part, hard and thick, and held it there as he grasped her hair with his other hand. He yanked, pulling her hair, arching her neck, and suddenly his mouth was on hers, cruel and merciless. He ground her lips against her teeth, used his hold on her hair to angle her head for his greater access. She felt the push of his tongue against her lips. For a moment she stopped fighting. She opened her mouth and let him in, hot and searching. She could taste the heady liquor on his tongue, feel the sudden gentling of his mouth as he got what he wanted. His kiss was overwhelmingly masculine. Overwhelmingly dominant.

Something clenched inside her—something primitive and needy, something that had nothing to do with love.

He groaned.

And she lurched back. Her hand came out of the water and she hit him as hard as she could across the face. The sound of the blow was loud in the room.

"No!" she cried, her heart pounding, her breasts aching. "*No*. You don't have the right."

He watched her retreat, his eyes lazy, and his body unmoving. A trickle of blood seeped slowly from the corner of his mouth. He let her get nearly out of the room before he spoke, "I may not have the right, Silence, me love," he drawled so soft she nearly didn't catch the words. "But I would've listened to ye. I would've believed ye."

Chapter Six

Now on the third night when dusk drew near, Clever John thought long and hard about the feathers he'd found on his person and the fact that he and his cousins could not stay awake no matter how they tried. He took a bit of candle wax from the castle and stopped up both his ears. Then he took up his position beneath the cherry tree and waited for nightfall....
—from *Clever John*

Mick woke the next morning to the sound of Lad retching by the fireplace.

"Don't ye dare!" Mick growled, lunging up.

Lad stood frozen on the hearth, tail between his legs, and tiny triangle ears flat to his head. The dog rolled his eyes at Mick.

Mick narrowed his. "Heave in me room, ye damned dog, and I'll spit ye and serve ye to the crew tonight for supper."

Lad whimpered and lay down.

Mick sighed and flopped back onto his pillows. A far cry this was from how he'd used to wake in his bedroom. No scented female flesh to warm his bed, only a sick mongrel on the hearth.

And the memory of his kiss with Silence Hollingbrook last night. Aye, and he hadn't acted the gentleman, had he? No, he'd seized and taken and he would not regret his actions in the light of day, for the kiss had been sweet and hot and all that he'd imagined that a kiss with Silence would be.

Well, not quite all. In his lusty thoughts such a kiss hadn't ended with her hitting him—nor stomping from the room. No, in his dreams, there'd been much more than that almost chaste meeting of lips. Enough to make his already stiff John Thomas twitch with interest.

He winced, feeling an ache in his arms from the unexpected swim last night. He needed to deal with the Vicar and soon, but first there was the matter of Silence Hollingbrook and her stomach. Harry had kept him informed and the maddening woman hadn't eaten all yesterday—despite being smuggled food. Perhaps she thought she was protecting the servants or perhaps she was refusing food in some sort of ridiculous protest against living with him. Or perhaps she was simply not eating to irritate him—and if that were so, well it was certainly working.

Women were something best bought, he'd found. Pay them, fuck them, and send them away in the morning. That way avoided tears, recriminations, and feminine disappointment. Oh, and small things like being slapped across the face. Mick rubbed his jaw. But Silence wasn't one of his whores, as Harry had pointed out. Mick couldn't send her away. And he couldn't let her starve herself—he wouldn't let anyone hurt her, including herself.

Which meant that much as it went against his instincts, he would have to take the risk of drawing her closer. Letting her in, just a tad, mind.

Mick O'Connor never admitted defeat, never backed down, but he might choose to change his plans, should he come head to head with a stubborn widow bent on hurting herself for whatever reason.

The course he'd originally taken with her was not working. Time to take a different tack.

SILENCE WAS DRESSING Mary Darling for the day when the door opened behind her.

The baby looked up and frowned. "Bad!"

Which was warning enough, Silence supposed.

She inhaled and turned to face Mickey O'Connor, biting her lip against the memory of that savage kiss last night.

He had closed the door behind him and was leaning against the wall, his frown nearly identical to Mary Darling's. "Will she ever find another name to call me, d'ye think?"

"I don't know," Silence said with commendable calm. If he wouldn't mention the kiss, well, then neither would she. "It might depend on if you ever call Mary something else besides 'she.'"

He grunted and shoved away from the wall. "Fair enough."

She watched him cross to the hearth and stare broodingly into the fire. Fionnula had gone down to fetch Mary's breakfast, so they were alone for the moment. "What did you come for?"

"Forgiveness?" he murmured.

She blinked, not sure if she'd heard him correctly. "What?"

"Yer not what I expected, ye know." The curl of his lips seemed self-mocking. "I thought ye'd sit in yer room and knit or do needlework. Come when called, go away when bidden. Upset me fine life not at all."

Her lips firmed in irritation, but she merely said, "You obviously haven't seen either my knitting or my needlework."

"No," he said. "I haven't. There's much about ye I don't know."

She shrugged, feeling restless—and hungry. She hadn't eaten anything since before yesterday. "Does it matter?"

"Aye," he said slowly. "I think it does in fact."

She stared at him, nonplussed. Why would he care to know her?

As if he'd heard her thoughts, he shook his head. "Don't let it bother ye. 'Tis me own worry and none o' yers. I came with two purposes. The first is to give ye this."

He strode forward and proffered an oilcloth-wrapped bundle.

Silence took it gingerly.

"Gah!" Mary stood and grabbed her arm, looking on curiously as Silence unwrapped a fine little book with gilt edges.

"Gentle," Silence chided as the baby grabbed for the prize. "We must be careful. See?"

She opened the book and then gasped herself when she found an exquisite little illustration. Tiny men sailed, crowded on a ship with a square crimson sail on a sea with towering cobalt waves.

"D'ye like it?" Mickey O'Connor's voice was gruff.

"It's lovely." She glanced up at him and was surprised to see an expression of uncertainty on his face.

He shrugged, the expression replaced with his usual insouciance. "I thought ye and the babe might find it entertainin'."

"Thank you."

He nodded curtly and moved to the door. "Me other purpose in comin' was to ask ye to attend me supper tonight. No"—he cut her off as she was about to reply—"don't give me yer answer now. Jus'...think on it will ye? Please?"

She stared. Had Mickey O'Connor ever begged anyone in his entire life?

He grinned, quick and rueful. "Oh, aye, the pigs'll be flyin' today, so I've heard."

And then he was gone.

"Well." Silence looked at Mary—just in time to rescue the beautiful little book from a curious taste.

Mary was still squawking her indignation when Fionnula came in the room a minute later, laden with a heavy tray.

"Oh, ma'am," she said, "Himself has ordered breakfast for ye!"

And while Silence watched in bemusement Fionnula began setting out a sumptuous breakfast. She'd never have thought that Mickey O'Connor would give in. He was a pirate—a cruel, unyielding pirate—and nothing else.

Wasn't he?

ISABEL BECKINHALL, BARONESS Beckinhall, stepped from the carriage that afternoon and immediately saw a half-naked wretch lying in the gutter.

She shuddered. "Amelia, darling, are you sure this is the place?"

"Quite sure," Lady Caire said briskly. She exited the carriage with the help of a brawny and impossibly handsome footman, then waved a hand. "Disregard the less attractive sights."

Isabel glanced about the awful neighborhood ruefully. "If I did there would be nothing at all that I might look at. Whyever did you situate the home here?"

Amelia sighed. "The orphans come mostly from St. Giles, so the area is inescapable. The building however is not. Unfortunately, we are still waiting for the new home to be completed. We hope in another month or so it will be."

She sailed ahead to a miserable little door in an equally miserable building.

Isabel sighed and picked up her skirts to carefully follow. This was her first time attending the Ladies' Syndicate for the Benefit of the Home for Unfortunate Infants and Foundling Children and she was beginning to think it would be her last. But Amelia had been quite persistent that Isabel join the syndicate. Amelia herself had been, along with Lady Hero Reading, one of the first lady patronesses of the home and she was rather enthusiastic about the endeavor.

Isabel glanced fondly at her friend. They were not close in age—Amelia would die a thousand deaths before she revealed her years, but since her son was in the latter part of his thirties, she couldn't very well deny that she was well past her fifth decade. Isabel in contrast was but two and thirty.

Despite the disparity in their ages, though, they had much in common. Both ladies had married young and subsequently buried their older husbands. It was true that Isabel suspected from small hints here and there that Amelia's marriage had not been nearly as happy as her own to her dear Edmund, but Edmund and the late Baron Caire did have one thing in common: they'd both been quite ridiculously rich. And while both titles and estates had been inherited after their deaths—in Edmund's case by a distant, much younger cousin—both men had left their widows very well off.

Which was why Isabel was about to attend a meeting of the Ladies' Syndicate for the Benefit of the Home for Unfortunate Infants and Foundling Children today. There didn't seem to be much in the way of requirements to join the Ladies' Syndicate, but wealth was definitely encouraged.

The door to the wretched house was opened abruptly by a stern-looking child of about thirteen. She made a very nice curtsy. "Good morning, my lady."

Amelia permitted herself a small, approving smile. "Good morning, Mary Whitsun. Isabel, this is Miss Mary Whitsun, the eldest orphan at the home and a great help to both Mr. Makepeace, the manager, and his sister, Mrs. Hollingbrook, the manageress. Mary, this is Lady Beckinhall."

Isabel smiled. "Mary."

"I'm very pleased to meet you, my lady," Mary said carefully as she dipped into another curtsy. She darted a glance at Amelia who gave an encouraging nod.

With this approval, Mary smiled and suddenly her grave little face lit up. She had rich, dark hair and a lovely creamy complexion. Once she'd grown past her adolescent gawkiness, she'd be a beauty if Isabel was any judge.

"Won't you come in?" Mary said in that same solemn voice.

They entered a hallway so narrow that the two could walk abreast only with difficulty. Isabel winced at the cracked and falling plaster on the walls. She could understand why a new building was needed.

Mary led them up two flights of stairs and into a windowless room.

"This is usually the children's classroom," Amelia said, "but Mr. Makepeace has graciously let us use it for our meetings once a week."

"I see," Isabel murmured, looking around at the cramped little room. Three other ladies were already in attendance, sitting in rather rickety chairs.

"I know," Amelia whispered, as if reading her mind, "'tisn't the most comfortable of places, but we—Lady Hero and I—thought that it best to meet where we could also immediately receive reports from Mr. Makepeace and also inspect the children, the premises, et cetera. Ah, Hero."

Amelia broke off to press cheeks with a tall young woman. "Hero, this is Lady Beckinhall. You remember Lady Hero, do you not, Isabel?"

"Of course. Lady Hero's cousin, Miss Bathilda Picklewood and I are friends." Isabel dipped in a curtsy as the other lady did, as well. Lady Hero wore an elegant silver and lavender gown, setting off her gorgeous light red hair. "Congratulations on your recent nuptials, my lady."

Lady Hero's pale cheeks pinkened. "Thank you, Lady Beckinhall. May I introduce you to my sister, Lady Phoebe Batten?"

The girl was not much more than a child, a plump little creature with a squint. She was obviously terribly nearsighted, poor thing. Still, she smiled cheerfully as she dipped into a curtsy. "I am pleased to meet you, my lady."

Isabel nodded to the chit with a smile.

"And this is my dear husband's sister, Lady Margaret—" Lady Hero began, gesturing gracefully to a pretty, dark-haired woman, when the door opened again.

"Goodness! What a dismal place!" A girlish voice exclaimed.

Isabel turned to see Lady Penelope Chadwicke blow into the room. Lady Penelope hardly ever simply entered a room—she was much too melodramatic for that. With glossy black hair, rosebud lips and pansy-purple eyes, she'd been declared a beauty the moment she'd come out, nearly three years ago. She wore a velvet cloak lined with swan's down, which she immediately doffed and threw to the much plainer woman following her. Underneath the cloak, her close-fitting jacket was champagne brocade overembroidered in pale rose and gold thread. Her skirts were pulled back to reveal a petticoat embroidered to match the jacket, the entire ensemble probably costing several hundred guineas.

But then Lady Penelope was the daughter of the Earl of Brightmore, one of the richest men in England and she was rumored to have a dowry worth a king's ransom.

"Is there tea?" Lady Penelope looked about the room as if a tea tray might be hiding in the corner, then pouted prettily. "Tea and cakes would be so nice. The carriage ride here was simply devastating. I think my coachman was actually aiming for the holes in the cobblestones. And St. Giles!"

For a moment Lady Penelope's gorgeous eyes widened as if struck speechless by the horror of it all. Then she turned with a snap and addressed the lady following her, who was still struggling with the velvet cloak. "Artemis, you must go see about tea. I'm sure you're just as weary by all of this as I. We need reviving!"

"Yes, Penelope," Artemis murmured and retreated out the door.

"And cakes!" Lady Penelope called after her. "I do so long for some darling little cakes."

"Yes, Penelope," the other woman answered from the hall.

Isabel noted rather wryly that Lady Penelope might include her lady's companion in her "weariness" but that didn't stop her from sending the woman off on a servant's errand. Amelia used the time to introduce the other ladies to Lady Penelope.

"Oh, Lady Hero, I'm not at all certain it is wise for the Ladies' Syndicate to meet in this part of London," Lady Penelope said, after the introductions were made. She gingerly lowered herself into one of the rickety chairs. "Is it quite safe?"

"I believe as long as we meet in daylight and bring along footmen as guards, we shall be perfectly safe," Lady Hero said. "It wouldn't do to visit St. Giles after dark, of course."

Lady Penelope shivered dramatically. "I hear that there is a masked man dressed as a harlequin who roams these parts, stealing pretty women away to his lair where he ravishes them."

"The Ghost of St. Giles is mostly a myth," came a deep, male voice from the doorway.

Lady Penelope gave a little shriek and Isabel turned to see a tall young man standing just inside the room. He was entirely in black, save for his white shirt, with no ornamentation of any kind on his clothes. He held a round-brimmed hat in his hand and his unpowdered brown hair was clubbed back very simply. He'd frowned a bit at Lady Penelope's shriek and the expression made him seem rather dour. As he glanced about the room, Isabel had the distinct impression that this man didn't approve of any of the ladies.

Isabel smiled widely—with just a hint of wicked flirtation. "Mostly?"

He glanced at her, his eyes flicking over her form so swiftly that for a moment she thought she'd imagined the look. She was suddenly conscious of the low, rounded neckline of her dark emerald gown. Then he met her eyes, his face perfectly expressionless. "A man dressed as a theatrical harlequin does roam the streets hereabouts, ma'am, but he is harmless."

The information didn't reassure Lady Penelope. She shrieked again and made to slump in her chair as if in a faint, but then seemed to remember the fragility of the chair and thought better of the idea.

"Let me introduce you all to Mr. Winter Makepeace, the manager of the Home for Unfortunate Infants and Foundling Children," Lady Hero said hastily. She introduced the ladies in turn and Mr. Makepeace bowed shortly to each. When he came to Isabel, she rather thought his bow was more a nod of the head.

"Mr. Makepeace," she drawled. Priggish gentlemen always managed to get her back up—and they were so very easy to tease! "How...*interesting* to meet you. I vow you look rather young for such great responsibility." Despite his grave air he couldn't yet be thirty. Certainly he was younger than she.

"I've managed the home since my father's death two years ago," he replied calmly. "And before that I was my father's right-hand man for many years. I do assure you my years are quite sufficient to run this home."

"Indeed?" She bit her lip to keep from smiling. He was so woefully serious! The man had probably never laughed in his life.

Lady Penelope's little companion returned at that moment with several girls bearing trays of tea. She was a bit out of breath, for she was carrying a tray of dainty cakes herself, and seemed almost startled as Lady Hero took the time to introduce her to everyone present as Miss Artemis Greaves.

Mr. Makepeace's expression softened—although he still didn't smile—as he was introduced to Miss Greaves. "May I take that?"

Without waiting for her assent he took the tray of cakes and placed it on the sole table in the room.

Miss Greaves smiled rather shyly. "Thank you, Mr. Makepeace."

"My pleasure, Miss Greaves," he replied, his voice a pleasing rumble.

So he did know how to comport himself in the presence of a lady—when he chose.

"Will you give us a report on the home, Mr. Makepeace?" Amelia asked as she poured the tea.

He nodded and proceeded to give a very dry account of the expenses of the home and how the children were situated. By the end of his little speech even Lady Hero was nodding.

"Er, thank you, Mr. Makepeace," she said when there was a little silence indicating he was finished. "Have you any suggestions as to how the Ladies' Syndicate may benefit the home at the present?"

"We need money, ma'am," he said without a hint of humor. "Everything else is extraneous."

"Oh, but couldn't we have little jackets made for the children? At least the boys?" Lady Penelope cried.

Mr. Makepeace looked at her. "Jackets, ma'am?"

Lady Penelope waved a vague hand. "Oh, yes! Scarlet ones—they'd look like little soldiers. Or perhaps lemon? Lemon is such an elegant color, I find."

She smiled brilliantly at the home's manager.

Mr. Makepeace cleared his throat. "Yellow also becomes dirty very easily. In my experience, children, especially boys, tend to run about and make a mess of themselves."

"Oh, pooh!" Lady Penelope pouted. "Can't you just keep them inside?"

Everyone looked at Lady Penelope. It was hard to credit, but she seemed quite serious.

Isabel felt a grin tug at her lips. She widened her eyes at the manager. "Yes, Mr. Makepeace, tell us why you can't simply lock the little dears in their rooms?"

He shot her a quick, dark look that made her catch her breath.

"I'm sure Lady Penelope understands the impossibility of keeping small boys immobile and clean at all times," Amelia murmured. "If that is all, Mr. Makepeace, we will not keep you further from your duties."

"Ma'am. Ladies." He bowed.

He was almost at the door when Lady Hero suddenly seemed to remember something. "But where is Mrs. Hollingbrook? I thought to see her today."

Mr. Makepeace didn't change expression, his body didn't jerk or stiffen, but somehow Isabel understood that the comment had given him pause.

He glanced over his shoulder. "My sister is no longer residing at the home," he said coolly and left the room before Lady Hero could make further comment.

Lady Penelope's high, silly voice broke the silence.

"Goodness! Surely he isn't thinking of running the home all by himself? A woman's touch is so important with children, I think, especially since Mr. Makepeace is a *bachelor* gentleman."

Several other ladies offered their opinions, but Isabel let the conversation flow about her as she bent her head in thought. Mr. Makepeace's gaze had met Isabel's in the second before he turned away, and she'd realized something in that instant: Mr. Makepeace might not show it, but there were strong emotions churning under that cold exterior.

His eyes had been black with anger.

SILENCE SQUARED HER shoulders that night outside the dining room door. She'd left Mary Darling happily playing with Moll, the maid from the kitchen, with Bert as guard, and now she was about to join Mickey O'Connor for dinner. After all, he'd *asked* this time instead of ordered. There was still that small part of her that was convinced she was making a mistake. But then she reminded herself that it had been he who had made the first move, had held out the hand of peace.

Surely that counted for something?

She pushed open the door before she wasted another five minutes pacing and dithering. The room within was long and, not surprisingly, gaudily decorated. Watered silks lined the walls in purple, deep blue, and green. Silence snorted under her breath. How appropriate: Charming Mickey had covered the walls of his dining room with the colors of a peacock.

Down the middle of the room several long tables had been set end-to-end, almost like what she supposed a medieval dining hall might have looked like. Mickey O'Connor himself lounged at the far end of the table in a crimson velvet chair. He hadn't looked up at her entrance, but she didn't make the mistake of thinking he hadn't noticed her.

Silence began making her way down the line of tables. This end of the room seemed to be comprised of Mickey's crew, quite a rough-looking lot. She'd gingerly passed the first couple of seated men when some type of signal was given. Suddenly all the pirates rose rather alarmingly, some so hastily their chairs crashed to the floor.

Silence blinked. "Ah...good evening."

"Good evenin', ma'am," the closest man said gruffly. Belatedly, he snatched the greasy tricorne from his head.

Each man greeted her in turn as she walked past them, and even though they were all rather murderous looking, Silence smiled shyly at them. She found a seat just past the pirates. It was across from Harry and next to a little man with spectacles who she'd seen before in Mr. O'Connor's throne room.

As she drew out the chair, the little man stood. "Not here, ma'am."

"I'm sorry?" she asked, confused.

"He'll want you with him," the little man said nervously.

"That's yer place," Harry said and nodded his chin toward the head of the table.

Silence looked at the head of the table and of course Mickey O'Connor was watching her. They were *all* watching her.

Silence lifted her chin and made her way up the table, conscious that all eyes were upon her, until she stood beside the empty place at the right hand side of Mickey

O'Connor. For an awful moment she thought he would ignore her, but then he uncoiled his long limbs and stood, pulling out her chair for her.

"Mrs. Hollingbrook," he murmured. "I'm that pleased ye've come down."

She nodded nervously and accepted the chair. She could feel his heat behind her as his hands took the sides of the chair and moved it forward to properly seat her. The scent of frankincense and lemons floated in the air, sensuous and somehow alarming. She thought she felt the brush of his fingers on her shoulder, but when she looked around he was already back in his seat.

He made a gesture and Tess and two other maidservants came in laden with trays of food. Incredibly—*decadently*—rich food. There were platters of thinly sliced pheasant, roasted rabbits, fish in wine, pigeon pie, fresh hothouse fruit, and enormous serving dishes heaped with oysters.

Mickey O'Connor seemed to sense her faint disapproval as one of the serving maids placed a bowl of oysters before them. He cocked a black eyebrow at her. "I'm proud of me table, Mrs. Hollingbrook. I like good food and me men work better for it."

She pursed her lips. "The price of those oysters could feed a St. Giles family for weeks, maybe months."

He smiled lazily. "Would ye rather I dined upon bread and water?"

"No, but—"

"Come," he said in his deep, black velvet voice, "the oysters are already cooked and they don't keep at all well. 'Twould be a pity to let them go to waste." He picked up a shell and pulled the pearly, succulent flesh free with his fingers, holding it out temptingly.

Silence's stomach growled and she flushed.

The corner of his mouth curved with roguish charm. "Tisn't a sin to enjoy good food."

"A special treat once in a while is one thing," she said severely, "but you spend your life in constant excess. Does it not become boring after a bit?"

He smiled wolfishly. "Never."

She reached for the oyster he still held, but he moved his hand back out of her way.

She looked at him coolly. "I'll not eat out of your hand."

His bold mouth compressed—he didn't like her refusal, but all he said was, "As ye wish, me darlin'."

He placed the oyster on her plate.

She bit into the savory oyster and contemplated telling him that she wasn't his darling, but it seemed a waste of breath. Besides, the oyster really was terribly delicious. She licked her lips and glanced up. Mickey O'Connor was watching her, his black eyes narrowed, a corner of his mouth faintly curled. For a moment she felt caught in his gaze, her heart beating faster.

Then Tess bustled over with a tray of tiny tarts.

More dishes were set in front of Mickey O'Connor and without asking he served her something from each and filled her glass full of what proved to be sweet red wine. Silence ate and for several minutes she was quiet, her entire being concentrating on the food and filling her empty stomach, for although she'd had a lovely breakfast it hadn't quite sated her after more than a day without food.

When she looked up again, she met Mr. O'Connor's gaze. He was leaning back in his chair, his own food untouched, apparently content just to watch her eat.

She swallowed. "It's all quite good and I enjoyed it very much, but..."

He raised his eyebrows.

"Your food seems very rich." The pirates were still busily shoveling in their meal. Harry had got up and left the room, and now he was replaced with Bert. "It can't be good for your constitution to eat such rich foods regularly. Aren't you afraid of gout?"

Mickey O'Connor grinned and ran his hand down his flat stomach, his rings flashing on every finger. "Never occurred to me, to tell the truth."

She shook her head. "No, I suppose it wouldn't. You do like to revel in excess, don't you?"

He raised a mocking eyebrow.

She tilted her chin toward his hands. "Those rings, for instance. They're so gaudy and they must be worth a fortune."

He spread his hands before him, fingers wide. "Oh, two fortunes at the very least, but I only started wi' one ring."

She peered at them curiously. His extravagant, jeweled rings seemed such a part of Mickey O'Connor that she couldn't imagine him without them. "Which one?"

"This." He held up his right index finger. A round ruby so dark it was nearly black sat in a worn gold ring. "Got it on a raid with me first crew. In point o' fact it were me only part of the raid, it were worth so much. I forfeited me portion o' the gold for this here ring."

She raised her eyebrows. "Why didn't you take the money instead?"

He sat back and eyed her and she realized suddenly that his playfulness had vanished. He was quite serious now. "Because a poor man don't wear a ring like this.

Everyone who saw me wear this could tell: Charmin'
Mickey's come into his own."

Silence stared down at a lone pear remaining on her
plate, thinking about his words. How odd. She'd never
been rich—certainly not as rich as Mickey O'Connor was
now—but she'd never really desired great wealth. Certainly there had been times when she'd looked longingly
at a fan or heeled slippers in a shop window, but those
were mostly fancies. Her everyday needs had always been
quite satisfied. In contrast, Mr. O'Connor, by his own
admission, had spent his childhood in poverty. Perhaps
that then was his basic reason for flaunting the wealth he
had. Once one had longed for something—hungered after
it day and night—would that well of want ever truly be
filled?

She shivered at the thought and looked up. "And the
rest of your rings?"

"Oh, picked up here and there. This one"—he waggled
his left pinky where a great black baroque pearl sat—"I
found in the chest o' a ship's captain. He had a bit o' a
reputation, that one. Wouldn't be surprised if he'd got it
piratin' from the Frenchies."

Mickey O'Connor grinned and popped a hothouse
grape into his mouth.

She looked hastily away from the sight of him lounging like a sultan, and saw Fionnula sitting a little way
down the table with Bran beside her.

"She worships Bran does our Fionnula," Mickey
O'Connor said quietly, following her gaze.

"Does he worship her, as well?" she asked, sharper
than she meant.

Mickey O'Connor cocked his head, considering the

matter. Then he shook it once. "I very much doubt it. Bran worships power and money and little else."

"Not so very different than you, I suppose." She wasn't sure why the information that Fionnula's sweetheart didn't love the girl as much as Fionnula did him troubled her, but it did.

"Did ye look upon yer William like she does Bran?" he asked so quietly she nearly didn't hear him.

Silence drew in her breath. He hadn't the right to speak William's name—he should know that. But she lifted her chin and met Mickey O'Connor's black eyes. "I suppose I did."

She'd thought to provoke him, but he merely leaned his head on his hand, studying her. "How did ye meet him, this paragon o' a husband?"

She smiled at the memory. "He saved my shoes."

"How?"

"I was out shopping with Temperance, my sister, and I'm afraid I got caught behind—I was staring in a shopwindow."

His lips twitched. "At gloves and lace?"

"At a cream cake, if you must know," she said with dignity.

He breathed a chuckle and she felt a flush start on her neck. "Father didn't approve of sweets so we only had them on special occasions—Christmas and the like." He was still smiling so she hurried on. "*Anyway*, I was rushing to catch up with my sister. I mustn't have been watching because all at once there was a great miller's cart right in front of my nose. If William hadn't grabbed me about the waist and pulled me back, my shoes would've been quite ruined." Silence sliced off a bite of the pear. "There was a puddle, you see."

He reached for his ruby-red wine. "Sounds more like Will saved yer life rather than yer shoes."

"The cart wasn't that close." Silence wrinkled her nose, because the cart *had* been rather close and the first thing William had done upon setting her on her feet again was to give her a scolding. *Not* that she was about to tell Mickey O'Connor that.

"I thanked him," she continued, "and went off with Temperance and thought never to see him again. But then the next day, he came calling to ask Father for permission to court me."

"And what did yer da say?" Mickey O'Connor asked as if he were greatly interested.

"*Father* was not at first pleased." Silence saw a look cross Mr. O'Connor's face and hastened to add, "William was a bit older than me, you see."

"How much older?"

Silence poked at the half-eaten pear. "Fourteen years."

She looked up to see Mickey O'Connor watching her and for the life of her she could not read his black eyes.

"It's not such a great age difference as all that," she said and heard the defensive note in her own voice.

"How old were ye?"

"Eighteen," she muttered, then said louder, "He sailed very soon thereafter, but before he left he brought me a posy of violets."

"He didn't get ye the cream cake ye were moonin' over in the bakery window?"

"I wasn't mooning," she said indignantly. "And, no, whyever would he buy me a cream cake? It's a gift for a child."

"It's what ye wanted," he retorted.

"Violets are much more suitable." She frowned. "While he was away at sea he sent me wonderful letters from his travels, with all sorts of descriptions of the foreign places he saw. Then when he came home he would call upon me. It was so lovely," she said dreamily. "William would take me to fairs and puppet shows."

"And then?" His voice was expressionless.

She shrugged. "I married him. I was one and twenty by that time so Father would not have been able to stop me. But I wanted his blessing and he gave it to us. He said that William had shown his devotion for three years and that he was satisfied that he'd make me a proper husband."

She paused, but Mickey O'Connor didn't say anything.

She looked down at her plate. She'd eaten the pear as she talked and she no longer felt hungry. The empty desperation was gone—all that was left was the vague queasiness from having overindulged. Some of the pirates were laughing now as they finished their meal, while Mr. O'Connor's little secretary had opened a book beside his plate and was making notes as he ate.

"We were happy," she said slowly. "We lived in Wapping, by the ships. I would go to the docks and watch the tall ships come in, looking for the *Finch*, even when I knew she wasn't expected back for months. And when she did dock"—she closed her eyes, remembering—"William would come to see me first thing. I always ran into his arms. We were happy. So happy."

"And yet when ye needed him most he didn't believe ye," she heard him murmur. "He didn't listen to ye."

"I only needed him to believe me because of what you'd done," she pointed out, but her voice lacked heat.

He didn't reply.

She wiped her cheeks. Where last night she'd felt rage, now all she held inside was a deep sadness. "Is that what you think? That because he didn't believe me, because he didn't listen to me, he must not have loved me? That our happiness was but a sham?"

She stared at him, but he merely took a drink of his wine, watching her.

Had her happiness been a sham? At the time she hadn't thought so. Life with William had been perfect, it seemed. He was away for long periods, true, but when he did come back it was like a honeymoon every time.

She frowned, troubled by the thought. What would her marriage have been like if William hadn't been a sea captain? If they'd lived together day in and day out like most married couples?

Silence heaved a sigh and looked around the table. No one was paying them any mind—although she suspected that was more because of Mickey O'Connor's presence than that they hadn't noticed her tears.

She turned back to Mr. O'Connor. "Where are your women?"

His mouth curved slightly. "What women?"

She waved a hand, wondering if she'd drunk too much wine with her meal. "The women you always have. Your . . . your *whores*."

He took a sip of wine and set down his glass. "Gone."

She wrinkled her brow. "Oh."

"Are ye disappointed?"

She bristled. "What do you know of how I feel or think?"

"I don't know," he said as he waved a youth over. The boy held a tray of sweets. Mickey O'Connor's hand hovered over the selection before he chose something with a candied cherry on top. He turned back to her with the sweet in his hand. "That's the fascinatin' thing about ye, Silence, m'love. I know what me men will think afore I tell them we're raidin', what me whores will think at the end o' a night, even what Lad will think about tomorrow— mostly me bed and a nice stew bone. But ye—ye I cannot fathom. I look into yer pretty green-brown-blue eyes, and I haven't the tiniest idea what yer thinkin' about. What ye truly feel."

Silence stared at him in wonder, then blurted, "Why should you care?"

"That," said Mickey O'Connor, holding the sweet to her lips, waiting while she accepted it into her mouth, then smiling almost as if he could taste the melting sugar on her tongue himself, "is a very good question."

Chapter Seven

As soon as dark fell in the king's garden, a bird's
song filled the air. Three notes and the other two nephews
were nodding their heads, but Clever John had his ears
stopped so he could not fall under the spell of the sweet
birdsong. As soon as the king's nephews were asleep,
a wonderful bird alit on the cherry tree. Its feathers were
every color of the rainbow. The bird began pecking at
the king's cherries. But up jumped Clever John and
seized the bird by its delicate neck.
Whereupon the bird turned into a lovely—and quite
nude—woman....
—from Clever John

Mick watched as Silence ate the confection from his fingers. He felt a strange satisfaction in feeding her himself that wasn't dulled even when she realized what she'd done and drew away, wrinkling her nose.

He was enjoying himself, he realized with something like surprise. He'd never chased a woman for more than a day or so—a week at most. They all fell at his feet, some within minutes. He knew, cynically, that his attraction couldn't all be put down to his pretty face. His power, his money drew them just as much if not more.

But not Silence.

Mick smiled to himself and sat back to select a sweetmeat. Silence disliked him, disobeyed him, argued with him, and was all but starting a rebellion amongst his people, and still he indulged her.

"I must be getting back to my rooms," Silence said and stood.

Mick frowned with displeasure. "Why?"

"Because of Mary Darling."

He shrugged. "One o' the maids is watchin' her."

"But if Mary wakes she'll want me."

"Why?" he asked again, biting into a sweetmeat. This discussion wasn't to his fancy, but sparring with her was.

"Because," she said slowly, looking at him as if he were lack-witted, "she's only a baby and she loves me."

"Babies," Mick pronounced, "are a great trouble."

She shook her head, not bothering to reply this time, and started marching to the door.

Mick sighed. "Have the rest o' the sweetmeats brought to me rooms," he told Tris and rose to follow her. Lad, who'd been lying beside his chair, got up as well, padding quietly behind him out into the hallway.

Silence didn't seem surprised when he caught up with her in the hall. "You should come to see Mary more often yourself. She is your daughter after all. Perhaps then she might learn to call you something else besides *Bad*."

She quickened her pace.

He shrugged, keeping up with her shorter strides easily. "Happens I've other things to do, and as I say, babies are a bother."

"Humph. You say that as if you've made a great discovery."

He didn't answer, just to irritate her, and she quickened

her step again. They were nearly running through the halls now.

"Whyever did you bother acknowledging her in the first place, then?" she asked. "Surely it would've been easy simply to turn her away. Unscrupulous men do it all the time."

She glanced over her shoulder at him as if she'd scored a hit with that "unscrupulous," but he'd been called worse in his time.

Much worse.

Still, it wouldn't do to let her think he was going soft on her. Mick stepped in front of her and slammed his hand against the hallway wall, putting the length of his arm in her path.

She squeaked and bumped into him, soft breasts pushing for just an instant against his muscles. Lad sat down in the hall, looking back and forth alertly between them.

Silence straightened and glared at Mick.

He leaned down close—close enough to catch the scent of lavender in her hair.

"What's mine is mine, m'love," he whispered, "and I won't be lettin' go o' anything that belongs to me."

She scowled at him. "Mary is not a 'thing.'"

"Aye." He smiled. "But the principle's the same."

"That's not how a father should treat a daughter," she said, her voice softening.

He narrowed his eyes at her—that tone might creep under his skin if he let it.

Her beautiful eyes widened pleadingly. "Didn't you have a father?"

He refused to let the memories surface. For a moment he was still, making sure they were properly stowed away, and then smiled. "Why, darlin' did ye think mine was a virgin birth?"

She blushed as he knew she would. "No, of course not, but surely—"

She might have said more, but he straightened away from her. Her questions were hitting too close to home.

She blinked and looked around.

"Ye were hurryin' to see the child, were ye not?" he asked and opened the door to her room.

"Her name is Mary Darling," she said as she sailed into the room. She halted suddenly and turned. "But it should be Mary O'Connor, shouldn't it? She's your daughter after all."

He stopped and blinked. Mary O'Connor. It was a good name. A proper name.

He shook his head to dispel the thought. "Off with ye now," he said to the maid, hovering near the door.

She bobbed a curtsy and left without a word.

Lad padded around the room, sniffing at corners, before going to settle by the fireplace.

Mick turned to look at Silence who was bending over the baby's cot. "Happen she mightn't want to be known far and wide as me daughter."

"Shh," Silence hissed, then glanced at him and whispered, "She's just a baby. Whyever wouldn't she want to be your daughter?"

He shrugged and came to stare broodingly down at the lass. "I've many an enemy."

The child's cheeks were flushed deep pink, her black locks plastered with sweat to her forehead. One chubby fist was flung over her head. She was a pretty little thing, there was no doubt.

Mick frowned. "Does she often breathe so loud?"

"No," Silence whispered worriedly. She laid the back of her hand against the child's forehead and something deep inside him twisted.

Her palms had been rough, but the back of her hand was soft and cool as she laid it on his forehead and smiled wearily into his eyes. "Have ye a fever then, Mickey, me love?"

Mick felt sweat start on his back. Those memories were buried deep—he'd made damned sure of it, but letting Silence in was resurrecting them. He had the sudden urge to order her from his rooms, from his palace. But he couldn't do that now. It was far too late. She was already in his palace, in his life. He couldn't go back—and wouldn't even if he could. She was so close to him now that it was as if he held her in his palm like a glowing ember—and gave thanks for the pain even as he inhaled the smoke from his burning flesh.

Mick's chest expanded. He breathed in Silence's scent, breathed in both pain and comfort. "Is she ill, then?"

"I don't know." Silence bit her bottom lip. "She's hot."

Mick nodded. "I'll send for a doctor."

She looked up, her eyes wide, the gray swirling with the green and the brown, her hand laid so tenderly on the baby's head. "If you think that's—"

He didn't stay to hear the rest of her sentence. The baby needed a doctor...and the room was haunted by memories.

SILENCE'S HANDS TREMBLED as she wrung out a cloth and patted Mary Darling's little cheeks. The toddler was so hot that Silence could feel the burning of her skin even through the cloth.

The heat worried Silence, but it was Mary's awful listlessness that struck terror in her heart. Mary'd had chills and fevers before. She'd once whimpered all night long, tugging on her ear fretfully, until in the morning a clear liquid had drained from the ear and she'd slept calmly. Silence had stayed up many nights rocking and walking Mary Darling when she wasn't feeling well. And in all those times Mary had been grumpy and sad and fretful, but she'd never been listless.

"Himself has sent for the doctor," Fionnula said as she came in with a fresh bowl of water.

"She's just so hot," Silence murmured as she wrung out the cloth and applied it again. "I've taken her out of her frock and stays, but she's still on fire."

"Me mam used to say as the fever was to burn away the illness inside," Fionnula offered.

"Perhaps so, but I've seen fever kill, as well," Silence murmured.

There had been a little boy, new to the home and rather sickly. Winter had suspected he'd not had enough to eat in his short life. The child had caught a fever and within two days had simply faded away. Silence had wept quietly in bed that night, holding Mary close to her chest. Winter had said with awful pragmatism that some children didn't live and one just had to face that fact. But even he had worn a drawn expression when he'd said it and he was especially nice to the small boys in the home for weeks afterward.

Silence shuddered. Mary couldn't fade away. She couldn't imagine living if the little girl died.

There was a murmur of voices in the hall and then the door opened to reveal Mickey O'Connor ushering in a rotund little man.

"What have we here?" the doctor asked in a bass voice that seemed too large for his body.

"She's burning with fever," Silence said. She had to fight to keep a quaver out of her voice.

The doctor placed a hand on the baby's chest and stilled.

Silence started to ask something, but the man held up his other hand.

After another moment he took his hand off Mary's chest and turned to Silence. "Pardon my rudeness, ma'am, but I was feeling for the wee one's heartbeat."

"I understand." Silence grasped her hands together at her waist to still their trembling. "Can you help her?"

"Of course I can," the doctor said briskly. "Never you fear."

He opened a black case, revealing a half dozen sharp lancets in different sizes. Silence rubbed her palms together nervously. She knew that the doctor meant to cut Mary.

Mr. O'Connor had been lounging by the fireplace, but he stirred at the sight of the lancets in their fitted pockets. "D'ye have to cut her?"

The doctor's face was serious. "It's the only way, sir, to let the evil drain from her body."

Mickey O'Connor's mouth tightened, but he nodded once before turning his face to the fireplace.

The doctor chose a delicately wicked looking tool and then fished out a little tin dish. He looked at Silence, his face grave. "Perhaps you can hold her upright upon your lap. If you can keep her from moving in any way, it'll be for the best."

Silence picked up Mary gently. She'd always hated bloodletting, ever since she was a little girl and had had to be bled three times for some childhood illness. If she could save Mary's tender skin the sharp scalpel, she'd offer her own arm, but this must be done. She knew that.

The doctor had been watching her and now he nodded at her approvingly. "Can you hold the cup for me?" he asked Fionnula.

The maid stepped forward and took the cup.

"Easy," the doctor murmured, and with quick efficiency, lifted Mary's chemise and made a cut high on her thigh.

Mary flinched but made no sound.

Bright red blood flowed from the wound.

It seemed to take forever before the doctor murmured, "I think that will do it."

He pressed a clean cloth to the wound and wound a strip of linen around Mary's leg, tying it off neatly.

"Now then," the doctor said as he wiped and put away his lancet. "A little broth will help enormously, I believe. Take a small piece of chicken and boil it with a sprig of parsley and two of thyme. Strain the broth and add a spoonful of white wine, the finest you can find. Serve this broth to the child thrice daily, making sure she drinks a full teacup if possible." He glanced at Silence sharply. "Do you understand?"

"Yes," she said, stroking Mary's hair.

"Good. Good. I also have this elixir." He produced a small blue glass bottle. "My own concoction and I fancy a very effective one. A spoonful in a small cup of water before bedtime. Now"—he picked up his bag and stared severely at Silence and Fionnula—"should she come out in spots or vomit up bile, you are to call for me at once, yes?"

Silence nodded again, her lips trembling. "I will."

The doctor laid his hand on Mary's head and turned toward the door without another word. Mickey O'Connor turned and silently followed him, pausing before he exited. "Do ye have all that ye'll be needing for her?"

Silence bit her lip to stop it trembling. "I believe so."

His hesitated and for a moment she thought he was about to say something, but in the end he left without a word.

"WE'LL STORM HIS cursed palace and take her out by force if need be!" Concord Makepeace declared ferociously the next day. "Bad enough that she's ruined her own reputation, but to sully the good name of the home is too much!"

Concord's graying hair was coming down from his queue and he looked rather like an aging Samson.

A hotheaded, aging Samson who'd not fully thought through the consequences of an attack on an armed pirate stronghold.

Winter sighed to himself. He'd known the drawbacks to informing his brothers of Silence's plight, but he couldn't in all conscious let them remain in the dark.

Even if Concord's undirected anger and worry were giving Winter a headache.

"The palace is a fortress," Winter pointed out calmly. "And we are only two. If we—"

"Three," came a voice in the doorway of the home's kitchen.

Winter met the green eyes of his brother Asa, his own eyebrow slowly raising. Although he'd sent word to Asa's rented rooms, he hadn't expected him to actually show up. Asa hadn't been heard from in nearly a year. For all Winter had known, his middle brother had sailed overseas.

Yet here he was, as brawny as ever. Asa had the shoulders of a bull and a mane of tawny hair like a young lion. The last year had given him a few differences, however. His scarlet coat was intricately embroidered at the cuffs and skirts, and his shirt, while plain, was of fine linen. Winter's eyes narrowed. Interesting. However his brother made his living, he was apparently doing quite well for himself.

"What are you doing here?" Concord, never tactful, asked aggressively. "You don't respond to letters, you don't bother to make an appearance at Temperance's wedding or the christening of my new daughter, or when Silence lost her husband at sea, and yet you think you can simply trot back home?"

Winter winced and murmured quietly, "We do need his help, Concord."

"Ha!" Concord folded bulging arms across his chest. Like Winter, he dressed plainly in black and brown, his hat round and uncocked. "We've done just fine without him for the last year."

"That was before Silence went to live in a pirate's house," Winter pointed out drily.

Asa, who'd propped one massive shoulder against the door frame, straightened now. "What pirate? You said in your letter to me that Silence was in dire danger. You never mentioned a pirate."

Concord snorted.

"Mickey O'Connor," Winter said quietly before Concord could go off on another tirade.

"Charming Mickey O'Connor?" Asa asked incredulously. "What is Silence doing with him? Did he kidnap her?"

"No."

Asa pulled out a kitchen chair and sat, planting his elbows on the table. "Then why?"

"Last year a baby was left on Silence's doorstep," Winter explained. "Silence named the child Mary Darling and brought her here to the home. This was after Temperance married Lord Caire and was no longer managing the home with me. Silence took her position. She cared for all the children, of course, but she made Mary Darling her special pet."

Concord stirred. "The baby was like her own. When William died, I think the child gave her comfort."

Winter nodded. "I returned home from a trip to Oxford several days ago to find Silence gone. When I confronted her at O'Connor's palace—"

"You went to Mickey O'Connor's house by yourself?" Asa interrupted.

Winter met his eyes. "Yes."

For a moment a startled look crossed Asa's face, and then he slowly nodded. "Go on."

Winter inclined his head. "She seemed quite as usual. She was dressed in her own clothes and frankly did not appear to be overly happy that I'd come to her rescue. She said that Mickey O'Connor was Mary Darling's father—"

Asa swore and Concord glared at him.

"—and that O'Connor had brought her and the child to his home to protect them from his enemies. I could not persuade her to leave so I came away again. Now, however, there are questions being asked about where exactly Silence is. If the truth that she's living with a notorious pirate becomes known…"

Winter shrugged. He didn't need to tell his brothers what such information would do to the home's good standing—and the money it needed from its patrons and donors. One whiff of impropriety and the fickle aristocrats would find some other charity to amuse themselves with.

"You should have picked her up and dragged her out bodily," Concord growled.

Winter arched an eyebrow. "Past O'Connor and a half dozen of his men?"

Concord grimaced.

Asa rolled his eyes. "Trust you to advocate a near-suicidal action based on moral outrage."

Concord half rose from his chair, bellowing incoherently. Asa rose as well and for the next several minutes the kitchen was filled with loud masculine rage.

Winter sighed and closed his eyes, raising one hand to gently rub his temple. He'd had a lifetime to observe the strained relations between his elder brothers. There were times when they could almost make it through a family meal without resorting to shouts, but those occasions were rare and becoming rarer. Concord dealt with the tension by assuming an unyielding line: He was entirely correct and by contrast everything Asa espoused was entirely incorrect. Winter had once overheard Temperance muttering under her breath that their brother should've better been christened *Dis*cord.

Asa's response to this ceaseless state of friction was to disappear. It was a constant worry for their eldest sister, Verity. She feared—and Winter privately concurred—that someday their brother would go away and simply not come back.

His brothers' voices died.

Winter opened his eyes to find both Asa and Concord scowling at him.

He raised his eyebrows. "Might we continue this discussion now?"

A smile tugged at the corner of Asa's wide mouth. "We might." He sobered. "What I don't understand is why Silence trusted this pirate to speak the truth about his supposed enemies. Has he seduced her, do you think?"

Concord banged a hard fist on the table. "How dare you question our sister's virtue?"

Asa looked at Concord coldly. "I find that people are capable of many different things. How do you know Silence wouldn't fall under Mickey O'Connor's spell? He's rumored to be quite pretty."

Concord opened his mouth, but Winter beat him to it. "We know because we have watched Silence in the last year," he said quietly, but pointedly.

A ruddy flush lit Asa's cheekbones.

"Silence might be as susceptible to sin as any other female," Winter said, "but she would never be seduced by O'Connor. You know her history with him. What you may not know is that after William's cargo was returned, relations between he and Silence were... strained. He perished on his last journey at sea and Silence blamed her confrontation with O'Connor for the sorrow in her marriage before William left."

For a moment none of the men spoke. Winter looked at his brothers and wondered if they felt as helpless as he. He'd wanted to break things—to kill O'Connor—when he'd seen Silence after her night with the pirate. He hadn't of course. Such violence would not have helped their sister.

That hadn't stopped him dreaming of blood for weeks afterward, though.

"So you see," Winter said quietly, "Silence must truly think that there is danger for the child. She'd never consent to be in the same building with him otherwise."

"Then that presents an additional problem," Asa said.

Winter arched an eyebrow in inquiry.

"Besides the difficulty of getting into the palace and rescuing her," Asa said, "we will also need to have a place where we can safely bring both her and the child. A place that neither Mickey nor his enemies can find."

Winter nodded slowly. "I believe your assessment is correct. She will never leave willingly unless she knows we can keep the child safe."

Concord leaned forward placing his massive forearms on the table. "In that case it's obvious who we should bring into this."

SILENCE WAS TEARING her heart out over the child.

Two mornings later Mick stood over Silence's bed and watched her sleep. There were smudges of exhaustion and fear under her eyes, her brown hair was coming down from a plait, and she clutched the sheet in one fragile fist like a little girl afraid of night terrors.

She slept as if dead—she'd not moved as he'd entered her room. He brushed a stray lock of hair away from her eyes. Her breath didn't even hitch.

Mick sighed and straightened. It was not yet dawn— still dark out. She'd spent the last two nights and the day in between nursing the child. He'd stayed away, but he'd had Fionnula report the happenings in the sickroom three or four times a day.

The child was growing thinner, her little body lit from within by a fire that would not die. If the fire consumed her—

Mick clenched his jaw and turned away from the bed. He left without glancing in the direction of the child's cot, crossing through his own room and out into the hallway.

Harry looked up as Mick closed the door quietly behind him. Mick nodded at the guard and turned to stride down the hall. If the babe died, Silence's heart would be torn from her chest as surely as if a wild animal had savaged her. He had no heart himself, but he'd heard they were delicate things and easily broken. Mick growled low under his breath as he made his way to the front of the house. He knew how to protect Silence from knives and fists, from poverty and want, but he had no idea how—or even if—he could protect her from her own soft heart.

Mick passed the half-dozen guards he'd stationed at the front door and went out into the new morning. He glanced up at the grayish-pink sky and then studied his palace. It was a peacock cleverly disguised as a crow. There was no indication of what lay behind the deceptively simple plain wood door. One would never know from looking at it that the door was reinforced from behind with iron.

There was one other entry to the palace—a door leading to the small courtyard behind—and that was guarded, as well. From the outside, his palace appeared to be a dozen or more narrow row houses, built right next to each other. In reality, it was all one building inside and the doors to the house façades had been boarded up from inside long ago.

Mick grunted and turned to walk up the street. He might seem overprotected against attack, but then he had an unrelenting enemy.

A shadow moved in a narrow alley as he passed it and Mick whirled, a knife held ready in his hand. Lad emerged into the weak light, his ears laid back, his head down in submission.

"Jaysus," Mickey breathed in disgust and shoved the knife back in the sheath strapped to his forearm.

He started down the street again and the dog trotted out happily and fell into step behind him.

The daylight people of St. Giles were already on the streets. The ones he passed now did honest work—more or less—porters, hawkers, chair men, night soil men, and beggars. They gave him a wide berth, careful not to meet his eyes. They knew him of course. He was their king and they were properly respectful. The river and the boats he lived on were to the east and he'd be nearer his work if he lived in Wapping or some other place in the East End of London. But Mick had been born and grown up in St. Giles. Had run the streets like a feral young wolf cub as a boy, had fucked his first woman here. Killed his first man. This was his home and when he'd made his fortune he'd built his palace in St. Giles.

And now there was one more thing that held him here.

He crossed a street and looked up. The spire of the new St. Giles-in-the-Fields loomed ahead. Mildew had destroyed the old church. Rumor had it that the mildew had fed upon the damp from the rotting plague corpses buried beneath the church flagstones. Certainly the air in the old church had held an evil stink. But no more. The modern church was clean and elegant, a far cry from the old building. Mick grunted. The new church had been built by nobles living outside of London City proper. He wondered what the locals—the ones who actually lived by the church—thought of the new building.

Mick skirted the church, coming upon the graveyard wall. A little way farther and the gate came into sight. He pushed it open. The graveyard was old, of course, the monuments moss-covered, some leaning as if the underground inhabitants had tried to push their way free from the earth. Mick made his way through the crooked rows, Lad padding silently behind him, and even though St. Giles lay just beyond a small wall, the clatter and hustle without was muffled. The graveyard held its own insulated atmosphere.

Mick watched carefully as he neared the grave he'd come to see, for he wasn't alone in the graveyard.

The Vicar of Whitechapel stood looking down at her headstone and the freshly mounded earth. For a man who had terrorized the East End of London for the better part of a decade he didn't look that intimidating. He was of average height, wiry rather than heavily muscled, his shoulder-length hair graying, and his features pleasant.

"She called your name," Charlie said as Mick halted on the far side of the new grave. "As she was dying. Pity you didn't see fit to visit her on her deathbed."

Mick smiled widely, easily, as if the news that she'd called for him wasn't a white-hot poker thrust through his chest. "Busy, wasn't I?"

Charlie turned then, looking at Mickey full on, and revealing the horror that was the left side of his face. His skin had melted or burned off his face. The eye socket was merely a hardened gouge, his nostril destroyed, his lips pulled down into his chin. The ear was a melted rim and the hair on the left side of his head was in tufts as if most of it had been pulled out by the very roots.

Mick's smile widened. "Yer gettin' handsomer by the hour, Charlie."

The Vicar's expression didn't change—but then many of his facial muscles had been destroyed. His remaining brown eye glittered with mad hatred, though. A wise man would step away from such vicious anger.

Mick leaned forward. "I'll not let ye drive me from me home, old man."

Charlie's eyelid drooped. "What makes you think you have any say-so in the matter, boy?"

Mick's smile hardened. "What makes ye think I don't?"

Charlie shrugged one shoulder—the other had scarring. "Might be because I know you've got your babe hid in that palace of yours—along with a woman called Silence Hollingbrook. I find that interesting, I do. Seems to me that it'd be a fair trade: your woman for my own."

Mick shrugged himself as if Silence didn't matter to him, but his heart had begun to beat in triple time. Of course the Vicar had found out about Silence. Of course he'd know that she was different simply because she'd stayed when none of his other women had.

"I never took yer woman," Mick said.

"Aye, but you tried to."

Mick raised an eyebrow. Charlie wasn't making sense, but then he'd long known the man was mad.

"And that babe?" The Vicar tutted. "I hear she's a sickly thing. Like to die soon. That must weigh upon your heart most sadly."

Mick looked at the Vicar. He was such a small man for all the malice he held inside of him. Long ago Mick had wondered why Charlie was made the way he was. What had carved away all sympathy, all respect for other men. What had made him the vicious, violent bastard he was.

But he'd learned to stop wondering. It made no never mind why the Vicar was the way he was. As well to ask why a viper struck and killed for no reason. It was simply the way of nature.

"Ye know as well as I that I lost whatever heart I once had long ago," Mick replied without emotion, a simple statement of fact. "If the babe lives, or if she dies, it makes no difference to me. I'll still eat sweetmeats on the morrow and taste the sugar on me tongue, still fuck women and feel the pleasure in me bollocks. And, Charlie—mark me well, now—I'll still kill ye and laugh in yer ugly face as I do it."

He walked away then, carefully not looking at the new headstone with the tiny angel carved at the top. Lad glanced up from sniffing a weed and fell into step with Mick as he passed. The temptation to attack now was almost overwhelming. His hands, balled into fists by his side, shook with the urge to strike the older man and put an end to this once and for all.

But Charlie never went anywhere without a half dozen guards. One lounged behind a tree, another two stood by the wall, and the remaining three were out of sight, but Mick had no doubt that they were nearby. Strange. Only a year ago, he might've damned the guards and attacked Charlie anyway. Now, Mick had the knowledge at the back of his mind that if he failed, he'd not be there to protect Silence—Charlie was mad enough to revenge himself on Silence even if Mick were dead. The realization was not a pleasant one—that only he stood between Charlie and Silence.

He nodded ironically to one of the Vicar's men stationed at the churchyard gate as he passed by. Six men could overwhelm him, he supposed, if the Vicar chose to attack now, but that wasn't the man's way. Charlie preferred the indirect hit, the slow poison that systematically destroyed a person before they were even dead.

Mick halted in the middle of the street and threw back his head to gaze at the blue sky overhead. It was going to be a rare clear day in London, the sun shining so brightly one could almost believe in a God and all his angels, of a mother's love and a boy's innocent dreams. He closed his

eyes and saw her brown eyes, sad and defeated and filled
with tears as she'd sung to him.

Take me in your arms, my love
And blow the candle out.

A shouted curse made Mick open his eyes and spin to
glare at a drover with a heard of sheep.

The man's eyes widened and he was stuttering apolo-
gies even as Mick turned away. Mick walked the rest of
the way home without conscious thought. When he got to
his own door Lad trotted up the steps behind him. Mick
shot him a look and for a moment the dog froze, one paw
still lifted, and rolled his eyes sheepishly at him.

Mick sighed. "In with ye, then."

Lad's jaw dropped open in a grin and he happily
capered into the palace.

"How were ye ever a bull-baitin' dog?" Mick muttered
to the animal as they tromped through the house. "The
bulls must've laughed themselves silly when ye were
thrown in the pit."

Lad panted beside him happily, not a thought in his
boneheaded brain.

They reached the upper floors and Mick strode down
the hallway quietly. Bert was dozing outside Silence's
room, but straightened hastily as Mick neared.

"Are they awake?" Mick asked softly.

Bert blinked sleepily. "Fionnula left jus' a minute ago
to fetch some tea. I 'aven't 'eard a peep."

Mick nodded and entered his room, shrugging out
of his coat and waistcoat. He preferred the freedom
of just his shirt in his own home. He crossed to the

connecting door and cracked it carefully, peering in. Silence lay on the bed, her form still, save for the slow rise and fall of her chest. He was about to shut the door again when a squeak came from the cot on the far side of the bed.

Mick was across the room in a second.

The child lay on her back, her eyes open, yawning sleepily. She saw him and her tiny pink lips trembled, her mouth turning down.

Mick frowned at her. "Hush."

His admonishment had the opposite effect from what he intended. Her mouth opened and she let out a fretful wail.

Mick glanced at the bed. Silence hadn't moved at the sound. She was exhausted from hours of nursing the brat. Fionnula had left the room and might not be back for some time, and Bert would be very little help.

Mick scowled at the toddler. "What d'ye want?"

She sobbed and lifted her arms to him.

He blinked, taken aback. Surely she didn't want him. But another wail gave him very little choice.

He lifted the little girl from the cot, bringing her close to his chest as he'd seen Silence do. She was as light as feather down from one of his fine pillows. His chest wasn't as soft as Silence's, but the baby didn't seem to mind. The fretful sounds stopped as she stuck a finger in her mouth and regarded him with wide brown eyes. Her eyelashes were spiked with tears, making them dark and long.

She'd be a beauty someday, he thought dispassionately, someone would have to guard her against the men who would be drawn to her. They'd swarm around her like bees to honey, wanting to lift her skirts, wanting to dishonor her, little caring of her feelings or who she was as a person. She'd be a piece of flesh to them, not a girl. Not someone's beloved daughter.

He scowled again at the thought.

The child whimpered, her face crumpling, tears pooling at the corners of her eyes.

"Hush now," Mick whispered.

Silence was still asleep. He crossed to his own room and entered, holding the baby. He bent to set her on the bed, but she clung to his fine lawn shirt, rumpling it, and sobbed.

"Hush away, sweetin'," he whispered. What did she want? He picked up a jeweled snuffbox lying on his dressing table and showed it to her.

She batted it away irritably and smashed her little head into his chest, still sobbing. He stared down at her, perplexed. She was so loud, so stubborn, and yet he could feel the delicate bones of her little ribs through her chemise. She was so small, so fragile, so easily hurt.

He walked to the fireplace and showed her in turn the items on the mantelpiece: an alabaster vase, a pink and white shepherdess, and a curved golden dagger that had once belonged to some Ottoman lord. She didn't seem very interested in his treasures, but she quieted a bit, still rubbing her face against his shirt. She'd ruin it soon if he didn't take it off. Her mouth opened suddenly in a wide yawn.

And he found himself singing to her softly, the words coming to him as naturally as breathing.

"Take me in your arms, my love
And blow the candle out."

Chapter Eight

❧

*Well, a bird that turned into a woman startled Clever
John very much, but he kept his hand about her neck
as he examined her. She was young and lithe, her face
lovely and unlined, and her hair waved gently about
her head in every color of the rainbow.*
*He plucked the candle wax from his ears and said,
"What manner of being are you?"*
*The woman laughed merrily. "My name is Tamara.
I am daughter to the dawn and sister to the four winds.
Let me go and I shall grant you three wishes." . . .*
—from Clever John

Silence woke from a dream of a singing angel. He'd been tall
and stern—like an angel carved in the door of a gothic church.
An otherworldly being of great virtue and little sympathy. But
his voice had been low and sweet, warming her from within
like hot honey, making her bones liquid with relaxation—
even though she'd known that the angel was a dangerous
being from another world. That she ought to keep on the alert.

For a moment she lay still in the big bed, blinking
sleepily, loath to move.

And then she realized that the angel's song hadn't
stopped on her waking.

Silence sat up. The tantalizingly beautiful voice was coming from the half-open door to Mickey O'Connor's room.

She rose, drawing a shawl about her shoulders and glanced at Mary Darling's cot. It was empty, but she felt no alarm. She thought she might recognize that voice. Moving as quietly as she could she crept to the connecting door.

The sight within made her draw in her breath.

Mickey O'Connor stood across the room by the fireplace, his back toward her. He was clad only in tight black breeches and jackboots, his upper body nude. His broad back was a smooth olive expanse, the muscles that delineated his shoulders and arms in firm, sensuous bunches. And he was singing, his voice a wonderful, soaring tenor. She'd never heard anything so beautiful in her life. How was it possible that Mickey O'Connor, a man with a soul as black as tar, should have a voice the angels would envy?

He half-turned suddenly and she saw that he cradled Mary Darling to his strong chest. The little girl's pink cheek was laid trustingly against him, her eyes closed in sleep. His hand moved gently in her inky curls, stroking her soothingly.

Silence must have made some sound at the sight. His eyes flashed to hers, yet he never stopped singing.

"My father and my mother
In yonder room do lay
They are embracing one another
And so may you and I
So take me in your arms, my love
And blow the candle out."

She felt her face heat at his words, even though they were part of his song. He didn't mean them for her. They were merely the words to an old ballad.

She knew that, yet she couldn't tear her gaze from his. His dark eyes seemed to be telling her something, something apart from the song he sang so beautifully. She lifted a hand to her belly and pressed to still the trembling there.

His song died on a low, liquid note and he continued to stare at her.

Silence cleared her throat, fearful her voice would come out a croak. "Is she asleep?"

He blinked as if he, too, were waking from a dream, and glanced down at Mary Darling. "Aye, I'm a-thinkin' she is—she's stopped fussin' at me."

Silence felt a huge smile of relief spread over her face. "She was fussing? Oh, how wonderful!"

He shot her a look, one eyebrow arching. "Ye've taught the child to bully me, too, now?"

"Oh, no," she said hastily, embarrassed. Did he really think she bullied him? What a silly notion! "It's just that she'd been so listless. If she's well enough to fret, then she must be feeling better."

"Ah." He glanced down at the baby's head, his look nearly tender. "Then I'll rejoice when she starts bawlin' again at the top o' her lungs."

"You should," Silence said as she crossed to him and gently took the sleeping baby. Mary mumbled something and snuggled against her bosom. Silence examined her anxiously. Mary's cheeks were pink, but they weren't the hectic red of before and her little body no longer felt as if it burned. *Oh, thank God.*

Silence looked up grinning. "I know I will. Far better a screaming baby than one that's too quiet."

"Aye," he said, watching them with a somber light in his eyes. "I can well believe ye."

She gazed down at Mary's sleeping head, avoiding his eyes. She should leave his room, but she was oddly reluctant to do so. "You have a beautiful voice."

He snorted. "Do I now?"

She looked up at him, puzzled by his dismissive tone. "You must know you do."

He grimaced. "Aye, I suppose I do at that. I spent enough time when I was a lad singin' for me supper." He caught her questioning look. "When there was naught in the cupboard, me mam would take me down to the street corner. She'd lay a handkerchief on the ground at our feet and we'd sing for pennies. It might take minutes or hours or all day afore we had enough to buy our supper."

Silence swallowed. He talked of begging for food so cavalierly, yet she knew now that the experience must've scarred him terribly. "How old were you?"

He cocked his head as if considering. "I don't rightly know. One o' me earliest memories is going to the corner on a freezin' night in winter."

"How awful!"

He looked at her sardonically. "There be worse ways to make a penny."

She bit her lip. There were indeed worse ways in St. Giles to make money. So many came to London from the English countryside, from Scotland and Ireland and even from the continent. There were far too many for the jobs available. She sometimes saw the women coming home in the morning after a night of walking the streets. And it wasn't just women who walked the streets. There were children, too, of both sexes.

Silence peeked at Mickey O'Connor from under her eyelashes. He was beautiful, his eyes dark and sensuous, his mouth mobile, his hair thick and black. He would've been a lovely child—too lovely.

"You're Irish," Silence blurted out and then felt the heat rise in her cheeks. The Irish were numerous in London—and almost universally despised.

He smiled, dimples creasing the corners of his mouth. "Aye, me mam came from Ireland lookin' for work. She was one o' ten children to a widowed mother, or so she told me. I never met me Irish kin. She came over alone." He bent his head as he donned the shirt he'd taken from the back of a nearby chair. "'Tis a far cry from yer own family, I'll wager."

She nodded. "My father's family has lived in London for generations. My mother's people came from Dorset and live there still, though we don't often see them."

"Ye've a sister and a brother, I know," he said.

"Two sisters and three brothers, actually," she replied, smiling a little. "I'm the youngest of six children. There's Verity—she brought up Temperance and me when our mother died, then Concord who took over Father's brewery on his death. Both are married with families of their own now. Asa is my next brother, but I don't know exactly what he does—he's something of the black sheep of the family. Temperance used to run the Home for Unfortunate Infants and Foundling Children before she married Lord Caire, and Winter is the next youngest above me."

She stopped suddenly, a little out of breath. He probably thought her a ninny for prattling on about her family.

It occurred to her that although her family was not rich, compared to his, she'd been quite well off. Further, in his world—a world of beggars and thieves—he had risen quite far. In his own way, Mickey O'Connor was a successful man.

"Ye'd a happy childhood." The comment was a statement of fact, but she had the feeling that the idea was a foreign one for him. Dear Lord, what might his childhood have been like?

"Yes, I was happy," she said simply. "My father was strict, but he loved all his children and made sure we each were properly educated. We may not have been rich, yet we never lacked for food or clothing."

He nodded, unsurprised. "He was a good provider."

"What of your family?" she asked tentatively. "What did your mother do when she came to London?"

He shrugged. "Afore I was born I've heard that she was a spinner for a time."

"And then?" Silence whispered.

He looked at her, his face devoid of expression. "And then she met a monster."

Silence covered Mary's little head with her hand as if to shield her. How bad would a person have to be for a river pirate to consider him a monster?

Mickey's beautiful mouth had twisted into a terrible snarl, his voice ragged and low. "She fell under his spell, this monster, for he was a silver-tongued man and knew well how to hide his evil. Hide it until she was too entangled in his web to free herself. He took her and made her his, blindin' her so that she could never look entirely away from his dark eyes, never think without his voice in her head. He had a still and she helped him make gin.

When the still wasn't makin' money, she'd whore herself for him, spendin' nights on the streets and turnin' out her pocket to him when she came home again. Sometimes he sent her out on the streets even when there was money, and she went without protest, so under his spell was she. 'Twas his way of keepin' her firmly beneath his fist. Keepin' her bewitched."

"And your father?" she asked bravely. Had he been born from one of his mother's nights walking the street?

He simply looked at her with those beautiful black eyes and did not reply.

MICK WATCHED THE color drain from Silence's face. Was she simply repulsed by his poverty-ridden upbringing and the fact that his mother had been a whore? Or had she some little care for him? A tiny bit of sympathy for the devil himself?

She stood before him clad only in a worn chemise and equally worn shawl, cradling the baby in her arms. He'd grown enormously erect in the last few minutes, simply from staring at her. He'd donned his shirt, but left it untucked from his breeches in feeble disguise. Silence's chemise hung only to her calves. Her lower legs were smooth and delicately shaped. He could just make out—if he squinted hard—the shadowed outline of her thighs. He fancied he could see a dark triangle as well, but that was probably the product of his over-heated brain. Still, his cock didn't seem to care between reality and fantasy.

Did she have no sense of self-preservation? he wondered, suddenly irritable. She knew what he was, his unremorseful cruelty, and yet she stood before him only half-clad and as innocently unaware as a lamb. Except that wasn't the entire truth. His gaze dropped to the child's curly black hair. Silence had been worried about the baby. It was her love for the child that made her vulnerable and he had an urge to protect that—both the woman and the maternal love she held.

That love within her was more precious than all the gold in his throne room.

"I-I had no idea how awful your childhood was," she said.

He blinked and had to think to remember the conversation they'd been engaged in. "No matter. Me tale is one that's often told in St. Giles."

"But it shouldn't be. Your mother should've protected you." He chanced a glance and saw she was nibbling on her bottom lip, her eyes uncertain. He nearly groaned.

He arched a mocking eyebrow. "The way of the world, isn't it? Children are born from sin and learn to look to themselves as soon as they can walk. Why should me childhood be any different?"

"Because we aren't animals," she said simply. "You deserved better."

He barked a laugh to cover the bloody pain her words drew from his breast. "Perhaps in yer world—"

"In yours as well!"

"A person cares about himself, and only himself," he said, suddenly weary of this conversation, "in yer world or mine. Me mam was no better or worse than any other and I didn't deserve more. Yer silly to think otherwise."

"*No.*" He felt the touch of her hand on his arm and looked down in surprise to find her gripping his arm with feminine strength. He raised his gaze and saw that her eyes blazed greeny-brown at him. "I may not be as sophisticated as you. I may not have constant, changing lovers, I may not carelessly disregard the law and common morals, I may not live the romantic life of a river pirate, but I know this, Mickey O'Connor: all children deserve a loving mother. And a mother who truly loved her child would do anything—*anything*—to protect and save him."

He looked into her fierce face, her delicate cheeks flaming with passion, her lips stained a rose red, and the small child she still held protectively in her arms and felt himself fall, tumbling helplessly, all thought stopped in his head. She took his breath away with her simple avowal: *A mother should protect her child.* Something came loose in his chest.

Dear God, he wanted this woman.

He remembered, as he stared down at her, the cold nights on the streets, the leather strap against his back, and that final, terrible confrontation.

"Perhaps me mother didn't truly love me then," he whispered.

Her magnificent eyes suddenly swam with tears. "Maybe not. But that doesn't mean that you didn't deserve to be loved."

And he couldn't help it. She wept—for him.

He touched his lips to hers and unlike their first kiss, this one was nearly chaste. He couldn't draw her body near because the baby was still between them. Still, he could savor her softness. He hid his claws and brushed his mouth against hers, as delicately as a butterfly's wings on a petal. She breathed a sound and he tilted his head, licking softly, tenderly, over her mouth. His cock was straining against the fabric of his breeches, but he made none of his usual decisive moves to take this further. He was strangely content simply to savor her lips. To savor Silence herself.

When at last he raised his head, her beautiful eyes were dazed.

He smiled a little, and stroked one finger over her soft cheek. She tilted her face toward his hand, as if without thought. He watched his finger stroke down her elegant neck, over her collarbone and onto the upper slope of her left breast, just revealed by the top of her chemise.

He swallowed, staring at his swarthy finger against her creamy skin. "Ye should go."

He raised his eyes to hers.

He didn't know what she saw there, but whatever it was, it made her turn away without speaking. She fled the room.

Mickey cursed under his breath, letting his head fall back against the wall. His cock still beat angrily against his clothing. Once he would've simply sent for a whore. Now that thought was oddly unsatisfying. He could have a willing woman, a woman who would do anything he might request of her, even the most exotic acts of sex, but instead his flesh wanted just one woman.

A woman who was as fierce in her maternal love as he had been as a boy in his will to survive.

Just thinking of her—the flush that had lit her face, her lips rose red from his kiss—made his cock leap eagerly.

Mickey swore and unbuttoned the placket of his breeches. He'd never been one to deny himself pleasure of any sort. He reached inside his breeches now and drew out his swollen flesh and looked down. Liquid had oozed from the tip of his randy member, making the dark plum head glisten. He spat on his palm and took the thing in his hand.

Jaysus, what would she do if she knew what he was doing right now? Her stormy eyes would widen in shock, he knew, if she could see him, but mightn't they also show a bit of interest as well? He chuckled breathlessly at the thought, and imagined her sitting in the chair before his fireplace, watching as he fisted his cock. Her eyelids would droop with desire. She might let her head fall back, revealing the vulnerable heartbeat in her throat.

He groaned and slid his palm faster over his straining rod.

Would she let her legs fall open? If she did he'd come closer. He might kneel at her feet, still achingly hard, and slowly lift her tattered chemise. He'd reveal white thighs, the tender crease separating leg and stomach, and that place between where soft, curly hair grew. Would her bush be full or merely a few wisps at the top of her slit?

Mickey lifted his lip in a snarl, canting his hips, stroking his other hand over his own belly and thigh, to reach his bollocks drawn up tight in lust.

He'd take his thumb and run it through that sweet cleft, watch the tender petals part, inhale the scent of her desire. And when he placed his mouth on her and suckled, she'd arch beneath his hand. He'd need to press his palm on her belly to hold her, but still she'd scream—

His crisis hit him hard and fast, making him groan as he spilled his seed on the floor.

He rested against the wall, still caressing his aching flesh. If merely thinking about the act with Silence was that explosive, then how would it be to actually lick her? A small smile curved his lips. He'd bet his next haul that her puritan husband had never showed her that particular pleasure. He'd give much to be the first one to lick her sweet pussy.

If she'd ever let him . . .

*   *   *

DEAR LORD.

Silence carefully, *quietly*, closed the connecting door to Mickey O'Connor's room and leaned back against it, her hand to her breast. She could feel her heart beating much too fast under her palm.

She'd known the moment she'd cracked the connecting door and peered inside that the scene within was not for her eyes. When she had entered her own room, she'd put Mary down and come back to say something to him—what she could no longer remember. The sight within had driven all thought from her mind. Mickey O'Connor's head had been arched back, his strong neck corded with strain, his black breeches unbuttoned and his hand had been working his manhood.

He'd been simply...*mesmerizing.*

She should've closed the door at once. Should have never dared to peek at what had obviously been a very private moment. But somehow she couldn't make herself close the door. It wasn't just curiosity. It had been something more. She'd talked to Mickey O'Connor. Not as supplicant to pirate, but as one human being to another. That simple act—*talking*—had changed everything. She no longer thought of him as just a pirate. He was a man now, a living, breathing man. A man who could be hurt.

A man she could be attracted to.

And once that line had been crossed, she could never go back. He was real to her now, and while the pirate evoked fear and dread and even revulsion, the man—the *real* man beneath—was infinitely alluring.

So she'd stayed at the crack in the door, watching breathlessly as Mickey O'Connor did something very earthly indeed. She'd remembered his kiss as she watched. It hadn't been like their first kiss. That had been wild and erotic and tinged with anger. No, the kiss he'd just given her was sweetly gentle—so gentle she'd found herself falling helplessly. He had been the one to pull back, he had been the one to tell her she must leave.

Silence tiptoed to her bed and lay down, still breathing fast. What had he been thinking as he stroked the shaft of his penis? Had he thought of her? She was hot just wondering, but surely it was not coincidence that he'd done *that* just after they'd kissed. The thought of bringing such a strong man, such a viral man to the point of using his own flesh—because of her....well, it was arousing.

She gazed at the canopy over the bed, remembering. His penis had looked very big in his hand and it'd gleamed in the firelight as if wet. She'd been married for two years, but William had been a properly modest man. She'd only glimpsed him nude once or twice. Sometimes, late at night, lying beside him as he slept, she thought about what he must look like, but she'd quickly shoved the speculations from her mind as immodest.

This must be the sin of Onan. She'd spent long hours as a young girl wondering what exactly Onan had done to spill his seed upon the ground. Later, when she'd been older, she'd heard whispers of this act that men performed. She'd even once broached the subject with William, in a single, stuttering question. He'd made it quite plain then that her curiosity over the matter was not proper.

But what Mickey O'Connor had done did not seem particularly sinful. It had actually been rather wonderful. He'd gripped himself with casual certainty. Obviously he'd performed this act before. She clenched internally at the thought. Did he not have enough women to satisfy him? Or was the act particularly pleasurable for him?

Dear God. She ached, wanting something that she knew was a sin.

Wanting a man who was sin itself.

"THE OWNER OF the *Alexander* has paid his tithe," Bran said later that day.

"Has he?" Mick replied disinterestedly.

He'd not seen Silence since he'd sent her away this morning, but their kiss haunted him. Even after taking care of his lust, his flesh still demanded her. He smiled wryly to himself. A kiss. A simple kiss and he was panting after Silence.

"Mick?"

And forgetting where he was it seemed. Mick glanced at his lieutenant. "Ye'll have to repeat yerself, Bran, me lad, I'm afraid me head is in the clouds."

"Your head has been in the clouds since you brought Mrs. Hollingbrook here," Bran said in a voice that cracked at the end of his sentence.

Mick had been sitting in his desk chair, his long legs carelessly flung over the arm. Now he slowly straightened and let his booted feet hit the floor heavily. "Have ye somethin' ye wish to say to me?"

The boy held his gaze—a feat that many older and brawnier men had failed to do. Mick noticed that Bran's jaw was darkened with his beard. A year or so ago, one could hardly make out the fuzz on Bran's cheeks. His shoulders seemed heavier, too—and was he an inch taller? Perhaps it was past time Mick stopped thinking of Bran as a boy.

"You always told me that a man must make his decisions with his head, not his cock," Bran said. "You said that a man entangled by a wench couldn't think straight. That he lays himself open to misstep and misstep leads to ruin."

Mick tilted his head, studying Bran thoughtfully. "Why, Bran, me lad, I had no idea ye'd taken me words so to heart."

Bran merely stared at him, looking a little sullen. "She's distracted you."

Mick felt a prick of irritation. "And what o' yer fair Fionnula, now? Hasn't she caught yer cock and yer attention?"

"No."

"No?" Mick laughed. "Come, Bran, ye needn't lie to me. Our pretty Fionnula loves ye true."

"She might," Bran said coldly, "but that doesn't mean I love her."

Mick narrowed his eyes. "Then ye'd give her up, were I to order ye to?"

"Aye."

"And if I told ye to bring her to me bed?" Mick asked softly. "Would ye bring the lass and sweetly hand her over to me?"

"In a thrice," Bran said stubbornly. "Is that what you want?"

Mick felt his mouth curve. "Oh, not at the moment, no, but I am that glad to hear ye'd whore out yer sweetheart should I want her. Such loyalty is more than a man should expect."

Finally Bran showed unease. A mottled red flush rose on his neck. "It's what you asked for."

"Was it?" Mick asked gently. "I wasn't exactly sure."

For a moment Bran stared at Mick, some kind of emotion working behind his features.

Mick watched him thoughtfully. They were all on edge after the deaths of Sean, Mike, and Pat, but something more seemed to be bothering Bran.

Mick came to a decision. "I want ye leadin' the next raid."

Bran's eyes widened in shock. "You've never let anyone lead but yourself."

"Aye, and perhaps it's time I did," Mick said. "Ye aren't tryin' to back out now, are ye?"

"No! I'd be happy to lead in your stead."

"Good," Mick said. "Ye'll need to make a plan and report back to me on it, hear?"

A grin split Bran's face. Suddenly he looked more like the oversmart scamp Mick had taken on so long ago. "Aye, Mick!"

He was out the door in an instant.

Mick chuckled to himself. He should've given Bran the responsibility months ago. Well, at least he'd done so now.

The door opened again and Harry's ugly mug appeared. "Mr. Pepper would like a word."

Mick nodded. "Send him in, then."

Harry made to leave, but Mick called, "Harry?"

"Aye?"

"How's the lass?"

Harry's broad face relaxed into a grin. "Mrs. 'Ollingbrook sent down for more vittles this afternoon—the babe is eatin' like a starvin' wolf cub."

Mick sat back, feeling like grinning himself. "She's better?"

"Oh, aye," Harry said. "She's been chasin' Lad 'round the room and even Bert 'as smiled at 'er play."

Mick's eyebrows shot up. "Bert smiled?"

"Well..." Harry considered. "'Is mouth twitched anyway. Might've been gas, but I like to think 'twere a smile."

"Huh," Mick grunted. If Bert was moved by the baby she was quite the charmer. He felt an odd sensation in his chest, something that might've been pride.

The rest of the day went by slowly as he examined the books with Pepper and discussed the special "insurance" investments that Pepper had made on his behalf.

It wasn't until Mick was walking to his dining room, feeling anticipation, that he realized Silence most likely wouldn't be there tonight. While the baby had been sick, he'd ordered food brought for both her and the child to their rooms. The toddler might be feeling better now, but Silence would probably still stay with her to make sure of her health.

He walked to his seat, barely acknowledging his men. What was it about the woman that his supper should be bleak without her? Every other woman he'd only valued for what lay between her legs. He wanted that from Silence as well—make no mistake—but he also had the strangest urge to simply talk with the woman. To flirt and provoke and watch her brown-green-blue eyes spark in outrage, soften with interest, warm with heat.

Mick sat and stared down at a plate of roast goose without interest, irritated by his own apathy. He'd eaten countless meals without the wench and been perfectly happy—joyous, even—why then should—

"Don't you like roast goose?"

He felt the grin stretch his lips before he even looked up. "It's me favorite."

She looked adorably confused—and a little shy. Perhaps she was remembering the kiss they'd shared that morning. The thought gave him a tender pang near his heart.

She licked her lips. "Then why were you staring at your plate as if you wished the goose was alive again so you might slaughter it?"

He shrugged, leaning back in his chair and propping his chin in one hand to watch her. She'd slept some since he'd last seen her, despite the baby's return to activity. Her cheeks were a light, healthy pink, and her eyes bright and alert. The sight gladdened him, though he frowned a little at her dress. She wore her usual black with but a white cap and white collar. He'd once seen her in brown, but that had been a year ago.

What would she look like in sparkling blue or deepest red? His gaze dropped to her breasts, barricaded behind worsted wool. She was slim, but still nicely rounded. He'd wager her breasts would look a treat framed by a low-cut emerald bodice, her fair skin shimmering in the candle-light. He'd give—

"Have some boiled turnips," she said, passing him a bowl.

Mick frowned. "Turnips? At me table? I'll have a word with Archie, I will."

"There's no need," she said blithely as she served him the misshapen vegetables. "I already have."

His eyebrows arched. "What do ye mean?"

"I mean," she said as she accepted a dish of boiled beef from Moll, "that I discussed with Archie the food you serve at your table and I've made a few healthful additions. I think you'll find that your digestion improves considerably."

He watched in bemusement as she added a heaping

mound of steaming carrots to his plate. She was serving him as if she had every right. As if she were the mistress of his table and his home. Strange that. He supported an entire household of people—pirates, servants, and until recently a bevy of doxies—but no one had ever attempted to care for him. The thought spread warm pleasure through his chest—even if the things she was serving did not.

"Vegetables and good English beef, simply prepared, are quite beneficial for the constitution," she said.

Mick grunted. He'd never been particularly fond of boiled anything.

"Try some," she said, her cheeks pink, her eyes bright and encouraging.

He looked down the table and saw that his crew were staring, appalled, at huge platters mounded with boiled roots and beef.

Mick narrowed his eyes. "Every man eats vegetables tonight, right?"

The pirates hurriedly began to spoon up carrots and turnips.

Mick forked up a turnip and bit into it, chewing bland mush.

"How is it?" Silence asked.

"Right tasty," he lied, swallowing.

"You seem distracted tonight," she said as she frowned at a platter of artichokes.

"Do I?" If he squinted a bit, he could imagine the shadowy curves he'd glimpsed beneath the chemise this morning. Tantalizing, elusive, damned unclear. Mick sighed and looked up to find Silence staring at him, her cheeks flagged red.

He cleared his throat. "I've et yer food. Can ye not taste mine?" He pushed the platter of artichokes closer to her, wanting her to eat the food he provided for her.

"Thank you." She examined the platter with a small frown. "Are you planning another thieving raid?"

"Pirate's raid." He propped an elbow on the table. There was a dish of boiled beef by his side, but he had the feeling it wouldn't taste that different from the turnips. "Why? D'ye hope I'll meet me bloody death at the end o' a sword?"

"Dear Lord, no!" She stared at him, appalled. "I wouldn't wish that fate on anyone."

"Even me?" he murmured.

She blushed as she hurriedly helped herself to an artichoke, avoiding his eyes. "Especially not you."

Something in his chest squeezed.

"Such a saint," he murmured low. He didn't want to share this banter with anyone else at the table. "I can almost see yer halo, a-glowin' in these curls at yer temples."

He reached out a hand to brush the curls in question. They were little wisps, escaping from the prim knot at her neck, innocently seductive against the delicate skin of her temple.

She caught his hand before he could touch her face.

"Mick," she whispered, and he felt a sudden thrill: it was the first time she'd used his given name. Her gaze darted down the rest of the table. His men were too smart to be openly looking, but he had no doubt that they were quite aware of what was happening at the head of the table. "Don't."

She abruptly dropped his hand.

"Ye wound me, love," he said lightly, and wondered if it were true. Heaven help him if it were.

"Don't be silly," she muttered. "I'm surprised you know what a halo is."

He grinned. "Oh, I do assure ye the Devil knows his opposite."

Her brows drew together. "Is that who you see yourself as? The Devil himself?"

He arched his eyebrows. "D'ye doubt it?"

"I didn't used to." She poked at her artichoke thoughtfully. "But now I'm no longer sure."

"Oh, be sure." He tapped the table with a fingertip for emphasis. "I am the Devil himself, born and bred."

"Are you? I wonder . . ." She looked at him thoughtfully for a moment and then down at her untouched artichoke. "What is this thing?"

"The artichoke?" His lips quirked.

"Is that what it's called?" She stared disapprovingly down at the vegetable. "I've never seen the like. It looks like a giant flower bud."

"Well, 'tis—or so I'm told." He gently took the fork from her fingers and picked up her knife, beginning to pry apart the dark green leaves. "They're grown far away in Italy. A sea captain gave me a crate o' the things some years ago."

"Gave?" She raised her eyebrows suspiciously.

He shrugged and flashed her a sly smile. "Gave, took, does it matter, love? To be sure the captain hadn't much choice, but the result was the same: a case o' artichokes ended up in me care and I've had a fondness for them ever since."

"Humph." She peered down suspiciously as he parted the leaves to reveal the choke. "That doesn't look very tasty."

"That's because it isn't," he said. "Pay heed: the artichoke is a shy vegetable. She covers herself in spine-tipped leaves that must be carefully peeled away, and underneath shields her treasure with a barricade o' soft needles. They must be tenderly, but firmly, scraped aside. Ye must be bold, for if yer not, she'll never reveal her soft heart."

He finished cutting away the thistles and placed the small, tender heart on the center of her plate.

She wrinkled her nose. "That's it? But it's so small."

"Ah, and d'ye judge a thing solely upon size alone?"

She made a choking sound.

He paused, the knife and fork still in the air. "Now what is it yer thinkin' about in that prim little mind?"

She shook her head mutely and pointed at the artichoke heart. "Go on?"

"Hmm." He took bit of soft butter and spread it over the little heart. "Well, I was thinkin' that sometimes the smaller the treasure, the sweeter the pleasure."

He cut the heart in half and held it out to her on the tip of the fork and found he was holding his breath. Would she let him feed her? Let him care for her?

She stared suspiciously for a long moment before accepting the morsel into her mouth. His heart leaped in triumph. He watched as the taste in her mouth was reflected in her bright eyes.

"So delicate, so buttery," he crooned to this fascinating woman. "Green and rich and smooth, but with a tiny bitter taste on top as if to keep yer interest."

She swallowed and licked her lips. "It's rather good."

He laughed breathlessly. *Have care*, part of his brain whispered. *This way only leads to pain.* But his cock was pressing hard against the placket of his breeches and he wanted to take her hand and draw her away to his rooms and keep her there until she learned to scream in pleasure.

Until she screamed his name and no other.

"Yes, rather good," he imitated her tones gently. "Well worth the trouble o' the thorns and the prickles to reach that sweet, meltin' center, I think."

Chapter Nine

*Now, it's well known that an offer of three wishes must
be carefully considered, lest the wrong thing be wished for.
Clever John thought on the matter for some time, while
he held Tamara's soft neck in his broad hand.
Finally, he looked at her and asked, "Must I make
my three wishes all at once?"
She grinned, as quick as a sprite. "Not at all. You have
merely to call my name and I will come to grant a wish."
He nodded and slowly unwrapped his hand from about
her neck. "I wish for a kingdom ten times the size of my
uncle's."...*
—from *Clever John*

Silence savored the exotic taste of the artichoke as she listened to Mickey O'Connor's deep, velvet voice talk about creamy centers.

She swallowed and looked down at the artichoke petals piled neatly on the side of her plate. Her center certainly felt like it was melting, growing soft and wet just from the rasp of Mr. O'Connor's voice. Why should a man already devilishly handsome also have a voice that could charm birds from the sky? It simply wasn't fair. And, goodness! Surely he didn't mean what his words conjured in her too heated mind? Silence took a hasty sip of red wine, casting about desperately for something—anything—to say.

"Did your mother name you Mickey?" she asked.

He blinked as if he were startled by the change of subject matter.

"I...I mean, well..." She inhaled, gathering her thoughts into a semblance of order. "It's from Michael, isn't it? Did she christen you Mickey or Michael?"

His mouth twitched as if he knew she was desperately trying to break the tension between them. "Well, now, I doubt very much that holy water ever touched me infant head, but me mam did name me Michael, sure enough."

"It's a lovely name, Michael."

"Is it, now?" he asked skeptically.

She nodded, tearing apart a piece of bread. "Saint Michael is one of the archangels. He bears a sword and leads the army of God."

"A militant fellow, then."

She nodded. "In the Book of Revelations he battles the Devil and all his minions and they are thrown out from Heaven."

Mickey's lips pursed, his dark eyes sardonic. "Not so very like me."

"I don't know..." Silence frowned. "After all, Saint Michael must be very hard, very fierce. He's a warrior who metes out God's justice. He did defeat the Devil, after all. In some ways he must be not unlike the Devil."

He chuckled.

Silence glanced up, horrified. "Is that blasphemy?"

He shrugged. "Ye ask the Devil to point out blasphemy?"

"I told you, you aren't the Devil at all," Silence muttered

distractedly. "In fact, you may just be a very frightening angel."

He threw back his head and laughed at her earnest statement, drawing surreptitious glances from his pirates.

He grinned at her when he'd calmed. "Don't matter. I'm not the one to judge blasphemy." He leaned back in his chair, cocking his head to study her. "Besides, ye know that given the chance I would've fought on the other side o' yer Saint Michael."

"Would you have?" she asked, serious despite his laughter. A week ago she wouldn't have questioned his assertion that he was the devil. Now she wasn't so certain. "Your mother must not have thought you so terrible. After all, she named you after a saint, not a devil."

He frowned.

It was her turn to eye him. "Unless she was naming you after someone else? A relative, maybe? Perhaps your father?"

He snorted. "No."

"Then who?"

"No one to me knowledge." He looked away from her as if bored with the conversation, yet his fingers gripped the table tightly. "She mightn't have had a reason."

"Perhaps she named you with the hope that you would be a fierce protector like Saint Michael."

He flinched. It was a small movement, hardly noticeable, but Silence felt as if she'd hit him. She reached out a hand to him before she could stop herself, laying it on his sleeve.

He stared down at her hand as if mesmerized by the sight.

"If that was why she named me," he said low, "then she was sorely disappointed."

"Michael," she whispered, whether in apology or question, she did not know.

His Christian name was somehow terribly intimate upon her lips. It suited him much better than Mick or Mickey. An angel, both terrible and violent, but also with the possibility of redemption. Saint Michael.

His eyes narrowed and it was as if he'd pierced her with his gaze. "Don't." He closed his eyes, shuttering that dreadful look. "Don't call me that."

She withdrew her hand, but she wouldn't back down. There was something important here. Something she very much needed to find out.

"Why not?" They might as well be alone. The rest of the dining room fell away and with it all the other people around them.

"Ye know why," he murmured, his eyes still closed. His black eyelashes lay on his cheeks like soot on snow.

If they'd been alone she might've taken him into her arms.

"I know why," she said softly, "but I have no intention of calling you anything else."

He chuckled low, a dry, broken sound now in contrast to his earlier laughter. "O' course ye won't. Sweet Silence. I may be named for an archangel, but yer the one who shines with a clear, pure light."

"I don't know what you mean," she whispered.

"Don't ye?" He finally opened his eyes and they were haunted. "Didn't ye lay down yer virtue for the husband ye loved? Haven't ye agreed to live with the devil himself for a child ye found upon yer doorstep? Ye, Silence Hollingbrook, are more awe inspirin' than any angel."

She didn't know where to look. It had never occurred to her that he might think her anything out of the ordinary. Her lips parted soundlessly and she stared into his eyes as if she would drown.

His gaze grew warm and the corner of his mouth quirked. "D'ye mean to eat that bread?"

Silence looked down and saw that she'd long ago crumbled the piece of bread to bits on her plate. "I—"

Mickey—*Michael*—snapped his fingers and the small boy hurried over with a tray of sliced meats. Michael took the tray from him. "Bring me the bread, as well."

The boy skipped away.

"I can't eat all that," Silence protested even as Michael piled savory lamb onto her plate. The platter of boiled beef seemed to have disappeared.

"Ye've been eatin' like a mouse while the child was ill," he said, still transferring tidbits to her plate.

She sampled a bite of the lamb. It was so tender it nearly melted in her mouth. She ate it a bit guiltily. Somehow Michael's lamb was much better than her own English boiled beef—even if it couldn't possibly be as beneficial for one's health.

Laughter from down the table made her look up. Bran had his head thrown back and was laughing. Fionnula was gazing at him and her entire face glowed with a look of love so intimate that Silence glanced away, embarrassed. She found Michael watching her.

Silence swallowed and reached for her wineglass, avoiding his eyes. They seemed to see too much behind her face. "Fionnula certainly adores Bran."

"She wears her affection upon her sleeve," he said, his voice strangely flat.

She glanced at him. "Bran is very young to be so much in your esteem, isn't he?"

Michael shrugged. "Maybe, but the lad has been with me for more'n six years."

"Really?" She glanced again at Bran and Fionnula. He didn't seem much older than twenty. "How did you come to know him?"

Michael sat back, a sugared grape in his fingers. "Our Bran was runnin' the streets wild. He and his crew—a ragtag troop o' lads, most younger than himself. They made their way by pickin' pockets, thievin' from chandler shops and hawkers, and general mischief. One night he'd decided to hunt bigger game."

Michael stopped to take a drink of wine. He carefully set his glass back on the table.

"Well?" Silence asked impatiently.

His mobile lips curved. "Our Bran decided to take a ship already marked by m'self."

Silence inhaled. She didn't know much about the details of how Michael made his living—didn't *want* to know, truth be told—but she knew he must be a ruthless competitor. "What happened?"

"We came upon the ship jus' after Bran and his boys had swarmed it. They were fightin' the guards when we came over the gunwales. Me and me men made quick work o' the guards, and then I found this lad, only half me height, mind, tryin' to shove a dagger in me gut."

Silence swallowed and glanced at Bran under her lashes. Any man, let alone a boy, was either very courageous or very foolhardy to challenge Mickey O'Connor. "What did you do?"

Michael toyed with his nearly empty wineglass, a

smile playing about his wide mouth. "Took the dagger away from him, that's what. And when he lunged at me with his bare hands I grabbed him by the scruff o' the neck and shook him. I might've simply tossed him into the Thames, but..."

He trailed off, a thoughtful look in his eyes.

"But you didn't," Silence supplied. "Why not?"

He glanced at her and finished the last gulp of wine. "Truth be told, he reminded me a bit o' m'self, once upon a time. A ragged boy, alone and fightin' for everythin', even his next meal."

Silence looked at her hands. He'd said he'd had a mother—and perhaps even a father. Why had he been alone, then? Her stomach cramped thinking of him, a pretty boy, fighting for something to eat.

It was as if he heard her thoughts. "Ah, never pity me, Silence, m'love."

She looked up and saw his black eyes, his sardonic mouth, and the haunted memories in his face.

He nodded, toasting her with his empty wineglass. "Whatever trials and tribulations I may've had, they were deserved. Most well deserved, mind."

"MICKEY O'CONNOR'S THE one behind our problems with gettin' grain," Freddy said.

Charlie looked up slowly from his supper. "Is he now?"

The information wasn't surprising. For the last week his grain suppliers had either been strangely reluctant to sell or had already been all sold out of their grain supplies.

Charlie grunted. "You'll have to find me new suppliers then."

Freddy looked unhappy at the news.

"What else have you heard?"

"There're soldiers in St. Giles," Freddy said gruffly.

"What of it?" Charlie said as he forked up a bite of beef. It dripped gravy as he brought it to his mouth. "Soldiers are everywhere in London."

"'Tis said these have been sent to clean St. Giles o' thieves and murderers and other crime."

"Have they?" Charlie sat back and glanced at his man. Freddy as usual was avoiding looking at his face—his gaze was focused mostly on Charlie's full plate of food. "That's interesting. Who sent them?"

Freddy frowned, digging furrows into his brow, which did not help his appearance any. "No one knows. They've been ridin' about in pairs, catchin' up anyone seen loiterin' about. 'Course the smarter ones went to ground as soon as the soldiers rode in. They get mostly the old women who sell gin and the like."

Charlie grunted. "Still, if they're after gin sellers they're bound to run into my business." He tapped his knife on the edge of his pewter plate, thinking. "Be best if we can point them in another direction. A direction we choose."

Freddy nodded slowly. "Where?"

A sudden thought appeared, fully formed in Charlie's brain. He took it and examined it, peering at it from all sides.

And then he nodded. "At Charming Mickey's heart."

"Mo'," MARY DARLING cried the next morning.

Silence obediently bounced the baby on her knees, chanting a song about a horsey. It was so good to see Mary pink-cheeked and well again! But it was also exhausting entertaining the baby in only one small room.

"Mo'!" Mary urged as soon as Silence paused in the bouncing game. "Mo'! Mo'! *Mo'!*"

"Oh, sweetheart, I think the horsey is quite tired out," Silence said as she put Mary down.

Mary fretted and then began making her way along the stuffed chair Silence sat on. She was heading to the fireplace, knowing full well that she was forbidden the alluring delights of the fire.

Silence pushed a strand of hair out of her eyes and cast about for a distraction. "Here, Mary. What do you think of this?" She opened her sewing kit on the floor.

The baby quickly dropped to her hands and knees and crawled over.

"Yer lettin' her play with yer needles?" Fionnula asked doubtfully from the door.

Silence looked up gratefully. "Oh, thank goodness, you brought tea. I was running out of things to do with her."

"I can see that," the maid said as she set down the tea tray.

"Well, it was better than the fireplace," Silence muttered, extracting Mary's busy fingers from a small skein of mending thread.

The thread was hopelessly tangled. Silence stared at it as Fionnula set the baby down and gave her some toast and a small cup of milk.

"Mary's just so bored here," Silence murmured. She was bored as well, she realized. Silence had spent the last several months running a busy orphanage, work that kept her occupied from sunup to well past sundown. She simply wasn't used anymore to sitting and doing nothing.

On that thought she looked at Fionnula hopefully. "Is Mr. O'Connor at home today, do you know?"

"Saw him goin' into his room just now." Fionnula nodded at the connecting door.

"Really?" Silence rose and crossed to the connecting door and knocked.

The door was opened almost at once.

Michael leaned a shoulder against the doorjamb, a wicked smile playing about his sensuous lips. He was so very big this close—every time it surprised her and made her breathless. "Well, now, and when did ye decide to start knockin' at me door?"

Silence fought to keep her face from flaming as she remembered the *last* time she'd peeked through Michael's door.

She swallowed. "We're bored."

"Is that so?" Michael glanced down.

Silence followed his gaze and saw that Mary had crawled over to investigate. The baby grabbed a handful of her skirt and stood up. She kept one hand on Silence's skirt and popped two fingers from the other into her mouth as she stared solemnly at Michael.

"She looks a rare treat," Michael said softly, watching the toddler.

Silence smiled down at Mary. "She does indeed."

She glanced up and her heart squeezed at the gentle look on Michael's face.

As if she understood she was the subject of conversation, Mary lifted her arms—to Michael. "Up!"

Michael arched an eyebrow. "Mouthy little thing, ain't she?"

But he bent and lifted the toddler.

Mary Darling looked so small in his arms. The pirate cradled her body against his chest, her face on a level with his.

Mary stared into his eyes and then took her fingers out of her mouth and poked him in the chin.

Silence caught her breath, but Michael merely laughed. "Bored, sweetin'? We'll have to do somethin' about that, won't we?"

He turned and started back into his room.

"Where are you going?" Silence asked as she hurried to catch up.

"Always demandin' answers, isn't she?" Michael murmured to the baby.

Mary looked back over his shoulder. "Mamoo."

"Aye, yer mamoo," Michael drawled as he opened the door to the corridor. "A lovely lady, I must admit, but a worrier, too, wouldn't ye agree?"

Mary had her fingers back in her mouth, listening to this blather very seriously, but she took out her fingers to point to Harry and Bert, standing guard in the corridor. "'Ert!"

For some reason Mary had taken a liking to the cantankerous man.

"Aye, Harry and ''Ert' shall come with us, as well," Michael said to her, nodding to the two men.

The guards looked at each other and then fell into step behind Silence.

She lifted her skirts to lengthen her stride—Michael's long legs were eating up the corridor.

"Now, I always find a bit o' fresh air quite invigoratin'," Michael continued. "Mind, we can't have ye out in the open—too many bad men about, see? But we do have a bit o' fresh air at the back of the house."

He came to a stairs and clattered down them, the trailing parade following. The stairs opened up into the kitchen and Archie the cook turned in surprise at their entrance.

But Mary Darling wasn't paying attention to the cook. "Goggie!" she exclaimed, holding both hands out urgently to Lad, who'd been dozing by the fire.

"By all means," Michael replied amicably, as if he and Mary were having a conversation. "Let's bring the mutt with us, as well. He's almost presentable now that he stinks o' roses."

The whole procession—Lad included—tromped into a small courtyard.

Silence looked around. The courtyard was paved excepting for a lone patch of dry earth in the middle. On all four sides it was bordered by tall brick buildings. Opposite the door to the kitchen was an ancient arched tunnel through the lower part of one of the buildings.

"Where does that lead?" Silence asked.

Michael glanced at the tunnel. "It lets out on an alley. No need to worry. There's a gate on the other and two guards in the tunnel."

Silence nodded, watching as Michael placed Mary down next to a wooden bench set against a wall. "Have you always had to live like this?"

"Like what?" he asked.

Mary was already making her way determinedly toward Lad.

"This." Silence waved a hand about the courtyard. "With guards and high walls and constant vigilance?"

He straightened and looked at her. Bert and Harry had followed Mary like lumbering nursemaids, attempting to keep her from poking Lad in the eye. She and Michael were, for a moment, by themselves in a corner of the courtyard.

"No." Michael turned his face up. It was near noon and the sun was straight overhead, shining down into the little courtyard. But in an hour or so, the tall walls on either side would shield the sunshine. Only in the middle of the day was the courtyard lit thus.

"What happened?" she asked softly.

He shrugged restlessly. "The more power a man has, the more enemies he takes on, as well, I've found."

"Really?" She frowned down at the cobblestones beneath her feet. "Have you ever thought that it may not be worth it? Your stealing?"

He cast an ironic glance her way. "And will ye be reformin' me now, me darlin'?"

She pursed her lips at his mockery, but lifted her chin to look him in the eye. "You have piles of riches—I've seen them."

"A man may never have too many riches." His mouth firmed irritably.

"Of course he may," she said. "You have enough to feed and clothe and house yourself and your men, what more do you need?"

His eyes narrowed. "Easy for one who's never been without to say."

She paused at that. It was true that she'd never gone hungry. But Mickey O'Connor had riches stacked in his palace! "Surely you no longer need to steal?"

"I could become a fat farmer, d'ye mean?"

"No." She couldn't even picture him as a country squire, fat or otherwise. "But there must be some other work you could take up?"

"Such as?" he asked silkily. "Would ye make me a shipbuilder?"

Well, that was a ridiculous idea.

"I don't know!" She planted her hands on her hips in exasperation. "But the life you lead is dangerous. Surely you realize this. It's only a matter of time before one of your enemies finds you—or you're brought before a magistrate for thievery. Why not leave this life while you can?"

"Worried about me, darlin'?" His words were flippant, but his look wasn't. For a moment Silence thought she saw vulnerability deep in those black eyes. Then he looked away. "Ah, best not to worry for me, m'love. I'm a pirate and a pirate has but one end in this world."

"What's that?" she whispered, feeling dread.

A corner of his mouth kicked up. "Why, the end o' a rope, what else?"

Silence shivered, though the sun's rays were warm in the courtyard. She imagined him swinging from a hangman's rope, his strong, lean body jerking in the throes of death. Something inside her couldn't bear the thought. Michael O'Connor had once been her enemy. No one had ever hurt her as deeply as he had. What he'd done to her—to William and their marriage—could never be forgiven.

But that was before. Before she'd come to know him, before he'd come to know her, for that matter. She knew that he might be a very dangerous pirate at the present, but once upon a time he'd been only a boy, small and vulnerable and with no one to take care of him.

The fact was that some part of her would wither away should Michael O'Connor leave this world.

Silence wrapped her arms about herself. "That's it, then? You'll simply wait to be caught and hung?"

Michael cocked his head. "Oh, there's no waitin' about

it, love. I'm livin' a full and happy life, in case ye haven't noticed."

"Are you?" She watched as Harry threw a wooden ball he'd produced from somewhere on his person. Both Mary Darling and Lad started after the ball. "You have your men and your riches, but you have no family, do you? Is that all that you want out of life?"

He didn't answer.

She turned to find him watching her intently.

Silence lifted her chin. "Well, do you?"

He shrugged. "'Tis well enough for many a man."

"It seems very lonely to me."

"Does it?" He stepped closer. "What about yerself, Silence, m'love? Ye talk about me family but what family d'ye have o' yer own?"

She looked at him in astonishment. "What do you mean? I have quite a large family. My sisters, my brothers, and my nephews and nieces."

Michael nodded. "Ye've brothers and sisters, nieces and nephews. But ye don't have a husband or children."

Silence tilted her chin. "I have Mary Darling."

"Is she enough?" He leaned over her until she could feel the heat from his body. "Someday she'll grow up. She'll find a man o' her own and live apart from ye. Ye'll be alone. Is that what ye want?"

Tears pricked at the corners of her eyes and she looked away. "I had a man—a dear, good husband."

"And now ye do not." There was no trace of compassion in his voice. "Will ye mourn him forever? Wear this dingy black until ye die yerself?"

He reached out and flicked the starched white collar of her gown.

She hunched a shoulder against him. He was too close, asking questions that made her too uncomfortable. "I loved William. You cannot understand it, I think, but he was my true love. The love of my life. I don't hope to ever find another love such as he in this lifetime."

She'd said the words so many times, the syllables were worn into her soul. She didn't even have to think what they meant anymore. But were they still true? She shook her head in confusion. She didn't want to be having this conversation with anyone, let alone Michael.

But his deep voice was relentless. "And without this true love ye'll let yerself wither away, is that it, darlin'?"

"As I said, I don't expect you to understand—"

"And I don't," he cut in. "Ye ask how I can live a life that I know will end with the hangman's noose. Well, at least I *am* alive. Ye might as well have climbed inside yer husband's coffin and let yerself be buried with his corpse."

Her hand flashed out before she'd thought about it, the smack against his cheek loud in the little courtyard.

Silence had her eyes locked with Michael's, her chest rising and falling swiftly, but she was aware that Bert and Harry had looked up. Even Mary and Lad had paused in their play.

Without taking his gaze from hers, Michael reached out and grasped her hand. He raised her hand to his lips and softly kissed the center of her palm.

He looked at her, her hand still at his lips. "Don't take to yer grave afore yer time, Silence, m'love."

Her heart was beating so fast that she was breathless. She could feel each exhale he made on her palm.

"He has no grave," she whispered inanely. "He died at sea and his body lies there beneath the waves."

"I know, love," he said tenderly. "I know."

Then the tears overflowed her eyes, there in the sunlight in the little courtyard. Silence squeaked, embarrassed and helpless, and felt him pull her against his chest.

"There, there, sweetin'," he murmured into her hair.

"He loved me, he truly did," she gasped.

"I know he did," Michael said.

"And I loved him."

"Mm-hmm."

She raised her head, glaring angrily. "You don't even believe in love. Why are you agreeing with me?"

He laughed.

"Because"—he leaned down and licked at the tears on her cheeks, his lips brushing softly against her sensitive skin as he spoke, "ye've bewitched and bespelled me, my sweet Silence, didn't ye know? I'll agree that the sky is pink, that the moon is made o' marzipan and sugared raisins, and that mermaids swim the muddy waters o' the Thames, if ye'll only stop weepin'. Me chest breaks apart and gapes wide open when I see tears in yer pretty eyes. Me lungs, me liver, and me heart cannot stand to be thus exposed."

She stopped breathing. She simply inhaled and stopped, looking at him in wonder. His lips were quirked in a mocking smile, but his eyes—his fathomless black eyes—seemed to hold a great pain as if his strong chest really had been split open.

HER EYES STILL swam with tears, blue-green and woebegone. Why the sight should pain him so Mick didn't know. He'd seen men gutted and killed, watched starving women prostitute themselves, seen beggar children lay down in the gutter and die. He'd fought with tooth and nail to reach the place where he was now—where he didn't worry over food or a roof over his head. He'd killed men and never thought about their faces again.

Yet the sight of Silence in tears nearly unmanned him.

He glanced away from her face uneasily. *That way lies pain.* "Come. I've somethin' to show ye."

He took her hand and led her toward the kitchen door.

"But Mary—" she protested.

He tilted his chin to where the toddler giggled as she pulled at Lad's ears. "She'll be fine with Bert and Harry to watch over her. We'll be only a moment."

She trailed after him, casting worried looks at the baby until they were inside. "Where are we going?"

"To me throne room." He led her through back passages and stairs until they reached the echoing hall that he received visitors in.

Bob, guarding the door, looked curious as Mick approached with Silence, but the guard merely nodded.

"See that we're not disturbed." Mick drew open the heavy wooden doors.

Inside he strode quickly to a chest he'd had set beside his throne. He threw open the lid and drew out a shimmering blue silk gown.

"What is it?" Silence asked as if she'd never seen such a dress.

He rolled his eyes. "It's a dress. For ye."

She backed a step, looking mulish. "I can't wear that."

Ah, now he had to be careful. He held up the dress, letting the light play on the gorgeous fabric. "Ye told me ye were bored. Wouldn't ye like to get away from me palace?"

"Yes, but—"

"But," he interrupted, "if ye wish to go out wi' me, ye must wear this. The dress yer wearin' now won't do."

She bit her lip, eyeing the iridescent blue silk.

"It was given to me," he lied, "by a sea captain wantin' me to do him a favor. I haven't a use for it m'self."

He held the dress against his chest, drawing a reluctant smile from her. In fact, like a besotted lover, he'd spent half a day searching for a ready-made gown especially for her. That information, however, was unlikely to make her want to take the gown. He knew instinctively that accepting such a costly gift—such an elegant gift—from him would outrage her puritanical morals.

"Or would ye rather be spendin' another evenin' by the fire in yer rooms?" he asked casually. His fingers trailed over the shining skirts.

Her eyes darted to his face. He could see she was wavering. "Where do you intend to take me?"

He shook his head. "It's to be a surprise."

Her brows knit and her lips parted as if to protest.

"But it's respectable," he hastily added. "I promise."

He held his breath, waiting to hear her answer. Wanting her to accept.

"I haven't anything else to wear with such a fine gown." She blushed at even the oblique mention of underclothes.

He fought down a grin, trying to look innocent instead. "I'm thinkin' ye'll find the items ye need in the bottom o' that there trunk."

"But—"

He was already striding to the throne room doors. She'd decided when she asked about things to wear with the dress. If he hesitated, she'd have time to rethink her decision.

Mick pulled open the doors and spoke to Bob. "Send two lads here to take a chest to Mrs. Hollingbrook's room."

Bob nodded. "Right ye are." He scurried off down the corridor.

Mick turned back to Silence. She was still standing by the chest, but she was looking about the room as well. "Why keep so many of your souvenirs in one room? Aren't you afraid of thieves?"

Mick smiled. "Ye think I'd be robbed in me own home?"

Pink tinted her cheeks. "No, of course not. But your men might be tempted."

"Pay them well, I do," Mick said simply. "Better, mind, than they could get anywhere else in London. And if they're still tempted, well…believe it or not, m'love, but I've somethin' o' a reputation amongst violent men."

She shivered and turned away, peering at a marble cherub. "I know."

He tilted his head, watching her. His violence upset her, he knew, but since he couldn't change who he was, he dismissed it from his mind.

"As to why I pile me goods in this one room"—he shrugged—"ye yerself told me it makes a certain impression."

She looked over her shoulder at him. "Is that the only reason for all your treasure? To impress others?"

He watched her for a moment, and then decided he could tell her. "Ye know o' me life as a lad. About beggin' for me supper."

She nodded hesitantly.

He grimaced and looked around the room at his booty. "Well, when I made me first haul I swore then and there that I wouldn't ever do that again."

Her eyes widened. "But...that was long ago. You've become a powerful man since then—a rich man."

"Can a man ever be rich enough?" he asked softly. "Powerful enough?"

"Oh, Michael."

Her eyes had gone wide, her sweet lips parted, and her face was filled with compassion—for him.

That look went straight through him. He took a step nearer, his muscles tensing, his hand lifting, reaching for her.

Just then two of his men clattered into the throne room.

Mick bit back a curse and pointed to the trunk. "Bring it to her rooms." He glanced back at Silence, still unmoving by the cherub. "Seven o' the clock tonight, mind now. Be ready for me."

And he turned and strode from the room, wondering if he was going to survive courting a chaste widow.

Chapter Ten

"As you wish!" Tamara cried.
At once they were transported to the top of a mountain.
Before them were spread rich fields and a huge, sparkling
lake.
Clever John's eyes widened. "All this is mine?"
"Of course, my King Clever John!" Tamara danced a few
delighted steps, her bright hair waving in the mountain
wind. "What else do you wish?"
But Clever John's gaze was on the wealth before him. "I
shall call you when next I need you."
Tamara nodded and quick as a wink turned into the
rainbow bird and flew away, leaving only one bright red
feather to float to the ground in her wake....
—from *Clever John*

"Mr. Makepeace."

Winter tamped down a surge of impatience and turned at the feminine tone of command. His morning had been busy enough before Lady Hero had decided to make an unscheduled appearance at the home—and bring Lady Beckinhall with her.

He'd thought the ladies well occupied with Nell, discussing the new venture of teaching the children how to spin, but apparently he was wrong. Lady Hero stood on the upper landing just outside the meeting room of the Ladies' Syndicate for the Benefit of the Home for Unfortunate Infants and Foundling Children. She smiled brightly and he immediately was suspicious. The lady was the least annoying of the aristocratic members of the Ladies' Syndicate, but he was beginning to realize that underneath her always pleasantly elegant exterior, she was a bit Machiavellian.

He bowed shortly. "My lady?"

"I have a particular favor I wonder if I might ask of you," she said.

He sighed, mentally girding his loins, for he had the feeling he wasn't going to like this favor. "Of course, ma'am."

She nodded, satisfied. "You've met Lady Beckinhall, the newest lady attending our meetings?"

"Indeed, ma'am."

"Lady Beckinhall would be a wonderful addition to the Ladies' Syndicate for the Benefit of the Home for Unfortunate Infants and Foundling Children," Lady Hero said. "But I'm afraid she's not quite certain if she would like to join us."

Winter looked at her blankly. "Yes?"

Her smile became firmer. "Yes. And I thought, if you gave her a special tour of the home, she might realize what very good work you do here."

"Ah..." For the life of Winter, his brain, usually quite a quick organ, was unable to come up with a suitable excuse which would get him out of wasting his time with a silly society matron for forty-five minutes or longer.

"Lovely!" Perhaps Lady Hero had gone deaf, for she beamed as if he'd acquiesced enthusiastically. "Lady Beckinhall is waiting in the meeting room for you."

And in another minute Winter found himself bowing to Lady Beckinhall.

He straightened and thought he caught a gleam of amusement in her eyes.

"How kind of you to volunteer to show me the home," Lady Beckinhall said. "I vow the prospect of inspecting children's beds fills me with wonder."

"Does it indeed, ma'am?" Winter replied woodenly. He turned on his heel and strode to the stairs, starting up them. His worry for Silence—both her person and the harm she might do the home—was ever constant and now he must pander to this woman.

There was a pattering and a breathless voice behind him. "My! Will this be the five-minute tour?"

Winter stopped and turned.

Lady Beckinhall stood, panting a bit, three stairs below him. From his higher vantage point he had an intimate view down her bodice. Her plump breasts were mounded softly, the cleft between them shadowy, mysterious, and far too alluring.

He looked away. "Pardon, my lady. I did not mean to make you run after me."

"No, of course you didn't," she replied.

He glanced at her swiftly. The lady's blue eyes were watching him mockingly.

Winter sighed silently and mounted the stairs at a slower pace. The next floor held a short, cramped hall with three doors. He opened the first and stood back to let Lady Beckinhall enter.

She swept in and glanced around. "What is this?"

"The children's beds you were so eager to inspect," he said without inflection. "This is the boys' dormitory. As you can see it is in need of repairs."

She glanced at him over her shoulder and then around the room. The ceiling was low, stains from previous leaks in the roof prominent. Two rows of narrow cots lined each wall. "But you'll soon be moving into a new home, won't you?"

He nodded. "That is our hope. I believe, however, that there is still a need for funds to pay for furnishings for the new building."

"Hmm." Her murmur was noncommittal.

They needed her money. Winter inhaled. "Would you like to see the girls' room?"

Lady Beckinhall raised elegant eyebrows mockingly. "Would I?"

Tamping down an urge to reply bluntly, he led her out of the room and into the next, which was nearly identical.

She paced to the far end of the room, peering at one of the cots lining the wall. "It's very Spartan."

"Yes."

Lady Beckinhall delicately touched the threadbare blanket on one of the beds with her fingertips. "Well, the coverlets leave much to be desired, but at least the beds are roomy enough for the children here."

Winter cleared his throat. "This dormitory houses some seventeen children. The children sleep two or three to a bed."

She swiveled in an abrupt movement, her rich burgundy skirts sweeping the bare boards of the floor. "Why?"

He looked her in the eye, this aristocrat who'd never known want, and said gently, "Because it's warmer at night."

He could see the logical question form in her mind and then her swift glance at the tiny fireplace. The coal scuttle was nearly empty beside it.

She looked back at him, and to her credit, she didn't try flippancy. "I see."

"Do you, my lady?" Perhaps it was his impatience coming to a head. Perhaps it was his very real worry for Silence, but suddenly he was tired of sophisticated sparring. Of wasting his meager time on beautiful, frivolous women.

When he spoke again his voice was hard. "They crowd into the beds at night and huddle close, but the hearths aren't big enough to keep the entire room warm, not with the thin walls. One of the maids must rouse herself in the middle of the night to stoke the fire again. The children who have been living with us awhile are well fed. They are fine, even if the night is cold."

"And the others?" she whispered.

"If they have come new, often—usually, in fact— they're thin and weak from starvation," Winter said. "They haven't the plumpness of a healthy child. The plumpness that keeps a child warm at night. Most do well after several months of being fed good, wholesome food. But for some it is too late. Those do not wake in the morning."

She stared at him, her face pale. "I thought you were supposed to tell me how sweet the children are. To woo my money with gentle words and flattery."

He shrugged. "You seem like a woman who has had more than enough flattery in her life."

She nodded once and swept past him.

He stared after her, startled. "Where are you going?"

"I think I've seen all that I need to, Mr. Makepeace," she said. "Good day."

Winter shook his head, disgusted with himself. Every day Silence lived at that pirate's home, the orphanage was in imminent peril of losing what funding it got from these aristocrats. All the more need, then, to placate women like Lady Beckinhall. The home needed money and if the only way to get it was by toadying up to wealthy widows, well then, he ought to toady and be happy.

Instead, he'd just driven away a potential patroness.

Fool.

LATER THAT NIGHT Silence nervously touched the ruching that decorated the neckline of her new dress. It really was lovely—the loveliest dress she'd ever worn. Before William's death she had worn colors, but she had usually dressed in brown or gray. Sedate colors, practical colors for a woman who, when she needed to go somewhere, did so by her own feet. London was a grimy city.

Certainly she'd never worn bright indigo blue. She turned a bit before the full-length mirror that had been brought into her rooms. The silk seemed to shimmer and change, sometimes more purple, sometimes more blue.

"It's simply grand, ma'am," Fionnula sighed from where she sat on a footstool near the mirror.

The maid had helped her to dress and had pulled back her hair into a knot with a few locks carefully curled at her temples and nape.

"Do you think so?" Silence asked shyly. She touched again the ruched ribbon at her neckline. The bodice was round and deeply cut, highlighting her breasts pushed into mounds by the embroidered stays she wore under the dress.

"Oh, yes," Fionnula said firmly. "Yer even more grand than the ladies that Himself used to have in his rooms."

Silence stilled, and wet her lips before asking with feigned indifference. "Used to?"

Alas, she'd never be a good actress.

Fionnula gave her a speaking glance. "Haven't ye noticed? He hasn't had a strumpet in his rooms since the day after ye arrived."

"Oh," was the only reply Silence could think to make, but her heart leaped willy-nilly with joy.

Fionnula rolled her eyes. "He used to have at least one woman a night, sometimes more."

"More?" Silence squeaked. "Than one? At a time?"

"Oh, yes," Fionnula assured her. "Sometimes two or three at once."

Silence simply gaped, her mind stopped on the thought of Michael entertaining two or *three* women in his bed at once. Had he ... serviced them all? In a single night? How ... ?

But Fionnula had grown quite chatty. "I never understand it myself. I mean, if it was backwards, as it were, and a woman could have any number of men she wished ... Well, I'd never have more than one, I think. Why, can ye imagine two men snorin' in yer bed? Or three? And what about the covers? When Bran lets me spend the night—which don't happen often, let me tell ye—he's always pullin' the covers off my shoulders in the middle of the night. I wake up, my shoulders numb with cold. No." Fionnula shook her head. "No, ye couldn't pay me to take more'n one man to me bed."

Fionnula turned at the end of this speech—the longest she'd ever made in Silence's presence—and looked at her expectantly.

Silence blinked and unfortunately an image of Michael, entirely nude, lounging in the middle of his huge bed came into her mind. In the image he was erect, his long penis lying hard and straight against his flat belly. It was ruddy and wide at the tip where—

Oh, dear.

She cleared her throat and said rather huskily. "No, one would be *quite* enough."

Fionnula nodded as if her argument was confirmed. "Sometimes I don't understand men at all."

"Gah!" Mary Darling cried as if agreeing with Fionnula. She'd slept most of the afternoon as Silence and the maid had worked on the dress, taking in the waist a bit. The baby toddled over and held out her arms to be picked up.

Silence stooped and carefully lifted the baby. "Will you be good and obey Fionnula while I'm out?" she whispered into the dark curls.

"Down!" Mary said, wriggling, so Silence kissed her hastily and put her on the floor, just as a knock came at her door. It was the corridor door, so it mayn't be Michael, but still she checked her reflection in the looking glass.

Fionnula opened the outer door.

Michael stood there in a fine deep blue coat over a white waistcoat embroidered in silver thread. Diamonds winked on the buckles of his shoes. His gaze went straight to her and something in his black eyes seemed to heat when he saw her.

She instinctively covered her décolletage with her hands.

"Don't."

He took three steps and was before her. Gently, he grasped her hands in his own and spread them wide, exposing her bosom framed by the low neckline of the dress. His gaze dropped to her breasts and heat flooded her cheeks.

"Don't ever hide yerself from me eyes," he murmured low so that only she could hear.

Her gaze darted to Fionnula by the door. "Please!" she whispered in embarrassment.

His smile was not quite kind. "Ye may cover yerself only when we're not alone."

Her breath caught at the sensual promise in his eyes. Did he mean to make their friendship more intimate? And if so, would she let him?

His eyes narrowed at the confusion in her face, but he didn't comment. He'd thrown a cloak over a chair as he entered the room and now he picked it up and drew it about her shoulders. It was velvet, rich and warm and lined with rose silk. He pulled the edges together under her throat and tenderly tied the cloak closed.

"There," he said when he was done. "A shield to hide yer modesty behind. And to hide yer identity..."

He held out a velvet half mask.

"Oh!" She'd been worrying all afternoon about appearing in public with him, though she wasn't sure how to bring up the subject. It was not for her reputation that she worried—that was already ruined—but for the orphanage. Now she looked at him gratefully. "Thank you."

He gave her an ironic glance and moved behind her. Gently he lowered the mask over her face and tied it behind her head. She could feel his male heat at her back and the whisper of his breath on her nape. Something warm and soft brushed her ear.

Her breathing went shallow.

Then he was beside her again, holding out his arm. His voice was husky when he said, "Come now or we'll be late."

She made her good-byes to Fionnula and Mary Darling and then he was taking her hand and pulling her into the hall.

"Late to what?" Silence asked breathlessly.

But he only glanced over his shoulder at her and grinned, white teeth flashing, and so handsome her heart seemed to leap into her throat.

He led her to the front door this time, nodding at the two guards standing there. Outside a carriage waited.

"Is this yours?" Silence asked, eyeing the polished lanterns hanging by the coachman.

"Aye," Michael said as he handed her in. He leaped in beside her and knocked on the ceiling. "I don't have much use for it, so I keep me carriage and horses at a stable."

"And the coachman?"

She saw the flash of his teeth again as he grinned at her in the dim carriage. "One o' me crew. He had a job as a stable lad in another life."

"I see."

Silence fingered the soft velvet lying over her lap, the realization suddenly hitting her that they rode in a small enclosed space together. She tried to keep her breathing even, but the feel of his broad shoulders leaning against her, the sight of his long legs stretched clear across the carriage floor, seemed to make breathing rather difficult.

"This is only my fourth carriage ride," she said nervously into the heavy quiet that had fallen.

"Oh?"

"Yes." She nodded. "Papa could not afford to keep one, but I once rode in a carriage belonging to a friend of his, Sir Stanley Gilpin, who helped to found the Home for Unfortunate Infants and Foundling Children. That was when he took us to a fair in Greenwich once. And when Temperance was married, her husband, Lord Caire very kindly provided a carriage for the family to ride in to the church and later the wedding breakfast." Silence stopped suddenly having run out of breath.

She darted a look at Michael.

His face was shadowed in the dark, but he seemed to be paying close attention to her babbling. "And the fourth time?"

She remembered and had to look down at her hands in her lap. "The fourth time was on the morning after I spent the night in your bedroom. Temperance rented a hack to come search for me. She found me at the end of the street after I'd walked it with my hair undone and…" She trailed away, unable to say the words.

But he was quite able to supply them. "And yer dress unlaced to show yer chemise and the tops o' yer pretty titties."

"Yes." She looked at him. The old anger and pain was in her chest, but it was dimmer now, allowing her to think. "Why did you make me do that? Walk up the street like a whore coming home from a night of sin? Did you want to destroy my marriage?"

"No." He shook his head sharply. "Had I thought enough to want to destroy yer marriage then me actions might be forgivable."

She wished she could see his face. It had never occurred to her that he might think what he'd done that day unforgivable—that he might care enough to *want* forgiveness. The idea was a revelation.

"Then why?" she asked.

"Why not?" he replied and the simple cruelty of his

statement sent a jagged shard of pain through her breast. "It was me whim, that and only that. I was bred and birthed in St. Giles. I clawed me way up to become king o' hell and now me every wish is granted, love." He shrugged, his expression filled with self-mockery. "If I should have a mind to crush a virtuous woman merely for me own entertainment, then I do it."

His honest depravity took her breath away, but her eyes narrowed in suspicion. Once she might've taken his words as simple fact. Now she knew him better. He might think himself a devil, but he was far more complicated than that.

Far more good.

"So you have no control over your desires?" she prodded skeptically.

"Sure and I have control." He closed his eyes as if disgusted. "Don't harbor false illusions about me, Silence, m'love. I *chose* not to control me desires when I met ye— even if that meant making an innocent walk, disheveled, up a street in St. Giles to fall into her sister's arms."

"How do you know I fell into Temperance's arms?" she asked. "You didn't escort me to your door—that was Harry's job."

He went still. "I watched ye with a spyin' glass from me windows. I saw yer courage—and I saw ye collapse into her waitin' arms."

"Why?" she whispered. "Why should you watch me?"

"Why shouldn't I share in yer pain?"

She shook her head, looking away from him, staring blindly out the darkened windows. "You say you chose not to control your basest urges that night, yet you did not harm me physically. You could've taken me to your bed and destroyed me, yet you did not." She turned and stared at him seriously. "You cannot tell me that you don't feel true remorse for the pain you caused me."

He looked startled for a moment and then he laughed, short and hard. "Ah, Silence, m'love, don't mistake me for a gentleman. I am a pirate, a thief, and a killer, and nothin' but."

"Then you would do it again, if you had the chance?" Silence demanded. "Make that terrible bargain with me? Send me into the street, disheveled and ashamed?"

His hesitation was so slight that had she not been paying careful attention, she might've missed it. But she didn't miss it. It was real.

He looked haunted—confused as if the very earth had shifted under his feet. "D'ye hope to change the stripes on a snake, darlin'? Rub as hard as ye might, they'll not come off and yer like to be bitten for yer pains."

"You didn't answer me," she whispered.

He turned to face her though she could not make out his expression in the dark. "And yer sure o' that now?"

She drew in a wavering breath. "You can *choose* not to do such horrible things in the future, can you not?"

"Can I?"

"Yes," she said firmly. "No matter what you were in the past, what you are now, you can *choose* to change, *choose* to indulge only your better desires, not your basest ones."

He stared at her and she wished that she could see his eyes clearly. Would a devil lurk there—or a militant archangel?

She opened her mouth, but the carriage shuddered to a halt at that moment.

"We're here," Michael drawled.

He pushed open the carriage door, revealing blazing

torches in the night, and jumped down before setting the step and offering his hand to her for assistance.

Silence took her skirts in one hand and carefully stepped down. She wasn't used to such an abundance of skirts and she rather feared she'd drag her hems in something awful.

"Come," Michael said and set her hand upon his arm.

She finally looked up and saw a lovely classical building. Lanterns lined the steps leading to the doors and streams of ladies and gentlemen were entering the building. At the edges of the crowd were hawkers calling their wares: oranges, walnuts, flowers, and sweetmeats. Michael led her up the steps and into the doors.

Silence looked up at the vaulted ceiling, lined with sparkling chandeliers. "Where are we?"

"Ye'll see," he said and mounted a curving stair.

The upper level held a corridor with doors along one side. Michael opened one and ushered her inside.

"Oh!" Silence exclaimed. "You've brought me to the theater."

"Not quite," Michael said from behind her. "This here is an opera house."

Silence looked about excitedly. She'd never been to either the theater or the opera as Father had rather frowned upon such things as frivolous.

They were in a luxurious box with several plush chairs and a table. Velvet curtains lined the box and could be drawn to give the occupants privacy. But beyond the railing the stage blazed with lights. Below a crowd milled in the pit.

"Let me take yer cloak," Michael said, lifting it from her shoulders.

Silence hardly noticed. She was busy peering into the pit and across the theater to the boxes on the other side.

"Take care," Michael warned. He placed his hands on either side of her waist. "Lean too far over and ye'll tumble out."

"I won't," Silence said, blushing. She must look a rustic country lass in her excitement. She sat on a chair with careful dignity, but then couldn't help putting a hand on the rail as she hissed, "Isn't that the king?"

Michael had taken a seat beside her and he casually turned his head to look where she indicated. "That'll be the king's son, the Prince o' Wales. He does bear a fair resemblance to his da, though 'tis said the king hates his son most strongly."

"The king hates his own son?" Silence felt incredibly naïve. How did Michael know this and she did not?

He shrugged. "The king and the prince are never seen together."

Silence tried not to stare at the florid man with the protuberant eyes. "Oh! And what about the lady beside him?"

"His wife, I think," Michael murmured. "'Tis rumored that he's devoted to her."

"Really?" Silence examined the princess. She wore a very elegant silver and white gown, but she was little more than a girl.

She craned to see who was in the boxes on their side of the opera house. "Do you come here often?"

Michael shrugged. "Once or more a month."

Silence looked at him then. She'd not thought when she asked the question that he would answer in the affirmative. "You do?"

He smiled, his face in profile to hers. He didn't lean

forward eagerly as she had done, but his attention was most definitely on the crowd, the stage, and the atmosphere of the opera house itself. "Aye, and is it that startlin' a savage such as m'self can find pleasure in music? Or is it the elegance o' the music I like that surprises ye?"

"I am surprised," she admitted. She was fascinated by the beauty of his profile, the severity of the straight lines of his forehead and nose, the sensual curves of his lips, and the arrogance of his chin.

He turned and caught her watching him and the smile left his lips. His eyes grew intent, his eyelids drooping, his eyebrows looking quite satanic and a little frightening.

She found him so tempting that she pressed her hand to her chest without conscious thought.

He followed the movement.

A corner of his mouth kicked up as he stared at her exposed bosom. He reached out and trailed his finger lightly across the upper slopes of her breasts. "Ye have no idea how long I've waited to see these."

She caught his hand in her trembling fingers, uncertain if she was thrilled or mortified.

He didn't try to pull away. "If I knelt right now at yer feet no one would see."

"I . . ." She glanced at the low wall in front of her. It hid her from the waist down to anyone looking at the box. An image of him kneeling at her feet popped into her head and she suddenly stopped breathing. "What?"

"I could kneel there and lift yer skirts," he murmured. "Ye'd have to be very still, mind. Very quiet. And no matter what I did ye couldn't let it show on yer face."

She stared at him, mesmerized by his deep, slightly

rasping voice as he told her his wicked thoughts. She blinked, unable to resist asking, "What would you do?"

A corner of his mouth curled and his black eyes were intent. His hand left her lax fingers and trailed over her bosom, down her stomach, to her lap. "Do, love? Why, I'd fold yer skirts up, careful like, a little at a time, until I could see yer sweet cunny, hidin' there between yer thighs."

He pressed with his palm on the place that he described and it seemed to burn right through the layers of cloth.

She bit her lip, unable to look away from him.

His nostrils flared as if he could scent her arousal. "I'd part yer sweet thighs and touch ye there, where yer pink and wet. I'd slide me finger through yer softness, up until I touched that little spot at the top." He tilted his head, watching her. "D'ye know the spot I mean?"

"I..." She swallowed, feeling the heat rising over her throat. She knew, of course.

"Tell me."

She closed her eyes. "Yes."

"And have ye touched yerself here?" He spread his fingers wide as if claiming possession of her femininity. "Tell me, Silence me love. Have ye touched yerself and thought o' me?"

She drew in her breath—to deny or confirm, she didn't know which—but a squeak came from the orchestra.

Michael lifted her hand to his mouth and kissed the palm, his lips warm and intimate.

Silence stared at him, her heart fluttering in her chest.

He smiled into her eyes, placed her hand gently back on her lap, and turned his gaze to the stage. "Hush. It begins."

*   *   *

MICK SMILED TO himself as he turned to watch the stage. He could hear Silence's quickened breathing, still saw in his mind's eye the pink tingeing her lovely chest. He was rock hard from their play and were she a doxie he might've pulled the curtains and taken her there.

But she was a lady true and he had no intention of making her flee. No, he'd take this slow, seduce with voice and imagination, and when he finally took her to his bed, well then, the victory would be all the more sweet for the anticipation. He sat back and swiftly made his breeches more comfortable as the music swelled.

The *musico* stepped out on the stage to calls of approval from the audience. The opera singer was Italian, well known, and had quite a following in London. He was unnaturally tall and a bit fat and he stood woodenly on the stage, his body ungraceful. But when he opened his mouth... what delight!

Mick closed his eyes as the mezzo-soprano voice flew, high and precise, confident even when the notes were rapid and complex. Mick had come to the opera a little more than a year ago on a whim and had been instantly enthralled. That a man could produce such a wonderful sound almost made him believe in a God.

Almost, but not quite.

Mick opened his eyes and turned to watch Silence. She was leaning against the rail, her expression utterly rapt. Her lips were slightly parted, her eyes wide, and a curl of her hair drifted against her fair cheek. It occurred to him that he was very content thus, watching Silence and listening to the opera. Was this what happiness was? Strange thought. He'd never considered happiness before.

That kind of prosaic life was not for him, he knew. But here, now... he had a glimmering glimpse of what happiness might be.

At the intermission he left her and fought through the crowds to a certain hawker he'd seen outside the opera before.

"What's this?" Silence asked when he returned with laden hands.

"Cream cakes and wine," he drawled, and felt the warmth light his chest at her delighted gasp.

He watched her eat the pretty cakes he'd found for her and drink the sweet wine and the satisfaction was so pure that it gave him pause. Was this all an illusion? Could he trust her as he'd trusted once before, long ago?

That time had ended in tragedy. Would this?

She glanced up at that moment, licking the cream from her sweet lips, and frowned. "What is it?"

He sat back, looking away. He'd break in half and die if she treated him as the other had. "Nothin'."

He felt her gaze for minutes that seemed to drag like an hour, but then, thank God, the orchestra began.

Mick hardly paid mind to the second half of the opera. It was time. Tonight he would take her to bed and end his restlessness. Once she was his, he'd no longer have this womanish worry that she'd betray him.

The decision made, he waited out the rest of the opera impatiently. Silence was hiding a yawn behind her hand by the end, so Mick gave her his arm and led her into the night air.

The carriage was around the corner and he was conscious as their footsteps echoed off the buildings on either side that this would be a grand spot for an ambush. He breathed a sigh of relief when they made the carriage and he grimaced ruefully to himself as he followed her inside. He was becoming a silly old woman it seemed.

He settled beside Silence, very aware of her smaller size and of the delicacy of her profile. Tonight he'd have her in his bed. Tonight he'd discover all that smooth, soft skin, and the woman beneath.

"Thank you," she said sleepily. "That was the most delightful thing I've ever seen."

"Ye liked it then, m'love?" he murmured.

"I did."

He smiled in the dark. He'd had years of practice with seduction, but this was different somehow. Final and just. After tonight he'd have no need to seduce any other. "What did ye like the most?"

"Oh, I don't know. I liked the lady singer and the dancer—imagine dancing without stays!" She stifled a yawn. "So scandalous, and yet she was terribly graceful as well, like watching swan's down float on the wind." She was quiet a moment. "It must be nice to see the opera or the theater whenever you might wish."

He tilted his head toward her. "Perhaps I'll take ye again."

He waited like a lovesick schoolboy for her reply and it took several moments for him to realize that she'd fallen asleep. He smiled in the dark. Best she get her rest now. Still, he could not help the impulse to carefully put his arm around her and gently tilt her head so that it lay more comfortably on his shoulder.

She murmured something and snuggled into his chest.

They rode thus through the night, she fast asleep trustingly against him, he with the smell of her hair in his nostrils. He was erect and throbbing in anticipation, but oddly he was content to sit thus with her.

More than content, if truth be told.

The ride must end at last, though, and the carriage shuddered to a halt before his palace.

She stirred and looked up, her eyes suddenly wide. "Oh! I'm sorry. I must have been a terrible weight."

"Not at all, m'love," he murmured. "Not at all."

He bent his head toward hers, drawn by her plump, parted lips, but the carriage door opened.

Immediately she moved away from him and he sighed. "Come inside and I'll give ye a taste o' some fine Spanish wine."

"Oh, I don't know," she said as he handed her down.

"Naught but a sip, I promise ye," he whispered into her ear.

He was so wrapped up in their gentle flirtation that it took him a moment to notice what he should've seen at once.

There were no guards outside the palace.

Chapter Eleven

Well, being a king was quite lovely, and for many years
Clever John was happy with the arrangement. But as
time went on, it became a bit…monotonous. Every
morning Clever John ate his breakfast off plates of
gold. He strolled his royal garden—ten times the size
of his uncle's—and then went riding about his kingdom.
By afternoon he'd usually exhausted all there was for
a king to do and was forced to take a nap.
So it was with more interest than trepidation that he
heard the news that his neighbor had invaded
his kingdom.…
—from *Clever John*

Silence was sleepy from the carriage ride, but
Michael's sudden stillness brought her to full alertness.
"What is it?"

"Get in the carriage," he ordered quietly and drew a
long, wicked-looking dagger from his sleeve.

"Michael?" she whispered. She couldn't see anything
to alarm him. The street was quiet, the moon high and
full overhead. Their carriage had stopped directly in front
of the palace's nondescript door. It looked the same as
usual except—

"The guards are gone," Michael murmured. "Me palace is under attack."

"Dear God," Silence said. "Mary Darling—"

He turned swiftly, his eyes burning with intense emotion. "No. Don't even think it. I'll get her and bring her to ye alive and safe. Wait here in the carriage."

"But—" She was suddenly filled with fear—not only for herself and Mary, but for Michael. He thought himself invincible, but he was only a man after all, made of flesh and blood and as mortal as any other.

She bit her lip, knowing that she couldn't distract him from his task, and started for the carriage.

"No, wait," he took her arm, halting her. "Might be this's a diversion to separate ye from me."

Her eyebrows drew together. Why would Michael's enemies care particularly about her?

"Follow me close like," Michael said, gripping her tighter for emphasis, "but not so close that ye interfere with me right arm. Understand?"

She nodded mutely, gathering her skirts in trembling hands.

He looked over her head at the coachman. "Stay behind her and guard her with yer life, ye hear?"

"Aye, Mick," the man replied.

Then Michael opened the door to the palace.

It was dark inside, the candles that should've been waiting already lit, had been snuffed. The coachman retrieved one of the lanterns from the carriage and held it up high behind Silence.

The gaudy golden walls jumped out in the flickering light, the multicolored marble floor sparkling. The entry hall seemed deserted—that is until Silence noticed a smear of blood on the rainbow marble. Michael advanced swiftly and bent over the two bodies lying in the shadows behind an ornamental urn.

He straightened almost at once. "Dead."

Silence clapped a hand over her mouth to still a cry of fear. What would the intruders do to Mary Darling?

Michael was already moving swiftly and quietly through the hall and she hurried to catch up, trying to keep the heels of her delicate embroidered slippers from tapping on the marble. Instead of taking the main, grand staircase, Michael drifted past it and pushed on a panel half-hidden in the shadows. The panel opened to reveal a narrow staircase. Swiftly he mounted the twisting steps and Silence found herself panting as she ran after him.

A minute later he abruptly halted before a small landing and another door.

"Remember to stay close," he whispered to her and kissed her hard on the mouth.

Before she could reply he'd opened the door.

The intruders were standing immediately on the other side.

Michael lunged soundlessly and the first man fell. Two other men turned, cudgels raised, and Michael made a flurry of swift jabs and darts. Someone grunted and Silence was pushed aside as the coachman came up the stairwell behind her. She saw now that they were in a hallway around the corner from the room she and Mary Darling shared. There were a few candles lit, but the hall was mostly a mass of violent, heaving male bodies. Silence gasped as the coachman was pushed back against her. He grunted and kicked the assailant away.

"Steady on, ma'am," he growled, but she wasn't reassured.

She'd lost sight of Michael and because of the melee she couldn't move closer to her rooms and Mary. A wild-eyed giant ran at the coachman, a cutlass raised over his head. The coachman somehow deflected the larger man's attack. But the coachman stumbled back onto Silence. For a moment she couldn't breathe beneath the man's weight.

Suddenly Bert appeared, his face ghastly white beneath a wash of scarlet blood. With a foul curse he bashed the giant over the head and pulled the gasping coachman off Silence.

"Are ye all right, ma'am?" Bert asked and for a moment Silence was simply stunned by the honest worry in the guard's ugly face.

Then there was a shout from behind Bert and Michael reappeared. His fine velvet coat was ripped at both shoulder seams and a line of blood trailed from the inky black of his hairline.

"We make for the babe's room!" he roared and seized Silence's hand, plunging into the mass of twisting bodies.

She gasped and fought to keep by his back as he hacked and kicked his way bodily through. For the first time she realized what sort of man it took to become a successful pirate. He was ruthless as he fought, a wolf made entirely of sinew and ferocity. He never hesitated, never seemed to rethink a thrust or hit, he simply fought with single-minded savagery. It was rather awe-inspiring, his primitive violence, like a lightning storm. And like a natural force, he was graceful, too, his body moving with sure and simple brutality.

Within a minute they were in sight of her room. The door burst open and a huge man ran out.

Michael bellowed.

The man took one frightened look at them and turned and ran.

Michael started after him, but Silence dug in her heels, halting him.

He turned on her, his face savage.

"Mary!" she said.

He blinked as if coming out of a dream state and nodded.

The other intruders, though greater in number, had fallen away from Michael's attack. Now they were retreating with Bert and the coachman in pursuit.

Michael ignored the stragglers. He turned and tried the door to her rooms and when it didn't open, backed a step and kicked it in.

The room was lit only by one candle. In the middle, Harry crouched over a body. Silence could hear Mary Darling crying, though, and she pushed past Michael.

"Silence!" he called behind her, but she was intent on the baby. She couldn't see her. Where was Mary? A low whimper came from somewhere near her feet. Silence looked down and saw nothing.

Almost instinctively, she dropped to her knees and peered under the bed. Two pairs of eyes stared back at her. Lad gave a low growl, but Mary held out her arms. Sobbing.

"Oh, baby!" Silence cried.

Lad stopped growling as he recognized her voice. Silence reached under the bed and caught Mary Darling by the shoulders as the dog crawled out.

"Oh, sweetheart," Silence murmured once she had the baby in her arms. Mary was sweaty and grimy from the dust under the bed, but she was entirely whole, entirely alive. Silence felt tears of relief flood her eyes as she buried her face in the baby's curls.

"What a good dog you are, Lad," she murmured wetly to the mongrel as he wagged his tail. "What a good guard dog."

She rose and turned, smiling, only to freeze in confusion.

Michael still stood by the door, staring down at Harry and the figure on the floor. Now she saw that it was a woman—and her heart began to beat faster. "Who—?"

She stepped closer and then gasped and turned Mary's face away. The body on the floor had no face. Or rather what had been a face was now a mass of blood and melted tissue. Silence squeezed her eyes shut. She knew who it was even before she felt Michael's arms close around her and Mary.

"It's Fionnula, I'm afraid," he said into her hair. "I'm sorry, love. She's dead."

MICK FELT THE tremor that went through Silence's body. He closed his eyes a moment and simply held her. The baby was bawling in his ear and he didn't give a damn. She was alive. They both were alive and unhurt. They weren't lying on the floor like Fionnula, her face a horrific mess. He grit his teeth at the thought and knew suddenly: *this was fear.* This terrible, cold hand clenching at his inner organs. This wild urge to scream at the awful thoughts running through his head.

What if—?

What if he'd delayed ten minutes longer at the opera? What if they'd thought to post an ambush by the front door? What if he'd been cut down as he'd entered? What if, at this very moment, Silence was in *his* hands?

Mick wanted to laugh. Doubts, worries, and fear of his mortality—those were all problems that other men had to deal with. He'd never bothered with them himself. Why should he? If he died, well, then he died. He'd led a good life—a fighting life. He'd leave no regrets behind.

But that was before. Now he had Silence to protect and worry over—and *Jaysus* a baby, as well. If he fell who would take his place to guard them? Who was as ruthless as he?

He looked up and his eyes met Harry's.

Harry nodded soberly at Bert, standing in the doorway panting. "Bert says the Vicar's men 'ave been run out o' the 'ouse."

"Good," Mick said.

"What did that man d-do to her?" Silence asked, her face was still turned into his chest.

"Vitriol," he said starkly. He didn't have to look at Fionnula's corpse again to see the effects.

He remembered the results of a vitriol attack well enough. The caustic liquid was used in the production of gin and was in common enough supply in St. Giles. Vitriol burned any surface it touched except glass, and that included flesh and bone.

"Dear God," Silence murmured. "I'd heard what vitriol could do, but this . . . it killed her?"

He stroked her hair. "It was quick," he lied.

In fact Fionnula had probably suffocated as the terrible liquid ate into her nose and the tissues of her mouth and throat. Her death would've been agonizing.

"Poor, poor Fionnula," Silence said. The baby had quieted into an exhausted slump against her shoulder. "Do you think Mary saw it?"

"Nah, she didn't. Fionnula must've saved the babe," Harry said somberly. He gently spread a handkerchief over the girl's ruined face. "The baby was already under the bed wi' Lad when I got 'ere." He nodded to the connecting door to Michael's room. "I came through there. Saw the Vicar's man standing over 'er, jus' lookin'. Then 'e turned tail and ran."

"And why weren't ye here afore the Vicar's men to stop them from enterin'?" Mick asked coldly.

Harry flushed. "There were a fire in the kitchen. We went down to 'elp put it out afore it spread to the rest o' the 'ouse."

"A diversion," Mick grunted.

"Aye," Bert said. "A diversion right enough, Mick."

Harry nodded. "The 'ole 'ouse was roused to carry the buckets. Weren't until we 'eard a scream from above that we realized we was under attack. By that time they'd made the upper floors and 'twas 'ell to fight our way through." He averted his eyes from Fionnula's pathetic body as if he couldn't stand the sight. "She were already dead by the time we made it 'ere."

"How did the fire start?" Mick asked.

But at that moment Bran shoved past Bert in the doorway. Bran's face was blackened, his hair straggling about his shoulders. He saw the still form on the floor and froze.

"No."

Harry turned. "Aw, Bran—"

"No!" Bran batted aside the hand that Harry would've set on his arm. "No, no, no!"

He sank to his knees beside Fionnula and carefully lifted the handkerchief from her face. For a long moment he simply stared at the horror and then he abruptly jerked aside and vomited.

"She were a brave lass," Bert said thickly, his eyes

reddening. "Must've jus' 'ad time to shove the babe under the bed afore they were in the rooms."

Bran had his hands over his face and was simply rocking as if too stunned to move away from his position beside Fionnula. His reaction was stronger than Mick would've expected—he'd never thought the boy as in love with Fionnula as she'd been with him. Perhaps it was the shock of her terrible death.

Or perhaps Mick simply didn't understand love.

Mick felt Silence shudder within his arms as she stifled a sob.

He stroked her hair. "A brave lass indeed. We'll give her a proper burial, Bran, never ye fear."

"Damn you!" Bran looked up, his face white and clear of tears. His eyes seemed to burn in the parchment of his face. "The Vicar had her killed because of your damned war, because of your damned pride! You whoreson! You should've killed him years ago, simply taken over his business and been done with him. But you're too high in the instep for gin." He spat, the glob of phlegm hitting the floor with a loud splat. "Damn you, her death is on your soul."

Mick watched Bran throughout this tirade, not bothering to defend himself, though he did put his body between the grief-stricken boy and Silence. He glanced at Harry and nodded.

"Come on now." Harry reached down and took Bran's arm. "Times like these's good for gettin' roarin' drunk."

"Damn you!" Bran tried to wrench his arm from Harry's grasp, but his heart didn't seem to be in it anymore. The big man drew him up easily and hustled him to the door.

Mick glanced at Bert. "See that the room's cleaned and Fionnula's taken to the cellars until we can bury her."

Bert nodded, his hangdog face heavy with sorrow.

Mick turned and left the room with Mary and Silence. He wanted them away from the scent of death and tragedy.

His own room hadn't been touched. For a moment Mick narrowed his eyes, considering. The palace was a large and deliberately labyrinthine building. Finding a specific room was hard for those not initiated into its secrets. Yet the Vicar's men had found Silence's room very rapidly and without error, it seemed. How—?

"Why did they kill her with vitriol?" Silence whispered.

Mick looked down, his thoughts scattered. "Because o' me."

Her face was turned up toward his, pale and weary. She'd been fond of Fionnula. She'd be in mourning, too, along with Bran.

Her brows drew together in dazed puzzlement. "Because of you?"

He nodded. This was not the time or place, but he was all out of deceits and whiles. "A long time ago I attacked a man with vitriol. Threw it in his face."

She recoiled. Well, and why wouldn't she? It was a horrific act, the action of an animal. Naturally she'd be appalled.

"Why?"

He felt his own eyebrows arch in faint surprise. To question why an animal would act in an animalistic manner seemed absurd, but he humored her anyway.

"Because I wanted to kill him and the vitriol was at hand."

She stared at him and blinked it seemed with an effort. "I'm very tired," she said carefully, "but I know there must be more to the story than that..." She trailed off and shook her head as if too weary to go on. "I can't ask the right questions tonight, but tell me this: Why should your attack so long ago lead to Fionnula's death tonight?"

"Because," he said, "the man I scarred with vitriol was Charlie Grady, the Vicar o' Whitechapel."

SILENCE STARED UP at Michael O'Connor, pirate, thief, admitted murderer. He'd confessed to a ghastly crime, one that led naturally to deserved retribution.

And yet...

And yet she refused to believe the worst of him—even if he believed it of himself. She knew him better now. All she saw at this moment, late at night in a dark room, was the sorrow in his eyes.

"Oh, Michael," she said, and laid her palm against his cheek.

His black eyes flared wide in surprise and she almost laughed. Was compassion such a strange thing to him? Impulsively she stood on tiptoe and kissed him.

The heat of his mouth was a shock. She held the baby between their bodies and she'd meant only a quick, careless kiss, but somehow nothing was careless with this man.

He opened his mouth and took control of the kiss, bending over her, surrounding her and Mary in a circle of protection. He tasted of the wine they'd drunk at the opera—so long ago it seemed now—and the memory made her want to weep.

She broke away, intending to lay Mary down, to seek his arms with nothing between them, to find out what it was like to kiss him as a woman kisses a man.

But an arm wrapped around Michael's throat and yanked him backward.

Silence opened her mouth to scream and a hand was clamped over her face.

"Hush," Winter whispered close to her ear. "Don't be frightened. We're here to take you away from him."

She stood still, her eyes wide over her brother's hand. No! They couldn't separate her from Michael now. She watched as Asa took the long knife from Michael's sleeve. Michael stood unnaturally calm.

He met her panicked gaze. "Don't let it worry ye, love. They'll not hurt me."

Beside her, Winter made the strangest sound—almost a *growl*.

Behind them, an aristocratic voice drawled from the bedroom door, "Oh, don't be too confident of that, O'Connor. Not if you've harmed my sister-in-law."

She turned her head within Winter's grasp and saw Temperance's new husband, Lord Caire. He was an intimidating man even under the best of circumstances—Lord Caire's hair was stark white, long and clubbed back, and he nearly always wore black in dramatic contrast. Tonight, though, his face was as grim as Silence had ever seen it, and her chest tightened in sudden fear.

She pulled Winter's hand, unresisting, from her lips. "Please. Don't harm him. He hasn't offered me any disservice."

"Oh, no?" Asa asked darkly. "Then what do you call the embrace we witnessed when we entered?"

Beside him, Concord scowled at Michael.

Silence could feel her face warming, but she tilted her chin up. "None of your business."

"Silence—" Concord began in a heated tone.

Lord Caire coughed into his hand, interrupting him.

"But you see my dear, it is, actually, our business—your well-being, both physically and spiritually. We've come to take you and Mary Darling away."

Only a few days ago she would've welcomed their interference. Now things were entirely different. *She* was different. She simply couldn't betray Michael. He'd been attacked and his palace invaded. He *needed* her.

Michael saw the torment on her face. "Go with them, love. 'Tis for the best. Me palace isn't safe anymore. I cannot protect ye by m'self."

Her eyes widened at the admission. He was backing down, conceding the field—for her. What must it have cost his pride to admit that he couldn't protect her in his own house? Tears suddenly pricked at her eyes, but she blinked them away fiercely. She wanted to keep his face in her sight as long as she could.

Lord Caire turned and gave Michael a considering look. Michael met his eyes and some male communication seemed to pass between them.

Her brother-in-law nodded. "Thank you, O'Connor."

Michael returned the nod, but oddly it was Winter he spoke to. "Ye'll need to guard her and the babe night and day. The Vicar o' Whitechapel is me enemy and he'll think either o' them a fine prize."

Silence looked up at Winter. It was obvious that he had no love for Michael, but he gave one jerky nod. "Understood."

Michael was suddenly in front of her, having apparently moved so swiftly he'd taken Asa unawares. He took her face in his palms. "Remember me." And then his mouth was on hers, hard and hot and open, his tongue thrusting into her mouth despite her brothers' presence.

There was a growl and he was torn from her. Silence was hustled into the hall. She held Mary Darling close as Asa, Winter, Concord, and Lord Caire formed a phalanx about them and escorted her from Michael's grand palace. They met no resistance, whether because Michael's men were busy elsewhere or because he'd called them off, she didn't know.

Abruptly a door opened and she was once again out in the chill night air. She glanced over her shoulder at the palace's shabby outlines, and then she was helped gently but urgently into a waiting carriage.

The door slammed, a man called something, and the carriage jerked forward.

"Silence," Temperance said, and Silence made out the dear face of her sister in the seat opposite.

For the second time in her life Silence burst into tears as her sister bore her away from Mickey O'Connor's fortress.

Chapter Twelve

*Clever John put on his armor and went to the top
of his mountain and called, "Tamara!"
At once the rainbow bird swooped down from the
clouds and circled his head before alighting and
turning into the girl Tamara.
She clapped happily at the sight of Clever John.
"How have you been, my friend?" she asked. "Do you
like your kingdom? Have you swum the sparkling lake?"
But Clever John merely frowned to the west where
his neighbor was even now marching toward his castle.
"I wish for an invincible army."
Tamara threw up her arms. "As you wish!"…*
—from *Clever John*

"I have a traitor," Mick said quietly just after midnight.
He watched Harry to see how the other man would react
to the news. He was almost certain that the traitor was
not Harry, but then until the events of tonight he would've
said that none of his men would betray him.

That was patently not true.

And what was more, he'd had to let Silence's brothers
bear her away because the palace wasn't safe for her or
the babe now. Conceding to anyone was not something

Mick was used to doing. If any man had told him a month ago that he'd let four men walk out of the palace with something—*someone*—he considered his, Mick would've laughed in his face. But that was before Silence and the babe had come to be important to him. More important than even his self-esteem and his reputation. If that made him a weaker man, well, then so be it.

Harry's ugly face creased as he frowned. He looked troubled at the announcement of a traitor, but tellingly, not surprised.

"Ye figure 'twas a traitor let in the Vicar's men?" Harry asked.

Mick nodded and leaned back in his chair. They were in his planning room—the safest place in the palace for a discussion such as this. The room lay against one of the outer walls, with thick interior walls on either side. The passage outside was the only entry point and Mick's desk lay across the room and out of earshot of anyone listening at the door.

He'd always been a suspicious man, just, it seemed, not suspicious enough.

"Did ye find out how the kitchen fire started?" Mick asked.

The big man scratched his head while regarding the ceiling critically. "'Twere a bit 'ard to figure out, truth be told. 'Ole place is a mess and Archie in a right fit about it. 'E said 'e'd gone to fetch some turnips and other victuals from the cellar and when 'e returned the kitchens were boiling with black smoke."

"The chimney wasn't stopped?"

Harry shook his head decisively. "Naw. 'Tis drawin' well now. But me and Bert we found a pile o' greasy rags—or what were left o' them—by the back door. They might've been lit and left to smolder while the traitor took to 'is 'eels."

Mick nodded. "Who gave the alarm for the fire?"

Harry screwed up his face, thinking for a moment. "Bran. Or maybe Archie." He shrugged. "Everyone were shoutin' at once."

"And when did you realize we were under attack?"

"We 'eard a scream—must've been Fionnula. They came at us as we tried to get back to the baby's rooms." Harry shook his head. "The 'all were full o' them, must've been near two dozen or more armed men. We was fightin' them when ye came from the other way and we finally got to the rooms." He shook his head sorrowfully. "They must've got to Fionnula almost at once. That vitriol doesn't kill fast like but she was already still when I found 'er."

Mick nodded. "The guards at the front door were hit from behind—attacked from *inside* the palace."

Harry scowled. "'E's a right bastard 'ooever 'e is. Lettin' men in to kill a babe and a 'armless lass. If it weren't for Fionnula's quick thinkin' Mary might be dead as well."

"No, not dead," Mick murmured absently. "The Vicar wanted her alive. She'd be a good hostage against me—she's me daughter. And the fact that he knows that, means the traitor has been tellin' him secrets for a bit. The Vicar knew about Mary, knew where she slept in me palace, and knew that I was away tonight. Come to think o' it, a traitor might be how the Vicar found out that she was hid at the orphanage in the first place."

Mick steepled his hands before him and stared at the rings sparkling on his fingers while he thought it out. The traitor's identity was obvious. He felt a small twinge of what might have been grief, but Mick ruthlessly shoved the useless emotion aside. The man had put both Silence and Mary Darling in danger. The only decision to be made was what to do about it. He could expose the traitor, have him killed as a warning to his other men. Or he could let the traitor think he was undiscovered and use the man against the Vicar.

Mick looked up at Harry, still standing patiently in front of the ornate desk. "We're goin' to strike fast and hard, mind. I want ye and Bert to see to the repairs to the kitchen. See to it that Fionnula is buried proper with a pretty carved headstone. This news o' a traitor stays with ye and me—I don't want it leavin' this room, d'ye hear?"

"Aye," Harry said slowly. "But where will ye be, Mick?"

"I'm goin' after me lasses—Mrs. Hollingbrook and Mary Darlin'." Mick grinned. "We're goin' to double-bluff the bastard. Whisper it about that I think the Vicar will be expectin' an attack so I'm delayin' me hand. Me leavin' London will add truth to the lie. But once I'm gone and he's restin' easy I want ye and Bert to attack the Vicar's gin stills. They blow easily, gin stills, nice and high. The Vicar will be thinkin' I'd attack his person, not his stills. We'll strike him where he earns his gold and cripple him."

Mick stood and began gathering papers on his desk. He still had to have a hasty meeting with Pepper if he were to leave London in the morning. The investments Pepper had made for him were now more important than ever.

Harry was silent and after a bit Mick glanced up at the man, half-expecting a protest.

Instead Harry merely looked sad. "'Twould be kinder to let 'er be."

Mick didn't pretend misunderstanding. "Aye, and if I could leave me Silence alone, none o' this would've happened in the first place." He stood a moment, tasting the bitter irony on his tongue. Then he looked at Harry. "Can ye do all that while I fetch her from whatever country wilderness her family has hidden her in?"

"Oh, aye," Harry said grimly. "We'll blow that old bastard sky 'igh, never ye fear."

"FOUR MEN KILLED and you didn't even get the baby," Charlie said softly. He looked at the carved marble headstone as he spoke, but he addressed the man at his side.

Freddy was standing close enough to hear Charlie's murmured words, but far enough away that he could swiftly duck any sudden blows. No fool, he.

"'E'd 'idden the babe," Freddy said.

"You should've found her." Charlie stroked the cold marble. Grace had been a good woman—a loyal woman. "That babe means a lot to me, Freddy. I think I made that clear, did I not?"

Freddy shifted uneasily. "Yes, sir."

"And the woman? The one you were supposed to kill with the vitriol?"

"She were out wi' Charmin' Mickey. Went somewheres in a fancy carriage, all rigged out in silks."

Charlie glanced up slowly. "Did she indeed?"

Freddy looked alarmed at his tone. "Sir?"

"Now that is of interest," Charlie mused. "He's never taken one of his doxies out before, has he?"

"She sits at 'is right 'and at 'is dinner table, too, so our spy says."

"Ahh. Then I'm glad you didn't kill her outright after all." Charlie drew a deep breath and tilted his head back, feeling the dawning rays of the sun on the right side of his face. He felt nothing at all on the left side, of course. He traced the ragged ridges and furrows, the unnaturally smooth valleys, with his fingertips. Not since that day sixteen years ago when a small, beautiful boy with hatred in his black eyes had thrown vitriolic acid in his face.

"I've waited years for this day," he mused.

"For what, Vicar?"

Charlie lowered his chin and smiled into Freddy's horrified eyes. "For the day that Mickey O'Connor chose a woman of his own."

THE DAY WAS well established when Silence woke from restless, dream-filled sleep. She lifted her head and immediately winced at the crick in her neck. Outside the carriage window the rays of the sun shone on gray fields rolling away to the horizon.

"We'll make Oxford tonight," Temperance said from across the carriage.

She held Mary Darling in her lap. Mary was cradling a brand-new doll, but she cast it aside when she saw Silence was awake and stretched out her arms mutely.

"Already?" Silence murmured as she took the babe. She'd not traveled much outside London in her life, but she knew they'd gone a great distance in the night. A great distance away from Michael.

"We changed horses in Chepping Wycombe," Temperance said, "but you did not wake. Caire tells me that we'll stop again in a bit for luncheon. There's a lovely inn in the next town with a cozy back room where we can sup in private. We stopped there on our way to Caire's estate in Shropshire after the wedding."

"That's where we're headed then? Shropshire?"

"Yes, we thought it the safest place—away from London where we can guard you and Mary properly."

At the mention of her name Mary made an impatient wiggle. The baby climbed from Silence's arms and sat beside her, though that certainly wouldn't last long. Mary hated sitting still, except when looking through the little illustrated book Michael had given Silence. She loved the little men in their funny boats and the strange monsters that rose from the tiny cobalt sea...

Silence remembered with a pang that the book was back at the palace. She'd probably never see it again.

She sighed heavily and showed the baby her dolly. "Where is Lord Caire?"

"He's riding outside," Temperance replied. "He thought we might like the time alone together."

Silence flushed, looking away from her sister's too-perceptive sherry-brown eyes. Temperance always had been maddeningly helpful and levelheaded. "I should thank you, I know."

Temperance pursed her lips thoughtfully, "But you won't?"

"No, no, I will." Silence took a deep breath, trying to organize her muddled thoughts. "Thank you, truly."

"But?"

"But I didn't need rescuing."

Temperance simply looked at her, eyebrows slightly raised.

"I *know*," Silence burst out. "He's a pirate and...and a

terrible, nasty person who hurt me badly before and I was in his clutches—"

Temperance cleared her throat delicately. "I heard you were rather enjoying his clutches."

"Winter tattled, didn't he?" Silence asked darkly.

A corner of Temperance's mouth twitched. "It was Asa, actually. He sounded a bit like an elderly maiden with shocked sensibilities."

Silence crossed her arms under her bosom and slumped rather mulishly in Caire's rich carriage seat. "I suppose he and Concord are riding outside, too?"

"No." Temperance shook her head. "Concord had to get back to the brewery. Asa rode with us as far as Chepping Wycombe last night, but then he muttered something about business that couldn't wait and left."

"Humph." Silence didn't know whether to be hurt that her rescue apparently didn't rate very high on Asa's to-do list or relieved that she wouldn't have to face him again over luncheon. "Winter?"

"He had to stay at the home, naturally," Temperance said gently. "They are rather short of help at the moment."

And that was her fault, as well. Silence bit her lip, looking out the window as the gray scenery passed. The sun had risen fully, but it was rather defeated by the late winter landscape. The day looked cold and unwelcoming.

She'd made a muddle of this, she knew. She'd gone to Mickey O'Connor's house initially intending to merely endure to the best of her ability—and she'd ended by calling him "Michael" and kissing him enthusiastically in his bedroom.

Well, but that was the thing, wasn't it? He was no longer Charming Mickey O'Connor, infamous pirate, to her. She found him charming, yes, it was true, but charming in a much more intimate, personal way. She'd never been tempted by the pirate.

She was deeply tempted by the man.

"That dress is quite lovely," Temperance observed in a carefully even tone.

Silence swallowed a lump in her throat. Her indigo dress *was* lovely—and she'd probably never have occasion to wear it again. He'd promised to take her to the opera once more and now he never would.

"He's seduced you, hasn't he?" Temperance asked quietly.

"Not in the way you mean," Silence answered without looking away from the dismal view. "I haven't gone to his bed. But, yes, I suppose I am seduced."

"I don't understand."

Silence shook her head slowly. "He's different than what everyone thinks him. Well, different and yet the same. He's so... so much *more*. More charming, stronger, more clever. I don't know if he has any sense of shame, but I do know he feels—and feels deeply. And... and that fascinates me—the difference between his public face and his private face."

"None of that sounds like he cares at all for you," Temperance said.

"Doesn't it?" Silence stared at her lap. "I think he does care something for me, actually. You haven't seen the way he's taken care of me, after all. But I'm not sure that really matters in the end—whether he cares for me or not. It has no bearing on my feelings toward him."

"Perhaps not," Temperance said, her voice hard now. "But you must see that it has a great deal to do with how

I feel about Mr. O'Connor. I don't want to see you hurt again. And I'm not the only one who feels thusly. I've never seen Concord so beside himself."

Silence winced. "Was he very angry?"

"I think it was mostly worry, but of course he showed it as anger—he is a man after all. It took Winter half the night to convince Concord to go home to his family. Otherwise your Mr. O'Connor might be sporting a blackened eye this morning."

"Oh, dear."

"Asa was quite upset, I think, though one can never quite tell with him, and Winter…Silence, Winter has been terribly grim. He loves you, you know, in his own quiet way, and I think he's spent the time you were away worrying constantly."

Silence closed her eyes. "I'm sorry. I never meant to make Winter worry. But Michael said we were in danger. And last night proved his concern quite real." Her lips trembled again at the memory of Fionnula's poor, ruined face. "The Vicar's men killed the girl who'd been looking after Mary."

"I'm so sorry," Temperance said sincerely. "Caire and Asa have been watching Mickey O'Connor's house for the last two days, waiting for a chance to come and get you out. When they saw the smoke and the commotion, they sent for Winter and went inside."

Silence nodded. "The guards were killed at the front doors. Otherwise they would never have made it past the front hall."

They didn't say anything for a while, Silence thinking of Fionnula and worrying about Michael, still in danger from his enemies. Mary played for a bit, then let her dolly fall to the floor and knelt on the seat to look out the window.

Finally Silence sighed and glanced over at her sister. Temperance seemed younger somehow, she realized. She wasn't more than eight-and-twenty of course, but for many years Temperance had been so grave, so mature and...and *stodgy*. "Marriage suits you."

She had the satisfaction of watching her elder sister blush. "Oh! Thank you."

Silence smiled a little. "It's nice, isn't it? Being loved. Loving in return."

Lord Caire might be an intimidating man, but when he looked at Temperance something seemed to go still behind his eyes and he became entirely focused on her. Silence shivered. Had William loved her with such all-consuming devotion? She realized, a little sadly, that no, he hadn't. She might've built a life around him—and the dream of him—but he had always been quite autonomous.

"It's simply wonderful," Temperance said, interrupting her gloomy thoughts. "Sometimes I find myself just looking at him and smiling. He'll catch me and give me the most puzzled look and I can't help laughing in his face and then he..." She shook her head and stopped. "Well, marriage *is* wonderful. I never knew it before."

"You didn't love Benjamin as you do Lord Caire," Silence murmured. Temperance had been married very briefly when she was only a girl.

"No, I didn't," Temperance said quietly. "I never knew I could be this close to another person. It was such a surprise to me. But it's not a surprise for you. You had this same thing with William."

Temperance's voice was gentle, but Silence still braced

herself for the arrow of pain at the mention of William's name. Strangely though, the hit wasn't as bad as she expected. Oh, the pain of William's loss was still there, of course. Perhaps it always would be. But it was dulled now and a little distant.

The pain that was close and immediate was the loss of Michael.

Silence sat stunned at the thought. She'd become intimate with him, it was true, but she never believed that Michael might mean something *permanent* to her. The notion was disquieting. After this morning she wasn't even sure she'd see him again.

"Silence?" Temperance asked tentatively.

Silence sighed and shook her head. "Oh, I've created a mess!"

Her sister smiled. "It can't be as bad as all that."

Silence gave her a speaking glance. "I think I may be falling in love with a pirate."

Temperance blinked. "Oh."

"Yes, *oh*." Silence leaned her head back against the squabs. "He's entirely the wrong man for me. Not like William who was calm and kind and—"

"And *good*," Temperance put in drily.

Silence glanced at her helplessly. "What am I to do? I'm not even sure I'll see him again."

"You won't want to hear this," Temperance said gently.

Silence scrunched her nose and turned back to the gloomy view. Still, she couldn't ignore Temperance's words:

"But perhaps it's for the best."

Chapter Thirteen

An army appeared at the base of the mountain, mounted
men in armor and warriors on foot, carrying shields and
swords. Quickly, Clever John ran down the mountain and
led his army into battle to defend the kingdom. The shouts
of men and the screams of horses were heard for miles
around. When the shadows began to grow long, Clever
John looked up and saw that his enemy was defeated.
Only then did he notice the blue feather stuck in the
links of the armor covering his right arm....
—from Clever John

Naturally, Lord Caire would have an overwhelmingly
elegant country residence. Silence listlessly perused the
great library in Lord Caire's country manor, hoping for
something—anything—to distract her from thoughts of
Michael. The late afternoon sun shone in the glass doors,
illuminating the great bookshelves that lined three walls
of the room.

She'd heard no word from Michael in the week since
she'd hastily left his palace.

She really ought to be more grateful. Huntington
Manor was huge and rambling with lovely food and servants to take care of her every need. Actually she hadn't

quite gotten used to the servants. The butler was a terribly daunting elderly man and Silence found herself flushing furiously every time she had to speak to him. Oddly, Temperance seemed right at home as the new Lady Caire. One would think she'd always been a baron's wife from the ease with which she consulted with the cook about meals and the housekeeper about decorations and such.

Silence shook her head and trailed her fingers over the spines of the books lined up like soldiers. The library, like everything else in Caire's country estate, was magnificently appointed. Histories, poetry, philosophy, and even a few works of fiction could be found here. She should be happy to have the chance to simply sit and read. She had no chores here, no tasks or worries.

"Gah!" Mary said, patting the glass on the French doors. They looked out over a terrace bordered by a mown lawn. Mary was carefully walking down the glass doors, admiring the view and the crows on the lawn.

Silence turned back to the bookshelf and pulled out a book at random. It was a treatise on Latin history—or so she thought. Her Latin was rather poor. She wrinkled her nose and replaced the book.

A week and no word from Michael. Well, it was silly to expect otherwise, wasn't it? He'd sent her away with Caire and her brothers and even though he'd done so to protect her, perhaps he'd been secretly relieved to see her go. Without her around he could have tarts in his palace once again—two at a time in his bed, if he wished!—and go back to his wastrel pirate ways.

Silence kicked the lower shelf.

"Goggie!" Mary Darling said from behind her.

"No, sweetie," Silence said, "those are crows."

"Goggie!"

A thump came from the windows.

Silence turned, alarmed that Mary might've fallen, but the toddler was still standing against the windows. And on the other side was a very familiar dog wagging his tail like mad.

"Lad?" Silence whispered. She swiftly crossed to the glass doors and looked out. Dusk was gathering, but she thought she saw something flash in the trees beyond the lawn. "Oh, my goodness."

There were guards, of course. The first thing Lord Caire had done on reaching his country residence was hire several strong men from the village to patrol the grounds. Silence craned her neck and saw two men just disappearing around the far corner of the house. She knew from watching them that they wouldn't be back around to this side again for another ten minutes or more.

That is, if they didn't reverse their course.

Hastily she found a pencil and flipped through the Latin book until she found a blank page. Silence wrote a short note to Temperance and left the book on a table, opened to the note. Then she scooped Mary up in her arms and went out the French doors. Lad immediately began jumping around them like a maddened hare, but fortunately he seemed to know enough not to bark.

"Where is he?" she hissed at the dog, feeling like a fool.

Lad pricked his ears forward and then turned to look at the trees.

Well, that was clear enough.

Silence darted across the lawn, arriving at the tree line breathless and with her heart beating in a staccato rhythm. She peered into the dark copse, but didn't see anyone. Disappointment seeped into her chest. Perhaps she'd been mistaken at the flash. Perhaps Lad had somehow followed them from London. Perhaps—

A hand clamped over her mouth.

"Hush," Michael murmured.

She nodded.

He lifted his hand and then just watched her. He was different—his clothing dark and plainer than any she'd ever seen on him. His coat was brown, his hat a simple black tricorne. And he'd covered his extravagant hair with an anonymous white wig, making his face appear leaner, his cheekbones sharper. His black eyebrows winging up so starkly against the white of the wig made him look more Satanic, more stern than ever.

"Will ye come with me?" he whispered.

And she answered without hesitation. "Yes, please."

WINTER SIGHED SILENTLY as he watched another elegantly dressed lady pick her way down the narrow alley leading to the Home for Unfortunate Infants and Foundling Children. Lady Penelope wore an elaborately worked yellow silk gown with an embroidered jacket, and a velvet cloak thrown over her shoulders. The lady held her skirts high as she carefully stepped along, the jewels on her slippers winking in the sunlight. Behind her, Miss Greaves trailed, much less richly dressed and holding a silly little white dog in her arms. Winter eyed the winking jewels on the slippers sourly. The cost of those slippers could probably keep the home in coal and candles for an entire year.

At least he no longer had to worry about Silence, now that Caire and Temperance had her safely hidden at

Caire's. Still that didn't quite make another day wasted with silly society ladies bearable.

"Oh, they do look splendid, don't they?" Nell Jones commented beside him.

Winter coughed. "Indeed."

"The children are so looking forward to singing for the ladies," Nell said. "And they've become quite good at singing the same words at almost the same time."

Winter arched an eyebrow. The last time he'd passed the classroom while the children were practicing, the sound had not been exactly melodious.

"And Joseph Tinbox has memorized the psalm he is to recite," Nell went on. "If only we have enough biscuits for all the ladies! That last batch didn't turn out quite right."

Winter, having spent years dining upon the products of inexperienced cooks—the girls of the home did most of the cooking—knew better than to ask what exactly had happened to the last batch of biscuits. "I'm sure the biscuits will do very well."

Nell flashed him one of her quick smiles. "Well, I just hope so. I wouldn't want to let you down, sir."

"You won't, Nell. That I'm quite certain of," Winter said as he stepped forward to welcome Lady Penelope Chadwicke and her outrageously expensive slippers.

"Oh, thank you, Mr. Makepeace!" Lady Penelope exclaimed. She wrinkled her nose as she let her skirts drop. "I do think you should do something to make the street cleaner. Perhaps you could see about having it repaved?"

"The home is only temporarily housed on this street, Penelope, dear," Miss Greaves murmured. "Perhaps we should save large projects like repaving the street for the permanent residence."

Winter shot Miss Greaves a grateful look. The lady smiled shyly back at him and he noticed that her eyes were a rather lovely dark gray.

"Oh, I suppose that's the practical thing to do," Lady Penelope said with a pout. "But I do think practical things are so boring, don't you, Mr. Makepeace?"

Winter opened his mouth, a little bemused by this frivolity, but was saved from having to reply by the sound of hooves clattering on cobblestones.

A trio of mounted soldiers pulled their horses to a halt before the home. The lead soldier, riding a huge black horse nodded formally.

"Sir, ladies. Have I the honor of addressing Mr. Winter Makepeace?"

Winter felt everything within him still. He looked up into the man's face. The officer wore the standard white wig like his men. Beneath, his pale blue eyes were sharp and intelligent. His face was long, with deep lines incised on either side of his mouth, giving the impression of a man who had been so hardened by life that he no longer made concessions for those less capable than himself.

"I am Winter Makepeace."

The officer nodded. "Permit me then to introduce myself. I am Captain Jonathan Trevillion of the 4th Dragoons."

"How do you do?" Winter said quietly. The ladies still stood by him, looking curiously up at the soldiers, but he made no move to introduce them to Captain Trevillion.

The other man noticed the omission with a tightening of his thin lips. "My men and I have orders to arrest any criminals we discover in St. Giles, with particular attention paid to the murderer called the Ghost of St. Giles."

"Murderer?" Nell exclaimed. "But the Ghost has never been proved to murder anyone!"

Captain Trevillion turned his gimlet eyes on the maid-servant. "He can defend himself in a court of law."

Winter snorted under his breath. The Ghost might "defend" his innocence, but only if he could afford to pay the magistrate. The courts were notoriously corrupt in London.

"I expect your cooperation in this endeavor, Mr. Makepeace," Captain Trevillion said coolly. "I shall be requesting the same from the other merchants and men of business in St. Giles, but as an educated man, I hope in particular to have your cooperation. Do I have it?"

"Naturally," Winter said. He laid a restraining hand on Nell. The maidservant seemed about to make another protest. "We will do whatever we can to help the king's men."

"Good." The captain nodded. "Whatever rumors you may hear will be of great help in hunting the Ghost of St. Giles and other miscreants. Indeed—"

"What a brave man," came a husky feminine voice, "to declare he will hunt the Ghost of St. Giles."

Winter stiffened even before he turned to see Lady Beckinhall. He'd been so intent on the confrontation with Captain Trevillion that he'd not been aware of her approach. The thought shocked him almost as much as the wash of quite inappropriate gladness that shot through him at the sight of her.

Lady Beckinhall wore a flaming red gown today, covered in silver embroidery. He felt a muscle in his cheek twitch. Her gown was at least as grand as Lady Penelope's, perhaps more so, and it set off her rich mahogany hair exquisitely. Yet it wasn't the expensiveness of her attire that perturbed him.

No. Disconcertingly, it was the woman herself.

Lady Beckinhall smiled quite blindingly and held out one slim hand to the man on the horse. "I don't believe we've met, Captain."

The soldier took her gloved hand and bowed over it. "Captain Trevillion at your service, ma'am."

"Indeed?" Lady Beckinhall drawled. "How charming."

A faint red stain tinged the captain's craggy cheekbones, poor bastard. "If you say so, ma'am."

"Oh, I do." Lady Beckinhall glanced around at the people gathered before the home's door. "To chase down a bloodthirsty murderer? Quite charming indeed."

Lady Penelope gave a shriek at the word "bloodthirsty." "Oh, my goodness! You told us the Ghost was harmless, Mr. Makepeace."

Captain Trevillion's stern eyes swung to Winter. "You have had some dealings with the Ghost of St. Giles, Mr. Makepeace?"

Winter shrugged. "Some. As I say, he never seemed particularly dangerous to me."

"He has been accused of several bloody murders," Captain Trevillion said.

Lady Penelope shrieked again.

Winter winced.

"But have no fear, darling," Lady Beckinhall drawled, "Captain Trevillion is here to protect us, are you not, Captain?"

"Yes, ma'am."

"Which is a good thing since we seem to have no other gentlemen as stalwart as the captain." Lady Beckinhall widened her eyes at Winter.

Winter felt his jaw tighten at the ridiculous insult to his

manhood, but he did his best not to let her see it. Instead he looked up at the captain. "If that is all, sir, I will bid you good day and see my guests inside the house."

Captain Trevillion bowed again. "Good day to you, sir. Ladies."

He wheeled the big black and set it to a trot, his men following behind. In another moment they were around a corner and gone from sight.

"My nerves are quite overset," Lady Penelope declared. "And I'm sure Sugar's are as well"—she waved vaguely at the little white dog, which appeared to be asleep in her companion's arms—"I do hope that even a bachelor establishment such as yours has some tea and refreshments available, Mr. Makepeace?"

A bachelor establishment? What odd phrasing. Winter pasted a polite smile on his face and bowed to the silly woman. "Of course, Lady Penelope."

He opened the door and watched her and Miss Greaves step inside. Lady Beckinhall was behind them and he cleared his throat as she drew abreast of him.

"I thought not to see you here again, my lady."

"Had you not?" Her eyebrows arched over mischievous eyes. "But then I've decided that the home needs my help, even if *you* don't think so, Mr. Makepeace."

And she swept inside, leaving him to follow her, his eyes narrowed in contemplation.

ALMOST A WEEK later Silence frowned over her knitting. It was always hard to make the heel of a stocking, but this one seemed particularly misshapen. Michael's carriage gave a bump and began slowing. She glanced out the window and saw that they were turning into a narrow, tree-lined country lane. Lad the dog raised his head at the change in speed. He lay on the floor of the carriage, taking up far too much room.

"Why are we stopping?" she asked. "This isn't a London inn."

The last week had been a blur of tedious travel over bumpy roads, interrupted now and again by stops at little inns where the food could vary quite drastically from good to inedible. Each night she'd fallen into a strange bed, exhausted, with Mary Darling snuggled close to her side. She'd woken in the mornings to find Michael already up from whatever bed he'd spent the night in and usually bringing her a pot of tea. He'd been kind and attentive and rather distant, now that she thought of it.

"We're in Greenwich," Michael said. "We're home."

She looked at him, sitting across the carriage with the baby on his lap, and as always the sight of him made her heart beat faster. "Home?"

He smiled crookedly, but didn't answer. He wore the same clothes he'd had on when he'd first come for her at Lord Caire's residence: worn and simple. She was almost used to this more sedate Michael. This Michael who might have been a traveling merchant or prosperous farmer.

What an odd thought. Silence peered out the window to try and find out what "home" was to Michael. The tree-lined lane opened up to a small circular drive in front of a mansion made of warm red brick. Ivy covered one corner, its branches still bare, and a half dozen chimneys rambled over the gabled roofs. Tender green shoots had begun to poke through the soil around the foundation of the house.

Silence looked at Michael in surprise. The mansion was

quite lovely, it did indeed look like someone's "home"—but certainly not a pirate's.

He gave her a wry glance as if he knew her thoughts. "Come inside."

He lifted Mary Darling in his arms, practiced now after a week of keeping her entertained in a cramped carriage. He descended the steps and held out a hand to help Silence step down. Lad bounded down from the carriage last, ran to water a tree, and then began running in wide circles.

Silence shook out her skirts and looked up. A short, stout butler had appeared on the front steps to the house, flanked by two young maids and an older woman.

"Good evening, Bittner," Michael called as they approached the steps.

"Good evening, Mr. Rivers," the butler replied. His round red face beamed under a snowy white wig. "I trust you had a pleasant journey, sir?"

Silence blinked and glanced at Michael, but instead of correcting the elderly man, he merely nodded. "Pleasant enough. Have you made the arrangements I asked for?"

"Oh, indeed, sir," Bittner replied. "Mrs. Bittner made sure to procure the very best nursemaids from the village. This is Rose and her younger sister Annie."

The girls curtsied shyly. The elder one was probably in her early twenties, while the younger was still a teenager. Both were fresh-faced and pretty with striking blue eyes.

"Rose has worked five years in the Johnson family nursery," Mrs. Bittner cut in eagerly. She was a couple of inches taller than her husband, but just as rosy.

"Indeed?" Michael said.

Mrs. Bittner nodded vigorously. "The Johnsons have seven children, would you believe?"

"Then she should be quite capable of handling one small child," Michael said. He glanced down at Mary who hid her face shyly in the lapels of his coat. He looked up again and drew Silence closer. "This is my friend Mrs. Hollingbrook. I trust you all will extend every courtesy to her while she is a guest in my home."

Silence felt a blush creep up her cheeks. Only one kind of woman resided unaccompanied at a bachelor's house. But she saw no trace of disapproval on the servants' faces. Indeed, they were quite respectful as they curtsied and bowed.

"Naturally so, Mr. Rivers," Mrs. Bittner said. "Shall I show Mrs. Hollingbrook to her rooms?"

"Please," Michael said.

"Come with me, ma'am."

Mrs. Bittner led her inside. The entry hall was neatly appointed, with wood floors and paneling gleaming with beeswax. Windows to either side of the front door as well as above it let in the late afternoon light, making the space warm and welcoming. A heavy wood staircase to one side of the hall led to the upper floors.

"This way, ma'am," Mrs. Bittner said as she mounted the stairs.

Silence followed after her, glancing about curiously. Oil paintings decorated the stairs, but they weren't in what Silence thought of as Michael's usual style. There were a few landscapes, but the majority depicted sailing ships of all things.

"Ma'am?" Mrs. Bittner called.

Silence had paused by a huge painting of a ship in harbor. "Coming."

She hurried after and found the housekeeper standing in the doorway of a bright little room. Silence entered, looking around. It was a beautiful room, done in several shades of blue. In fact, it rather reminded her of her rooms at Michael's palace. She turned to look at the walls and saw the connecting door almost immediately.

No need to ask whose rooms lay beyond.

"I'll have the girls bring up some hot water," Mrs. Bittner was saying. "We'll have supper at seven. That'll give you several hours to refresh yourself and rest."

"Thank you," Silence replied. She hesitated, then blurted out. "How long have you known Mr. Rivers?"

Mrs. Bittner had been drawing the curtains. She paused and looked over her shoulder. "Bless you, dearie, it's been five or more years since Mr. Rivers hired me and Bittner to look after Windward House."

"Windward House?" Silence asked, utterly charmed. "Is that what it's called?"

Mrs. Bittner smiled, the corners of her eyes crinkling. "As long as anyone in the area can remember. We thought Mr. Rivers might want to change the name to Rivers House, but he said Windward House suited him fine."

"And he's lived here ever since?" Silence asked, just to see what the housekeeper would say.

"Well, when he has a chance he does," Mrs. Bittner replied. "His business takes him away most of the time, poor gentleman."

"What is Mr. Rivers's business?"

"Don't you know, ma'am?" Mrs. Bittner's brows crinkled. "He's a shipbuilder, is our Mr. Rivers. Makes the finest ships to sail out of London."

"Oh," Silence said because she couldn't think of what else to reply. A shipbuilder? How fanciful! And yet dressed the way he'd been for the last week, with his hair hidden sedately under the ubiquitous men's white wig, Michael might indeed be a prosperous shipbuilder.

"Will that be all, ma'am?" Mrs. Bittner asked.

"Yes, thank you." Silence smiled absently.

The door closed behind the housekeeper and Silence went to part the curtain and peer out the windows.

What other secrets had Michael hidden so well from her?

Silence only had time to notice that her room had a lovely view of a garden in back before the water arrived. It was pleasingly warm and Silence washed her hands and face before lying down on the soft bed.

But within minutes she was up again. She was simply too curious to lie abed when she could be exploring Michael's secret house.

Outside her door was a hallway. She knew whose room was beside her own, and after opening a few doors she saw that the rest of the rooms in the hall were empty bedrooms.

Well, that was rather boring.

The stairs led both up and down. Up would almost certainly hold the nursery. She mounted the stairs and found the upper floor lined with windows facing south, the late afternoon sunlight pouring in. At the end of the bright hallway was a door.

She opened it and peeked inside.

Mary Darling sat in the middle of a large, beautiful nursery. The room was situated on a corner of the house and had windows on two sides with new bars to keep Mary safely in. There was a small bed and tiny dresser, and though there were only a few playthings, Mary's new dolly had already been installed on top of the pillows on the bed. Anne was showing Mary a little wooden wagon with flocked horses to draw it, but on her entrance Mary looked up.

"Mamoo!" The baby got to her feet and toddled to Silence.

"And how are you, Miss Mary?" Silence smiled. The baby was freshly washed and wearing a new rose-colored dress that contrasted nicely with her glossy black hair. Silence looked at the nurse who had sprung to her feet. "Do you mind if I take Mary for a walk, Anne?"

"Oh, no ma'am."

Silence picked up Mary and bore her away. "Shall we see what we can find downstairs?"

She descended the stairs, holding Mary. Below, they startled a little maid, dusting the pictures in the hall. They paused for a moment to examine the portrait of a funny spaniel dog before continuing. Further along the hall was an open door on the right. Silence tiptoed in and guessed from the masculine furnishings and the huge desk that this must be Michael's study. She spent a few minutes peering at the sketches of ships and sails on the walls, and then Mary Darling indicated that she was bored.

"Very well," Silence murmured. "Let's see what else we can discover."

Across from the study was a closed door. Silence gently pushed it open, expecting a little sitting room perhaps.

The room took up the entire south side of the house and was lined with French doors that let in the sun's rays. A vast carpet covered the floor in muted shades of cream, apricot, and grass green, and scattered here and there were comfortable groupings of plush chairs and polished tables. The walls were lined with honey-colored wood, and everywhere there were books. Big books, small books, books on tables, books laying open as if abandoned by a recent reader. Some were old with crumbling spines, some looked so new they might never have been read, and all were illustrated.

"Down!" Mary said, and Silence absently set her on the floor.

This room was so elegant, and at the same time so comfortable. It was as if Michael had taken his library at the palace and made it something a person might actually want to spend time in.

Days in.

Silence looked around in wonder. By the window was a simple wooden stand with an enormous book opened on it. Silence went to it and looked down. An azure butterfly lay on the page, trembling and delicate, and almost alive. Carefully she turned the page and found an exotic black and white striped butterfly.

This was his butterfly book, she realized. The first book he'd kept. The one that had taught him that there was beauty in the world. She'd found Michael's treasure, the heart he'd kept hidden.

She looked up and saw that at the top of the walls, where it met the ceiling, the wood had been carved. Butterflies cleverly flew all around the room.

"D'ye like it?"

She spun and was unsurprised to see Michael standing in the doorway, Lad by his side. "I do. It's.... wonderful."

He smiled and nodded at the windows where Mary stood. "Mary wants to see the garden."

"There's a garden?" Somehow the information made her want to smile, as well.

"There is in summer. It's not much more than bare earth at the moment."

"Oh, can we see?"

In answer he crossed the room and opened one of the French doors. Outside a paved terrace separated the house from a garden. Low evergreen hedges demarcated earthen beds, most of them barren.

"Look." Silence crouched over the nearest bed. Someone had planted crocuses and they had spread on their own, like a living carpet, spilling into the lawn. Their delicate purple petals fluttered in the spring breeze.

"Bye!" Mary said. She crouched in mimic next to Silence and pointed one stubby finger at a small, azure butterfly, sitting on a crocus.

The butterfly startled at Mary's gesture and floated up, drifting on the breeze, its wings sparkling blue and bright in the late afternoon sunshine.

Silence watched it, enthralled, and then her eyes met Michael's.

A corner of his mouth cocked up. "Welcome home, m'love."

MICK GAVE A last tug to his neck cloth and scowled at himself in the small mirror over the dresser. His rooms at Windward House weren't nearly as ostentatious as those in his palace, but he had kept one thing the same: his bed here was just as big as the one in his palace. He glanced around his rooms. It had taken him years to outfit this hidey-hole, this refuge where no one knew him as Charming Mickey O'Connor, and at first he'd felt foreign in this house. After all, he wore different clothes, used a different accent. He was a different man here. But somehow over the years, that different man had become merely another facet of him. Now he felt nearly as comfortable wearing Michael Rivers's staid clothes as he did Mickey O'Connor's flamboyant costume.

So if revealing his other identity to Silence wasn't the reason for his present nerves, what was? He'd supped every meal with Silence over the last week. There was no reason then for this missish skittishness.

He cursed and thrust himself away from the mirror. No reason, and yet here he was delaying by playing with a plain neck cloth—he who usually wore silks and velvet!

Mick strode out of his room and down the hall. Bittner had already announced supper and Cook did hate it when he was late. But that was not what made his pace quicken. It was the thought of seeing Silence again. Mick snorted. Oh, he had it bad! Like a lad with peach down on his cheeks with his very first tart.

Except that if Silence were a tart, he'd be much more sure of what to do with her. No, he'd had to go and fall for a respectable lady. A lady with swirling hazel eyes that hid secrets he wanted to spend the rest of his life exploring.

Mick paused outside the dining room to catch his breath. And now he'd brought her to his secret hidey-hole that only Harry, of all his men, knew about. He was exposing himself, he knew. Ah, well, and he couldn't even regret doing it. She and the babe needed to be hidden while Harry did Mick's bidding in London and this was the safest place.

With that thought he opened the door to the dining room.

Silence was already inside, sitting primly on the right hand side of the head of the table. She wore a simple blue and white print gown—one that he'd had sent up to her, for she'd fled her brother-in-law's house with only the clothes upon her back. It gave him a satisfied feeling to see her in clothes that he'd provided for her and he smiled as he prowled down the length of the room toward her.

She met his gaze steadily though her cheeks stained pink. "I was beginning to wonder if you'd join me, Mr. Rivers."

He cocked his head. Had he imagined her emphasis on his assumed name? "And leave a lovely lady like yourself alone? I think not."

"Humph."

He sat and looked at her. "How is Mary Darling?"

"Fast asleep after playing and having a bath," she said. "The nursery is lovely."

"I'm glad you like it."

"Rose and Annie are obviously practiced nursemaids, and what is even better, they seem to like Mary, and she them."

He grunted. "It would take a hard heart to turn away from my Mary Darling."

A smile curved the corners of her lips. "You didn't seem too enamored of her when you first met."

"She has a forceful personality, as do I. We just took a bit to get to know one another."

She eyed him suspiciously. "I think your Irish has mysteriously disappeared from your speech, Mr. *Rivers*."

No, he'd not imagined the emphasis. He shot her a warning look as Mrs. Bittner entered with a steaming dish.

The housekeeper bustled around the table serving roasted chicken, boiled vegetables, jellies, and fruit. A little maid trailed behind her, acting as acolyte to the service.

"There now," Mrs. Bittner exclaimed when the table was laden. "Will you be wanting anything else, sir?"

"Thank you, no," Mick murmured.

The housekeeper nodded in satisfaction and left with the maid.

"Will you have some chicken?" Mick asked as he reached for the dish.

"Yes, please," she answered quite politely. "Are you in disguise here?"

He ought to have known she wouldn't let it drop.

He gave her a wing and some breast meat. "Not exactly, but I find it . . . useful to have a place where I'm not known as the pirate Mickey O'Connor."

She waited until he'd served himself and then tasted the chicken. "Then you're a simple English gentleman when you're at Windward House."

He nodded. "More or less."

"And do you really build ships?"

"Yes."

"How?"

"How did I come to be a shipbuilder, do you mean?" He cut into his chicken. "Several years ago I hired Pepper to manage my money. He advised me that it would be wise to invest some of it in a business that wasn't linked to my pirating."

"But why shipbuilding?" she asked. "You could've chosen anything, couldn't you?"

"I suppose." He ate a bite of chicken and chewed as he thought. "I've always admired the ships that dock in London. I used to sit and watch them for hours at a time when I was a lad. Shipbuilding seemed a natural business to invest in. Too, there was an established shipbuilder—his business has been in his family for three generations—who was in need of financial backing. That was where I came in."

"Then the investment has worked well for you?"

He shrugged. "I make nearly as much from the ship-building business as I do from pirating."

She frowned a bit, drank a little of her wine, and set the glass carefully down.

He tensed with foreboding. He expected her to bring up again the topic of him retiring from pirating, but she spoke about something entirely different instead.

"That night when the palace was attacked," she said, "you told me that you had thrown vitriol in the Vicar of Whitechapel's face, but you did not tell me why." She looked up at him, her hazel eyes dark in the candlelight. "Can you tell me now?"

He froze as her question caught him off guard. He'd been expecting the question all this long week, yet she'd chosen to ask it when he'd at last come home. For that at least he supposed he should be grateful.

He took a sip of the wine because his mouth had grown dry. It was a French wine and of an excellent vintage, but it tasted like vinegar in his mouth.

"I was a boy," he began and then stopped. How could he tell her? This was the most wretched part of his life—the most wretched part of *him*. How could he expose her to it?

She waited, sitting quietly, her back straight, her eyes clear and innocent, and he could only stare at her, the words clogged in his throat.

"Michael?" she whispered at last. "Michael, can you tell me?"

And her voice was like a drought of sweet water relieving his thirst, quenching his pain.

"I was a boy," he said again, holding her gaze, for it seemed the only way he could speak this terrible evil.

"And me mam and I lived with him, Charlie Grady, the Vicar of Whitechapel, though back then he was only Charlie Grady. He made gin in St. Giles and he sent me mam out to walk the streets at night."

She didn't say anything, but her eyes seemed filled with sorrow. Sorrow for him, that innocent boy, long dead now.

"Sometimes she'd bring her customers back with her, but mostly she sold her wares out on the streets, and she never said naught to me about those nights, but once in a while I'd hear her crying..." His voice trailed away and he watched his hand as he fingered his glass.

He hated to think about that time. Mostly he was able to push the memories to the back of his mind. Try to forget them, though he never could. Truth be told he didn't want to think about it now. But she wanted to know, so for her he'd dredge up this foulness.

He took a drink to rinse the taste of evil from his mouth.

"She would sing to me in the evenings afore she went out, and her voice was sweet and low. She did her best to shield me from him, for he had terrible rages and then he'd beat me. He never liked me much." He shrugged. That part of his story was common enough in St. Giles. "But when I were thirteen or thereabouts she got sick. It was winter and grain was running low. He couldn't pay for it, the price had ridden so high, and without the grain he couldn't make gin. And she—she was too sick to go out at night."

He paused and the room was very quiet. From without, distantly, they could hear someone laughing in the kitchen.

He looked up at her because he wasn't a coward and he wouldn't have her pity him for one. "I was a fair lad, pretty as a girl, and there are those who like such things, you understand?"

Her face had gone marble white, but she held his gaze and nodded her understanding once. No coward either, was his Silence.

"He said he had a taker for me and that I was to do as the man said or he'd beat me until I couldn't move. Well." Mick inhaled, still holding those beautiful hazel eyes. "I was an innocent, had never touched a girl in me life, but I knew the kind of thing that would be expected of me. And I knew it wouldn't be the once. After I'd done it, Charlie would want me to do it again and again until I was naught but a boy whore, despised by all. I wasn't going to be that thing. We were in his distillery and he had the vitriol in a basin to use for the gin. I knew what it could do, had watched it burn through wood. I took that basin and dashed it in Charlie Grady's face and then I turned and ran as fast as I could."

Silence gave a kind of shuddering gasp and spoke. "You had no choice. What he wanted you to do was abominable."

He shrugged. "Maybe. But me mam never forgave me for it. She spoke but once to me after that."

"Why?" she cried, the outrage in her voice a balm to his soul. "Why would she take his side against yours?"

"Because," he said low, "Charlie Grady is me father."

Chapter Fourteen

*Now Clever John's kingdom was safe from attack.
With an invincible army the people grew used to peace
and prosperity. And if Clever John found his days a little
dull, he amused himself by climbing to the top of his
mountain and surveying all he owned and controlled.
But an army has many mouths to feed, and one day
Clever John found his kingdom's coffers bare.
It was with a light step that he went to his garden
and called, "Tamara!"...*
—from *Clever John*

Michael's greatest enemy was his father.

Silence lay in bed late that night, sleepless and thinking of the things that Michael had told her over dinner.
At the time, when he'd revealed what his father had
done to him—had done to the mother Michael so obviously loved—she'd been too stunned, too sickened to ask
anything more. They'd finished the dinner in near quiet.
Now, as she lay staring sightlessly up at the dark canopy
of her bed, questions and thoughts teemed in her mind.
How could a mother let anyone, even a child's father, do
such horrible things to a boy? And once the child had

defended himself, how could she take the part of the adult who cared so little for his soul?

She shivered in the dark. So much about Michael was explained by his terrible history. She'd wondered how a man could become so cynical, so devoid of common pity, and now she had her answer. Pity had been seared out of him by his monster of a father. Charlie Grady might bear scars on the outside of his body, but they were nothing to the scars that lay within Michael's soul.

Yet now she realized there were questions she should've asked of him—what had he done all alone at the age of thirteen? What had become of his mother?

Well, she wouldn't get any sleep tonight wondering and thinking. Silence turned her head and looked at the door that connected her room to Michael's. A faint light shone under it.

Impulsively, she got up and tiptoed to the door. She pushed it open as quietly as possible. If he were already asleep...

Michael was sitting bare-chested in a huge honey-colored wood bed. He had some papers scattered about the coverlet and a candelabra on the table next to the bed to give him light.

He looked up as she entered.

For a moment he stared at her, frozen.

Then he set the paper he was holding down. "Silence."

She bunched her chemise skirts in one hand nervously. "I have two questions to ask you."

He nodded gravely. "What?"

He hadn't invited her in, but she came forward anyway and perched in a chair near the bed. "What happened to you after you ran away from your father?"

He began to gather his papers together. "I did what any young boy does who finds himself alone in London. I worked."

She waited.

He squared the edges of his papers and laid them on the table by his bed before looking back at her. "I ran away from St. Giles. I knew Charlie had survived the vitriol and while he lived he was a danger to me. So I begged for a bit and stole, as well, but it's perilous for a lad by himself. There's gangs o' pickpockets and thieves who don't like others poachin' on their territory—not to mention the danger o' bein' caught. After a bit I made me way to the river and hired on to a wherryman, helpin' him row and load and unload goods. That was durin' the daytime. At night the wherryman and me stole what we could from the cargo ships."

He was matter-of-fact as he relayed this dangerous life. Sitting as he was now—large and fully grown, a man aware not only of his strength, but of his ability to command other men—he looked like he could handle anything and anyone.

But he wouldn't have been like this back then. Back when he was only a boy of thirteen. She knew about young boys—she'd spent the last year taking care of them. They were tough and reckless and yet at the same time so very sweet and vulnerable. Their cheeks were soft and their eyes apologized even as they fought to assert their independence with too smart mouths.

At that age Michael's broad chest would have been narrow and thin, his arms long and skinny. He would've had the same brown eyes, but they probably would've dominated a thinner, more youthful face. She could almost see that phantom boy, lost and alone, determined to make his way by himself, because there was no one to help him.

Her heart nearly broke.

She inhaled. "Where did you live?"

He shrugged. "On the river. At night I'd sleep wherever I could find a place to lay me head. There're houses where ye can rent a bed for a night or part o' a night, but they can be dangerous for a young boy, too. Often I slept on the boat if the weather was fair."

She watched him. He sat like a king in that great bed, his olive skin shining as if burnished in the candlelight. The coverlet was bunched carelessly at his hips and for the first time she wondered if he wore anything beneath the sheet.

Hastily she raised her eyes. "And then?"

"And then one night me master and me were set upon by a bigger crew o' river thieves. We were beaten and the haul we'd taken that night stolen from us. And I knew then, as I crawled into a corner to lick me wounds, that I couldn't survive as I was."

"What do you mean?" she asked.

He held out his hands in front of him, palms up, weighing his long ago choice. "I could be a wolf or a rabbit, it was that simple. I chose to be a wolf. The next night I went to the crew who'd attacked us and offered me services. They beat me again, jus' to show me that I was at the bottom o' their pack, but I began to raid with them."

He held her gaze and closed both hands into fists. "And when I was stronger, when I was no longer at the bottom and had learned to use a knife, I challenged the leader o' the gang and beat him so badly he never walked straight again. I was fifteen and the leader o' that river crew then."

He lowered his fists to the coverlet and looked at them. "In another couple o' years I was the most feared river pirate on the Thames. I moved me crew to St. Giles and met up with Charlie again. He'd recovered from the burns to his face, but he wasn't nearly at his peak. I could've killed him then, but I didn't."

"Why not?" Silence whispered.

He looked up at her, but she knew it wasn't her he was seeing. His dark eyes were haunted. "*She* ... she begged me. I hadn't seen her for seven years and she got on her knees to beg for his worthless life."

Silence drew in her breath. What must he have felt to see his mother on her knees begging for the life of the man who had abused her—had abused Michael?

"I let him go, more fool I, because of her, and he went and made his home in Whitechapel, schemin', plannin', buildin' his power until he became the Vicar o' Whitechapel." Michael shook his head as if disgusted. "I should've squashed him like a bug."

"Your mother would never have forgiven you," Silence said and she wanted to weep for him.

He looked up. "She never forgave me anyway. I never saw her again alive."

"You tried to?" she asked gently.

He snorted bitterly. "Many a time. He wouldn't let me near her and I knew 'twould only bring her trouble if'n I saw her in secret. She loved that bastard until the end."

She'd loved Charlie more than her own son. Michael didn't say the words, but Silence knew he thought them.

She looked down at her hands and found that she'd squeezed her chemise into hopeless wrinkles in her fists. Carefully she opened her hands and smoothed the fabric.

"When did she die, your mother?"

"Four weeks ago."

Her head jerked up. "That recently?"

He nodded. "It's why I had to bring Mary and you to the palace. Once me mam was gone, there was nothin' to hold him back from makin' me pay. I knew he'd try and draw his blood price from anyone close to me, particularly a woman. He's always liked hurtin' lasses."

"Your mother held Charlie Grady back from attacking you?"

He looked away and nodded.

She held out her hands urgently. "Then she did care for you, didn't she?"

He glanced back at her, his eyes raw.

"She must've," Silence whispered. "Even if she never saw you, she still loved you enough to keep your father from hurting you again."

He shook his head, and she could see that he was having trouble believing her. It would be hard, after a lifetime of seeing only one truth, to open oneself to another.

His deep voice interrupted her thoughts. "You said you had two questions."

She looked up and saw that he was watching her intently, his black eyes hooded. She felt her face heat. Had he known what she was thinking?

"Yes." She clasped her hands together in her lap, trying to look calm. This was important. How he answered might change everything. "Why did you tell me all this?"

He blinked as if the question wasn't the one he'd been expecting. One corner of his wide sensuous mouth curved up ever so slightly. "Oh, love, I think ye know the answer to that one well enough."

Did he mean what she thought he meant? That he wanted her to know about him? Wanted to let her into his life? Her breath caught on the possibility. On the hope that he wanted from her what she wanted from him.

And while she thought, he got up from the bed and answered the question she'd asked only in her mind.

No, he wasn't wearing anything at all.

He was tall and broad and everything that was male, from the mounded muscles of his shoulders to the faint black hairs on his feet. And he was proudly erect.

"Now, I have a question for ye," he drawled, low and thrillingly dangerous. "Will ye be comin' to me bed tonight, Silence Hollingbrook?"

Silence lifted her chin, refusing to back away as Michael prowled closer, large, naked, and dauntingly male. "Yes."

He cocked his head as if unsure that he'd heard right. "Yes, what?"

She swallowed. He was an arms-length away from her now and she could feel his heat. Could feel the responding excitement within herself. "Yes, I'll stay."

With one stride he was next to her, overwhelming in his nudity. "Be sure, Silence, mine. Once I take ye to me bed, I won't be stoppin' if ye have any sudden maidenly qualms. Right now I'll let ye walk through that door and away. In a minute more, I'll not."

She reached out and did what she'd been wanting to do for weeks—she laid her palm against his naked chest. His skin was smooth and so hot she felt as if he'd branded her hand. She'd carry the mark of his flesh forever. "I may have qualms, but they aren't maidenly, I assure you. I want this."

The sound that came from his lips was very close to a growl as he moved swiftly and decisively. Silence found herself suddenly lifted in strong arms as Michael bore her to his big bed.

He laid her down on the soft mattress and placed a knee on the bed. Then he stilled, the muscles on his shoulders bunched and ready. He seemed to restrain himself with effort. "Am I frightenin' ye?"

She shook her head slowly, her heart contracting at the fierce worry in his eyes. "Only in the best of ways."

He closed his eyes and she saw that his big body was trembling. He gripped the coverlet in both fists. "Ye must tell me if anythin' I do frightens ye. I don't want to hurt ye. I—"

She placed her fingertips against his lips and he froze. His black eyes snapped open and he watched her, wild and dangerous.

But not to her.

Never to her. She didn't know how she knew this, but somehow, deep in her bones, she knew now that Michael O'Connor would never hurt her physically. He might hurt her emotionally, but even that wouldn't be on purpose. One couldn't blame the animal for the instincts he was born with.

The thought was a little sad, so she banished it and focused on the man beneath her fingers instead.

His lips were soft. She rubbed them lightly and they parted to lick at her fingertips. She smiled and let her hands drift over his jaw, rough with a day's growth of beard. He was very still, watching her with waiting eyes. She stroked down his neck, feeling the cords of his tendons, and over to her favorite part: his smooth chest. She flattened her hand there and pressed. The muscles of his chest were hard and strong and gave very little. Curious, she scooted closer on her back, putting herself almost under him, so that she could touch him with both hands. Why he stayed so motionless and simply let her explore, she did not know, but she was grateful. She'd always been indecently interested in what lay beneath a man's clothes. William had been a very modest man, so her curiosity had not been assuaged.

Here, now, though, Michael seemed willing to let her explore as much as she wanted. And she was determined at last to discover all she could about this man—in both body and mind.

She smoothed her hands up to his shoulders, shaping the sloping muscles that led to his neck. Women didn't have such muscles and she found it fascinating. She trailed her hands down his upper arms—and then laughed in delight when he flexed them beneath her palms, the bulges of his muscles moving under her hands.

His expression didn't change, but somehow his eyes laughed, too, a great predator, indulgent.

She peeked up at him from underneath her eyelashes as her hands touched his wrists. How far would he let her explore?

She trailed her fingers over his ribcage. A swirl of black hair circled his navel and she traced it, amazed that men should have such hair where women did not. She glanced up and saw his eyes were nearly feral now, watching her with half-lowered lids. His look made her breath quicken.

Hastily she lowered her gaze again. Below his navel the hair narrowed to a line that led to the inky curls around his penis. She followed the line with her fingertips, her mouth going dry at her daring. The fine curls wrapped themselves around her fingers as if drawing her in. He rose strong and hard in the space between her hands, but she didn't touch him yet. Instead she fingered the lean lines of his hips, returning again and again to the center of his manhood, drawing out the anticipation. His breathing had roughened as she played and she thought she heard a low growl.

Only then did she bring her hands together and cradle the prize she found there. She smiled as she held Michael O'Connor's cock. Oh, it had been so very long and holding a man's cock was a wonderful thing. He was soft like a fine kid glove, but if she gave a little squeeze, the flesh beneath was hard as a rock. Her fingers didn't quite wrap around him as she circled him and something feminine inside her quaked. This part of him would be inside her body soon, large and foreign and male.

She inhaled and delicately traced the head of his penis. His foreskin was pulled back, the glistening, swollen head entirely free. At the very tip was a drop of clear liquid and she caught it on her fingertip, bringing it to her mouth to see what a man tasted like.

At her gesture Michael cursed and caught her hand, falling suddenly atop her.

She stared up at him wondering what bedchamber faux pas she'd committed.

He groaned at her look. "I'll let ye pet and play all ye want—*after*. Now I need"—he pushed her chemise to her waist, parted her thighs, and settled between them—"to be inside ye."

There was a flag of red in his cheeks and his mouth had turned dangerous. She could feel his hard cock prodding insistently against her thigh.

He reached between them and touched her, probing and parting her folds. Her eyes widened, watching him as he watched her and touched her where no one else had put a hand save she herself. Her face was hot, she wanted to look away, and she knew she was already embarrassingly, naively moist. Was this what sophisticates did in the bedchamber? She had certainly never done this in her marriage. Did his other women take this type of touch in stride, perhaps with a knowing smile?

The thought of his other women made her mouth tremble and he misunderstood.

"Have I hurt ye?" he asked, his voice like gravel.

He took his hand away and turned with her so that all at once she found herself laying on top of him, her face only inches from his.

He scowled at her. "Ye must tell me if I'm too rough, if I hurt ye. Damn it! I had no intention o' causin' ye pain, m'love."

"Shh!" She pressed her palm to his mouth to stop the fast, angry voice. "You did not hurt me."

"Then why did ye frown?" he demanded.

"I..." She lowered her gaze. How could she be having this conversation? She with her chemise rucked up, her wet sex against his hairy thigh and his erection still pressed to her belly? This was a mad dream.

"I'm not used to this sort of lovemaking," she said in a rush before she could think better of the words.

He was quiet for a moment. Then she felt his hand on her chin as he tilted up her head to meet her eyes. His mouth was still hard and dangerous, his face drawn into even more severe lines if that were possible, but his words were quiet if not soft. "Forgive me for a thoughtless lout. Truth be told, I'm not exactly used to this kind o' bedsport, either."

Her brows drew together. He'd had many lovers. "But—"

"Hush." He placed his own far bigger palm over her mouth. "Let me..."

He gripped her bottom with one hand and drew her legs up on either side of his hips, spreading them wide. In this position his cock was pressed intimately against her folds.

"Oh!" Her exclamation was muffled behind his hand, but since her mouth was open anyway, she stuck the tip of her tongue out and tasted him.

He hissed. "Brat."

She wasn't entirely sure, but she thought that might be a compliment.

He took his hand away and caught her hips in both hands, arching beneath her. The movement drove his cock over her, rubbing the peak of her sex.

The sensation was exquisite and before she could control herself she'd made a needy, moaning sound.

He grinned, though his face was strained. "That's it, love. Use me to make yerself feel good."

She flushed. Surely he didn't mean—?

But he moved again and she lost all thought. He was driving her wild, driving her into some kind of madness. He helped her to sit up and brace her hands on his chest and she found herself moving against him in a sensual haze. His big penis was against her folds, slick with her wetness, and he moved deliberately, knowingly, making her excitement spiral higher. Surely this wasn't right. It must be some sort of sin for it to feel this good, but at the moment she simply didn't care. She bit her lip and ground against him as he held her bottom in his hot hands, and—

And suddenly she was there, racing past the point, flying with dizzying speed. She gasped, her head falling forward, her body convulsing once, twice, three times in quick succession with impossible pleasure.

She opened her eyes, dazed, and saw him watching her with the most satisfied male look she'd ever seen. But his mouth was drawn as well and she realized that his swollen cock was still ragingly hard between her folds.

Sweat was beaded on his upper lip. "My turn." He lifted her and grunted. "Put me there."

Her eyes widened and she reached between them. He was hot and wet with her moisture and he was also so very large. She took one look at his face and knew she must at least try though. She moved him, brushing the head of his penis through her sex.

They both gasped.

She found the right spot and guided him before letting go.

He groaned, loud and male, his eyes turned to feral slits.

She swallowed and tilted her hips, feeling the head of his cock breech her. There was no pain, but she felt a stretching at her opening.

"Michael!" she panted.

"Jaysus," he breathed. His head was arched back, his neck taut with strain.

She bore down, swiveling her hips a little.

He closed his eyes, his mouth open, his nostrils flared.

She pulled back just a fraction and he flinched and flexed his hands on her bottom. She hastily came back down again, watching him as another inch of his length entered her. He looked almost like he was in pain and she felt a sudden power—only she could ease this ache he felt.

She leaned down and brushed her lips gently over his jaw, pushing back with her bottom, taking more of him within her body.

He whispered something under his breath and she sat back, bearing down, gasping, taking the entire length of his cock. She felt stuffed full, her tissues stretched wide over the base of him. He was still, panting, groaning every now and then, his hands twitching convulsively on her buttocks.

Carefully, slowly, she rose on her knees, his cock pulling as it slid from her warmth.

She lowered herself, inching him back inside and he swallowed, his strong throat working. He was such a beautiful man—and he was all hers.

Perhaps she was doing it wrong. Perhaps he really was in pain. She leaned down and brushed a soft, nearly chaste kiss over his lips.

It was as if she'd put spur to him. His tongue was in her mouth, his hips arching off the bed and his hands holding her down as he drove his length into her again and again. His passion was intense, nearly overwhelming and she hung on, determined to ride him out. Determined to bring him as much pleasure as he'd brought her.

Suddenly he pulled from her kiss, his teeth gritted, his head arched back, and he shouted. At the same time she felt the scald of his semen rushing into her.

Silence watched in wonder. She'd never before seen this moment. It was as if he was possessed by a demon or perhaps an angel—some otherworldly being come to give both unbearable pain and exquisite pleasure. Maybe one and the same.

Gently she brushed kisses over his damp face, luxuriating in the intimacy of the moment as he recovered.

Finally his hand rose and he stroked her back with fingers as light as a butterfly. His touch seemed so tender, so loving almost, that it brought tears to her eyes.

Michael looked at her.

She blinked. She was still astride him, his penis inside her, though she could feel it retreating. What did sophisticates do now?

"Come here," he growled, and pulled her down on top of him.

"I-I should go to my own bed," she protested feebly. "I'm too heavy on you."

"No," was all he said in reply. He wrapped one arm across her bottom and flung the other over his head.

She laid her head on his chest. It was amazingly comfortable to lie on a man. He was warm and she could hear his heartbeat, strong and steady.

For a while she listened as his breathing grew deeper and his heartbeat slower. She'd always enjoyed sharing a bed with William, but what they'd done there had never produced the kind of excitement that Michael had given her. Making love with him was wonderful and wild and very, very pleasurable. Everything and more than she'd dreamed.

Which was why it seemed so strange when she began to cry a half hour later.

Her brown eyes swam with tears, overflowing, splashing down, scalding his hands, his face, drowning him in salty sorrow. Mam wept as Charlie stood over her, berating her, beating her with words and fists, and Mick was too small and weak to stop him.

But then Charlie faded and she lifted her head. Mick saw that it was Silence who wept and he could do nothing to comfort her, to console her terrible, unrelenting grief. For he had been the bringer of evil and death, the wellspring of her salt tears. He'd grasped with greedy hands and in so doing had crushed the very thing he'd sought to hold.

But hold her, he would. She was his, weeping or not, grief-stricken or not. And if he could not comfort her perhaps her hot tears would scald away the poison in his suppurating soul...

Mick woke from the nightmare, his body slick with sweat, and for a moment thought he still dreamed.

He could hear Silence weeping.

Weeping after he'd made love to her.

If he'd had a heart it would've contracted in pain then. But since he had no such organ, he reached for her. She was in his bed, finally, and he could not regret it. If he was incapable of love or comfort, so be it. But he could at least hold his woman and feel her tears on his face.

Share in her pain.

"What is it, me darlin'?" he asked, his voice rasping with sleep—or perhaps some new emotion.

She stiffened as he touched her, hunching her shoulder, but he gave no clemency. He was a pirate, after all, and what he took he held and she was his now—whether she knew it yet or not.

He pulled her into his arms. "Sweet Silence, tell me."

Her body relaxed all at once, as if she conceded defeat. "I lied. All this time, I lied."

He had no idea what she meant, but he made soothing

noises at the back of his throat and kissed her neck. "What d'ye mean?"

When she shook her head again and didn't answer, he gently turned her face so he could see her.

The sight sent a bolt of iron through his middle. It was just like in his dreams, her hazel eyes bright with crystal tears, her cheeks wet and reddened. "Dearest one."

She hiccupped and said, "I said William and I had true love. That our marriage was perfect, but oh, Michael, it *wasn't.*"

He sighed and laid his cheek against hers. Of course her marriage hadn't been perfect. Her husband, from the sound of it, had been a stuffy sod. But he was also a *dead* stuffy sod. He knew well enough that mourning had nothing to do with how kind or unkind the person had been while alive.

"I just…just wanted to have a perfect marriage, I think," she whispered, and he could feel the tremble in her voice as she said it. "He was away so much and I was always waiting for him…it was like we never truly settled into everyday married life. And when something difficult came up…" She sighed forlornly. "We didn't know what to do. How to talk to one another."

"I'm sorry," he murmured into her hair.

"And doing this…," her voice squeaked, "this between you and me…I guess it just made me realize that William and I were truly over. Our marriage, our life. I can't even lie to myself that it was perfect anymore."

He stroked her back, waiting.

She lifted her head, her beautiful eyes still shining. "You must think me so foolish."

He smiled at her tenderly, for she made something

in his chest squeeze. "Nay, love. I jus' think ye've a soft heart, and I cannot be displeased with that."

She smiled, though her lips trembled.

He threaded his fingers through her fine brown hair. So lovely it was. "And I'm that sorry the memories give ye pain, but I'm afraid I'm not sorry for what we did here."

"Oh." She blinked. "But I'm not sorry."

"I'm that glad to hear it," he murmured, running his mouth over the corner of her lips.

She gasped and then opened her mouth shyly, and he never hesitated. He kissed her deep, thrusting his tongue into her warmth, tasting the dregs of her sorrow.

He didn't particularly like the memories of another man in her thoughts, but he figured he knew of a way to drive them from her mind. Turning her, Mick pulled her close until her plump arse rested against his loins. His rod was already stiff and hard. He wrapped his upper arm over her shoulders and scooped one luscious breast into the palm of his hand.

He'd not had time to properly appreciate her lovely titties earlier—his lust had been near out of control once she'd shown her willingness. In the daylight he'd strip her naked and examine his new prize, but here in the dark he merely held her. He weighed her softness—her plump breast fit his palm perfectly. Her breath caught and her nipple was pointed and eager. He thumbed it, flicking it gently through the lawn of her chemise, feeling her body quiver against his.

He played leisurely, lazily with her nipples for a few minutes and then his hand stole lower. Her chemise was tangled high about her thighs, which served his purpose well. He laid his palm over her cleft. This was his now, a private garden of delight open only to him. Her breath hitched again as he delved his fingers into her honeyed slit. She wept here, as well, and the discovery was gratifying. This at least he could do for her. He found that tender bud at the apex of her cunny and delicately slipped a fingertip around it, not quite touching the little peak, teasing instead. Around and around his finger slid, until she sighed restlessly and moaned his name—*Michael*—the only one who called him so.

But he allowed it, for she was a fair prize, this softhearted woman. And if she were his woman, well then, he supposed in a way he must be her man.

"Hush, darlin'." He tongued the back of her neck tasting salt and womanly allure.

She bumped her hips demandingly into his and he chuckled low. At last he touched her where she wanted his fingertips. He pressed firmly, rubbing and circling until a high wail came from her throat. The sound was a balm to his blasted soul.

She would've jerked away then, but he was having none of it. He anchored her hip and tethered her in the most basic way possible. He lifted her upper leg, draping it over his own hips, and thrust into her warm, welcoming wetness.

Then he went back to playing. He bit at her shoulder as he stroked her pretty cunny, his own body still. He had what he wanted: her pinned to him, unable to escape. He slid his fingers through her sweet folds until he touched the base of his own flesh where it met hers. His cock was buried within her body as his hand played upon her delicate flesh. She moaned low and he licked where he'd bitten her shoulder, then moved to catch her earlobe. She tried to rub against him, but he was stronger and he easily held her still.

Fingering. Softly tapping.

She was swollen now, his hand drenched with her readiness. He could feel her flexing about his rod and the sensation was an exquisite torture. He treasured her, treasured her tears, treasured her love for others. Her heart might even be big enough to fill that empty space in his own chest. Perhaps she could be his heart as well.

"Michael," she whispered, a siren unaware of her song.

"Yes, love?"

"Michael, please."

"Turn yer head to me, love."

She did and he devoured her mouth, licking salt tears from her lips, thrusting his tongue deep within, a pirate demanding tithe.

She arched and he could no longer hold himself back. He flexed his hips and drove deep within her, holding her cunny in the palm of his hand. He speared within her clenching valley, plundering all that was sweet in her. She opened her mouth wide in a silent scream and his release caught him, hard and fast as he kissed her openmouthed. He tore his mouth from hers and shouted his triumph. She was his, now and forevermore, until the end of time, until the seas ran dry and man no longer roamed the earth, amen.

His and only his.

She slumped against him, the scent of their passion musky in the night air.

"Sleep," he murmured to her, and held her against himself, his cock still buried deep.

She was caught and he had no intention of ever letting her go.

Chapter Fifteen

*The rainbow bird swooped low from the sky and
flew in happy cartwheels around Clever John's head
before alighting and turning into Tamara.
She threw back her rainbow head and laughed merrily.
"Clever John, you have gray in your hair and
your strong back has begun to bend! Has it been
so many years, my friend?"
But Clever John was looking toward his castle with worry.
"I wish for a chest of gold and jewels that is always full."
Tamara smiled a little sadly and raised her arms to the
sky. "As you wish!"...*
—from *Clever John*

Silence woke to the feel of a man's body around her. It
was such a nice luxury that she sighed in pleasure. His
broad shoulders cradled hers, warming her all the way
through. The soles of her feet were against his calves and
she flexed her toes, feeling the rough hair on his legs.

Only then, with that small movement, did she realize that
he still lay within her. Silence froze, her eyes wide in shock.
She'd slept linked with Michael. Even now she could feel
the twitch of his penis within her depths. The sensation was
utterly decadent.

Utterly wonderful.

In one night she'd shared more with Michael than she'd ever had with William. It was more than the fact that Michael was a slow, *thorough* lover. He'd listened to her weep without male embarrassment. Had stroked her and comforted her. The thought gave her hope. If he was able to listen to her tears and disappointment, then surely if they argued, if they disagreed, he'd talk about it with her—not turn aside as William had. And if Michael was able to talk to her...

Well. Then they might have a future together.

Always assuming, of course, that he *wanted* a future with her. Silence frowned at the thought. He'd not mentioned marriage, or indeed even making her his mistress. Did he have any plans for her? Or was he—

Michael's breathing had been sonorous, but she realized suddenly that it had lightened. She stilled, suddenly cautious. What must he think of her tears last night? Surely he wasn't used to such things? Her overabundance of emotion was gauche, she knew, but it was something she could do little to change. She'd lived so long with the fantasy of a perfect love with William, that putting it aside was a hard thing.

"I'm sorry," she whispered.

"For what?" he asked, his voice blurred with sleep.

"For weeping," she said softly. "I know it must have irritated you, it's just that—"

"I wasn't irritated," he said, his breath whispering against the back of her neck. "Never apologize for what we two do here."

"But you must not want a weepy woman in your bed."

He grunted and stirred, withdrawing from her. She

only had a moment to be disappointed and then he flipped her to her back and rose over her, powerful and male. He casually parted her legs with his knees and thrust into her again, hot and hard.

She gasped at the swift invasion, the lovely feeling, and then his face was next to hers, his big palms cradling her cheeks.

"What I want," he drawled, "is ye. Nothin' else."

She opened her lips to ask what exactly he meant by that, but his mouth covered hers, and all thought fled her mind.

He kissed her leisurely then rose, bracing his upper half on his arms and thrust into her. This position was an old one, a familiar one, though not with him. Somehow with Michael she felt much more vulnerable. More intimate. He watched her face as he inserted and withdrew himself, completely in control, arrogant in his dominant manhood.

"Yer mine now," he whispered, his eyelids at half-mast. "D'ye understand, Silence, m'love?"

She didn't, not entirely. She wanted to ask him to tell her more, to explain exactly what he meant by "mine" and if he envisioned it lasting for a week or the rest of their lives. She wanted details and explanations, but he was moving on her—moving *in* her—in the most wondrous way and she simply couldn't form the words.

So instead she stretched her arms above her head, reveling in the heavy thrust of his hips. Her breasts jiggled with the movement and his gaze lowered to stare at her bosom.

"I've wanted to see these forever," he murmured, and hooking his fingers into the neckline of her chemise, tore the garment from her.

She gasped, his casual violence somehow terribly erotic.

"Aye," he growled.

He lowered his head and tongued her quivering nipple, his hips still moving rhythmically.

She felt a restless rising, a desperate yearning for something that might not be entirely physical. This lovemaking was wonderful, but it was not love. Was it enough? If he couldn't ever find it in himself to love her, would she be content?

She pushed aside the thought and dug her fingers into his hair, sliding so silkily over his shoulders. Her touch seemed to spur him on. Suddenly he was pounding into her, his thrusts fast and sure. She wanted to raise his head, to look him in the eye and see if there might be something driving him on beside lust.

But her own ecstasy caught her and threw her high. She closed her eyes, gasping, feeling as if she were the recipient of some kind of pagan offering. She spread her legs wide, her toes pointed, and accepted everything he had to give her.

He groaned against her breast, his big body suddenly stiffening as the spasm took him. She dropped her hands to his shoulders and felt the ripple as his muscles tightened.

When she opened her eyes the very air seemed golden, crisp with promise.

For a moment he lay heavy upon her.

Then he rolled aside and propped himself on his elbow. Michael's beard blued his jaw and his eyes were still lazy from their lovemaking as he watched her with tenderness. Was that love in his eyes? Or something close enough? But she felt too shy to ask him. She felt shy looking at him.

He was so wantonly seductive it made her self-conscious. Surely her hair was mussed from sleeping, her face puffy from crying the night before. She drew the coverlet over her breasts.

A corner of his mouth curled at her action, making him even more sensuously handsome. "Bittner usually readies a bath for me in the mornin'—he knows me routine. Would ye like me to have one brought to yer rooms for ye?"

"Oh, yes, please," she said shyly. A bath was a rare luxury, especially this early in the morning.

His half smile turned to a grin at her enthusiastic reply. He leaned down and kissed her—hard and thoroughly.

A knock came at the outer door.

Silence squeaked, embarrassed. "The servants—"

Michael shook his head, rising from the bed. "The servants know better than to disturb me—unless it's important."

He crossed to the door and cracked it without bothering to dress.

Silence couldn't see who was outside the door, but she could hear his voice.

"A word, Mick," Harry said.

And somehow Silence knew their imperfect idyll was shattered.

"'E BOLTED LAST night near midnight," Harry said as he matched his stride to Mick's. The two men were headed in the direction of the small stable behind the house. "We followed 'im like ye instructed, but we 'ad no notion o' where 'e was bound until we fetched up 'ere this mornin'. Didn't think ye'd want 'im showin' up all unannounced, so I put a 'and on 'im and came for ye."

Mick could feel his muscles tensing, his stride

lengthening as he neared the one who had betrayed him. "Ye did well."

They went out through the kitchens, ignoring the startled squeak of a single scullery maid bent over a mountain of dishes. Outside the day was gray as if the skies reflected this grim business. The stable was across a cobblestone yard and their boots rang on the stones. Inside the stable one of the carriage horses whickered in greeting. Bran was standing in an empty stall with Bert watching him narrow-eyed.

Mick looked at his former lieutenant. Bran no longer could be mistaken for a boy. Several days' growth of beard shadowed his jaw. His face had new lines about his mouth and his eyes looked sunken. Bran glanced at him and then away again as if too ashamed to meet Mick's eyes.

"Wait for me outside," Mick said to Bert and Harry without taking his eyes from Bran's face.

The two men left.

Mick took one giant stride forward and hit Bran in the jaw, putting all the force of his shoulder—and his pain—into the blow.

Bran staggered, struck the back of the stall and abruptly sat.

"Why?" Mick rasped.

Bran had his hand to his face. A blow like that could break a man's jaw, make it impossible to properly eat or talk ever again.

Mick didn't care. "I brought ye up from the streets, boy. Took ye into me own home, fed ye me food, put clothes on yer back. And *this* is how ye repay me? By betrayin' me to me enemy? By lettin' his men into me house to kill an innocent lass?"

Bran licked at the blood seeping from a split on his lip. "I didn't know he'd kill Fionnula." His voice cracked on her name.

Mick shook his head. "What did ye think he'd do?"

Bran shrugged, glancing about the stall vaguely. "Take you down."

"Ye wanted me crew."

Bran looked at him finally and Mick was surprised to see defiance still in his eyes. "You told me, over and over again, about how *you'd* made your way. About how you'd taken down the leader of that pirate crew when you were merely a boy. What did you expect from me but that I would do the same?"

Mick squatted on his haunches, feeling weary to his soul. "I expected loyalty."

"Loyalty?" Bran shook his head and then winced at the movement. "You told me never to trust anyone. That any man who does so is a fool. You taught me that no one would champion me but me. That I must look out for myself and *only* myself. I could recite your lessons in my sleep. Not once did you mention loyalty, but now you expect it from me?"

"Aye!" Mick remembered those offhand remarks, the lessons given casually as they'd raided ships and analyzed the strengths and weaknesses of their men and of their enemies. But he'd considered Bran one of his own—his lieutenant, damn it. His friend. How could Bran have taken his words and turned them against him? "I expected loyalty from ye and every man under me command."

"Under your command, exactly," Bran said. "I had no way of bettering myself. I wanted to be like you."

"Ye *were* like me," Mick roared. "I took ye into me

confidence, made ye a man. What the *fuck* were ye thinkin', Bran?"

"I was thinking of freedom!" Bran shouted. "You kept us under your thumb, made us live in your house, eat at your table. You dealt out the spoils as you saw fit and consulted no one else. You never listened to my suggestions or plans. I was nothing but a lackey to you when what I wanted to be was your equal."

Mick stared. He'd spent years never knowing where his next meal would come from. He'd made the palace into a fortress, not only to guard his wealth, but to guard his men. And now Bran threw back his generosity in his face?

Mick turned his head away in disgust and stood. "Try and put the blame for yer betrayal on me, but it won't work. Fionnula is dead because o' ye and ye alone."

"Oh, God." Bran squeezed shut his eyes, moaning so low Mick had to lean close to hear the words. "Oh, God, don't you think I know that? Her pretty face was burned off. I keep seeing her in my dreams. I can't sleep at night."

Mick grunted. "How did ye find me house?"

Bran shook his head. "I snuck a look in Pepper's book."

"And have ye told the Vicar where I am?" Mick asked, low and deadly.

"No!"

"Why come here?"

Bran opened his eyes, the tears stark upon his face. "I thought to warn you about the Vicar. He wants Mrs. Hollingbrook. He talks of nothing else now."

Mick laughed though he felt no mirth. "And don't ye think I know that well enough? Why did ye really come, Bran?"

"I'm sorry, Mick," Bran whispered. "I didn't know what he was like. If you'd told me..."

"What?" Mick sighed. "If I'd told ye he was mad ye wouldn't have betrayed me to me own father?"

Bran stared, the color leeching from his face. "Your father? The Vicar is your *father*?"

"Aye." Mick inclined his head, his mouth twisting bitterly. "Come full circle, hasn't it? Betrayed by me father, and betrayed *to* me father. The old man's probably right pleased."

"Mick—"

Mick threw out a hand, stopping the other man's words. "Get out o' me sight afore I kill ye."

Bran rose wearily. "Will you forgive me, Mick?"

His words cut a cord within Mick, letting loose the grief within. Mick drew his dagger and before Bran could move he had the knife at his throat.

Bran froze as a drop of blood welled under the dagger.

Mick looked into the face of the boy he'd held dear as a friend. "I can't forgive ye, Bran, no. Ye banished that hope the moment ye put Silence and Mary Darlin' in danger. They might've died because o' yer stupidity. For that, for puttin' them at risk, I should slit yer throat here and now and throw yer rotten corpse in the river."

For a moment he stood, the knife against Bran's neck, staring into the other man's light blue eyes. They'd once laughed together, drunk brandy, and planned raids. Bran had been as close to him as a brother . . . or a son.

It could've been Silence with that ruined face.

Abruptly Mick swung away, putting the length of the stall between him and Bran as he strode to the stall door.

"Harry!" he roared.

The guard appeared a second later. He glanced in the stall and blinked, looking confused to see Bran still alive.

Well, and hadn't Mick killed for far less than Bran had done to him? "Take him." Mick jerked his head back at Bran.

"Take 'im?" Harry asked cautiously.

Mick winced. He wouldn't put the burden of Bran's death on Harry, either. No, Bran was his own responsibility and he'd see him out of England himself. He sighed and stretched his neck. "Take him to the cellar and lock him in well. I'll be bringin' him back to London and a ship bound for a distant shore tonight."

The relief was plain to see on Harry's face, but it was fleeting. When the big man turned to Bran his expression was as cold as Mick had ever seen it.

"Come on, then." Harry took a firm hold of Bran's arm and marched him from the barn.

Bran cast one helpless look over his shoulder, but Mick ignored it. He'd made up his mind.

Mick waited, listening to the retreating footsteps, then stayed many minutes longer, trying to get his anger under control. He didn't want her to see him this way. She wouldn't understand. She came from a foreign land where people could forgive one another, where it wasn't weakness to let live the boy you'd taught to be a man.

Mick threw back his head and stared blindly at the dusty rafters of the stable. He couldn't change who he was. He'd been bred from the loins of a demon in human form and there was only so much humanity in him.

"Michael?"

Her voice was soft and sweet in the stable's still air. For a moment he wanted to hide. To not let the disease of his soul touch her. He felt filthy with sin.

But she was ever relentless was his Silence. She poked her head around the stall door. "There you are."

He straightened from the wall. "Aye, here I am."

She hesitated by the doorway as if aware of the blackness in his soul. Perhaps the truly good had a sort of inner compass that swiveled around when in the presence of evil.

"What did Harry come to say?" she asked.

He shook his head. "Nothing ye need worry about."

He started for the stall door, but she didn't move aside. Instead she hugged her arms across her chest and looked at him with those damned beautiful eyes. "What if I want to worry about it? What if I want to share your troubles?"

He stared at her nonplussed and couldn't help thinking that he'd never had this sort of problem with any of the whores he'd taken to bed. He wanted to brush past her and leave her and her damned questions, but he had a feeling in his gut that to do so would somehow be an act not easily mended.

Mick sighed. "Harry brought Bran to see me."

She stood immoveable and simply raised her eyebrows.

"Damn ye," he hissed, taking her by her slim shoulders. "Why can't ye leave it alone? 'Tis a man's business and none o' yer own."

"I think it is," she replied, bravely tilting her face to look him in the eye, stubborn thing. "I've given you my body and more. I think in return you can give me some small confidence."

"It that what this is? A test?" He felt the anger rise in him again, seeking a victim even if she might be innocent of any outrage against him.

"Perhaps it is," she said slowly. "I need to know that I'm more to you than a woman in your bed, Michael."

"Ye know full well yer more than that," he growled in outrage. "What d'ye want from me?"

"Truth," she whispered, powerful in her softness. "Honesty. Friendship. And perhaps love."

The words sent icy fear through his belly. He could storm a ship, could knife a man, could lead a gang of near-feral pirates, but the things she asked of him were impossible for him to do. He was the son of Charlie Grady, a man who'd never felt compassion, let alone love in his entire life. What softness Mick had had in him had been burned away sixteen years ago as surely as Charlie Grady's face had melted. He'd had to armor himself in layers of granite to survive, to fight to where he was now in the world. And she? She wanted him to simply strip his armor away—let it fall and stand naked and vulnerable in the sunlight.

Her gaze was clear and direct and too terrible for words as she waited for something from him—something he wasn't sure he *had* in him.

"Damn ye," he hissed again, and brought his mouth down on hers.

He'd been bedding women since the age of fourteen. He knew well their sweet parts, their soft sighs. This he could do. She would have to learn to be content with it. He knew no other way to keep her.

MICHAEL'S KISS WAS overpowering. Silence struggled to remember that he'd not answered her questions. But her body had become attuned to his mastery overnight it seemed. She found herself curving toward him, opening her mouth, running her hands through his lovely hair. Already she was quickening, anticipating whatever he might want to do to her.

But he hadn't told her what Bran had come for. He'd refused to share that information and more importantly some small part of his everyday life. If she was to be more to him than merely a body in his bed, he must learn to open himself, he must—

Michael began gathering her skirts in great handfuls and her thoughts scattered.

She tore her mouth away. "Oh! What if someone comes?"

"Hush," he murmured, his voice lowered to a deep rasp. "No one will interrupt."

He'd bared her legs now and was backing her into the stall wall. She leaned there and watched, dazed, as he dropped to his knees.

"Michael!"

He ignored her urgent hiss. "Hold yer skirts."

"Oh, dear Lord." She obediently took the material in her hands even as she craned her neck to watch for intruders. What if Harry came back? Or Bran? Did Michael keep a groom?

He laid both hands on her now, stroking up over her calves, smoothing over her knees, and delicately tracing her thighs.

She shivered. What did he intend to do? She could feel heat gathering at the apex of her thighs and if he reached up there—

She squeaked as he bent to kiss the inside of her thigh.

"Raise yer skirts higher, love," he whispered.

She groaned under her breath. If she pulled up her skirts any farther, her most intimate parts would be exposed. It was one thing to frolic nude in the dark, quite another to do so in the light of day.

But his voice was like liquid sin, dark and dangerously seductive. She did his bidding, her fingers trembling with want, and felt the cool air caress the juncture of her thighs.

"That's it," he said approvingly. "Hold it there, love, and spread yer thighs jus' a wee bit wider."

She swallowed and did as he bid.

"That's me girl." He whispered against her skin, his hot breath making her shiver.

His mouth trailed up beside her mound, licking and kissing, but very leisurely, as if he had all the time in the world. She tilted back her head, impatient, nervous, on edge from suspense. He drew closer to her center and tongued the crease next to her thigh.

Silence bit her lip, trying to make no noise—surely they would be discovered if she did.

She felt him run his thumbs through her maidenhair and down to the plump outer lips of her sex. He thumbed them apart, exposing her wet inner folds.

"Michael!" she whispered, as loud as she dared.

But he ignored her. He blew on her wet curls and she shivered—more from the sensation than the chill. Then he leaned forward and touched his hot tongue to her center.

She jumped at the contact, nearly hitting her head against the boards of the stall. Oh, dear Lord! "What are you doing?"

He chuckled low and restrained her quivering body with his hands, then he drew his tongue through her folds, slow and thorough, the most intimate contact she'd ever experienced. His tongue was wet and hot and felt indescribable.

He didn't seem to care that they were in an open stable, that she was jerking in reaction from each touch, that what he did to her must be some kind of wicked indecency. Michael O'Connor didn't care at all. He just kept licking and tonguing her until she thought she might go mad with the intensity of the feelings he was provoking in her. Each swipe of his tongue burned exquisitely on her nerve endings. Each deep kiss drove her ever nearer to an edge. She was shaking, panting, damp with her own need, and he simply would not stop.

She found herself spreading her knees wider, tilting her hips to give him better access. She might very well expire from this torture, but she would die in bliss. Her head was back against the old stable wall, and she watched the rafters overhead blindly, thinking that she'd never be able to enter a stable again without blushing.

And then he took her little knot of flesh between his lips and suckled it as deeply as he had her nipples this morning. Dear God, she could not hold back. She tumbled over the precipice, sweetly unaware, joyously free. Her back arched, her legs tightened, and she had to stuff a hand in her mouth to keep from screaming.

She was still trembling when he stood and took her into his arms. She rested there grateful and limp, for she wasn't sure she could stand on her own feet after her ravishment. But when she made to let her skirts fall he placed his palm possessively on her mound.

"D'ye like that, darlin'?" he drawled.

"You know I did." Her tongue felt thick and her words were slow. "But you did it to distract me."

He pulled back and looked her in the face, his own wary. "Ye never give up, do ye?"

"Won't you tell me, Michael?"

He shook his head, looking away and curled his fingers

into her cleft, sensitive now from her peak, and gently stroked.

She moaned, clutching at his coat.

His breathing had quickened as he felt her dampness. "Yer so wet, so hot and swollen."

He flicked a finger across her bud and her hips jerked. "Michael—"

"I had meant this only for ye. I had meant to try and play the gentleman, but it seems I cannot." His hand moved away from her and began working at the fall of his breeches. "I mus' have ye."

She watched him from half-closed eyes. She should protest, should tell him they must go inside and talk about why he'd looked so desolate after meeting Bran, but she found she couldn't.

She simply couldn't deny him when he needed her.

He drew himself out and her gaze dropped. He was fully erect, the veins standing out around the stem of his penis, the head ruddy and round.

"Come here," he said, and took one of her legs and wrapped it around his waist.

This brought his hips close to hers and she felt him rubbing against her—just a bit too high.

She moaned in frustration.

"Hush, darlin'," he murmured. "I'll make it all better, I promise. Jus' ..." He caught her other leg and she found herself braced against the wall, both of her legs wrapped about his waist now.

He had his hands on her bottom and was holding her full weight. She felt quite safe, but more importantly, his penis was now at the right height.

"Put me where ye need me, sweetheart," he whispered.

She reached between them and grasped him, conscious of his muttered curse as she did so. She couldn't help a quick stroke up and down. He was so hard, so beautiful.

"Silence...," he warned.

She couldn't wait any longer. She put him at her entrance, biting her lip at his heavy heat. It felt so good—so right. For a moment she stilled. Would she ever be able to recover from this height if he walked away from her someday? She felt as if she were giving a part of herself. Something that could never be taken back again.

He twisted and shoved and began to breach her and she looked up as he did.

Michael—her Michael—was watching her, his nostrils flared, his lips drawn back from his teeth.

She held his fierce gaze as she reached up and traced his cheek. "Make love to me."

He expelled his breath in a gust as he pulled out of her nearly all the way and then slammed back in. His pace was fast, nearly frantic and she held onto his shoulders and fought to keep from wailing.

Oh, God, he was so powerful! She watched him. A bead of sweat dripped down the side of his face, his lips curled back with his exertion. She wanted to kiss him, to embrace him and tell him he was everything to her, but all she could do was hold on and try not to fall apart when the explosion came.

For it was fierce—as fierce as he. A burning, ripping tide of pleasure nearly as violent as it was wonderful. She felt as if her world was tossed up in the air and came down completely re-pieced. This was earth-shattering.

This was love.

She gasped at the realization and watched as it took

him, as well. His head arched back and he shouted as he came, his body jerking against hers. He was magnificent, he awed her, but she felt a pang of melancholy. What did this act mean to him—if it meant anything at all?

He laid his head against her shoulder, gasping as he caught his breath, and at first she didn't hear him.

Then the words rang too clear. "He betrayed me, m'love. Bran betrayed me."

Chapter Sixteen

*A great chest appeared before Clever John, as long
as a horse and nearly as tall. When he lifted the lid
he found gold coins, long strands of pearls as big as
his thumb, and sparkling gems of every description.
For a moment he merely stared in wonder. Then,
belatedly, he remembered Tamara. He raised his head
to thank her, but the girl was gone. Clever John
stood alone in his garden with all the riches in the
world. Only a single orange feather floated gracefully
on the wind. . . .*
—from *Clever John*

"We took out four o' the Vicar's stills in Whitechapel,"
Harry said to Mick late that afternoon. "And we toppled
one o' 'is wagons fair full o' gin barrels."

Bert, lounging against the wall, grunted. "That were a
pretty sight to see. Gin spillin' everywhere and poor sods
runnin' to lap it up out o' the channel in the middle o' the
street afore the soldiers came to drive them away."

Mick winced. He'd never had any sympathy for those
who made and sold gin, but the thought of gin drinkers
actually trying to drink spilled gin out of a foul channel
was grotesque. "What soldiers?"

Harry scratched his head. "There've been soldiers patrollin' St. Giles, like, in the last few weeks."

Mick frowned. Soldiers didn't just turn up out of the blue. Someone ordered them. Someone sent them. "Who commands them?"

"Captain Trevillion," Bert said.

"And who gives him his orders?"

"That we 'aven't found out," Harry admitted. "No one seems to know. But Trevillion's a right prick. Strict about arrestin' any gin sellers 'e finds, though they be mostly old bawds."

Mick snorted. "The Vicar must not like that."

Harry chuckled. "Naw, 'e don't, and that's a fact. 'Is men 'ave been arrested, as well."

Mick leaned back in his chair, considering. The Vicar might be feeling harried by this Trevillion, but he'd dealt with soldiers before—most often by bribing them. They wouldn't stop him for long.

He let the chair legs thump down. "Ye've done well, lads. But I've one more job for ye and it's an important one." Mick looked both men in the eye. "I need ye to guard Mrs. Hollingbrook and Mary—with yer lives."

Harry and Bert exchanged cautious glances.

"O' course," Harry said. "But where will ye be, Mick?"

Mick set his jaw and said quietly, "I'm goin' to London to put Bran on a ship to the farthest corner o' the globe. And then I'm goin' to kill the Vicar."

Bert's hairy eyebrows drew together. "Can't ye send someone else to do the deed?"

"No, this is somethin' that must be done properly," Mick said grimly. "I'll see to it m'self."

Harry licked his lips nervously. "Why?"

"Bran said that the Vicar won't stop until he kills Mrs. Hollingbrook or me Mary Darlin', and I believe him."

Bert hawked as if to spit and then glanced about the orderly study and thought better of it. "'E was a fuckin' traitor was Bran. Can ye trust anythin' 'e says now? Per'aps it's some type o' trap."

Mick studied the papers on his desk without seeing them. Bran had been pale and sweaty—sick with remorse, if Mick was any judge. "He betrayed us all, aye, but in this, I believe, he spoke the truth. He has no love for the Vicar now, I'm thinkin'. Fionnula died by the man's order, mind."

Both Harry and Bert looked troubled at that reminder. But it was Harry who spoke for both of them. "Ye can count on us, Mick."

"Good," Mick said quietly, "because I'm trustin' me most precious possessions to ye."

"Right ye are, then," Harry said.

"They're upstairs," Mick said, "in the nursery. I don't want ye to let them out o' yer sight once I've gone, d'ye understand? I'll leave tonight after supper."

The big man nodded and stumped out, followed by Bert.

Mick sighed and studied the papers in front of him. With Bran gone and both Harry and Bert occupied guarding his lasses, getting into the Vicar's house was going to be a delicate matter. He leaned back in his chair to think.

By the time Mick left the study it was evening and he had a plan that should prove effective. But he was still mulling over the problem of a lack of men he could truly trust when he entered the dining room.

Silence was already seated and for a moment all thoughts of his raid disappeared. He remembered her insistence that he tell her about Bran, her worried concern when she heard that he'd been betrayed. She soothed his soul, this woman.

She wore a light green dress he'd had made for her, and the sight brought him a deep satisfaction. The dress was more modest than he would've liked—she'd wrapped a lace fichu over her shoulders and tucked it into the low neckline—but he'd provided it for her and she'd worn it. His eyes narrowed, studying the pretty picture she made sitting at his table. He'd have to order more gowns. Several morning dresses and at least one more elegant gown she could wear to the opera.

She smiled suddenly, the sight bringing a rush of warmth to his heart. "Why are you looking at me like that? Should I be nervous?"

He pulled out a chair and sat across from her. "I'm thinkin' on the gowns I'll have made for ye."

The smile remained on her face, but her eyes somehow looked sad. "Are you? Then you think I'll be living with you for some time?"

He froze in the act of lifting his wineglass. "D'ye have any doubt?"

She shrugged. "We haven't discussed the matter and I don't know your mind. You are an extremely hard man to read, Mr. Rivers."

He took a sip of wine while he considered her words. She hadn't said she was against living with him, simply that she hadn't known his mind.

"I do wish ye to stay," he said slowly, setting his glass down. "I can give ye many fine gowns—rooms full, if it's yer wish."

"That's quite generous of you," she said in a gentle voice.

He looked at her sharply. There seemed to be some sub-text of this conversation that he was missing. "Ye can live here wi' little Mary Darlin' and do as ye wish with yer days. I'll buy ye a carriage and there's the garden to tend."

"How kind."

His mouth tightened. Pushing. She was always pushing him. From this afternoon's argument over Bran to this now. He'd already let her in, already offered her his house and himself. "What more do ye want? It's more than yer husband provided for ye, ye must admit."

"Yes," she said coolly, "but William married me."

His head reared back as if she'd struck him in the face. He started to say something more, but Mrs. Bittner and the maids entered at that moment with their dinner.

He waited until the servants left, thinking hard on his reply.

When the door at last shut, he said, "I do not wish to quarrel wi' ye on the memory o' yer husband. I know he meant much to ye."

She nodded. "Thank you."

"If ye wish for somethin' more from me," he said care-fully, "books or clothin' or even a lady's maid, ye have but to ask. I'll fulfill yer every wish to the best o' me ability."

There was no mistaking the sadness in her eyes now. "Yes, I know that, Michael."

"Ye'll be the mistress o' Windward House. I'll place it in yer hands to do wi' as ye like." He felt a rising panic, a desperation that he'd never encountered before. "I'll come to see ye as often as I'm able, perhaps three or four days o' the week."

She set her fork down very carefully. "You do not intend to live here permanently?"

"Ye know that's impossible." His jaw flexed. "Me business is in the city."

"You mean the business of pirating."

He stared, confused and angry. "Yes."

"You will continue to rob people for your living," she said. Her face was so still it might've been made from carved marble, but her sweet hazel eyes seemed to burn.

Burn like his mam's. He couldn't give her what she needed. Couldn't prove himself worthy.

He lifted his head proudly. He'd not simper and whine for something she wouldn't give. "Aye, I'm a pirate. I've never hidden the fact."

"No, you've never hidden your sins, have you, Michael?" Her lips were thinned, her face strained. "I had hoped, though, that now with Mary Darling and myself in your life, you might consider retiring. For us. For *me*."

"Haven't I changed enough for ye?" He laughed, short and hard. "Where d'ye think the money comes from to pay for this house, the food we eat, the clothes upon yer back? From piratin'!"

"But I don't need your money, Michael." She shrugged and looked around his fine dining room. "It's very nice, but it's not necessary."

"Me riches might not be necessary for ye, but 'tis for me," he said impatiently. "I've lived in the gutter, mind, and I won't go back there, not even for ye."

"But there's no threat that you'll go back to the gutter," she said and finally her voice rose. "I've seen your throne room. You could live like a king off the treasures in there. You could live off your shipbuilding business."

"No," he was already shaking his head, the specter of his starving childhood flapping tattered wings before his eyes. Even with his shipbuilding business there was not enough money. *There was never enough money.* "No, ye don't understand. Ye *can't* understand. The money—me *piratin'*—is all that I am. 'Tis me power. I can't simply give it up."

"Why not? Your pirating is based on robbing people like my husband!" she shouted, rising from the table. "Have you any idea the suffering you inflict on innocents?"

He laughed. "Most are far from innocent, no matter your pretty illusions."

She braced her arms on the table, leaning over it toward him. "William was innocent, *I* was innocent. William would've gone to prison had I not come to you. Don't pretend that what you do is without victims, for I know otherwise. You hurt us, Michael, hurt us badly. I cannot live with a man who chooses to inflict harm on others for his business."

He stared at her, so passionate, so angry. He wanted to bend her over the table and settle this argument in the most basic way a man can with a woman.

Instead he inhaled. "I'm sorry."

She bowed her head as if to steady her emotions.

"What d'ye want me to do?" he asked, controlling his voice with difficulty.

Her head rose and she looked him in the eye, his brave Silence. "Become the man I know you can be. Be a father to Mary. Be a husband to me."

"Ye'll cut me bollocks off, will ye?" he asked softly. "Make me half a man, bent to your will? Have me sippin' tea with me pinky in the air?"

"No," she said, shaking her head slowly. "I don't care if you ever drink tea, pinky or not. I want you to do something far simpler. Far easier. Just stop. Please, *please* stop pirating, Michael. For me. We could live here together. Be married and have a family. Don't you see? Everything is within our grasp. All you have to do is choose. Choose me."

His chest grew cold. It might seem easy to her, but his money—his pirating—was the only thing he had to guard himself against want. Against starvation. Pirating had saved him when he was abandoned, fed him when he'd had no food, given him a life and a future when his had been destroyed. His mother might abandon him, Bran might betray him, even Silence might someday leave him, but at least he still had pirating. At least he had the money.

His money was his strength. Not even for this woman would he make himself weak.

He looked into her lovely, determined face. "No."

She held his gaze a moment more and he thought he saw despair in her eyes.

Then she turned and left the room.

THE TEARS HAD dried on Silence's cheeks by the time Michael came to her room that night. She watched from the bed as he laid an assortment of knives and a pistol on her dresser and began to arm himself.

"What are you doing?" she asked.

He stilled as if he hadn't known she was awake. "I'm takin' Bran back to London and then I've some business to be attendin' to. It won't take long. Harry and Bert'll guard ye and Mary here until I return."

It was just before midnight. If he left now and rode to London, he would be about his "business" for most of what remained of the night. He probably wouldn't return until well past daybreak tomorrow.

"What business?"

He paused for a fraction of a second—if she hadn't been watching him she'd wouldn't have seen it—then he shook his head once and Silence realized he wasn't going to tell her.

Her heart shrank.

"I didn't want to leave without sayin' me farewells." He strode to the bed with a small knife in his hand. "And I've somethin' for ye."

She looked at him and then at the knife, blinking sleepily. Did he expect her to become a pirate, too?

"Ye need to know how to defend yerself—defend Mary Darlin', too." His voice was gentle. "Come, I'll show ye."

He didn't say that Harry and Bert would have to be dead if it came down to her defending Mary Darling herself, but then he didn't have to.

Silence got out of the bed and stood before him in her chemise.

"Ye want to jab, quick and sharp like," he instructed. "Don't swipe, for yer knife is easily tangled that way."

He demonstrated a lightning fast blow.

Silence looked at him dubiously. "I'm not that quick."

"Ye will be with practice," he said. "Tomorrow I'll bring back padded jackets and ye can learn how to use the knife on me."

She raised her eyebrows. "You want me to stab you with a knife?"

"Aye," he said seriously. "Ye need to know how to kill a man."

She shook her head, folding her arms. She felt cold. "Even if you show me how, I won't ever do that."

He set his lips. "Then maim him. Thrust for the eyes, the throat, and the belly. That'll back off even the most insane o' men."

She shivered. Was the Vicar insane? She supposed he must be to pursue Michael so blindly. To send someone to kill a woman with vitriol. If it meant protecting Mary Darling from such a beast, she would learn how to wield a knife.

"Here," Michael said, offering her the knife. "Feel the weight. That's Spanish, that is, made by a fine swordsmith."

She didn't ask where he'd gotten the deadly little knife. She took the dagger and saw that it was rather pretty. The blade had been engraved with flowers of all things. The hilt was curved and fitted her palm perfectly. She weighed it. The dagger was heavy for its size.

Michael stood in back of her and wrapped his right arm around her to hold her hand and show her how to thrust the dagger. With his left he held her by the waist and prompted her movements. After several minutes Silence was panting, but Michael was not even breathing hard.

"Ye can keep it in a pocket under yer skirts or in yer garter," he said.

Silence wrinkled her nose. "Won't it rub?"

His eyelids drooped. "It'd better not. I wouldn't want yer tender skin chafed for the world."

She turned in his arms, the dagger falling to the floor, and looked up at him. His black eyes were weary and she could see worry for her in his face. The blue-black stubble of his beard shadowed his jaw and his wide, sensuous lips were slightly parted. She reached up to stroke through his hair, feeling the locks curling around her fingers in welcome. He hadn't told her what his business was in London, but she knew by his refusal to answer her question that it was something to do with his pirating—something dangerous. What if he were wounded—or worse, killed tonight? She might never see him again.

The thought sent an awful tremor through her belly. A world without Michael in it would be utterly dismal. Even if she lived apart from him, she wanted—always—to know that he was somewhere.

She stood on tiptoe and brushed her lips over his warm mouth, tasting the wine they'd drunk at dinner.

She heard him mutter a curse, then he was sweeping her into his arms and carrying her to the bed, placing her gently there.

"Why?" he whispered as he leaned over her, supported on one arm. "Why must ye be the one that haunts me dreams? I've seen ye weepin' night after bloody night since the day I sent ye from me palace with yer dress half undone. If I had it to do over again, I'd cut me own right hand off rather than hurt ye so. Will ye never be able to forgive me, Silence love?"

"I already have," she replied, cradling his cheek in her hand. "Long, long ago."

And it was true. She understood now the man he'd been that day—and the man he was today. The two men were the same—her Michael, cruel and gentle, autocratic and kind. If she loved him for his best parts, then she must in some way love him for his worst as well.

"Darlin'." He skimmed his warm lips over her cheekbone, down to her jaw.

"Michael," she whispered, longing, hoping. "Can you not—?"

"Hush." He turned his head, laying his cheek against hers. "Let us not argue."

She swallowed past the thickness in her throat. They'd

already been over this at dinner and come to an impasse: he refused to give up his pirating. There was no more to say on the matter—he was right: discussing it now would only lead to an argument and she didn't want that just before he went into danger.

So she smiled—or tried to at least, with lips that trembled—and stroked her fingers through his beautiful hair. "Will you lie with me, Michael O'Connor?"

He rose to look at her and she thought she saw something close to love in his black eyes. "If I were at death's door I'd stand and come to you."

She'd love this man for the rest of her life. Silence sat up and drew her chemise over her head, baring herself entirely to him. Then she lay down and opened her arms. "Come to me then."

He needed no further urging. He took her mouth like the marauding pirate he was. She opened gladly, accepting him, catching his tongue and sucking it. He growled and laid himself flat on her, pinning her to the bed. The feel of his coat and breeches against her bare skin was exotic. She wriggled a little, enjoying the friction on her thighs and belly, trying to push the coming sorrow from her mind. She couldn't change him, after all, only Michael himself could do that. If he refused to act, then she must accept that fact.

Accept and try to recover from the grief.

But he was moving lower now, going from one nipple to the other, licking and gently biting. She grasped the sheets in her hands, gasping at his fierce lovemaking.

"Spread yer legs for me now, sweetin'," he rasped as he sat back on his knees to unfasten his fall.

She complied, widening her thighs, watching him prepare himself for her.

He palmed his thick erection. "Will ye be wantin' this now, madam?"

"Yes, please," she whispered. She wanted to engrave the sight of him thus, about to make love to her, in her mind.

He nodded and taking her by the hips pulled her toward him. He settled her bottom in his lap and pushed the tip of his cock down to rub at her entrance.

She whimpered from the pleasure, the anticipation of what was coming next: joining her body with Michael's. Submitting to him.

Slowly, slowly he inserted himself in her. The angle was extreme, but because of it, his penis seemed to slide against something sensitive inside her. She felt herself already beginning to break apart—and he wasn't even all the way in.

"Is it sweet, m'darlin'?" he asked, panting.

She only sighed an answer—the act of speaking seemed too difficult.

Suddenly he was over her, his weight pressing her into the mattress, his cock sinking to the hilt in her. He was over her, *in* her, powerful and male. "Answer, m'love. Is it what ye want?"

Oh, she knew well what he really asked. She raised her eyelids languidly as he stroked out and then into her again, his penis rubbing against sensitive flesh, his body dominating hers. "Yes, it's what I want."

"And this?" he asked, face flushed, mouth grim. "Does this meet wi' yer pleasure?"

He twisted his hips, grinding his pelvis against her, his hips widening her legs until she was completely open, completely vulnerable.

She swallowed, awash in a sea of pleasure, close to tears. "You know it does."

"Ah, good," he breathed as his great chest rose and fell faster. "For I cannot imagine a thing more sweet than me cock in yer cunny. This is everythin' good and right in the world. This is what ye and I were made for."

She blinked back tears, for he was telling her that he cared for her—as much as he was able.

"Is it enough?" he rasped, his strokes growing swifter, his cock grinding against her clitoris.

She closed her eyes, drowning in his lovemaking, pushing everything else aside.

"Silence," he said. "Is it enough?"

She opened her eyes with an enormous effort and smiled up at him. "I love you."

His eyes widened at her words and he roared, still pistoning in and out of her. The feel of his loss of control, the rush of emotion made her come as well, sudden and hard. A warm bubble expanded inside her, reaching her belly, her chest, her limbs and her fingers, until she shook with love and fulfillment.

Until she thought she might die of ecstasy and sorrow.

He collapsed on her, panting, and the rough abrasion of his coat on her tender nipples sent an aftershock to her center.

"Thank ye," he said, stroking her hair. "Thank ye."

But she turned her head away, afraid he would see the grief gathering in her eyes.

In a moment more he got up from her and set himself to rights as she lay there, her damp body cooling in the night air.

"I'll be back by luncheon tomorrow, m'love," he murmured and bent to kiss her mouth.

She summoned a smile, the hardest thing she'd ever done in her life, but she didn't want him to remember her sad with grief.

He frowned. "Are ye all right?"

She raised her brows, saying lightly, "Your lovemaking can be quite devastating."

He grinned and she stared at him greedily, trying to memorize the sight.

"I'll wear yer scent on me body tonight," he said wickedly. "And every time I smell it I'll know yer waitin' here for me."

He turned then and left the room, his stride brisk.

Silence lay there, feeling the seep of his semen from her body, and counted to one hundred.

Then she got up and washed quickly. She dressed in the plain brown gown she'd had on when he'd come for her at Caire House—so long ago it seemed now. There was very little to gather—the Spanish dagger and some things of Mary's. She hesitated over the little book with the courageous sailors, but in the end she took that, as well. He'd meant it for Mary, after all.

She made one quick trip to Michael's room and then opened the door to the corridor—and found Harry dozing in a chair. She'd only taken one step when his eyelids rose.

"Goin' for a midnight stroll, are ye?" he asked amiably, but she wasn't fooled. Harry was eyeing the small bag she carried her things in.

She squared her shoulders. "I'm going home, Harry."

THE DAWN WAS just breaking when Mick rode up the lane to Windward House, weary in both mind and body. He'd found a ship for Bran easily enough—bound for the West

Indies, a long voyage. The boy had said never a word to him all the long way to London. He'd seemed beaten in both mind and body and Mick hadn't the heart to try and talk to him.

Putting Bran on that ship had been the last thing that had gone simply. Through bribery, guile, and sheer ruthlessness Mick had been able to enter the Vicar's house—only to find Charlie Grady gone. Either the man had been warned or his damned luck had held out. Mick had been forced to slink away and hope for another opportunity to strike. So it was with a sense of welcome relief that he caught sight of the house.

He pulled his nag to a halt and sat just looking at it a moment. The early sun made the brick glow pinkish-orange. The green shoots around the foundation had lengthened and grown yellow buds. Soon the daffodils would bloom. Mick smiled tiredly. How he looked forward to showing Mary Darling the pretty flowers when they bloomed. He and the baby would pick a posy for Silence and present it to her and then the three of them would sit down to luncheon or tea or some other meal and he would listen as Silence chided him about his food being too rich while he tempted her with some exotic dainty.

God, it was good to be home.

Mick rode around the back and impatiently threw the reins to a sleepy groom. He went in through the kitchens, waving to Bittner and Mrs. Bittner, enjoying their morning tea. Lad, who'd been dozing by the hearth, stood and wagged his tail.

"Sir—" Bittner called as Mick strode past, but Mick didn't stop.

He took the stairs two at a time and then paused at the

top. Where was Harry? Damn it, if Harry or Bert were sleeping, he'd dock them their portion of the next haul.

Mick burst into Silence's bedroom in a rush, only to pull up short when he saw that the bed was empty. He went through the connecting door to find that his room was empty as well. Only a pair of stockings were laid neatly on his pillow.

Mick stood a moment, staring at the stockings, an awful foreboding crawling up his spine. Slowly he picked them up. They were of different sizes, the heel of one completely wrong. He recognized them as the stockings Silence had knit in the carriage all the way from her sister's house. They hadn't been done when they'd arrived at Windward House, but now they obviously were, folded neatly as if they were a present.

For a moment Mick held the ugly stockings in his hand, his mind blank. With an effort he made his legs move, climbed up the stairs to the next floor, and checked the nursery.

A maid slept in the bed next to Mary's empty cot.

Mick shook her awake roughly. "Where are they?"

The girl rubbed her eyes. "They went away in the night wi' Mr. Harry and Mr. Bert, sir."

But Mick was already turning away, dazed, disbelieving.

She'd left him. Silence had left him and taken Mary Darling with her.

Chapter Seventeen

Well now Clever John had everything he'd ever wished for: a large and prosperous kingdom, an invincible army to defend his lands, and a treasure chest that never could be emptied. He was awash in wealth and good fortune. Kings and princes sent their daughters, seeking a match with the powerful King Clever John. But no matter how lovely the princess, Clever John merely turned his head aside, his gaze searching the skies for the glimpse of a rainbow wing....
—from *Clever John*

Caire House in London was even more opulent than Lord Caire's country estate. A week later Silence sat in one of the "lesser" sitting rooms in the fashionable town house, almost too afraid to move. All around her were elegant furnishings, fragile bric-a-brac, and plush carpets and drapes. Actually, she thought with a pang, the richness of the rooms reminded her a bit of Michael's palace.

Except everything was terribly tasteful here.

She watched as Mary Darling played with a stack of wooden bricks that the housekeeper had found for her. The sight should've brought Silence joy: a happy, healthy baby innocently playing. But nothing seemed to bring her joy anymore. Silence sighed, propping her chin in her hand. What was the matter with her? She'd lived well enough, *contentedly* enough, before Michael. Could she not do so again?

A maid entered the sitting room. "Would you like some tea, ma'am?"

Silence pasted on a smile. "Tea would be lovely. And could you make a pot for Mr. Harry and Mr. Bert, too, please?"

The little maid blushed and rolled her eyes. "They've already had two pots of tea this morning. Cook is spoiling them something awful."

One corner of Silence's mouth curled up at the thought of Harry and Bert wheedling treats from the female servants in the kitchen. Both Harry and Bert guarded her now, as well as a half dozen of Michael's crew. The men had simply appeared the morning after Silence had knocked on the door of Temperance's London home. She was lucky, since neither Caire nor Temperance were in residence, that the housekeeper knew her by sight.

Silence twitched at a thread on her old brown dress. Apparently Michael had moved quickly to safeguard her and Mary Darling when he found them gone. Silence was grateful, if a little guilty, to have the guards. She could just see one of Michael's pirates lounging outside the sitting room as the door swung closed behind the maid.

Harry had given Silence strict orders to stay inside Caire House until Michael dealt with the Vicar. Such a restriction might've made her restless in the past, but no longer. She couldn't seem to find the enthusiasm to do much of anything.

There was a commotion from the front hallway and Mary Darling looked up.

Temperance swept into the sitting room a moment later. "Goodness! Where did all these brutish men come from?"

"They're guards." Silence wrinkled her nose apologetically. "Michael insisted on them."

"Well, I should hope so!" Temperance crossed to Silence and gave her a hug before pulling back and looking in her face. "How are you, dear?"

Silence bit her lip to keep it from trembling. "Fine. I'm sorry to have taken over your home."

"Don't be silly," Temperance said.

The maid returned with a tray of tea and Temperance waved for her to put it on a low table in front of the settee.

"Thank you, Perkins," Temperance said as she sat on the settee beside Silence. She waited for the maid to leave before turning to her sister. "I take it that you're not safe yet."

Silence grimaced. "No. Not while the Vicar is still alive."

"Which brings me to the subject of how you left Caire's country estate," Temperance said.

Silence winced. "I'm sorry."

"We spent hours searching for you and Mary Darling," Temperance said in a much too calm voice as she poured the tea. "It wasn't until one of the maids confessed that she'd glanced out a window and saw you walking away with a 'tall, handsome as sin man,' that we realized what had happened. I was all for traveling at once to London, but Caire persuaded me to wait a bit." Temperance gave her a jaundiced look. "I think he rather feared what I might do to you."

"I never meant to make you worry so," Silence said in a rush. "I did leave you a note."

"Not a very helpful one," Temperance said darkly.

"It's just that he asked me to come with him—"

"And so you did." Temperance sighed and sat back with her dish of tea. "Without a thought for us."

"I'm afraid so," Silence said in a small voice.

Temperance took a sip. "He's bad, you know that, and yet you went off with him without a backward glance."

Silence took her cup of tea and held it near her face without drinking. She inhaled the fragrant steam. "I've left him."

Temperance set down her cup. "Have you?"

Silence only nodded.

Temperance eyed her. "Well ... I suppose that's good."

Silence closed her eyes.

"Isn't it?" Temperance asked.

"I don't know."

"Why did you leave him exactly?"

Silence shook her head, staring at her steaming cup of tea, trying to put into words the decision that had seemed so cut and dried a week ago. "He won't quit his pirating, even though he has enough money, from what I can see, to live happily the rest of his life."

"You asked him to quit?"

"Yes."

"Well," Temperance picked up her teacup again, murmuring over its rim, "that by itself would be enough for me to leave him."

"Would it?" Silence traced the edge of her teacup, considering. "I think it would've been enough for me as well—before I went to live with him."

"But now?"

"Now ..." Silence leaned forward, looking at her sister

intently, trying to convey what was in her heart. "He's no longer just a pirate to me. He's Charming Mickey O'Connor, notorious river pirate, but he's also Michael, a man who loves butterflies. Who told me about the worst parts of his childhood. Who took me to the opera and sat as if entranced by the music. Who sings to his daughter. Don't you see? I might be fascinated by Charming Mickey, but I could never love him. Michael I can—I *do*—love."

Temperance gave her a level look. "Even though he's a pirate?"

Silence met her gaze, lifting her chin. "Yes. I hate how he makes his money, but I love Michael."

Temperance sighed. "Then why did you leave him?"

"Because I don't think he'll ever truly see me as an equal, a partner, someone to trust and love for all time. Someone who is a person in her own right. Someone worthy of making a commitment—*changing*—for." Silence's lips trembled. "I wanted him to choose a life with me instead of a life of pirating—and he couldn't."

"Oh, sweetheart."

Silence gasped, trying to smile and failing. "I love him, Temperance, and I've been trying to see how I can stop, but there doesn't seem to be a way."

Her elder sister sighed. "No, I don't really think that love is something that one can control."

"And it's not like the love I thought I had with William," Silence said, closing her eyes. "That was sweet and light—a girl's fantasy of love. This...*this* is violent and emotional, and sometimes I think I don't even like him. How can that be?" She looked at her sister. "How can I love him and dislike him at the same time?"

"I don't know," Temperance said. "But sometimes I

feel the same way about Caire. Sometimes he says or does things that drive me to distraction. Yet I know always that I love him and that he loves me." She bit her lip. "Does O'Connor love you?"

"I think..." Silence paused to pat at her eyes with a handkerchief. "I think he does, though he's never said so. You don't truly know him. He can be very gentle with Mary Darling and me. He showed me how to eat an artichoke, and he has a big ugly dog that adores him and follows him everywhere, and...and..."

Well, she certainly couldn't tell her sister about Michael's lovemaking! Silence blushed at the thought.

"He has been kind to Mary Darling?" Temperance asked slowly.

"Yes! So loving and kind, you would not credit it."

"Then shouldn't you have left Mary with him?"

"I thought of it," Silence said quietly. "He is a good father. But he refuses to give up his pirating. What sort of life would that be for her?"

"Well, then," Temperance said, "that settles it, doesn't it? You did the right thing in taking her away."

"Do you think so?" Silence asked.

"Yes." Temperance smiled tenderly. "I know it feels like the end of the world now, but you'll get over him, I know you will. And when you do, we'll find a good man for you. One who loves you and can take care of you."

Voices came from outside the hallway. Michael's guard was saying something loud and angry.

Temperance sighed and stood. "I suppose your guardians are shooing away one of my afternoon visitors. I'd better go see who it is."

Silence nodded absently. Her sister's earlier words

were kind, but they were useless. For while her head knew she had done the right thing in leaving Michael, her heart was not so sure. Her heart didn't want a good man at all.

Her heart wanted a pirate.

MICK LOUNGED ON his throne, a near-empty bottle of brandy beside him, and watched as silver and gold coins fell from his fingers. There were shillings and guineas, but also coins from shores far distant from England. Coins with eagles stamped on them, coins with the heads of princes and kings, coins with symbols he didn't recognize.

When he was a lad he'd found it fascinating that there were so many kinds of money in the world. Sailors often brought back souvenir coins from the countries they'd made port in, and Mick would find the coins as he hurriedly searched the ships he raided. He'd take them and later examine the coins, turning them over in his fingers, looking at the strange marks, the stylized profiles. And then he would place the coins in a carved ivory box he'd stolen from a ship's captain.

The ivory box was open on Mick's knee as he stirred the coins within. It might be a king's ransom that he had in the box. He didn't know since he'd never bothered counting the coins. He held a particularly large one up, as big across as the length of his thumb. Mary Darling would like it, he thought. She'd grab for it and all the other coins in his box like a greedy magpie.

But Mary Darling wasn't here.

With a sudden movement, he swatted the ivory box off his knee. Coins flew, sliding across the marble floor and the box itself hit the tiles with a *crack*, breaking in half. Lad, who had been sleeping beside the throne, jumped up, his tail between his legs and ran to hide behind a statue of a Roman matron.

Pepper cleared his throat at the door behind the throne.

"Get the hell out, Pepper," Mick said without heat. All he felt was a vast, terrible weariness.

He'd left Windward House a week ago. He couldn't stand the place without Silence in it. Every room reminded him of her. He kept turning, thinking he'd seen her out of the corner of his eye. He'd been going mad, so he'd come here to his palace and commenced drinking. But no matter how drunk he got, he still dreamed of her tear-stained face every night. She'd left him, but she continued to haunt him, damn her.

"I would retreat, sir, as I did the other times you ordered me from this room," Pepper said precisely, "but I feel I should tell you that your men are worried."

Mick laid his head in his hand. "What the fuck do they have to be worried about?"

Pepper cleared his throat again. "They wish to know when you'll go raiding again and if you'll be returning to the dining room for supper in the near future."

Mick felt a headache start in his right temple, dull and throbbing. "Tell them it's none o' their damned business when I want to raid and where I take me supper."

"Ah," Pepper said. He sounded nervous. Mick couldn't remember Pepper ever sounding nervous. "Then might we discuss your various investments? The price of gold has tripled in the last five months. I thought if we were to sell some of your gold and reinvest the money in, say, jewels or silver plate, we would see a tidy profit, perhaps of—"

"Damn the money," Mick muttered.

Pepper paused, cocking his head inquisitively. "I beg your pardon?"

"I said damn the money!" Mick roared, rising from his throne. "Fuck the gold! Bugger the silver plate, damn the jewels, the furs and silks, the china, the books, the spices and tea, and the furniture!"

"But . . . but . . . ," Pepper stuttered.

"Fuck all me money!" Mick bellowed. "It don't bloody matter anymore!"

He kicked a barrel, tipping it over and sending cloves spilling across the floor. Lad whimpered from behind the Roman matron.

"Sir," Pepper began.

The door to the throne room opened and Bob thrust his head around it, looking wary. "Letter."

He ducked back, holding the paper out from behind the door.

Pepper hurried over and took it, breaking the seal. Something fluttered to the floor.

Mick casually knocked over a China vase, watching with bitter satisfaction as it shattered to pieces in the cloves.

"Sir, you need to look at this." Pepper was suddenly by his side, trembling, but proffering the missive bravely.

Mick took it and glanced down.

I have them. Meet me where your mother lies.

He was still staring down when Pepper shoved something into his hand. Mick looked at it and froze. It was a tiny lock of hair, as inky black as his own.

The guards he'd sent, Harry and Bert, all of them, they'd all failed.

"Saddle a horse for me," Mick whispered. His chest had constricted with dread.

Pepper ran from the room.

Mick strode to his bedroom, splashed water on his face

and neck and made sure he carried his knives on him. He took up a pistol, loaded it, and wrapped a wide belt about his waist to stick it in. Then he ran down the stairs. He couldn't let fear rule him. They were alive and well.

And if they weren't, he'd rain bloody retribution down on the Vicar.

The horse was out front and he took the reins without word to the boy waiting there.

Pepper stood anxiously by. "Won't you take some of the men with you, sir?"

"No," Mick said and wheeled the horse around. "This's between me and the fuckin' Vicar."

He urged the horse into a canter, weaving in and out of the late afternoon bustle. He made it to St. Giles-in-the-Fields church in under five minutes, dismounted, and tied the nag to the fence.

Inside, the churchyard was quiet. He turned a corner of the graveyard path and saw the Vicar standing by Mam's grave. No one else was in sight. Which didn't mean his usual guards weren't about.

Mick was on him in another two strides. He grabbed the older man's neck cloth. "Where are they?"

The Vicar stared up at him with his ruined face and laughed. "Oh, Mickey boy, how should I know?"

Mick took the lock of hair from his pocket and thrust it into the Vicar's face. "Whose is this then?"

"Your mother's," Charlie Grady said softly. "She gave me a lock of her hair when we were courting and naturally I kept it all these years. Your mother had that same black curly hair as you and the little lassie." He winked. "You ought to've introduced me to my granddaughter, Mickey. Now I'm afraid I'll have to be doing it myself."

"I'll see ye in hell first," Mick breathed, shoving the other man away.

Gravel crunched beneath a booted foot behind him.

Mickey whirled, but the Vicar had succeeded in distracting him just long enough. He was a fraction too slow. A split second too late. The knife was knocked from his hand and his arms were seized. Suddenly there were soldiers everywhere in the graveyard.

Charlie tutted. "Oh, I have no doubt we're both destined for hell, son, but I fancy you'll see it afore me."

"Fuck ye," Mick spat.

An officer in a white wig limped up to Mick. "Mickey O'Connor I arrest you on the charge of piracy."

"ARRESTED!" SILENCE LAID down the knife she'd been using to butter a piece of bread for Mary Darling's tea. They were in the lesser sitting room of Caire's town house, the sun shining brightly on the silver tea set in front of Silence. She stared dazedly at Bert and Harry, both men solemn and standing shoulder-to-shoulder in solidarity as they brought her the horrible news. "But how? Michael's been an outlaw for most of his life. How was he captured?"

Harry looked uneasily at Bert and then squared his shoulders. "'Twere a trap, ma'am, laid by the Vicar 'imself. Word is, the Vicar said 'e 'ad ye and the babe."

"Dear God." Michael had rushed to save them and in doing so had walked into a trap. She swallowed and stared at the bread on a pretty china plate. The sight made her stomach roil.

"You must leave as soon as possible," Temperance said from the doorway. She was out of breath as if she'd run from wherever in the town house that she'd heard the news. "If the Vicar has Mickey O'Connor, he'll come after you next. I've ordered the carriage made ready. We can have you out of London before dark."

"No!" Silence stood. "I'm not leaving London."

Harry looked uneasy. "The Vicar'll still be lookin' for ye and the babe, ma'am."

"I realize that," Silence said. "And I'll take all possible precautions, but I'll not leave while Michael is in prison."

"But dearest," Temperance protested, her sherry-brown eyes wide and distressed.

"No. You can't ask it of me." Silence looked at her sister and drew a quavering breath. "You know full well what the likely outcome of a trial will be."

Temperance closed her eyes, but didn't reply. She didn't have to.

The punishment for piracy was hanging.

"To the completion of the brand-new Home for Unfortunate Infants and Foundling Children!" Lady Hero raised her small glass of sherry high.

"Here! Here!" Around the cramped meeting room the members of the Ladies' Syndicate for the Benefit of the Home for Unfortunate Infants and Foundling Children obediently raised their wineglasses in toast.

Isabel Beckinhall smiled and sipped her wine. Who'd have thought over a month ago when she'd attended her first meeting that the Ladies' Syndicate would turn out to be so much *fun*?

She selected a scone from the tray Mary Whitsun was carefully holding and looked at Lady Hero. "When are the children due to move into the new home?"

"Next week, we hope," Lady Hero said, still flushing prettily from the triumph of her toast. "Lady Caire and I examined the new home just yesterday, before she left town, but I think Mr. Makepeace will have to do a final inspection as well with one of us."

"Can't you go, my lady?" Lady Penelope asked, her pretty face creased into a confused frown.

"I'm leaving tomorrow with Lord Griffin," Lady Hero said. The color which had begun to recede from her face rushed back. "He's to show me the ruins at his country estates to the north."

Lady Margaret, who was Lord Griffin's sister and thus Lady Hero's sister-in-law, snorted delicately. "That's not the only thing he'll show you at his estate, I'll wager."

"Megs!" Lady Hero's shocked gasp was rather ruined by a giggle. "How much of that sherry have you drunk?"

Lady Margaret squinted at her glass. "This's only my second glass."

"The wine is very good," Miss Greaves broke in tactfully. "Simply perfect to toast our success with."

Lady Hero shot her a grateful look.

"Hmm," Isabel murmured as she took another scone— really it was the orphan girls' best pastry. "The sherry is delicious, but it's a pity you were forced to smuggle it past Mr. Makepeace."

"I didn't exactly smuggle it," Lady Hero said with dignity.

"But you did have it packaged in a box with no markings," Lady Margaret pointed out.

Lady Hero wrinkled her nose. "It's just that Mr. Makepeace is so…"

"Dour," Isabel said.

"Stern," Lady Phoebe piped up from where she sat next to her sister.

"*Religious.*" Lady Penelope shuddered.

"And rather lacking in a sense of humor," Isabel added to round the whole thing off. She bit into her tender scone.

"But he is quite handsome nevertheless," Miss Greaves said judiciously.

Lady Penelope tossed her head. "Handsome if you like severe, unyielding gentlemen." The faint curl of her lip indicated that *she*, at least, did not. "I do think that the home is sadly lacking in a female influence now that Mrs. Hollingbrook has abandoned her brother."

"We're a female influence!" Lady Margaret said somewhat indignantly.

"But we're not here all the time," Lady Penelope pointed out. "'Tisn't the same."

"What about the female servants?" Lady Isabel asked, amused. She herself did not subscribe to the idea that Mr. Makepeace needed female help—or any help, for that matter—to run the home, but she was fascinated by Lady Penelope's prejudiced and somewhat convoluted thought process.

"*Servants,*" Lady Penelope sniffed and that seemed to be her entire argument.

Isabel hid a smile and popped the last bite of her scone into her mouth.

"In any case," Lady Hero said hastily, "we need someone to meet Mr. Makepeace at the new home the day after tomorrow. Someone tactful, charming, and able to deal with Mr. Makepeace's er...sternness." Her eyes met Isabel's and Lady Hero smiled sweetly—and rather craftily. "You'd be quite perfect, Lady Beckinhall."

Chapter Eighteen

> *The years went by and Clever John grew old. His once*
> *black hair turned snowy white, his broad shoulders*
> *stooped, and his strong hand shook. And in all those years*
> *he never again saw Tamara. Finally the day came when*
> *he knew his time on earth was drawing to a close. He sat*
> *on his grand golden throne in his wonderful castle, with*
> *his treasure chest beside him overflowing with jewels but*
> *he had eyes for none of that. Instead he examined five*
> *brightly colored feathers upon his lap....*
> —from *Clever John*

Mick O'Connor lay on a bed of straw in Newgate Prison's castle—the strongest cell in the prison—and contemplated his life.

The life that very well might end on the morn tomorrow.

After a month of prison he had an escape plan, of course, for he was a man who'd spent a lifetime planning. The castle was near break-proof, and a dozen of Captain Trevillion's dragoons had been assigned to guard him. They were immune to bribes, but that didn't mean he couldn't see visitors. Pepper had made several calls, helping Mick to set his affairs in order, and it'd been child's play to smuggle out an escape plan to the rest of his men.

Mick had calculated that the best time to make an escape was just before the execution cart reached the gallows tomorrow morning. There would be crowds of people, families out for a holiday, hawkers selling meat pies and fruit, and of course scores of soldiers. But the soldiers would be hampered by the crowds. If his men made a commotion just as the cart neared Tyburn gallows, they would draw the attention of both the soldiers and the crowds. During the confusion a second group of his men might be able to rescue him.

It was a long shot escape plan, but it was his only chance. He'd gambled before on his life and won. Why not now, as well?

On the whole Mick had few, if any, regrets. He didn't regret pirating, he didn't regret the men he'd killed in his life, and he sure as bloody hell didn't regret throwing vitriol into Charlie's face and saving himself from a buggering at the age of thirteen.

There was one thing he did wish he could change, though. He regretted that he hadn't found the proper words to make Silence stay with him. He should've lied, should've told her he'd give up the pirating, give up the palace, give up anything she damned well wanted if she'd only stay with him. Hell, maybe he should've really given up the pirating for her. He wanted only to sit at a table with her and feed her exotic foods that made her beautiful hazel eyes widen with wonder. And later he'd make her eyes widen in other ways. He'd caress her creamy skin and tell her—

Tell her what?

Jaysus. He'd tell her that he loved her. That she was the only woman save his poor mam that he'd truly loved.

Mick squeezed his eyes shut, ignoring the laughter, the

moaning, and the cries that were Newgate Prison. If he had it to do over again he would've chained her to his bed and made sweet love to Silence until she admitted that she couldn't live without him.

Because God knew that he couldn't live without her.

He'd stay with her always, perhaps even marry her, if she insisted. He chuckled to himself to think of Charming Mickey O'Connor domesticated. And if they someday had a babe—

His eyes suddenly snapped open on that thought.

He'd never considered—because he'd always thought she'd *stay*, damn it—that she might be with his child.

Jaysus! Mick jumped to his feet, pacing the length of his leg irons, barely six feet. If Silence were with child, she'd be frantic. He didn't give a damn or not if his child were born a bastard, but she would be deeply ashamed. She'd be an outcast. Her family loved her, but they were very strict. Would they toss her into the street? Where would she find the funds to care for both Mary Darling and a new babe? Dear God.

"Thinkin' on that noose?" the gaoler, a dirty little man who was puffed with pride that he was guarding the notorious Mickey O'Connor asked. Of course the real guarding was done by the dragoons, but that didn't bother the gaoler. His ugly face appeared at the barred window on the cell door, fingering his own neck. "The last one we 'ung 'ad 'is neck stretched near a foot."

Mick ignored the man, going to sit on the clean straw pallet he'd purchased at an exorbitant sum, his head in his hands. After a bit he no longer heard the gaoler's voice, so the man must've grown weary of taunting a prisoner who wouldn't respond.

But that didn't matter to Mick. All that mattered was Silence and what he might've done to her.

Mick closed his eyes again and did something he hadn't done since he was thirteen.

He prayed.

THE STREETS WERE still dark, the dawn only an hour away when Silence made her way to Newgate prison.

"This's barmy," Bert growled. "Sneakin' about the streets in the dark. 'Imself will 'ave our 'eads."

"Don't think even 'Imself can 'ave us punished, where 'e's now," Harry said soberly.

"I need to see him, Bert," Silence said. "Don't you understand? I love him. I can't just let him go to his—"

She cut herself off with a choked sob. *No, not now.* There would be time afterward to weep and wail. Now she had to be strong for Michael. She hadn't seen him in over month. Winter and Temperance hadn't wanted her to visit him in Newgate Prison during the trial. Only with his death sentence had they relented, admitting that it might be best for her to see him one last time.

Harry patted her shoulder awkwardly. "We do understand, ma'am. Like a fairy story it is, yer love for 'Imself. And we'll make sure ye see 'im afore . . ."

Harry broke off and gulped.

The two guards might be stoic about it, but Silence had seen their faces on the day the news of Michael's sentence had been announced. Harry's big ugly face had sagged into permanent lines of sorrow, while Bert had surreptitiously swiped at his eyes when he thought no one was looking.

The men kept close to her as they neared the prison.

Silence held the lantern so they might have their hands free should anything untoward happen.

Silence shivered and pulled her cloak more firmly about herself as Newgate Prison loomed suddenly in the dark, hulking and ominous. The ancient gate spanned the road, but next to it was the slightly newer prison. A guard with a light was dozing by the big double doors. He woke and glared at them as they approached.

"We're 'ere to see Mickey O'Connor," Harry said pleasantly.

"No one's to see the pirate," the guard snapped.

Harry tossed a coin at the man, which the guard caught easily.

The guard looked at the coin and sneered. "A shillin'?"

Bert bristled. "A shillin's quite fair!"

The guard started to say something more, but Harry sighed and gave him another coin.

This time the guard smiled. "Ye'll be gettin' closer."

"'Ighway robbery is what this is!" Bert exploded, advancing on the guard.

"All right! All right!" the guard said, backing a step. "I'll let ye see 'im, but I'm makin' a special deal jus' for ye."

Bert muttered something rather offensive about "deals" and the guard's parentage, but fortunately the guard didn't seem to hear. He opened the big door, leading them inside a gloomy corridor. It was still dark and so the inmates of this place were mostly asleep. But here and there could be heard the sounds of humanity: sighs, mumbles, snores, and coughs.

The guard led them through a courtyard with sleeping forms and up a series of steps. On the upper level were barred cells to one side of the corridor and a locked door at the end. The guard opened it to reveal a small anteroom and a dozen or more armed soldiers, standing or dozing in chairs.

The guard went to the cell door at the back of the room and scraped his huge key ring across the window bars, making them clang. He unlocked the door, stepped inside, peering, and shouted, "Oi! O'Connor! Ye got—"

An arm shot out from the dark cell and caught the guard by the throat. Michael stepped forward, still holding the guard, and looked at Silence.

His inky hair was down about his shoulders. He was in his shirtsleeves, despite the chill of the prison, the fine lace at neck and sleeves incongruent with the surroundings. Thick chains rattled when he moved for he had leg irons on both feet. But his cell was surprisingly clean and furnished with not only a pallet, but a chair and table with quills, ink, and papers on it as well. A small brazier glowed near the pallet. Michael looked, on the whole, as arrogant and strong as the first time she'd seen him sitting on his throne. Not even prison, it seemed, could daunt Michael O'Connor.

Something inside Silence rejoiced at his brutal power.

His black eyes glittered in the lantern light. "Bert, take this vermin and fetch the prison chaplain."

He let go of the guard who fell back several steps, gasping. The soldiers had risen at the interruption and one approached. "What's this then, Mickey?"

Michael shook his head. "Nothin' that need bother ye, George. Seems I've visitors."

George the soldier frowned heavily. "The captain won't like that."

"He's not here to care, is he?" Michael asked him,

but his eyes were on Silence. Absently he twisted off the moonstone ring from his finger and tossed it to the guard.

He was looking at her as if trying to memorize her every feature.

She bit the inside of her cheek to keep from sobbing at the thought. She must be strong.

"I prayed ye'd come," Michael said low to her.

The soldier, apparently satisfied that Michael wasn't trying to escape, pocketed the ring, and stepped back along with Harry.

Silence came closer. "Is there any way to get you out of here?" she whispered. "I could have Harry and Bert bring the rest of your men."

He shook his head a faint smile on his lips. "No one escapes from this part o' Newgate Prison, darlin'. Besides, they fear me so much that they've brought in dragoons to guard me. A rescue try would only lead to me men dyin' without me gettin' free."

"Dear Lord." Silence stared at him, not knowing what to say.

"I've had a bit o' time to think in here, love, and I wonder if ye might do me a very great favor," Michael said softly.

"You know I will." Silence searched his dear face.

His wide mouth quirked. "There ye go, agreein' to things without knowin' what they might be."

She sighed and touched his shoulder with a trembling hand. "I'd do anything for you, Michael, you know that."

"Except stay with me?" He tried to step toward her, but the leg irons brought him up short.

She shook her head, a tear slipping past her lashes. All

her arguments and fears meant nothing now. "That . . . that was different. If you had only—"

He laid a warm finger against her lips. "Never mind. I'm sorry I spoke o' it. I didn't mean to aggrieve ye."

She looked at him, mutely, her eyes swimming with tears despite her best efforts.

"Come here," he whispered and pulled her into his warm arms. He leaned his forehead against hers. "I'm sorry, so sorry, I made a mess o' things at Windward House. I should've known ye and the babe were all I need—all I'll ever need. The money, the piratin' they were jus' shields I was holdin' on to, fearful-like. 'Twasn't me best decision, love."

"Oh, Michael." She closed her eyes, willing the tears back, for his honest admission made her love him even more. If only this wasn't their last moment together. If only they had weeks and years to discover everything about each other . . .

"But I've somethin' important to say to ye now," Michael rumbled softly. "What I meant to say when ye came in was that the very great favor I'd like o' ye is for ye to marry me."

She pulled back and stared at him in shock. "Is that why you sent for the prison chaplain?"

"Aye." He smiled, dimples slashing into his olive cheeks. "He'll do most anythin' if the money's right. Not what I'd like for ye, love, but beggars can't be choosers. Will ye marry me, Silence Hollingbrook?"

It was silly but her heart leaped at his words, even here. She didn't even hesitate to think. "Yes, oh, yes, I'll marry you, Michael."

He grinned and kissed her fast and hard just as Bert came back with the guard. An elderly man with a shock of white hair and a bleary expression from having been woken up accompanied them.

The chaplain turned out to have a lovely, resonant voice. Silence stood in a dazed and delighted fog and in a few minutes found herself married to Michael.

"Here," Michael said, taking his ruby and gold ring off his little finger and putting it on her thumb. "That's to remember me by."

She stared down at the worn gold and the rich beauty of the dark red ruby. It was his first ring, she remembered, touched by his gesture. The ring was a little big, so she wrapped a piece of thread about it to hold it on her thumb. She had to blink hard then because it all seemed like both a dream and a nightmare. They were married—and he'd be hung by the neck in only a few hours.

Michael beckoned George over and had a whispered consultation with him at the end of which he gave the rest of his rings to the soldier.

"Only for an hour, mind," George said.

Michael held out his hand to Silence. "Spend a little time with me, Mrs. O'Connor."

She went into his arms gladly, and the cell door was locked behind her.

She sighed, laying her head on his warm chest, listening to the strong beat of his heart. He stroked his hand through her hair, his touch gentle, but she felt the tremble in his fingers. Suddenly it was too much, the sentence, the marriage, all the years after tomorrow without him.

"Oh, Michael." She closed her eyes, despair overwhelming her. "I...I don't know if I can live if you—"

"Aye." His voice was firm, commanding. He took her face between his big palms and looked into her eyes. His black eyes were fierce even in the dim light. "Aye, ye can live. For me, for Mary Darlin', for yerself. Promise me that, love. Promise me, ye'll live, and ye'll thrive, no matter what comes tomorrow."

She swallowed. She couldn't be weak when he needed her strong. "Yes. Yes, of course."

"That's me girl." He brushed his lips over her forehead, breathing the words. "That's me love."

The tears overflowed, coursing down her cheeks. "I love you, Michael."

He laid his cheek against hers. "I've written out a will for Pepper, me man o' business."

She tried to protest, but he pulled back to look her in the eye. His face was grave. "Hush, now, love, ye must listen to me words. I've left instructions for Pepper to manage yer money for ye. I think it best ye and Mary go to live at Windward House. It's quiet there and secret. Me servants and Harry and Bert can take care of ye. I'm hopin' that the Vicar might see it in himself to be satisfied once I've gone, but we can't take that chance. I've made arrangements for me men to guard ye until Charlie Grady is dead. And that, too, I've arranged for."

Silence stared at him, stunned. He'd planned it all, made sure she and Mary Darling would be well taken care of after his death. He hadn't said he loved her, but his actions spoke much louder than any words could.

"Silence?" he asked. "Do me plans meet with yer approval?"

"Yes," she gulped. "Yes, of course."

He leaned his forehead against hers. "I want ye to be happy, me love. Ye and Mary Darlin'."

She choked then, unable to speak. What words were

beautiful enough, sublime enough to convey all her heart wanted to express in this moment? They simply didn't exist.

His eyes were sad as he watched her as if he knew somehow what she was thinking. "Come lie with me, m'love."

She wrapped her arms around his neck and hugged him close.

But when Michael began to tug her toward the back of the cell and a pallet, she clutched at his shirt. "What if they look? The soldiers?"

He shook his head. "I paid them well not to peek. Bert and Harry will make sure o' it."

Silence glanced over her shoulder and saw that all the men outside had moved away from the barred window in the door. The only light in the cell came from the little window, leaving the back wall—and a pallet against it—in near darkness.

She looked back at Michael, peering in the gloom.

His voice was deep as he squeezed her hand. "Come and be me wife."

He was her husband now.

Despite the sorrow of this place, despite what would happen all too soon, that small fact lit a spark of joy within Silence. She was married to Michael O'Connor.

She was married to the man she loved.

And since time was short, she lifted up on tiptoes and drew his face down to kiss him.

"I love you," she whispered against his lips. "I love your voice and your Irish burr. I love the way you look at me just before you say something outrageous. I love the way you hold Mary Darling so tenderly. And I love that you wanted to make me your wife. I love you, Michael O'Connor, I love you."

The words made him tighten his hands on her waist and pull her closer. "Silence, me love. When I knew ye'd left me it felt as if a chunk o' me heart had been torn from me body. Only yer presence here can stop the bleedin'."

His mouth opened over hers and he took control of the kiss, biting at her lips, impatient and savage. She was aware that a dozen men stood only yards away, but she shoved the thought from her mind. She wouldn't let modesty keep her from showing her husband how much she loved him.

How much she would always love him.

So she took her mouth from his and skimmed it over his strong neck, tasting the salt of his skin. His hands rose to her shoulders, but he made no move to stop her. She tongued the V of his chest, revealed by his shirt, and as she did so she slid her hands to the front of his breeches where his erection was trapped. Feeling, learning in the dark she began unbuttoning his fall.

"Silence?" he whispered.

"Shh," she admonished as he had once done to her. "You mustn't say a thing."

And then she dropped to her knees.

She heard the harsh intake of his breath. He stood very still as she finished unbuttoning him and pulled his breeches and smallclothes open. She leaned forward, blind in the darkness, but she could scent his male musk. Her hands found his cock, stiff and ready, and so beautiful that she wished she could see it. She didn't have time for modesty or shyness. For slow learning. This would be the last time—

But no, she would not think about that. Instead, she explored the man before her. She slid the fingers of her left hand down his shaft, memorizing each veined ridge until she reached the spot where his penis met his body. His sack was drawn up tight under his cock and she fondled it gently, feeling the stones within.

He made a muffled sound above her and she thought that perhaps he liked to be touched there. Or perhaps it was what she did with her right hand. She was squeezing gently on his thick shaft. In any case, she certainly wasn't done. If this were to be their—

No, don't think about it.

She swayed forward and licked the head of his cock.

Michael went absolutely still.

His hands dropped to her hair and for a moment rested there as if stunned. Then she opened her mouth and took him inside. When she began sucking gently, his hands clenched. He tugged her hair as if to pull her away from himself. But since he was only tugging carefully, she stayed just where she was. She drew back and licked around the head of his cock. Without sight her other senses were heightened. She could taste him—man and musk—and beneath her tongue his skin felt warm and soft and pliable.

She kissed him and then thought to scrape her teeth gently over the tip of his penis. It jumped and he hissed softly. She smiled and took him into her mouth again. There was something terribly enticing about having such a strong man at her mercy. She was in a position of servitude, but she didn't feel servile. She felt very feminine, very sensuous as she stroked around the flange of his cock with her tongue. His hands had stopped pulling on her hair. Instead he gripped her as if unsure whether to push her away—or pull her closer.

She let go of his cock head to lick leisurely along the

underside of his shaft and something seemed to snap in him. He bent and picked her up by the waist. He pivoted, his chains scraping and clinking, and placed her flat on the pallet, following her down to lie on top of her. She gasped and then felt cool air on her thighs. His hands were under her skirts, caressing her thighs, trailing up until he touched her wet center. He stroked her there once and then his hand was replaced with his cock.

Someone coughed and she was suddenly aware that only a door separated them from a roomful of soldiers. He swirled the head of his cock in her moisture even as she had the thought.

She bit her lip and he began to push his way into her. It had only been a matter of a month, but she seemed to have forgotten how large he was. She held her breath as he shoved again. The sensation was so lovely, so perfect, that she was afraid she'd make some betraying sound.

He paused, half in her, and adjusted her position, burrowing his arms under her legs, prying them wider.

He withdrew a tiny bit and then very deliberately pushed again with constant, relentless pressure. He breached the muscles at the entrance to her sheath and, suddenly, he was all the way inside. She felt his breath against her cheek. Felt as his chest expanded as he inhaled. She wanted this moment to stop so she could live it forever. Here, now, there was only the two of them, occupying a wonderful island apart from the rest of the world.

Then he was withdrawing, slowly, steadily. Without a sound.

She gripped his shoulders and his mouth came down on hers. His tongue swept in and he kissed her so gently she wanted to cry. How would she live without him? Without ever again feeling this intense closeness to another human being?

She'd found paradise only to lose it.

Well, then she'd enjoy it while she could. She wrapped her arms around him, wishing they could both be nude, but glad of what contact they had. She tasted salt tears, seeping into both their mouths, and wondered if they were hers or his. Had she brought the great Michael O'Connor to tears? She bit down gently on his tongue, suckling it, holding it within herself. Perhaps if she held him hard enough he would stay with her forever.

Perhaps with this act they created eternity.

She could feel his shoulders bunch as he controlled himself, each thrust exquisitely slow and even. It was as if she'd been primed just for him. Only for him. Each inch of his hard flesh burrowing into hers, each drag against her folds as he withdrew oh, so slowly, built a fire within her, burning, burning, ever hotter.

But more, he was forging a bond between them, an unbreakable iron chain that would link them together forever. This was their true marriage ceremony, more solemn, more holy than the words said over them by an old man.

She held him and breathed with him and waited for the flames to climb higher, to burn white hot. And when he reached between them and thumbed her little nub they did. They flared together. She arched into him as her core melted. The flames seemed to sear her with ecstasy, bonding them together as if they were fired within a crucible. He thrust hard, burying himself and at the same time he covered her mouth and inhaled her moan and his own.

And as her crisis took her, she saw a rainbow form

from the ashes of their combined heat. A rainbow so fragile, so fine that she thought it must be real. That their lovemaking had shattered the prisons of mortal men and that
they were free.

Together and free.

But all things must end eventually and so, too, did the
rainbow. Silence opened her eyes, her husband still atop her,
his beloved weight heavy and comforting in the dim cell.

The dawn was coming soon.

Chapter Nineteen

Clever John called for his cook and made a special order,
and then he waited for the cherry pie to be brought to him
in his throne room. His voice had grown weak with age, so
he was only able to croak her name. "Tamara."
At once a beautiful rainbow bird flew through the window
and alighted at his feet, turning into Tamara. She was as
young and as lovely as she had been all those years ago
when he'd first seen her, but she didn't smile.
Instead her eyes were grave when she asked,
"Why have you called me?"…
—from *Clever John*

They came for him at dawn, just as promised, a new set of soldiers to replace the dragoons that had guarded him all night.

Mick kept his eyes on Silence even as the soldiers opened his cell door and tied his wrists in front of him. He'd dressed in his best with Silence's loving help—blue velvet coat and breeches, gold brocade waist-coat, and lace-trimmed shirt. He wore the stockings that Silence had knit for him—crooked and sagging in places—and they were the most important things on him. His fingers were barren of rings—he'd given them all away to spend an hour with Silence, but he'd not regret that in this life.

Or the next.

The soldiers hustled him from the cell and along long, dank corridors until he emerged, squinting, into the morning sun.

Silence stepped from Newgate Prison behind him, trailed by Harry and Bert.

"Go now," he said gently to her and nodded at Harry. Both Bert and Harry were forlorn, but from Harry's look he knew what Mick wanted.

A public hanging was a nasty thing and she didn't need to see him kicking his heels in the air. With any luck it'd not come to that. His men should rescue him in time—but he wasn't about to tell Silence that. There was still the chance that his plan would fail, and he didn't want to get Silence's hopes up for naught.

She looked at him, her eyes red, but dry, and said nothing. The expression on her lovely face was enough. Not many men were so fortunate as to have the love of a woman like Silence.

He expected to see her again in another couple of hours, but if the escape attempt failed, he'd die content.

Mick nodded to her as they led him toward the cart, already laden with his coffin and a chaplain. "Be well."

"How romantic," a terrible voice said.

The Vicar and a half dozen of his men emerged from the prison behind Silence and her two guards.

Harry began to look, but was knocked to the ground before he could fully turn. Bert backed away as two pistols aimed at his heart. In the wink of an eye Charlie had Silence, holding her by the throat as if she were a dog. She scrabbled at the fingers holding her, her eyes desperate as they met Mick's.

"Is this your lady fair, Mickey?" the Vicar asked, his mangled face tilted grotesquely.

No. *No.*

Harry was on the ground, his head bleeding, but struggling to sit, so he was still conscious at least. Bert had skipped out of the way of the Vicar's henchmen, but he couldn't get near Silence with their pistols trained on him.

"She's nothin' to ye," Mick said, trying to control his voice. *Not now.* Not now when he was trussed like a goose and helpless. "Let her go, Charlie."

"Oh, I might," the Vicar replied. "After I've taught her how to properly serve me. After all, your mother's dead, Mick. I need a replacement. And I've waited patiently since your arrest so that you might fully enjoy this moment."

Bile roiled in his stomach. Mick met Silence's eyes.

They were wide and frightened, but calmer now. "I love you, Michael."

He squeezed his eyes shut, then opened them to glare at the Vicar. "Anythin'. Just name yer price."

Silence threw her weight suddenly against the Vicar's grip. He stumbled under her force, but righted himself too soon, yanking her back into his terrible embrace.

Charlie smiled, a horrible lop-sided parody of a smile. "I already have my price, boy. Your death and your woman. I might get my granddaughter, as well, but she'll just be a sweet bon bon. This"—he shook Silence by the neck—"this is the meat on my table."

Mick bellowed, lunging at Charlie, but he was knocked to his knees by the soldiers surrounding him.

"Will ye allow the kidnappin' o' a lady?" Mick

demanded of the soldiers. They'd been simply standing there as if blind and deaf to the outrage being played out in front of them.

Charlie laughed. "They will if properly paid. This lot isn't like Trevillion's dragoons—they like gold in their hands, and never mind who gives it. Now, remember this as they tighten the noose around your neck, son: I'll be fucking your woman even as you're breathing your last."

And with that the Vicar motioned to his men and simply walked away. Silence gave Mick one last horrified glance, still struggling in the Vicar's grasp, and then the Vicar jerked her around.

The soldiers were manhandling Mick into the cart now. The chaplain studiously looked the other way. They'd all been bribed by Charlie, there'd be no help here. His men planned to rescue him at Tyburn, but if they did, no one would help Silence.

His life meant her death.

His death meant her life.

"Go!" he shouted at Bert and Harry. "Go tell Winter Makepeace what has happened. Tell him to take me men and get her back. Tell the crew to belay any other order. D'ye understand? *Nothin'* stops them from rescuin' Silence!"

The cart started and Mick craned his neck to see Bert helping Harry up and both men taking to their heels, Harry lagging badly. Bert had been with Mick for over five years, and had in that time served him well. But Bran had served Mick well, too—until the day the boy had betrayed him. Mick was going to his death. He had no way of repaying Bert for his loyalty. What if Bert decided simply to run away? Mick would only know if his men showed up at Tyburn as originally planned.

And Silence would pay the price.

Dear God, let him hang.

The cart ride was a trip through hell. The cart rocked into Oxford Street and they were already waiting. People lined the streets, calling to him, some in sympathy, some in derision. They were three and four deep, packed as full as the street would allow. Mick stood, head held high, feet braced wide apart so he wouldn't stagger as the cart began its journey through London to Tyburn. A young girl threw a wreath of flowers into the cart at his feet and Mick stared down blindly at them. He was notorious in London, and there were those among the poor who thought him something of a hero.

A hero, he who had done naught but steal all his life.

Others heckled and threw rotting fruit and worse. He hardly noticed. Where was Silence now? God! Was the Vicar raping her, extinguishing that sweet, hopeful light in her eyes? He wanted to kill at the thought. To wreak bloody mayhem. But he was tethered like a wild animal in a cart.

They stopped at a tavern on the outskirts of London so that he might buy a last drink. And Mick did, praying as he drank that he wouldn't be rescued. Let his death be price enough for Silence. He knew what the Vicar did to women in his power. He'd watched his mother weep for what the Vicar had made her do.

Let Silence live. Let her be happy.

Finally, *finally*, the tall Tyburn gallows came into sight, the distinctive triangle top foreboding against the gray sky. Wooden platforms had been built to one side with viewing seats, but the majority of the crowd milled about on foot. Mick saw a woman with a tray of pies on her head, steadily making her way through the mass of people. She was shadowed by a pickpocket who took advantage of her customers while they paid for the pies. A pack of boys with several dogs ran alongside the cart, shouting. Farther on, a juggler entertained a small circle, handily tossing a man's hat, an orange, a knife, and a posy of flowers into the air. He was quite good, but a group of drunken apprentices to the side were calling insults anyway.

Mick was grimly amused to see that his rescue plan would've most likely worked. The cart had to stop again and again as the crowd pressed around it, struggling to catch a glimpse of him. Hands reached inside, pulling at his coat, his breeches. A piece of fabric from his clothes would make a nice souvenir of the day—one that could later be sold to ghoulish collectors. There were soldiers to be sure, dozens on horseback, but the milling people separated the soldiers from the cart.

The cart drove right up to the gallows with no sign of his men and Mick at last breathed a sigh of relief. Perhaps they had gotten Bert's message. Perhaps even now they and Makepeace were rescuing Silence.

Dear God, he prayed so.

Mick descended the cart and was led up the gallows steps as the chaplain murmured prayers. The crowd was loud, a yammering, shouting, mass of mindless idiots.

Mick nodded to the hangman, a tall, bent figure, and handed him a guinea. The hood was put over Mick's head and his legs tied together. He felt the heavy noose drape over his shoulders and then tighten. He breathed in and out, calm and steady, his breath hot under the hood.

A lever was pulled and he dropped into nothingness.

His mouth opened wide, gasping for the air that could not enter his throat.

He spun, jerking involuntarily as stars lit in the darkness behind the hood. He was dying, his body painfully fighting the inevitable. His ears rushed with incomprehensible noise and he suddenly saw Silence's face, beautiful and as clear as day.

And then he hit the ground.

He lay there, stunned, taking deep, grateful breaths as someone loosened the noose around his neck. He didn't know if he were dead or alive until the hood was pulled from his head and he saw the Ghost of St. Giles.

"What the fuck are ye doin' here?" Mick choked out, his throat raw.

"She needs you alive, pirate," the Ghost said in a familiar voice. He knelt to cut the ropes around Mick's legs. "Don't make the mistake of thinking I'm doing this for you. I've sent your men ahead. Now go save Silence."

"Arrogant bastard," Mick muttered, but the crowd was swarming and the Ghost whirled to fight off two apprentices bent on being heroes.

"Go!" shouted the Ghost.

And Mick did, simply by rolling into the crowd. His hands were still tied and he worked the little penknife he'd concealed up his sleeve loose as people stumbled over him. He was kicked twice in the legs before he could cut the cords. Then he threw off the noose and looked up. A stunned walnut hawker was staring back at him and Mick reached up and pulled the man to the ground, scattering nuts everywhere. He simply shucked his velvet coat and tore the man's plain brown coat from his back. Mick had on the tattered coat in a thrice, took the man's battered tricorne for good measure, rubbed dirt on his face and white shirt, and stood.

The spectators were all looking to where the Ghost was in a mismatched fight with four soldiers.

A woman noticed him and began to open her mouth.

"Oi!" Mick shouted. "The pirate's gettin' away over there!" He pointed in the opposite direction from the Ghost.

There was a surge as the news spread through the crowd. Mick saw the Ghost fall and then get up again. Some of the crowd were still intent on him, angry for having their entertainment snatched from them. But the Ghost of St. Giles had proven himself a capable fighter more than once. As Mick watched, the Ghost dodged away, slipping back into the milling masses.

Mick drew the collar of his coat up around his cheeks and made for a mounted soldier on the edge of the crowd.

The soldier's horse was already agitated from the noise and movement of the crowd. All Mick had to do was give the soldier a good push and he tumbled from the nag.

Mick swung up in his place as the horse reared. People screamed and struggled to get away from the horse's flailing hooves. Mick kicked the nag and they were off at a cantor.

Charlie Grady lived in Whitechapel. Mick rode as fast as possible in that direction. He passed soldiers riding toward Tyburn and what was no doubt a riot now, but they didn't even look in his direction.

Mick rode hard and as he did all he saw was Silence's face. A bell began to toll. It had been at least three hours since the Vicar had taken her.

Jaysus, was she alive?

SILENCE SAT AS still as if she were in the presence of a viper. Except the man in front of her was much more dangerous than any snake.

She must survive.

Even if Michael no longer lived, even if this human snake attacked her, she must find a way to learn to live. Mary Darling depended on her and it seemed that Mr. Grady was quite obsessed with Mary.

Or rather he was obsessed with anyone who had any connection to Michael.

They were in an untidy bedroom that still bore the faint sour smell of the sickroom. From that and the feminine accessories on the dressing table she surmised that this must have been Michael's mother's room.

The room she'd died in.

Silence shivered and then froze as Charlie Grady swung his hideous face toward her at the movement. He sat in a chair across from her, his left hand constantly rolling two grimy dice. The left side of his head was almost entirely bald, only a few long strands of gray hair grew here and there. His ear was gone as was most of the left side of his nose. The skin that remained was burned a dark, leathery brown and rippled quite disgustingly. Had she seen him in the street, she would've turned aside in sympathy.

Here, she was frozen in fear.

Both of their chairs sat in front of a small, unlit hearth. They'd been here, sitting like this for nearly three hours as much as she was able to judge—there was no clock in the room. And that entire time Mr. Grady had been speaking in a low monotone. Any person entering would think he spoke to her, but in reality she might have been another chair. Charlie Grady wasn't really talking to her.

He was addressing his absent son.

"Thought you could turn her against me, didn't you?"

he said, only one half of his mouth truly moving. "But I soon showed you the error of that! She was ever loyal to me, was my Grace. Loyal though you tried to take her away. Ha! Didn't work, did it my lad? Now I have your woman and soon I'll have your little lass. Won't be able to laugh then, will you, Mickey O'Connor? Not when I've fucked your woman and turned her out into the streets."

It was rather strange to sit here and listen to years of hatred pour from this man's mouth. She might find it in herself to pity him—were it not for the fact that he quite often in his monologue made reference to what he intended to do to her. Outside the door was a room where half a dozen of Charlie Grady's men lounged. He'd informed her with chilling indifference that if she tried to escape he'd give her to them to be abused.

A bell began to toll.

Mr. Grady cocked his head, listening. "Right, then, he's hanging now. Shall we see how lucky you are?"

Silence felt a thrill of horror at his words. Was he finally addressing her? She watched in morbid fascination as he threw his grimy dice upon the hearth. They rolled and turned up a three and a four.

"Tch," he said, shaking his head. "Not lucky at all, are we?"

And he stood and began loosening his breeches.

Chapter Twenty

*Clever John watched Tamara stick her finger in
the pie. "I thought of all the possible mistakes I could
make in phrasing my wishes, and still I made the most
fundamental one of all: I asked for the wrong thing."
Tamara ate a cherry thoughtfully and nodded. "Yes,
but I cannot help you—you've used up all your wishes."
Clever John closed his eyes wearily. "Then might I ask for
one of your feathers, sweet Tamara? A purple one?
I shall go to the next world with a rainbow of feathers
in my hand."*...
—from *Clever John*

Mick rode around the corner leading to Charlie Grady's
street and into chaos. His pirates were attacking the house.
Men were screaming and moaning, some lying on the
ground dying, others fighting hand to hand with the Vicar's men pouring from the house.

Mick leaped from the horse before the animal had
come to a full stop.

"Throw me a knife!" he yelled hoarsely at one of his
men and then caught the dagger that came flying through
the air.

They'd arrested him.

They'd kidnapped his woman.

And they'd fucking *hanged* him.

Mick O'Connor was in no mood for any who stood between him and Silence. He flung himself on the first man, grabbing his shoulder and burying the dagger high in the man's gut. His opponent's eyes widened and then Mick yanked out the bloody dagger and kicked the body aside.

The next man swung a club at him but Mick ducked and kicked him hard in the knee. The man howled as his knee broke and he went down.

The third man took one look at Mick and simply fled.

Fine with him.

"Into the house!" Mick bellowed.

He charged the door, ramming his way through, and encountered men in a small entryway. Someone was fool enough to shoot a pistol. Smoke billowed and Mick felt a stinging burn on his face. He grabbed the pistol from the shooter and used it to club him over the head.

"Search every room!" Mick ordered his men.

He mounted the stairs three at a time, his heart pounding in his chest. If she weren't here, if this were a ruse, he didn't know what he'd do. Mick had no other idea of where the Vicar would've taken Silence.

At the top of the stairs was a room with a round table and several chairs. One lone guard was still left and he rushed Mick from above. Mick shifted to the side, pushing the man as he did so, tumbling him head over heels down the stairs.

Mick continued up and saw that two doors were off the outer room. He shoved open the first and saw it was a bedroom, plain and neat and entirely empty. The second door was locked and he kicked it open, the door ricocheting off the wall with a *crack*.

Inside he saw Silence.

He froze.

She sat, weeping, on the rug next to the hearth. Her hair straggling down the side of her neck, the bodice of her dress was ripped to the waist, and the sweet swells of her breasts were revealed over her stays.

There was a reddened mark across her tender breast.

Dear God, he'd come too late.

WHEN MICHAEL FIRST came through the door Silence thought she'd gone mad. The horrible events of the last hours must have weakened her mind, mocking her with visions of her husband.

Then he opened his mouth and spoke. "I'm sorry."

His voice was a thready rasp, but she didn't mind. She was up off the wretched hearthrug in a thrice, rushing into his arms, uncaring of her state or the dirt and powder burns on his face. She wrapped her arms around him and simply held on.

"I'm sorry," he said again, his lips tracing her cheek so softly. "Please forgive me, Silence. I'm so fuckin' sorry."

She murmured and tried to capture his lips with hers, but he pulled back and she saw with wonder that there were tears in his eyes. "I'll kill him for ye, never fear. Jus'…Jus' don't give up on us. I'll take care o' ye while ye heal. And ye *will* heal, I promise."

She stared at him, bemused. "Whatever are you talking about?"

"The Vicar"—he grit his teeth and exhaled hard—"*hurt* ye."

"But he didn't."

"What?"

She took his hand and led him around the bed, pointing without looking. She'd taken one look afterward and it had been quite enough.

She swallowed and whispered, "He tried to…to… well, you know, and I waited until he thought I was quite cowed and then I took the dagger you gave me from my stocking and I killed him."

She gestured again to the Vicar's body, lying prone on the floor by the bed. "I'm afraid I didn't aim for his eyes or his belly like you told me to. I just stabbed him in the back."

"Ye…" Michael looked, bemused, between her and the body. "Stabbed…"

"Him. Yes." She wrapped her arms about herself. Charlie Grady was his father after all. Perhaps Michael was in shock or grief. Perhaps—

Michael threw back his head and roared with laughter. "Ye killed the Vicar o' Whitechapel!"

"Well…yes," she replied, nonplussed.

"The most dangerous, the most insane bastard in all o' London, and ye, *ye*, Silence, killed him with one blow." Michael wiped away tears of laughter.

"Er…yes?"

He kissed her, hard and fast and for a moment all she did was revel in the feel of his still-smiling lips on hers.

Then he led her away from the body. "God, how I admire ye. Yer so calm and sweet and such a ferocious little thing all at the same time. But why were ye weepin'?"

"Dear Michael." She laid the palm of her hand on his cheek. "I was weeping for *you*. I thought you hanged and dead. How did you escape from the gallows?"

"The Ghost o' St. Giles." He gave her a thoughtful look. "He came and cut the rope as I was swingin'."

"Oh, God." She shut her eyes, suddenly feeling ill at how close a thing it must've been.

"And ye, me darlin'? What happened here all this time since he took ye from me?"

"He brought me here and talked and talked for hours, it seemed. And then." She gulped. "He came for me. But the Vicar never got very far with what he intended. I was not raped." A sudden, rather awful thought assailed her. "You do believe me, don't you?"

A wide grin spread across his handsome face. "Darlin', I don't believe in God, but I believe in ye."

"Michael, that's blasphemy," she chided, even as she couldn't keep the corners of her own mouth from turning up.

"No," he said, very serious now, "that's love. I hear ye, I believe ye, and I love ye, me darlin'."

She looked at him mutely, too afraid to ask.

But he nodded as he drew her into his arms. "I love ye, Silence O'Connor, with all me black heart."

"I don't think your heart is all that black." She smiled though tears sparkled in her eyes again. "I love you, too."

She stood on tiptoe and pressed her mouth to his, simply glad to feel his warmth, his breath. But then a thought occurred to her. She pulled back to look him in the face urgently. "But the soldiers will be looking for you."

"Aye." He took off the ragged coat he wore and wrapped it about her, concealing her ripped bodice, then he took her hand and pulled her toward the door. Outside in the anteroom they found Bert just coming up the stairs.

"The Vicar's men 'ave all been thrashed," Bert panted, "but one o' our crew says there's soldiers comin' this way."

Mick nodded. "The Vicar's corpse is in the bedroom. Have a couple o' me men get it. And if you don't mind, I'll borrow this." He took Bert's gray wig, leaving Bert's bald head naked.

"But you've been condemned to death," Silence cried. "Won't we have to flee the country?"

"Aye, we might," he said with a sly smile. He plopped Bert's wig on his head. "Were it not for Mr. Rivers."

"I don't understand," she said as he led her out the door and down the stairs.

"Charming Mickey O'Connor is goin' to meet a tragic death. It'll have to be at the palace, I fear, more's the shame, but it won't be believed otherwise. I'll have Harry and Bert take the Vicar's body there and set it alight. Set the whole palace alight."

"So they'll find a burned body afterward and think it's yours?" Silence shivered at the gruesome thought. "But where will we go?"

He stopped just inside the door and caught both her hands. "I'm to be a respectable, Englishman shipbuilder now, Mr. Michael Rivers. And you, my love will be Mrs. Rivers. We'll send for Mary Darling and live in Windward House in Greenwich."

His accent changed as he told her the news, becoming once again the thoroughly English Mr. Rivers.

Silence gazed up at him, and whispered. "So you'll give up your pirating? Just like that?"

He cleared his throat. "Someone I love—and respect— told me that I could be a better man than a pirate."

"Oh, Michael." He was giving her everything she'd asked for.

He was giving her a family.

They were out on the street now and Silence saw with relief that Harry was among Michael's men. He had a great bandage about his head, but he seemed well enough. He'd be able to wheedle any number of sweets out of female servants looking like a wounded hero.

Silence hurriedly put her hair back up as best she could with her remaining pins, while Michael shrugged on one of his men's coat.

Bert led over a horse. Michael mounted first and Bert handed her up to sit before him. Then Bert stepped back and saluted.

Michael nodded to him and nudged the horse into a trot.

Silence looked around nervously. She could hear shouts and hoof beats in the distance. She felt at her hair. It was up off her neck, but Lord only knew what it looked like.

"Steady on," Michael whispered into her hair. "Remember, we're simply Mr. and Mrs. Rivers, returning home after a jaunt into London. I'm just a shipbuilder."

"Won't you miss your palace?" she murmured anxiously. "Your gold walls and marble floors?"

"I'll not miss a whit of it. Gold nor silks nor fancy books and statues. I can live without them all. What I cannot live without is one Silence Rivers. I love you, my wife."

"And I love you, my husband. I look forward to being just plain Mrs. Rivers, I do." She leaned back and whispered in his ear, "But perhaps you can still be Charming Mickey O'Connor the notorious pirate—in our bedroom."

He winked at her as he bent to catch her lips. "Oh, to be sure, m'love, to be sure."

Epilogue

*There was a patter of bare feet and when Clever John
opened his eyes again Tamara knelt by his side. "Why do
you want my purple feather?" she asked softly. "What
possible use could a man who has everything he's ever
wished for have for a simple feather?"
He reached out a hand that shook with palsy and touched
her smooth cheek. "The rainbow feathers remind
me of you and everything I should've asked for."
"And what is that?"
"You," he said. "I should've wished for you and only
you, sweet Tamara, for I have loved you all these years
and without you my wonderful riches are but bones
and dust to me."
"Is this true?" she whispered.
"Oh, yes, it is true," Clever John replied sadly.
"I am a foolish old man who has lost everything he
might've had in this life."
But as his last words died away there was a great
rushing as a powerful wind blew. Everything—
the kingdom, the invincible army, and the treasure
chest—disappeared, and Clever John found himself
once again in his uncle's garden. His limbs were
young and strong, his hair black once again, and
Tamara stood before him, her rainbow hair shining
in the dawning sun.
Clever John threw back his head and shouted
with laughter. "How?" he asked as he caught up Tamara*

by the waist and swung her joyfully around. "How is this
possible?"
Tamara grinned down at Clever John. "Your wishes may
have been used up, but mine certainly aren't!"
Together they went to wake the king and tell him that the
cherry thief was discovered and Clever John the new heir
to the kingdom. And was Clever John sad that the kingdom
by the sea was smaller and not nearly as rich as the
magical one he'd wished for? Oh, no, he was the happiest
man alive, for he ruled his tiny kingdom by the sea with
Tamara by his side.
And that, Gentle Reader, made all the difference in the
world....
—from *Clever John*

The harlequin leaned against a brick wall, panting. He thought he might be nearly to St. Giles, but he couldn't be sure. They'd run him through the streets like a bull to slaughter.

Blood was seeping from a wound on his thigh, soaking into his tunic and leggings, growing cold and making him shiver in the late spring air. He looked up, trying to judge the time, but since the sun was hiding sullenly behind gray clouds, it was impossible.

It had taken him almost an hour to lose the rabid crowd. They'd been promised a hanging. They'd dressed in their Sunday best and gone out cheerfully to Tyburn for a festive spectacle and at the very last minute they'd been denied their entertainment.

Natural, then, that their ire had turned to him, the source of their disappointment.

The harlequin straightened away from the wall, testing

his feet. The street swirled and dipped sickeningly and he abruptly emptied his stomach into the channel. Must've gotten knocked on the head. Strange how blurry everything seemed.

Somewhere in his mind a tiny alarm bell began sounding.

He tried walking but found he had to grip the wall to stay upright. A further few feet and even that support failed. Blackness was crowding in on his vision and he fell to his knees. He heard the clip-clop of hoof beats nearby, and slowly, agonizingly turned his head. A carriage was turning the corner.

His sword dropped from his fist, clattering to the cobblestones. And then his cheek was on the cold, filthy stones. His eyes were slits as he watched the carriage draw nearer.

His last thought before the darkness took him was how surprised they would be when they discovered who he was.

Then Winter Makepeace, the Ghost of St. Giles, fell headlong into the enveloping black.

If you love historical fiction watch out for . . .

SCARLETT

Claire Lorrimer

*She was the daughter of an English aristocrat and a
young and gentle governess. She was lovely, intelligent, and
had a quality that drew all men to her, ensnaring
them fatally in a web of charm. Stubborn in her loyalties,
passionate in her affections, her one flaw was her
uncontrollable and tempestuous nature . . .*

Sir John Danesfield, captivated by his illegitimate
daughter's spirit, takes her to Regency London to live
with his mistress. At the age of fifteen, Scarlett falls in love
with the Vicomte Gerard de Valle, an impoverished French
nobleman. Believing him lost to her, she enters a
loveless marriage arranged by her father.

But Scarlett can never forget the man who had captured
her heart, and embarks on an epic journey across the
Napoleonic war-ravaged wastes of Europe and the snowy
battlefields of Russia, in search of the man she loves,
and the destiny that awaits her.

978-0-7499-5437-6

Do you love historical fiction?

Want the chance to hear news about your favourite
authors (and the chance to win free books)?

Mary Balogh

Charlotte Betts

Jessica Blair

Frances Brody

Gaelen Foley

Elizabeth Hoyt

Eloisa James

Lisa Kleypas

Stephanie Laurens

Claire Lorrimer

Amanda Quick

Julia Quinn

Then visit the Piatkus website and blog
www.piatkus.co.uk | www.piatkusbooks.net

And follow us on Facebook and Twitter
www.facebook.com/piatkusfiction | www.twitter.com/piatkusbooks

piatkus